DRUM WARRIOR

Mike Nettleton

and

Carolyn J. Rose

DRUM WARRIOR

Mike Nettleton

and

Carolyn J. Rose

2012

CHAPTER 1

Spid, the underworld's most arrogant and ambitious troll, shifted his massive backside on the polished black marble of the imperial throne. Set at the pinnacle of a column of basalt thrusting upward from the floor of an enormous cavern far below the surface of the earth, the throne was a symbol of his position as ruler of all that lurked in the realm called Beneath. It was also cold, hard, and uncomfortable.

Shifting once again, he watched his multitudinous minions marching on the pockmarked lava flows of the Plain of Misery. He, the Exalted Garboon, had recruited a vast army of ogres, trolls, skrees, gammits, and gronnks. Turning to the squat, muscle-bound ogre hunkered beside him, he chortled. "It won't be long now, Yurk. All of earth will be mine."

"Yeah, Boss. All of it. Yours." A glob of green drool slid from the protruding lower lip of Spid's second-in-command. Beady eyes set into the ogre's massive chopped-meat face, darted from side to side as if yanked on strings.

1

"Mine," Spid repeated, dreaming of victories, conquests, captives, and custom-made padded cushions for his throne. "All mine."

Acrid smoke from smoldering coal torches rose along with a hellish mantra from the assembled multitude below. "Heek hak horg. Heek hak horg."

Spid bowed his head in reverence, translating the ancient words into English, the language he'd mastered in order to communicate with those he would soon dominate. "If we take it, it is ours."

Craning his neck, he squinted into the smoky, reeking air and saw a thousand skrees circling in formation, razor-sharp talons flexing in rhythm with the beating of their featherless wings. Their limited vocal cords could not form the words of the chant so they screamed their own names at deafening volume. "Skree. Skree. Skree!"

It's taken me hundreds of years to achieve this, Spid thought as he watched another wave of troops pass his reviewing stand. Every waking moment since the last convergence of the full moon, the planets, the summer solstice, and the mating dance of the Darksuckers, those inhalers of perpetual night. "But I brought them all together," he muttered. "Through bargaining, bullying, and bloodshed, I bent them to my will, honed them for the battle to come."

He scowled and twirled the thick ring encircling his stubby forefinger. The stone glittered like a snake's eye. Yes, his troops were ready for the battle. But before sending them to murder, maim, and terrorize, he must pry open the portal to the outer world. If he failed, ten centuries would pass before the rhythms were right again. A millennium would go by before he, Spid the Devious, son of the troll king Glaub the Oblivious and his captive consort Dismalia, queen of the gammits, could force enlightenment and discipline on the pitiful creatures of

Above Skin. This might well be his last chance to harness the power of the Darksuckers for the good of...well...basically of himself.

He scowled again. Only two people stood between him and his dream—a mere boy and his younger sister.

They would be dealt with.

Immediately.

If not sooner.

CHAPTER 2

Alone at the edge of the continent, Noah Keene let his gaze slide west across the rolling swells of the Pacific to the fiery corona of the setting sun. Looking right at it, doing what his mother had often warned him against, helped lock her fading image in his mind and triggered a memory echo of her voice. Then a red laser stabbed his brain.

"Ow."

Squeezing his eyes closed, he dug his fingers into the rough rock of the narrow ledge while dancing stars lit the inside of his eyelids. When they twinkled out, he shaded his eyes with his right hand and moved his gaze to a spot on the blue-green water just short of the sunset. Whitecaps lapping at the horizon doused half the orb's fire, but the rest raged crimson up the cloudless Oregon sky.

Noah wondered if someone, maybe a kid feeling as lonely as he did, sat on a rock watching the sun rise in an eastern sky. Where would that sky be? He tried to remember his geography and time zones. Three to the east coast. Three more to England? Then a few more. Maybe some kid in the Middle East. Perhaps an Israeli girl on one of those communal farms. Or a boy in Afghanistan, staring out of a bombed-out apartment, worrying about his family's fate. Just as Noah wondered what was ahead for his family.

Not that they acted like much of a family anymore—not since his mother died. More like three people occupying separate dimensions within the same four walls—him, his father Sean, and his sister Abby. Dad, silent, unsmiling, on edge, and working too hard. Abby lost in her world of books and chess. And him thrashing on the drums hour after hour, trying to drown out the roar of silence and grief.

A passing gull canted its wings and hovered eye to eye with Noah, the June breeze puffing its feathers.

"I don't have anything for you." Noah held up his empty hands and the bird swooped away, gliding toward a nearby outcropping where dozens of other gulls guarded their nests. The pungent aroma of their droppings mixed with the sharp scent of gorse and the rank and salty smell of what the tide deposited on the beach below.

Only a thin rind of sun remained when Noah spotted two fishing boats, stragglers from the small fleet at Port Anvil. Their bows slapped the waves as they powered toward twin jetties bent like beckoning fingers into the Pacific.

They're running wide open. Racing the night.

He traced the jetties to the shore, to the broad curving sweep of sand that began at Massacre Rock and dead-ended several miles south at Humbug Mountain. A few beachcombers meandered along the tide line, searching in the twilight for agates, sand dollars, and treasures overlooked by others.

Noah glanced at the vinyl-banded watch on his wrist. Almost nine. Almost curfew. Dad would be hacked off. As

5

usual. But he wouldn't say anything, just point to the kitchen clock and motion for Noah to go to his room.

Tonight he wouldn't bite his tongue and slouch off in silence. Tonight he'd force his father to talk, maybe say something like, "Why are you making such a big deal out of it?"

He spun the scene out in his mind. His father would counter with something like, "Rules are rules, Noah. I expect you to follow them."

"But dad, tomorrow's Saturday," he'd argue. "And school got out today."

"Makes no difference. Nine o'clock is late enough."

"Can't we have different rules for summer?"

"Horsehockey, Noah. Nine o'clock."

"But Mom would have—"

And that would end it. His father's face would compress into the grim mask he wore since he and Noah's mother came back from the doctor's office the day before Noah turned fourteen. Cancer. She'd been gone more than a year.

His father was stuck.

So he was stuck.

No matter that he was almost a grown-up.

He considered that strategy, saying he and Abby were older, should have some say in making the rules. But he knew his father wouldn't listen. And what was the point, anyway? With Mom gone nothing made sense.

He kicked at a clump of ferns sprouting from a crevice below his ledge. "It wasn't fair!" A frond broke off and twirled to the rocks below. "It isn't fair."

It didn't seem like Abby missed Mom as much as he did. Or maybe she hid it better. And Dad's rules didn't appear to bother her much. Dad called her level-headed. Thirteen going on thirty, he said. At school they had her doing college math. Calculus. Noah heard one of his teachers call her a child prodigy. He knew that meant she was way ahead of everyone else, including him. Not that he was dumb, but sometimes his little sister made him feel almost backward. She could spot him two pawns at chess and checkmate him in a few dozen moves. Of course, she did that to most everybody; she was one of the best players in the state.

Her IQ measured 161. He remembered Mom and Dad's amazement when the test results came back. And even though his nickname for her was Ab-normal, most times he was proud of his little sister's brains.

He wouldn't let her help him with his math homework, though, even if it took him half the night. "Stubborn as a mussel shell clinging to the pier," Dad had once said. He wouldn't back down. That's where Abby got her nickname for him. No-way.

Noah got his feet under him and stood, glancing south along the coast to the looming mountain. Even in the dusk he could make out the grassy strip and the rocky knob at the top.

Strange. Most of the time a layer of fog covered that. In fact most of the time the whole upper half of the mountain was shrouded in mist.

That was probably the reason for some of the spooky stories about the mountain, about sightings of the hermit, and Sasquatch, and even the ghost of Noah's musical idol, Felix Delacroix. A gifted jazz-rock drummer, Delacroix blazed through the music world twenty years ago. He married a talented young actress and set out on a honeymoon tour in a small plane. Caught in a near-hurricane-intensity storm, they crashed into the mountain a month before Noah was born. Their bodies were never found.

As a little kid, Noah believed every tale about Humbug Mountain. Some claimed they heard Delacroix's moans on the wind, heard him calling his wife's name over and over. Hikers reported sighting a woman melting in and out of the mist twining through the dense woods on the steep slopes. His father claimed people made that stuff up. His mother had thought perhaps the tale-tellers imagined things when they were tired or had too much to drink.

A gust of wind sent a shiver through him and made him hyper-aware of his isolated perch and the foaming surf and jagged rocks far below. A faint taunting voice spoke from a dark and hopeless place deep within him, "Why not let go and fall? Dad won't miss you."

"No!"

He leaned away from the edge. Mom never gave up, not even at the very end.

Shrugging his backpack over his shoulders, he scrabbled up the brushy trail hacked into the cliff face, fifty feet to the lip of the bluff and the Cape Misfortune lighthouse. From up there, no one could see the ledge because of gorse and Scotch broom and a jutting brow of rock. Noah thought of the ledge as his secret spot even though he knew it was no secret. Often he found cigarette butts, beer cans, and fast-food wrappers. He collected the litter and carted it away, furious at those who left it.

Finding grips and footholds he used hundreds of times, Noah climbed the last fifteen feet, pausing for a final look at the purple smudge on the horizon and the first star winking overhead. "Goodnight, Mom," he whispered.

Below the probing beam from the lighthouse, the old keeper's cabin was a dark cube in the gathering night and he strode to it with a long-legged but awkward gait. Twice he snagged his toes on rocks or roots and once tumbled to his knees. Geez, he was uncoordinated these days. Was that normal? Would he grow out of it?

He freed his bike, wrapping the chain around the seat stem and securing it with the combination lock. Running to build momentum, he threw his leg over and started the fifteen-minute ride home. Sometimes he felt like a baby, still riding a bike. All of his friends were learning to drive, but Dad wouldn't even consider that. "You don't pay attention, Noah. You're oblivious to your surroundings. That could get you killed."

The last thirty yards Noah stood on the pedals, huffing and puffing his way up the sloping street. At the mailbox, he hopped off, panting as he walked the bike up the driveway. Abby lounged in the porch swing, reading by the light of the naked yellow bulb beside the front door. As he came around a gnarled rhododendron bush, he noticed that his father's pickup wasn't parked in front of the garage. Good. No curfew lecture.

He laid the bike over on the scraggly lawn and let himself down onto the concrete steps, calf muscles twitching. "Hey, Ab-normal. Where's Dad?"

Abby didn't look up from her book, Stephen Hawking's *A Brief History of Time*. Theoretical physics, she explained when Noah asked. He wondered if she really enjoyed it or felt like she had to read egghead stuff to meet everyone's expectations. Personally, he liked science fiction and Mom's favorites, murder mysteries.

"He's out," she said without looking up.

"Well, yeah, duh, Abby. His truck's not here."

"Oooohhh. Amazing powers of deduction Dr. Watson." She raised her right hand and twirled a strand of ebony hair around the forefinger, eyes still focused on the book.

He sighed. "Okay, Sherlock, where's out?"

"The movies."

Noah eyes widened and his jaw went slack. His father worked, cooked their meals, labored in his vegetable garden, and read books about history. Serious stuff. "But, he hasn't been to a movie—"

"—since way before Mom died." Abby finished the sentence and set the book aside. "And he has a date. Cool, huh?"

Noah felt the words rip into his heart. A date? What about Mom? "Who? Who did he go out with?"

"Mrs. Ramsden from down the block."

Noah felt a surge of relief. "That's not a date. She's married."

"Nuh uh. She's divorced, No-way. Don't you ever pay attention? Mr. Ramsden left six months ago. Moved to California with that lady who used to work at the souvenir shop."

No. No. No.

The word pounded in Noah's brain.

"Anyway, they drove up to Coos Bay to see some chick flick. It's supposed to be funny. I hope it makes Dad laugh." Abby motor-mouthed on. "He left you some meatloaf in the refrigerator. And Mrs. Ramsden brought us chocolate chip cookies. With nuts. I divided them up, fifty-fifty. Yours are in the sack on the counter. She wants us to call her Jennifer."

"Never. No way!" Noah leaped to his feet and tore open the screen door.

"Where are you going?" Abby called after him.

"Garage," he shouted. Passing through the kitchen, he seized the sack of cookies and slammed it into the wastebasket. "No!" He tossed his backpack on his bed and went out the back door. "No. No. No."

Abby sighed, set the book aside, retrieved the sack of cookies, and returned to the porch. Munching, she lay back in the swing, tapping one foot to the wild beat of

Noah's drumming drifting on the night air. Even though he put up makeshift soundproofing, lining the walls and windows of the garage with leftover egg cartons, it only dampened the thumps, thuds, and crashes. Tonight the noises were louder than usual, discordant and arrhythmic.

He's angry, she thought, angry that Mom's gone, angry that Dad doesn't seem to hear us, angry that it can't be like it used to be.

Sometimes Abby wished she could let it all out like Noah did, scream at the top of her lungs, hit something, run along the beach until she collapsed with exhaustion. But that wasn't in her nature.

She could almost hear Mom's voice, feel her soft hand against her forehead. "You're the one with common sense, Abby. You're the logical one. It's up to you to help your Dad and Noah keep it together when I'm gone."

She ate another cookie, closed her eyes and imagined her mother telling her the story about Noah's first drum. A Christmas present from Aunt Susan, it had been nearly as big as the two-year-old boy. An hour after unwrapping it he was keeping time to Christmas carols and leading their old dog Ranger in a parade around the house.

By the time Abby was old enough to have memories of her own, Noah had acquired a complete drum kit. Over the years he saved money to buy congas, timbales, and other percussion paraphernalia at yard sales and secondhand stores. He even fashioned a Caribbean-style steel drum out of an empty oil container they found on the beach. Mom helped him clean it and bought little mallets he could strike it with. Sometimes he'd play a calypso rhythm and she would dance around the garage, her hair swirling.

I should go talk to him, Abby thought. But she knew he'd locked himself in and wouldn't hear her pounding on the door. He'd have a turntable spinning an old jazz or

11

rock LP. With the heavy black headphones plugged in to the amplifier and the volume maxed out, Noah could ignore an H-bomb exploding next door.

She made the mistake of slipping on the headphones one time when he set them down. "Aooooooh," she'd howled, snatching them from her ears. She thought her head would explode.

Noah just gave her that silly grin—Mom's grin—and said, "I know, it rocks, doesn't it?"

Maybe girls had more sensitive ears than boys.

She smiled. Girls had other skills, too.

Darting to her room, she slid the nail file out of the manicure kit Mom gave her when she turned ten. The simple knob lock on the side door to the garage was old and worn. In less than two minutes she clicked it open, ducked inside, and shut the door as fast as she could. Neighbors complained about the volume of Noah's drumming.

The aroma of old motor oil, mold, and rusty tools filled her nose as she watched Noah snap out syncopated rolls and riffs, moving from snare, to tom-tom, to cymbal, all the while keeping a steady thump-thump going with the foot pedal on the bass drum. She didn't know beans about drumming, but she sensed that he was special, talented. Someday he'd make a name for himself; his picture would be on a poster like those stapled to the egg-carton-covered walls. Keith Moon, long-haired and shirtless, sweating and attacking his drums. He'd played with a group called The Who. He was dead now. So was Buddy Rich, a lounge-lizard-looking jazz drummer on the next poster. Next to that was Noah's favorite. Dela...Delaroy? She looked at the banner across the bottom of the poster. Delacroix. That was it. Lix Delacroix. Anyway, he was dead too. Crashed his plane into Humbug

Mountain. She once asked why Noah didn't like any live drummers. He just groaned and cranked up the volume.

Noah hadn't noticed her come in. No surprise. He mostly played with his eyes squeezed shut. Told her it helped him feel the music. She moved closer, waving her arms, hoping the fanning air would alert him. No luck.

Finally, she walked around him, to where the snakelike black headphone cord plugged into an ancient amp. With her index finger she punched the power button in. The tone arm skidded to a stop on the turntable.

"Hey, what the—? Abby!" Noah opened his eyes, but kept his headphones in place. "What's the big idea?"

Abby pulled one side of the headphones away from his ear. "We've gotta talk, dude. Take those things off."

"Nothin' to talk about, Abby."

"Horsehockey, Noah."

Glaring, he thumped one more short and angry riff on the snare and cymbal, then set the sticks on a low stool, slid the headphones off, and laid them beside the drumsticks.

Abby jumped right in. "Why can't you cut Dad any slack?"

"Me cut him slack? Like he does for me with all his stupid rules?"

The veins in his neck stood out and he reached for the drumsticks, then snatched his hand back. "Okay, fine. He can have all the slack he wants. It's not like he cares about what I think."

Abby glared at him. "Noah, you're always saying Dad is stuck. Well, tonight he's not. Maybe it will be good for all of us if he finds a lady he likes." She felt sorrow crash over her like a wave. "Mom's been gone more than a year."

"You don't have to tell me how long she's been gone! *I'll* never forget her. And your precious Jennifer will never replace her." He seized the drumsticks. "Never."

13

"I didn't say she could replace Mom. I just think—"

But, by then, her brother had punched on the amp, sheathed his ears with the headphones, and was thumping an insistent beat with the kick pedal. The bass drum vibrated so much she thought the face would burst. When Noah began a machine-gun sequence on the other drums, he threw back his head and howled at the top of his lungs.

Abby covered her ears and backed out of the garage, closing the door behind her.

Noah sat on the edge of the bed and tied his tennis shoes. Two a.m. Time to split.

He considered the capacity of his green canvas backpack. A glorified book bag. Still he could cram in all the junk he'd need for the trip: three extra pairs of underwear, two T-shirts, socks, cut-offs, and fourteen dollars and seventeen cents left from his lawn-mowing money. He regretted the twelve dollars spent on a movie and video games last weekend. No way of knowing he'd need it now.

The only thing left from last week's splurge was some salt water taffy in a plastic bag. He tossed it into the pack. A toothbrush, a mangled tube of toothpaste, a comb, a small tube of spicy fragrance deodorant, and his drumsticks joined the bag of gummy candy.

He glided to the kitchen, wrapped a slice of cold meatloaf in aluminum foil, snagged an orange from the bowl on the table, and filled his battered canteen with water. Tiptoeing to the hall closet to retrieve his sleeping bag, he stepped on a squeaky board and halted, holding his breath.

The door to his father's room was closed. Around midnight, Noah had heard Dad's pickup ease to a stop in the gravel driveway. Face to the wall, he'd listened to his father whistle that song about Jeremiah the bullfrog as he walked up the steps. He and Mom used to embarrass Noah by singing that at the top of their lungs when they were happy. Now it sounded like betrayal.

When his father opened his bedroom door to look in on him, Noah faked sleep and used silence as a weapon. The dead air had seemed to press in on him, making it hard to breathe.

But that didn't matter now. None of the things left unsaid mattered. By the time Mrs. Ramsden moved in and took over, Noah would be long gone.

Abby's door was also closed. Unusual. She was skittish about the dark and always slept with it open.

He wished he could take one more look at her but what if she heard him and woke up? She'd want to know where he was going. She'd argue with him. Wake up Dad. He'd be grounded for the summer.

Back in the living room, he stopped at the piano to peer at a picture of his mother, slim and smiling, holding three-year-old Abby up to pluck an apple from the ancient tree in the backyard. Noah pulled a T-shirt from his backpack, wrapped the picture, and wedged it into the center of the pack where it wouldn't break. The photo of Mom and Dad in the porch swing he left on the piano.

Time to go.

But where?

He slipped the pack over his shoulder. Somewhere. Anywhere. For tonight it was enough just to escape.

The bicycle lay where he left it. With care, he set it upright and walked it halfway down the driveway before hopping on. The night was still clear; stars twinkled by the thousands and the moon shone over his shoulder. Bright, but not full. In a few days though. He wondered where he would be then. Somewhere in California, he hoped. Mom's sister, Noah's Aunt Susan, lived near Los Angeles. She'd take him in.

He gripped the handlebars and pumped his legs harder. Could he ride all the way? Five hundred miles? Eight hundred? What if he got a flat or the chain broke?

Well, then he'd hitchhike. Or walk. It didn't matter. As long as he kept moving.

At the stop sign at the bottom of the hill, he looked both ways and turned onto Old Coast Road. Off to his right, the black ocean rumbled, louder in the stillness of the night. He heard the lonely clang of a harbor buoy. The slender beam from the lighthouse swept above glistening whitecaps and shot over his head. He pedaled faster, faster.

His eyes on the revolving light, Noah didn't see the pothole until his front wheel rammed into it. He flew over the handlebars, his head thumped the pavement, and blazing pain zigzagged behind his eyes.

"Owwwww!"

Rolling from side to side, he clamped his hands to his forehead. Colors flashed through his head—reds and yellows and whites.

Eventually, the pain receded and he sat up, rocking for a moment before he clambered to his feet. A trickle of something warm and wet rolled down his cheek. Blood? He wiped it away with the back of his hand.

He was about to retrieve his bike when a hand clamped on his shoulder.

CHAPTER 3

"Noaaaah. Noaaaah Keeeeene."

Menace dripped from the gravelly voice.

An icy fork of fear scraped Noah's backbone, paralyzing him. Gory scenes from every horror movie he'd ever seen thrashed through his imagination. A wave crashed against the rocks far below, the retreating water hissing like a giant snake.

The grip on his shoulder loosened and a puff of warm breath tickled his ear. "Tee hee."

Fear seeped away, leaving him weak and rubber-legged, then burning with anger. "Abby! Dang it anyway." He shook off her hand. "You scared the living peemore out of me."

He whirled to see her convulsed in laughter, the moon casting an eerie orange-yellow light on her tousled hair.

"Sorry—" she choked off another giggle. "I wasn't gonna, but I couldn't stop myself."

Noah clenched his fists, scowled, then eased himself onto the guardrail and turned his face from hers. Sometimes she reminded him so much of Mom that it hurt. She had the same hair and olive skin, the same flashing eyes, the same way of waving goodbye using just her fingertips. Even the "tee hee" came right from Mom's catalogue of gentle teasing. Noah took after his father—fair haired and freckled with lanky limbs, just a pound this side of skinny. The tendency to brood came from Dad also. And, he admitted to himself, the tendency to get angry and then clam up.

For a moment, he considered revenge. Abby was starting to slim down, but at thirteen she still carried some baby fat. Sometimes he teased her about it, calling her "chubby cheeks," even though he knew that would make her cry and argue that he ate lots more than she did. Three times as much. It seemed like he was always hungry.

He remembered the cookies he trashed and wished he'd brought them along. Then he recalled where they came from, remembered his father and that song, recalled the faint fragrance of something flowery in the kitchen. Her perfume. How long before Dad replaced Noah and Abby with other kids?

"Yo, big brother. Earth to No-way."

Abby's voice snapped him back. "How the heck did you find me, Ab-normal?" He felt another trickle of blood dribble down the bridge of his nose and wiped it with his fingers.

Abby pulled a tissue from her jacket pocket and dabbed at the cut on his forehead. "Hey, I'm a brain, remember?" She adopted a comic French accent. "I made use of zee leetle gray cells, *mon ami.*"

Noah groaned. The other night they'd watched a mystery show with a short, fat detective who pronounced his name Hair-kewl Pwah-roe. He was what, French? No, Belgian. He'd made a big deal about that. Ever since, Abby had been mimicking him and spouting off about her "leetle gray cells," and how everything was "quite simple, *mon ami.*"

"When I hear someone rummaging in the refrigerator in the middle of the night, it is of no consequence." Abby brought the words up through her nose like the Belgian detective. "But when zat same person begins rummaging in zee dresser drawers, then I say zere is zee fox in zee hen house." She dropped the accent. "Or, as Sherlock Holmes would say, 'the game is afoot.'"

"That's stupid, how can a game be a foot?" He pointed down at his shoe. "That's a foot, not a game."

"It means that what you're hunting is— Oh, never mind, you jerk."

"Take's one to know one." He pointed back up the hill. "You need to go home, Abby. Now. If Dad finds out you're gone he'll—"

"He'll what? How about you, dude? Way I figure it, you're out," she glanced at her watch, "about six hours past curfew. You'll be grounded until I graduate from college."

"Until next year then, right, genius?"

She made a face. He returned it. "Dad can't ground me if I don't go back."

Abby raised her chin. "You have to go back, Noah. Dad will worry."

"He'll be busy with Jennifer. He won't even notice I'm gone."

"Oh boo hoo. Poor No-way. Nobody loves him."

Noah's fists clenched. "Shut up, Ab-normal."

"I won't shut up, Noah. Dad loves you. He just has trouble showing it. He's not like—"

She didn't say "Mom." She didn't have to. They both fell silent. The lighthouse beam swept by them again and again.

Abby touched his arm. "Where are you going, Noah?"

"California. To Aunt Susan's. Maybe she'll let me sleep in her garage or something. I'll get a job mowing lawns, save my money, buy some drums, get into a band."

Abby threw back her head and laughed.

"What's so funny?"

"Aunt Susan moved. To Ohio. Last fall."

"No way."

"Way."

He felt his face flush with embarrassment. "How do you know that?"

"Return address on her Christmas card." She flashed him an impish grin. "Plus she wrote: 'Greetings from snowy Columbus.' What did you think, she was talking about the guy who discovered America?"

Noah hung his head. "I guess I forgot or something."

"Or something." Abby put a hand on his shoulder. "Guess I'll have to tag along whether you want me or not. Somebody's got to be the brains of this outfit."

"Nuh-uh!" Noah shook his head. "You'll just be in the way."

She grinned. "Yeah, I sure would have been in your way when you got to California and started looking for Aunt Susan."

Noah fought the grin for a few seconds, then let it spread across his face. Smart aleck little sister. He'd really miss her. He made a fist and laid it gently against her temple. "Twirp. I oughta..."

"Yeah, but you won't, because you love me even if I am a pain in the rear. And besides, I brought a blanket and more food and some money, cuz I broke open my piggy bank, and I even snagged us a bag of frosted animal cookies, see?" The words came out like they were chasing one another. She fished around in her backpack, found an iced cookie, and popped it into Noah's mouth.

"Mgfff. Pfanks," he mumbled. He should take her home. But how would he make her stay? Wake up Dad? Ask him to ground Abby while he ran away?

"Poor Noah. He's having a bad brain day." Abby stood, stretching her arms above her head, then rubbed her shoulders. "I'm cold. It will feel good when the sun comes up."

The sun?

Noah bolted to his feet. The one valid part of his plan had been to be off the road by sunrise in case his father called the police and they organized a search. He ran to his bike. "I've got to get going."

"Not without me you aren't." She raced after him, shrugging her backpack onto her shoulders.

"No, Abby. Go home." Noah swung a leg over his bike, found the pedal with his right foot and stood on it. The front tire went sideways. The bike bucked and screamed. Metal grated.

"You blew out a tire," Abby informed him. "Bent the wheel, too."

"Yaaaargh!" Noah screamed in rage and frustration. He leaped from the bike and slung it against the guardrail, hot tears blistering his eyes. Why couldn't anything go right?

"Take my bike," Abby offered in a businesslike tone. "I'll ride on the handlebars."

"How many times do I have to tell you? You're. Not. Coming."

"Might as well take me. I'll follow you anyway." She sighed melodramatically. "There I'll be, walking along the highway. All by myself. At the mercy of every weirdo around. Gangsters. Thugs. Ax murderers. Tourists."

Noah glared at her for a ten-count, then kicked the wreckage of his bike and growled, "All right, let's go. I

21

don't want to be on the road in the daytime. We can make it to Humbug Mountain before sunrise."

"Humbug Mountain?" She peered down the coastline at the hulking headland.

"Yeah. There's a big flat area on a ledge up from the beach, but you can only get to it during low tide. Which oughta be," he glanced at his watch, "in about two hours." He straddled her bike, helped her balance on the handlebars, and they wobbled down the road.

"Noah?" Abby's voice was a quavering whisper on the quickening wind. "You sure you wanna sleep on the side of that mountain? Aren't you scared of...of...you know?"

Payback time. He formed an O with his mouth and made a spooky moaning whistling sound, then did his best creepy monster impression. "You mean, the Homicidal Hermit of Humbug Mountain." He capped that with a cascade of diabolical laughter that echoed from the rock wall hemming the road on their left.

"Quit it you creep. Knock it off."

"Oh I see. It's okay for you to sneak up on me and get my shorts in a bunch, but when it's you who's scared it's dif—"

"The hermit *is* different, Noah," Abby said in her I-make-the-rules voice. "You don't joke about the hermit."

"Whatever," Noah puffed. He didn't have the breath to argue anyway, in fact, he didn't say another word until after they turned off the road, hid Abby's bike in a patch of gorse and struggled across rocks and logs to the beach.

A stiff breeze blowing from the south lifted Abby's long hair and rippled it out like a dark contrail. Noah dug his stocking cap from his pack and offered it. She shook her head and trudged on, taking three steps to each of Noah's two.

They stayed close to the water where the sand was packed hard and made steady progress toward the

22

looming mountain. An earthy perfume blew into their faces—a pungent stew of sea brine and decaying shellfish. Two crows, silhouettes against the slate gray sky in the east, circled down to the sand and an early breakfast buffet spread by the retreating tide. The surf was a steady roar; white noise as Noah struggled to memorize a to-do list. Build a fire. Get warm. Figure out how to get little sister to go home.

"Darn." He hadn't packed matches. He hoped that Abby, the organize-ma-tron, had.

"Abby?" He paused and tilted his head a little, expecting to find her just off his left shoulder. But she had stopped a few paces back and stood staring out to sea.

"What?"

She pointed to the west, where the moon cast a chilly light on the thrashing waves. "That bird. It's like it's riding the moonlight."

Noah squinted. Was it an osprey? Fish hawks, some of the locals called them, because they sometimes swooped down and took fish right out of the water with their talons. He'd seen ospreys down by the mouth of the river. They nested on the pilings there.

"It's an osprey," Abby said. "I can tell by the way it holds its wings."

The raptor dropped lower, gliding along the path blazed by the moon. Pale light glinted off something clamped between the bird's talons—it glittered blue, then red, then yellow.

"Wow," Noah said. Abby stood silently, intent on the approaching bird.

With harsh cries, the two crows swept into the sky and swooped at the osprey. The raptor rose to meet them, striking one crow with the object in its talons. With a sharp cry, the black bird tumbled toward the two spectators.

23

"Abby, duck!" Noah pulled his sister to the sand.

He felt an eddy of air as the crow pulled out of the dive, wings beating.

"Oooh, ick." Abby covered her head with her arms. "I think that crow pooped on me, Noah. Did he poop on me? Don't tell me if he did. Yuuggh."

Noah checked. There didn't seem to be any crow crap on her face or clothes, but he owed her for scaring him. "It's all over your head, Abby. There's a ton in your hair."

"Arrggghhh!" Leaping to her feet, Abby ran into the surf and started splashing water over her head.

With a scream, the osprey plummeted from the crows' assault and hurtled right at Abby, releasing the object in his talons.

"Abby, look out."

Abby did a little squealing frog jump, but before she could shield her head, the object splashed in the surf beside her. The osprey cried out once more, then tilted on the wind and flapped away with the crows in pursuit.

Something approximately the size and shape of a large orange glowed and pulsed in the surf. Abby waded toward it. Noah jogged after her. "What is it?"

"Whatever it is, it's mine." She turned and shot him an angry glare. "You lied about the poop."

"I owed you one."

"And now I owe you one back."

Abby stooped and took the globe in her hands. "It's kinda like glass only not. Check it out, you can see down inside." She tromped beyond the reach of the waves, the object in her outstretched hands. Sure enough, a twinkle of light played at the center of the orb.

Being a beach kid, this was not the first glass ball Noah had seen. Glass floats once broke free of Japanese fishing nets and drifted across the Pacific. He'd heard his Dad tell of times they'd been plentiful, but now they were fairly rare and crack-of-dawn professional beachcombers, who sold to gift shops, scooped up what rolled in on the morning tide.

Abby stretched her arm out as if offering the orb to the moon. "Look at how it glows. Like it's alive almost."

The smooth, round stone seemed to cast a light of its own, a greenish luminescence that shifted to violet and then to an icy white. "Yeah. Cool. Maybe we can sell it to a gift shop for some traveling money."

"No." Abby rubbed it on her shirttail and nested it in her backpack. "We can't sell it. It's important."

"Important? Why? For what?"

"I don't know." She frowned and gazed toward Humbug Mountain. "I just know it is."

Arguing with her—about this or anything—was hopeless, so Noah just shrugged. "Let's boogie." He strode ahead.

Abby ran to catch up. "Noah, what about Dad? I don't want him to freak out." She stumbled over a piece of driftwood and Noah stretched out a hand to steady her. "What if he finds your wrecked bike? He'll think you got hit by a car. He'll think I was kidnapped. It's not fair, Noah."

Fair? Didn't Abby know by now that life wasn't fair? Noah sighed. "You can call him later on, after we catch a little sleep." They'd have to find a pay phone. They didn't have cells. Dad said they cost too much. "Okay?"

She chewed her lower lip, then nodded. "Sure. I guess."

"You can tell him we caught a couple of rides last night and got as far as Eureka. Then the cops will look for us there. Meanwhile, we'll go east, to Ohio."

Abby worried her lip again, but then patted her backpack. "I brought a map. You can't find the right way without one. We'll take Highway 199, south of Brookings."

25

Dang. She was so efficient. "I knew that."

She made a "no you didn't" face, then pointed. "Hey look up there."

Several hundred yards ahead, a campfire flickered in an archway in the face of an enormous rock. Maybe it was someone who would offer them a ride. Or breakfast. "Let's go see," Noah said.

Abby clutched his arm. "Maybe we oughta walk around behind them." She jerked her head toward a jumble of logs littering the high tide line. "We can get through there as soon as there's enough light to see by."

"No. That will take too long. And we'll have to cut back to get to the trail to the ledge." He glanced up at the mountain, feeling something drawing him. It was almost as if he felt a rhythm, a barely audible heartbeat.

Abby relaxed her grip. "Let's walk by them fast though, okay?"

Noah put his arm around her shoulders. "Sure. As fast as we can."

They hugged the retreating surf, heads down, sneaking glances toward the campsite. As they drew opposite it, Noah heard the fire crackle and spit and picked up something else, too. Music. One of his Dave Brubeck jazz LPs had a cut where the drummer, Joe Morello, kept a syncopated beat like that. A tango? He ventured a look toward the fire and saw two people, illuminated by the flickering flames, advancing and retreating, whirling and dipping. Strange. And magical.

He halted and turned to Abby. "Weird, huh?"

"Shhh." She put a finger to her lips. "You said we'd keep going."

Noah nodded, but couldn't seem to take another step. The dancers moved gracefully, almost as if they were one person; they gained speed as the music built to a climax and, with a chattering of castanets and a crash of a cymbal, ended. The two separated and honored one another, he bowing stiffly from the waist, she answering with a prim curtsy. The man stepped to what appeared to be a boom box and punched a button.

"We need to go talk to them." Noah heard the words leave his mouth as he started toward the fire.

Abby grabbed his sleeve. "You're crazy, Noah. We don't know who—"

"It'll be okay. Really." Noah pulled away and strode to where the two people had collapsed on the sand. He heard Abby's feet scuffing and something humming inside him—something he couldn't define.

"Welcome children." The woman's husky voice conveyed a smile. "Sit down. Enjoy the fire."

Noah obeyed, but Abby hesitated at the edge of the firelight.

"Dry your shoes, little one," the woman urged. "Get warm."

After a moment, Abby sidled closer to the blaze. She didn't sit, but squatted, tensed and ready to run.

"You kids runaways?" The grizzled man put something in a brown paper bag to his mouth.

"Of course they are, George," the woman answered. "What else would they be, out here at this time of the night? Or should I say, this time of the morning?"

As she spoke, Noah recognized her. Old Hannah. Almost every day she hobbled up and down Highway 101 picking up bottles and cans and putting them into a supermarket shopping cart. He'd never seen her up close before, and it surprised him to discover she didn't look all that old. She was small, probably not much taller than Abby and her brown hair hung in tangles, like she'd stood in the wind and ocean spray. Soot from the fire had smudged her face but her eyes twinkled as she smiled.

27

"We're hitchhiking," Noah muttered. "Heading south."

"Better go stand alongside the road then. Ain't many cars pass by on the beach." The old man cackled at his own joke, took another pull at whatever was in the bag, and punched a button on the boom box.

Old Hannah locked eyes with Noah, stood, and swayed as the opening chords of another song roared from the speakers. She held her hand out and Noah took it, wondering what force was animating his body. As she led him toward the surf he saw Abby gaping. The old man, belched, swigged from the bottle, and slapped out time with his hand against his knee.

This song didn't swirl and bounce like a tango. He recognized a 3/4 beat and the orchestra played it slow and dreamlike. Old Hannah guided Noah in a flowing whirl, shedding her usual rocking, limping walk for a supple glide.

Noah had never danced. Mom had promised to teach him before— He submerged the memory as he spun and shuffled, retreated and advanced, his eyes locked onto Hannah's. His feet moved as if they'd rehearsed a hundred times. The complex steps sent the two of them flowing over wide stretches of beach, forward right to the edge of the water, sideways down the packed sand at the tide line, then into a series of spins and stutter steps that brought them back to the fire. Images passed from her piercing green eyes to Noah's mind—words, pictures, even sounds and smells so jumbled and fractured he could make no sense of them.

And then he heard the snap and pop of the fire and a hiss of white noise from the tape player. Hannah curtsied and, without thinking he bowed from the waist. "Don't ever be afraid to dance, Noah," Hannah counseled. "Remember the steps. Can you do that?"

"I...uh...think so."

"Good," Hannah said. "You will need them. Soon." Her eyes flashed into his again, sealing something in his brain.

Noah rubbed his eyes, then nodded. "We can go now, Abby."

Her brows arched above goggling eyeballs, Abby stood and scuttled to his side. "Mundo strange, big brother. Dancing with the bizarres." Her voice quavered a little. "How'd you learn to move like that? How did Old Hannah know your name?"

"It was—" He tried to find words to explain but couldn't. He glanced back at the fire and saw his dance partner and the man huddled together, the bottle in the bag passing between them. The homeless woman turned her head and flicked her fingers at him, shooing him on his way, then picked up a walking stick and limped to a rock at the edge of the darkness. Noah raised his hand tentatively, then turned his back and shrugged, letting silence replace the answer he didn't have for Abby's question.

Even though the tide had retreated, they had to take off their shoes and wade through ankle-deep brine to reach the pathway Noah knew about. As they slogged along, Noah tilted his head to look up the sheer west face of the mountain. Ominous, cold, and impossibly high.

The face of the rock was slippery, but they found enough handholds to scrabble up the trail to the broad mossy ledge. Too tired to talk, they ate a few cookies, unrolled their sleeping bags, spread them beneath an overhang, and crawled into them. Abby fell asleep almost immediately, but Noah lay awake for a time, looking out at the brightening sky and listening to the tide. When he closed his eyes and let sleep take him, he dreamt of his mother and father, Abby, and the couple at the campfire.

And then his dreams became strange and horrible, filled with dark passages and weird creatures, dwarfish baboon-like animals with wild dreadlocked hair and round black blotches for eyes. The stench of the creatures, their warm and foul breath, filled his nostrils.

When Abby screamed, he realized the horrible truth.

He was not asleep.

And a nightmare face was just inches from his own.

CHAPTER 4

Noah tried to scream but managed only a strangled gargle. He squeezed his eyes closed tight, employing the childhood defense against imaginary monsters under the bed.

It didn't work.

The beast was real.

He heard the rhythm of its breathing, a snuffling, snorting intake of air. A lip-quivering fooof. Then again. And again. He smelled sickly-sweet, rotten breath. The stench lay across his face like a mildewed washrag. He stifled the impulse to throw up, forced himself to remain utterly still.

Then Abby screamed again. "Get your hands off me, you scuzzy little dirtbags. Noah! Noah, help! They're—" Her words were cut off with a smothered "mmffk."

"Aaaabbbbbyyyyy!" Noah kicked his sleeping-bag-covered legs as hard as he could. His knees made contact with something. He heard a whoomp and a squeal.

He willed himself to open his eyes. Gray light surrounded him. Dawn? Twilight? No way he'd slept *that* long. He tried to stand, tangled with the sleeping bag, managed to kick it off.

31

"Abby! Abby!" His shout bounced off the mountain. "Abby, where are you?"

Please don't let them hurt her.

He swung around and saw the creature he kicked rubbing its midsection and backing away.

It's scared of me. Good.

He took two steps toward it. The creature cowered but didn't run.

Noah figured it to be about a foot shorter than he was, but much brawnier and with sickly gray skin. A cascade of braided hair fell from the top of its otherwise bald head. A fringe of feathery black hair hung from its waist to its knees and clumps surrounded each foot. The feet themselves resembled hands and reminded Noah of monkeys he'd seen at the Portland Zoo.

Noah bent his knees, preparing to lunge for the creature and throw it down the rocky slope. Then he saw the other two perched on a narrow outcropping thirty feet above him. One carried Abby, slung over its shoulder like a sack of potatoes. The other's huge gray hands were clamped over his sister's mouth.

Abby's eyes pleaded silently with him to do something, anything.

But what?

"Where are you taking my sister?" he bellowed. "Let go of her right this minute."

Abby's eyes widened even farther and she looked down. Noah clapped his hands over his mouth. Why did he always make things worse?

The creatures laughed, a sound like bacon grease spitting from a hot frying pan. The one covering Abby's mouth pointed at Noah and shook its finger. It was then he noticed they all wore sunglasses—specifically Ray-Bans. He had a pair in his backpack. He'd saved for two months and bought them because he thought they'd make him look cool, look like his drumming idol, the immortal Lix Delacroix. Abby had laughed and said that other than being too white, too young, too short, too skinny, and too alive, he was a dead ringer for Delacroix.

"Tuh-cht-cht-cht-cht-cht." The creature Noah had kicked made a clicking sound with his tongue. The one holding Abby answered with another clucking rhythm and scaled the cliff using its one free arm and both legs. Its companion took its hands from Abby's head and followed, carrying her backpack slung over its shoulder.

"Noaaahhhh!" Abby screamed. "Help me!"

Noah whirled on the creature he'd kicked. "You tell them to bring her back or I'll throw you in the ocean."

The nightmarish beast, looking somehow pathetic and perplexed, bared its teeth, showing red tinged gums, and raised its arms in a karate-like stance.

Noah kept coming, rage engulfing him. "You make them bring Abby back or I'll kick your butt."

The creature backed away, shaking its head, snarled braids flopping like worms. With a final "Cht-cht-cht-cht," it turned and scampered up the rock face.

Juiced up with anger and determination, Noah pursued. The rock was slick, with only small crevices and knobs, and he fought for each grip. Glancing up, he saw the creature he'd kicked only a few yards above. Abby and her captors, however, were distant blobs of color, hundreds of feet away.

"Oh, Abby," he moaned, "I'm so sorry. I should have taken you home. This is all my fault."

Reserves of strength and agility he didn't know he had kicked in and he clawed his way upward like a mountain goat. As he pulled himself onto an inch-wide jut and groped for another handhold, he saw his quarry just a few feet away, its head cocked as if it were listening to something. He pressed his chest against the rock and heard a low thoomp, thoomp, thoomp, like the beat of a massive kettledrum.

And then he heard it. "Thoomp, thoomp, thudda thoomp. Thudda thoomp, thoomp, thudda thoomp." The heartbeat of the mountain he sensed on the beach vibrated around him, in him.

The creature hugged the rock face with all four of its hand-like feet, swaying to the beat. It seemed oblivious to Noah, oblivious to anything except the rhythm.

Noah found another foothold and pulled himself closer, mesmerized by the rhythm of the mountain. And then he realized something strange. The rhythm he heard, the sound that the creature moved to, was identical to the beat of his own heart. He couldn't tell where his pulse ended and the vibration from the mountain picked up. "Thudda thoomp thoomp, thudda thoomp."

He shook himself. He had to save Abby!

"Aaaaaaaaaah!" he howled, lunging to grab a hairy ankle.

"Cht!" The creature kicked. Noah clung with strength multiplied by fear and fury. The dreadlocked animal kicked harder.

"You tell them to bring back Abby!" Noah shrieked. Lodging his toes on another small outcropping, he thrust himself upward and clutched the creature's other ankle.

The mountain continued to thump, faster now. "Thudda thoomp, thudda thoomp, thudda thoomp." Noah's heart remained in lockstep with the rhythm.

His adversary growled low in its throat and reached a pudgy paw down to swat at Noah's hands. The movement threw its center of balance backward, toward open air.

Noah felt himself peeling away from the rock.

"No."

He bent his head, tried to push himself against the cliff face. Too late. The creature's weight peeled him farther away.

Time slowed to a near standstill. Two words repeated over and over again in his mind, providing a strangely calming mantra as his left foot came loose.

Uh oh, he thought. Uh oh, uh oh, uh oh, uh, oh.

Wind rushed around him. He somersaulted through the air, hands clamped around the creature's ankles.

Their eyes locked for a moment just before they hit the water.

The animal's mouth opened. "Uh oh," it moaned.

CHAPTER 5

Abby peered at the rock walls of her chamber and munched on a mouthful of the dried fish she'd been given. Salty, but okay. At first, she'd been too frightened and confused to take anything from the contrite little semi-hairless grungoid who delivered a tray of strange-looking food, but eventually hunger and common sense took over. She needed strength so she could think. Think and plan her escape.

Her watch had broken as she struggled with the creatures that kidnapped her, so she didn't know the time. She tried to calculate how many hours had passed since 5:22 a.m. when it stopped, but found she couldn't even guess. Four hours? Eight? Time seemed to twist around itself in her mind. At least she'd gotten beyond her terror. Now she viewed her situation like a difficult chess match in its opening stages—just a few moves made and no clue what her opponents might try next.

As Abby chewed, she noticed her jaws keeping time to the throbbing rhythm of the inner mountain. The deep percussion she felt vibrating through her bones as the grungoids toted her up the cliff had subsided for a time, but now the mountain seemed to pick up the beat. The sound served as a tympanic reminder of her plight. Was it random? Was it caused by the shifting of rock strata expanding and contracting with changing temperatures? Or did it mean something?

Noah could probably figure it out. After all, he knew everything about drumming. He once told her that all the rhythms he heard in his head and conveyed through his arms and wrists and feet to his drums, were born in the earth. She'd scoffed. "Really woo-woo, Noah. What else do you believe in? Voodoo? Trolls and ogres? Warrior princesses?"

He'd sulked, retreating to the garage to pound on his snare, tom-toms, and bass drums. She'd felt a little bad about that, but not very. After all, you could explain everything around you with science. Rational people didn't believe in... Abby pictured the strange creatures that snatched her off the mountainside. "Grungoids."

She shivered. "Noah where are you?" Tears rolled down her cheeks. He'd come after her captors and she squirmed in their grasp, almost gagging at their musky body odor, trying to keep her eyes on her brother. But the distance between them widened and soon Noah was only as a speck.

And then the speck disappeared.

Had he fallen? Was he hurt? Dead?

Abby sobbed for a few moments, then knuckled the tears from her eyes. Crying wouldn't do her any good, wouldn't do Noah any good, either. She had to think, had to recall and memorize everything about how she got here—in case she got an opportunity to escape.

She remembered the second rhythm. After her kidnappers carried her almost to the top of the mountain, they stopped on a rocky ledge. The one with her backpack hefted a large stone and thumped it against a chipped and gouged spot on the wall in front of him. Two heavy thumps, a pause and then three lighter ones. The grungoid waited then, as if listening for a response, before it clubbed the wall three more times, pausing to let the echo of each hit die before making the next.

Abby heard a loud click and a section of what appeared to be seamless rock wall swung open. Four tunnels converged onto a narrow landing inside the door. After they passed through, that door pivoted shut behind them and the squat, muscular creature set her down but kept a tight grip on her hand. The grungoid tugged her into the tunnel on the right, a tunnel so constricted she had to duck. As she stumbled along the rocky path, the second grungoid prodded her with its bony finger.

Something occurred to her and made her smile at her own preconceptions. Why did she call the call the creatures "its"? She assumed they were male. But assumption without evidence wasn't scientific. Without parting the fringe that hung from their waists she couldn't tell. And she wasn't about to try that. But the grungoids, as she decided to call them, could well be grungettes.

The word caused her to giggle despite her fears.

She decided to think of them as male—sometimes you had to pose a hypothesis in order to test it—and returned to her review of a perplexing hodgepodge of twists and turns. Terrified as she'd been, Abby knew she could find her way back to the stone door if she had to. The same visual memory that allowed her to think six or ten moves ahead and overwhelm her older brother at chess, would allow her to retrace the route.

In the meantime, she was a prisoner. One of the grungoids paced between her and the door and this particular one disgusted her. From time to time, it—he, she reminded herself—would plop down, use a gray thumb and forefinger, and extract some kind of little bug from his hair. After examining it for a moment, he would pop it gleefully into his mouth.

Ooh. Ickkk!

Abby shuddered at the thought of what that morsel might be.

She'd given up trying to communicate with them. After she calmed down, she attempted several questions about what they meant to do with her, asking her guard where she was in English, Spanish, and French. In frustration she even tried Igpay Atinlay. But Pig Latin only brought a blank stare. Even acting it out didn't work. Her pantomime only drew another "cht-cht-cht-cht." Variations on that sound seemed to be the long and short of their language.

But there had been pleasant surprises. She'd dozed on a waterbed—or, to be more accurate, a bed filled with some kind of squishy stuff—gel, maybe. Abby knew this because one of her friends at school let her lie down on her parents' undulating mattress one time. It felt just like this, sort of squishy but still fairly firm. Someone had built a crude wooden frame around this one and there were matching sheets and pillowcases to go with several quilts. How these primitive creatures obtained bed and bedding and transported them into the mountain was a curiosity.

Something else about her quarters baffled her—the lighting. At first glance, she thought a solid panel illuminated the entire high ceiling of the chamber. But soon she saw individual little pinpricks of light, clustered so tight together they melded into one galaxy of luminosity. Like the Milky Way except they cast a different kind of glow—fuzzy, but at the same time warm and clear.

Intrigued, she'd climbed on her bed for a better look, but couldn't get close enough to see if there were wires or sockets. Strangely, when she laid her head down and tried to nap, the lights dimmed. She thought at first the grungoid had done it, but when she opened her eyes and sat up, the light increased. The grungoid hadn't touched anything other than the buffet he knew as his body.

After eating some of the dried fish stuff and a cooked root that reminded her of squash, which she hated, she pushed the tray away. One of the other grungoids, not her guard, came to take the leftovers and handed over something sealed in its original wrapper that totally boggled her mind. Deep within the mountain, held prisoner by nightmare creatures that spit instead of talking, and feasted on their personal parasites, Abby had found herself eating a Twinkie.

She thought again of Noah and blinked back fresh tears. This was all her fault. Somehow she should have forced him to go back. Or gone home and finked him out to Dad. She visualized her father, sick with worry, trudging up and down the highway where they left Noah's bike or plunging into the surf after a log he imagined looked like a body. No matter what Noah thought, she knew Dad loved him, worried about him, and would mourn him if he died.

Abby dabbed at her moist eyes with the back of her hand and sat up straight. Maybe Noah wasn't dead. Maybe he'd survived. Another hypothesis. She'd hold to it until she had proof—one way or another.

Despite the revulsion she felt about her captors, she didn't worry about her safety. Something told her they wouldn't hurt her.

"Cht-Cht-Cht-Cht."

Abby snapped from her trance to see two more grungoids enter the chamber. She thought she recognized the one who carried her up the mountain, but she wouldn't swear to it. They were different sizes, but their faces all looked the same. And they all wore sunglasses like the ones she'd seen on jazz musicians on Noah's posters, the ones he'd bought for himself.

Given the dim light in the cavern, she found the dark lenses surprising. Still, the eyewear didn't seem to impede the dreadlocked duo. They moved swiftly to her side, took her hands, and pulled her to her feet.

"So where are we going?" Even though she didn't think they understood her, talking helped her stay calm.

"Big plans for you. It gonna be too cool."

"What?"

"Cool, chickie, cool."

"Y...Y...you talk?"

"Every chance I get, little chickie. Every chance I get."

Not only did he talk, but he sounded like...like...that beatnik character she'd seen on the channel that showed old black and white sit-coms. The guy with the goatee and the ripped-up sweatshirt. The actor who played Gilligan in another old show.

"Why didn't you say anything before?"

"You and me only, like just now, met. And the others can't fling people lingo, dig?"

The strange-talking grungoid tugged at a tuft of hair that sprouted from his chin. Not a goatee. Just some random out-of-control hair. Thoughts swirled in her brain like fish in a feeding frenzy. "Where are we? Who are you? Which big plans? What happened to my brother?"

"Good job, little princess. You got all the big doubleyuh questions in there. But cool your jets. All in good time."

"But—"

The grungoid turned and drew a finger across his mouth. "My lips is zipped, chickie baby. Don't waste your wind."

41

Abby ducked to squeeze into the passageway, debating whether to ask another question. The grungoid seemed to read her mind.

"The Grand Exalted Pettifog has the answers, dudette." The grungoid's grip tightened on her wrist. "But he don't deal 'em out often. Or easy."

CHAPTER 6

Turbulent dreams savaged Noah's sleep. He saw himself on a towering precipice, twinkling unearthly light above him, a crowd of—what were they? Not people. Beings. Creatures, with humans mixed sparsely among them. An ebony giant pointed at him. He peered down, saw Abby in the giant's shadow.

Abby! He found her!

Like a bulb that burns out, all light retreated into the void. He heard the howl of the wind. Or was it the keening of some voracious beast, closing in? He felt his nostrils flare at a rank animal odor. He flailed his arms, tried to lift his feet to run, to get to Abby.

Something metallic clicked against his teeth and another pungent aroma replaced the first. A taste—organic, tangy and foreign—made him sputter and cough. He jerked his head. Hot liquid ran down his chin onto his bare chest.

"Careful boy. You'll be burnin' us both." The voice, guttural and gruff, filled his ears.

A disheveled man, long tangled gray hair afly, eyes like stone, and smelling of earth and fire, spooned brown-green liquid from a clay pot and extended the sludgy substance toward Noah's mouth. "Eat some. But go slow. You hacked up the last."

"Whuh...what is it?"

"Scrubbage stew. Good for what ails you. Don't worry boy. I'm not trying to kill you. You came close enough to doing that yourself."

Before Noah could ask what scrubbage was, the spoon found his mouth. This time he swallowed without problem. On second tasting, it wasn't bad, kind of a cross between broccoli and carrots, with maybe a dash of celery tossed in. Propping himself up on his elbows, he accepted more while he studied the rocky chamber in which he lay. "Where am I?"

"Not under the Pacific Ocean, that's where ye be. Lucky for you I happened along," the grizzled codger cackled. "Saw you peel that little worm-headed thing off the cliff."

In a rush of images, Noah recalled the frantic climb up the rock wall after Abby. He remembered grabbing the squat little creature's ankle and then...uh oh. The rough mattress below him made crunkly noises as he sank back for a moment, his head swimming. He breathed slowly, concentrating, then sat up, facing the thin, hunch-shouldered man. "Abby. My sister. Where is she?"

"Can't rightly say. Never saw her. Just you."

The geezer's eyes narrowed and Noah wondered if he was telling the truth. "Who—?"

"Am I? Good question. I am who I am. Except when I'm not. I live here. In and around the mountain."

"Humbug Mountain you mean?" What he'd teased Abby about came back to him. The hermit, the bogey-man of local campfire stories. Noah never believed he existed. But this man did and he sure looked like the hermit people claimed they'd spotted from a distance. And, like the legend said, he lived inside Humbug Mountain.

The old man ladled more stew into Noah's mouth. No question, it made him feel better, but he'd never relish the taste. He sucked it from the spoon, his energy level inching up. As soon as he could, he'd find Abby. But his eyes still felt heavy. Time jumbled. As hard as he fought it, he couldn't stop himself from slipping back into sleep.

It was pitch dark when he opened his eyes again, but immediately, as if it sensed his consciousness, a warm light glowed above him, illuminating an oval-shaped chamber defined by four rocky walls with an opening opposite the bed. As he sat up, the mattress-stuffing made a scrunchy sound beneath him. He wondered what it was stuffed with. Peanut shells? Scrubbage?

His ears also picked up a distant mumble. The hermit?

He stood, walking wobbly-legged across the uneven rock floor, realizing he was quite naked. He shivered a little and blushed at the picture of the hermit stripping his wet clothes from him. The flush subsided quickly. After all, the scruffy old codger was a guy. No big deal.

Noah looked around and saw his clothes on a sort of natural table formed by the rock. Still shaky, it took him a few minutes to pull them on. Bending down to double knot his tennis shoes, he felt the room spin and the floor tip. He sat with a thump. The dizziness passed.

It was then he noticed his backpack and sleeping bag on the floor beside him. But how? He'd left them behind when he chased Abby's kidnappers.

Hadn't he?

He checked through the zippered pockets, his hands pausing for a moment on the drumsticks. Nothing was missing except his wristwatch. He must have lost that in the water. He felt a little lost without it, having no idea what time it was or how long he'd been unconscious. After tying the sleeping bag to the pack, Noah shrugged himself into it, and staggered to his feet.

"Got to go. Got to find Abby. Or get out of here and get help."

His words echoed from the walls and he realized how impossible his mission sounded. Go where? How would he get out? And if he did get out, what would he tell his father? What would he tell the cops? Little monsters kidnapped his sister and he fell into the ocean trying to catch them? The hermit of Humbug Mountain rescued him and fed him scrubbage stew?

No one would believe him. Never in a million years. They'd think he'd been drinking or doing drugs. They'd lock him away.

A spasm of fear and revulsion twisted his stomach. They might even think he hurt Abby. Killed her.

"Got to think." He crossed back to the bed and sat, trying to slow the images zooming through his brain. After several moments, he became aware again of the one-sided conversation coming from the next room. The hermit. Talking to someone. But who? Who else was in this cave?

If they got in, I can get out.

Making his way to the door, he found himself in a larger chamber. Twenty yards away, the hermit sat in the lotus position, his eyes lifted toward the high roof of the cavern. Noah followed the old man's gaze, but saw only the same soft glow that illuminated the smaller room.

As he walked toward the hermit, moving his gaze from the ceiling to the floor so he wouldn't trip and fall, he noticed something strange. As the old guy spoke, rocking back and forth on his haunches, his hands forming a tent in front of him, the lights changed color. Not only that, but pinpoints of light rearranged themselves on the surface of the rock ceiling, forming images and patterns. Noah also heard a faint humming, like a whispered chant filtered through a thick quilt.

Approaching the hermit, he cleared his throat. "What are you—?"

"Shhh." The old man raised a hand, then pointed at the ground. An order to sit. Noah obeyed, sprawling with his face turned upward.

"And if he can overcome that obstacle, what will come next?" The hermit intoned toward the ceiling.

Noah heard the distant hum change pitch and rhythm. The light shifted hue again and formed a pattern unlike anything he could identify.

"Of course, the mountain's pulse will quicken before it begins to fail. That will be the signal old Spid has been waiting for."

Test? Mountain's pulse? Old Spid? Noah squirmed on the cold rock and watched the shapes shift again and the light become a violet, then an almost-lemon yellow.

"What will he need to do?" The whispered growl floated another question toward the lights. "What is his destiny?" The hermit turned slightly and studied Noah before looking to the lights for the answer.

Is he talking about me? Noah squirmed again. Crazy. This was crazy. This old guy, this hermit, was a certifiable lunatic. He wondered, for just a moment, if he might still be asleep and dreaming. He pinched the flesh on the back of his hand and felt pain, a reminder that the visage of this disreputable old vagabond hadn't sprung from his imagination.

"I see." The hermit rocked slowly, nodding his head in affirmation. "The girl will be critical then, to his quest."

The girl? Abby? "Are you talking about Abby? Where is she?"

The hermit turned his gaze on Noah for a moment, and Noah recoiled from the pinwheeling power he felt emanating from the man's eyes. Images flooded through his brain. He felt himself falling, then flying, felt a throbbing beat reverberating in his chest. Then the hermit returned to his communication with the pulsating glimmer on the ceiling. As he spoke, the pattern changed once more. The colors undulated into shades of red, from crimson to soft cherry. "His sister. He wishes to know if he will find her."

Noah sat transfixed as the lights danced on the surface above him and the hermit rocked back and forth, back and forth. "If Spid doesn't lure her to his side first," the hermit acknowledged the message from the lights. "He must rescue the Methuselah Stone from the Temple of Cheltnor and return to help the Pettifog finish the ritual and seal The Skin? And how will he—?"

Noah felt as though his head would burst. Leaping to his feet he yelled "Noooo!" at the top of his lungs.

Crazy talk. All of it. A quest? Who was Spid, and why would he want Abby? What temple? What stone? Why him? He was no hero.

Maybe he'd lost his mind and this is what it felt like. He had to escape—breathe outside air. He staggered away from the hermit and broke into a tangle-footed run.

"Wait," the hermit called. "Come back."

"No!" Noah stumbled across the rough floor. He found another opening and ducked into it, running with his head down. He went only a few yards before the glow from the big room faded behind him. Fearful of the dark, Noah stopped, panting, feeling sweat cold and clammy on his back. He looked over his shoulder, expecting to see the hermit loom in the entranceway, but there was no sound, no movement.

Think, he told himself. Think like Abby would.

Up, he decided after a moment. He needed to go up. Eventually he'd reach the top of the mountain and find a way out. There had to be openings to the outside or there would be no air.

Encouraged by this logic, he continued onward, keeping one hand in front of him and one on the tunnel wall. His nerve-endings tingled at the very surface of his skin. He felt a light spray of water splash onto his forehead and dribble down his nose and onto his upper lip. He licked it. It had a strong mineral flavor. Maybe he'd find an underground stream to follow.

Noah soon lost track of how long he'd been walking. He tried counting seconds and adding minutes, but gave up after realizing the exercise made no sense. If he didn't know what time he started, how could he calculate what time it was now?

The head-high tunnel wound around and around, tightening in some locations, opening up in others. Noah fought off claustrophobia and kept trudging ahead. After a time, he spotted a dim dimple of light. Outside! He made it!

Jogging the last few yards, Noah emerged into a lighted room about twice the size of the one he'd slept in. With a final burst of strength, he ran to its center, hoping to glimpse the sky, the sun. But the only light came from a blanket of glowing pinpoints on the ceiling.

He slumped to the floor, tears of frustration burning his eyes. "Where am I?"

The whisper sifted into the air around him and the lights on the ceiling seemed to dim. Noah felt the weight of exhaustion and despair on his shoulders, the hopelessness of his situation flooding through him. Abby gone, probably dead, him trapped inside Humbug Mountain, with some maniac, probably an escaped mental patient who talked to tiny fluorescent lights and thought Noah was supposed to save the world.

"Keep going," he told himself. "There's got to be a way out." Looking around, he saw three openings cut into the rock wall. Three! Which one would take him out? What if he chose wrong? He might die inside this mountain. He imagined spelunkers, years from now, finding his skeleton.

Noah covered his eyes with the palms of his hands. If only he'd listened to Abby.

He felt a small hand on his shoulder.

Abby!

If they were together, it would be okay. He smiled and relaxed, waiting for her "tee hee" giggle.

Then a musty aroma reached his nostrils. He heard a small, strange, warble of a voice say the words that had been on the nightmare creature's lips as they fell together into the ocean. "Uh-oh," the voice chirruped. "Uh oh."

CHAPTER 7

The biggest, brownest, baldest man Abby had ever seen hung upside down from an apparatus built into an arch in the middle of the rocky cavern. The immense man wore a pair of cream-colored canvas painters' pants and a small gold tambourine earring dangling from his left earlobe. As she approached, his eyes fluttered open and a sly smile curved downward.

"Little princess." The soft, low voice rumbled musically from the inverted giant. "Just five more crunches. I'll be wid you in a shake." At that, he drew his muscular upper body toward his gravity-booted feet and paused in an *L* position. Exhaling smoothly, he lowered himself until his head hung at the level of her knees. In a moment, with another slow intake of air, he pulled himself back into the *L*.

His pleasant voice and deferential manner took the edge off Abby's fear.

But what if that's what he intended?

Senses tingling, she inspected her surroundings—a large chamber with a great distance to the rock ceiling and only one entrance, the one through which she and the odd beatnik grungoid had trudged. Mellow amber light, emitted by the same kind of wispy, luminescent pinpoints she'd noticed earlier, bathed the chamber. A pleasant, sweet, almost fruit-like fragrance drifted through the space, cutting the faintly moldy smell. Incense? Air freshener?

"Five-Fwoo." The giant exhaled once more and the mellifluous voice rumbled, "Time to descend to earth orbit. If I was you, I'd motor backways a little, *ma petite*."

Abby checked over her shoulder to avoid bumping into the strange, jive-talking grungoid and his two sunglass-sporting sidekicks, then scuttled back a few yards. They shuffled along with her, never more than an arm's length away.

"*Merci.*" The strange man rewarded her with his upside down grin again and flexed his shoulders and neck. His accent reminded her of a travel show about Cajun people in Louisiana she'd watched a few days ago. His patois mixed French and English and was infused with some of the same jive the gross little dreadlocked grungoid spoke. And, even though he was upside down, she recognized his face. She just couldn't pin down where she'd seen it before.

The man jack-knifed so his head was at his ankles. In one almost-too-fast-to-follow motion, he used his teeth to yank open the fasteners on the gravity boots, bent his legs and somersaulted one and a half times in a tucked position. He landed with a soft slapping of bare feet.

A perfect ten, she thought. Except the Austrian judge would give him a nine-five. He never gave tens.

It was only as the giant gymnast raised his arms in the classic Olympic dismount pose that she noticed had no hands and no forearms. Both his arms ended in rounded stumps approximately halfway between shoulder and elbow.

Abby gaped, too stunned to speak.

"The Grand Imperial Pettifog of Humbug Mountain at your service, Mademoiselle Keene." He bowed from the waist. "I hope we shall be friends."

Any fear Abby felt dissolved in an explosion of anger. "Friends? You order these demented baboons or whatever they are to kidnap me. You hold me against my will in some smelly cave and feed me dried fish and gakky squash, and you want to be friends? Get a life."

The man's grin stayed firmly in place, but his eyes narrowed.

The grungoid who'd spoken to her laughed. "She got a definite point there, Lix. I, like, feel her pain, man. Can you dig it?"

Lix? Abby felt another twinge of recognition.

"A point she does have, Chillout. Deny I can't, no." The huge man motioned at the grungoids and bowed to Abby again. "They mean you no harm. But when you scream, they freak out, you know? They went up to that ledge for a little confabulation and got doinked by the fuzzy, frapulations of fate. Couldn't be helped."

Doinked? Frabulation? Before Abby could decipher his words, the man motioned for her to follow to a small cove. He lowered himself into a lotus position on one of three fringed pillows and waved Abby toward another

She approached with dragging steps. "How do you know my name? I've never met you."

"Ah but we know of you, little chickie," chortled the creature the Pettifog—is that what he'd called himself?—referred to as Chillout. "We grok you the most."

"Grok me?" Abby backed away, clenching her hands into tight fists. "If you touch me I'll scream. I'll—"

"Calm yourself, little princess," the brown behemoth insisted. He made a disapproving face in the direction of the grungoid. "Big goof, no? I read *Stranger in a Strange*

Land to him. He spit out whole everyting he hear. What he mean is, he admires you. Please, sit you down."

Abby considered that. The man's calm, matter-of-fact tone calmed her. Plus, she reasoned, if they meant to harm her it would have happened right after they snatched her away from Noah. She felt tears scorch the corners of her eyes. "Noah." She squeezed her eyes shut against the pain, saw him tumbling toward the ocean.

"Your brother survives his plunge into the sea, Abby. The Darksuckers they have the message sent."

She opened her eyes. "Noah's okay?"

"He grooves on, chickie," the grungoid spoke. "He's digging the hermit."

The hermit? Abby felt off-center. Images and thoughts swerved and dove around her head like bees. Noah and the hermit? Darksuckers? Grand Imperial what? This must be how Alice felt when she tumbled down the rabbit hole.

"I know, Abby. It seem like one big borgle right now. But it all gonna be revealed in due time. Trust, *ma cherie*."

She lifted her eyes to see the armless man gesturing again for her to sit on the soft cushion beside him. She sank to her knees, then tried an awkward imitation of his lotus posture.

"Most excellent." He favored her with a warm smile.

Sitting so close, she noticed that his head was not entirely bald. A short fringe of curly dark hair created a sort of horseshoe effect with the open end toward his broad, handsome face. He also sported a frazzly clump of hair just under his lower lip and another under his chin.

"Can I offer you some refreshment? Soda, bubbly water, cranapple juice? Oh yes, and we have espresso, of course. But a little young you probably are for that habit. *Non?*

"Uh..." Abby tried to think of a good reason not to accept his offer and couldn't come up with one. Espresso? He had an espresso machine down here?

For a moment, suspicion crept into her thoughts. Maybe she shouldn't touch anything he offered. But he hadn't poisoned the food. And she was thirsty. Very thirsty. "Uh, juice would be nice."

"Chillout, could you could?" The man turned his head a few inches toward the grungoid. Without a word the beast shuffled off, touched a spot on the wall, and ducked through the opening that appeared.

Still stunned at the strangeness of it all, Abby sized up the gigantic armless acrobat. Analyze the situation. That was the first rule of chess. Think about what you see. Try to understand the goals of the opponent. Try to figure out what he might do, and how you'll respond to your moves—the "what ifs." The more "what ifs" you could visualize, the better player you became. Her coach, Mr. Prentiss, told her that Bobby Fischer, at his prime, saw the board sixty or seventy moves ahead.

But Abby didn't understand this game *or* this board. Her opponent was still a shadow. A shadow with a familiar face and friendly manner, but a shadow nonetheless. She decided to attempt a move and see what happened.

"My brother's not with any old hermit. He went to get the police."

The Grand Imperial Whatever pursed his lips, bent one flexible leg upward, and scratched his chin with his big toe.

How did he do that? It hurt just thinking about it. "Well? Are you going to let me go, or what?"

This provoked a deep-throated chuckle. "Or what is the correct answer, Abby. Or what. Your jailer, I am not." His voice changed, became deep and mournful. "Fate is your jailer. As it is mine. We dance to the music of the spheres until the solstice. We listen to the heartbeat of the mountain. And then," he gazed at the ceiling, "poon shazam, all will be decided."

The gravity of his voice and words sent a creeping chill through her chest. The feeling of apprehension she felt watching Noah dance with Old Hannah returned and she remembered something else, the mysterious orb the osprey flung into the surf.

He seemed to read her mind. "You hold the Chameleon Stone, Abby. It is magical and it is a tool to help you play your part. Noah must also follow his path, play his part. His journey begins with the hermit, little princess. He must meet his fears, conquer them, and join us at The Skin. When he arrives with the Methuselah, we will kick-start the mountain's heart. He and I and you. If we are ready, if we are worthy, we will send evil back into the depths for a long sleep." He sighed. "If not, nothing more will matter."

Nothing more will matter? What did that mean? What was the evil and how would they send it back to sleep? What fears did Noah have to conquer? What was the Methuselah and where would he find it? What was The Skin?

As questions flew around in her mind, her frustration and fear grew. Why her, why Noah? It wasn't fair. She didn't want to play this game. She wanted to go home. With Noah.

Before she could speak, Chillout returned with a tray and two glasses filled with ruby red liquid. Both drinks had straws with accordion joints as well as wedges of lime anchoring miniature paper umbrellas in turquoise and pink. Leaning down, he set a pink paper napkin on a level spot beside Abby and placed her juice on it. Moving to the right side of the Pettifog, he duplicated his actions. Then, bowing at the waist, he spoke in an affected, almost effeminate voice. "I'm Anton and I'm like, your waiter for the evening. The fresh fish special is braised bass and the soup is cream of rock worm. I'll be back in a moment with your breadsticks."

At that, he jumped into the air, clicked his heels together, and pranced out of the chamber. Forgetting her anxious questions, Abby rolled her eyes and tried to stifle a giggle.

The big brown man smiled and leaned to sip his drink. "A smartass, yes? I'm almost sorry I taught him people talk. But I am desperate for conversation down here after so many years, you know. So..."

"Is he the only one?"

"Who can talk? Yes. The others understand some of what they hear but are not interested. Except for Chillout they are all a little, how-you-say? Dense? Not the sharpest pencils in the packet?"

"What are they? What are they called?"

The Pettifog raised his eyebrows an inch and pronounced a word that sounded to Abby like someone gargling a razor blade.

"I could never pronounce that. I call them grungoids."

"Grungoids? Hmmm. Like it, I do, princess. Easier to say." He repeated the gargle. "Grungoids we call dem from now on."

Abby noticed that as he spoke, the toes on both feet wiggled. It reminded her of Noah. He had the same habit, only with him it was his fingers, twirling his drumsticks even when he wasn't holding them. "Where's my brother?"

His eyes wandered to a spot above her head. "Somewhere. Not far, but many, many miles away."

"But that doesn't make—"

"I got no more answer right now. It all have to play out, you know?"

The worst kind of a response, a wait-and-see response. She took a sip of her juice. It smelled pungent and fruity and tasted sweet and tangy. "Is your name really Pettifog? How did you get into the mountain?"

"Ahhhh." The man took a deep draw on his own drink and regarded her. "Pettifog is only a title. Necessary it is, yes?" He shrugged his shoulders. "Here, they are very fond of their titles, and the roles people are expected to play. Pettifog is the role I play, the cog I have become in the machinery of the mountain."

After another sip he continued. "But my mama-and-papa-given name is Delacroix. Felix Delacroix. Lix for short."

The name jangled within her tangled mind, but she couldn't draw out what it meant. She felt slow and stupid and decided to try a memory trick she'd used before—change the subject. "Why do you wiggle your toes all the time?"

"Aha!" Delacroix was gleeful. "She cuts to the chase."

"I do?"

"*Oui.* Don't you recognize me Abby?"

"No. Uh, well, maybe yes. But I can't figure out from where."

"Chillout!"

The grungoid who appeared as suddenly as he'd disappeared. Delacroix made a quick gesture with his head to draw the little creature closer and they huddled for a whispered conversation.

"I'm hip, Lix," chortled the grungoid as it scampered out of the chamber. "I'm picking up what you're layin' down."

Delacroix clucked his tongue in mock disapproval but Abby recognized the great affection the big man felt for the bizarre creature. How did they all get inside the mountain? Where did the fruit juice come from and—

The sound of a needle dropping onto a phonograph record interrupted her train of thought. An amplified hissing surrounded her and she swiveled her head. Where were the speakers? She saw nothing but solid rock. Not too solid, she reminded herself. After all, the grungoid had passed through a door in it.

Delacroix smiled. "The needle searches for its groove, yes?"

Abby nodded, noticing that his toes had stopped moving for the first time since he sat down. The hissing noise ended with a pop and piano notes wandered wildly up and down the keyboard. A soulful sax sang and sputtered and soared. A bass guitar explored the bottom of the improvisation.

"Cool, yes? Delacroix beamed. "The music it is all on compact disc, too, and coming out of computers and very tiny devices." The giant's toes wiggled in time to the music. "But I for one am devoted to the black wax. The notes sound purer, more alive." He cocked his head. "Here come my moment. The others they provide the rain, I bring in the tunder and lightning."

Abby heard the thud, thud, thud of a bass drum and then the click and tat-a-tat-tat of a snare. She recognized the style instantly, amazingly delicate and intricate, yet impossible to ignore with its penetrating clarity. The drumming provided both a framework for the rest of the piece and stood on its own. Point and counterpoint. The drummer created rhythmic stories, journeys with beginnings, middles, and heroic endings.

A shock of recognition forced Abby to acknowledge exactly who sat beside her on the tufted pillow in the bowels of this mysterious cavern. She'd heard Noah playing along to his music just days before. Lix Delacroix.

Noah's hero. The man Noah called the greatest drummer who ever lived.

But this couldn't be Felix Delacroix. Felix Delcroix was dead. He and his fiancée died when their small plane crashed into the top of Humbug Mountain, years before Abby was born. Searchers speculated the two were thrown from the cockpit and their remains scattered by scavengers.

The man on the cushion smiled serenely. Was he lying? Was he someone else? Or had Felix Delacroix survived? If he had, why hadn't he let anyone know? Why was he living inside the mountain? And what had become of his fiancée?

CHAPTER 8

For a moment, Noah couldn't move. The gray thing he'd peeled off the cliff, the "uh oh" creature, had followed him to wreak vengeance. Then, strangely, that realization made him feel calm and ready. Energy coursed through his veins and he conjured up a mental picture of the animal he was about to engage in mortal combat—short, muscular, smelly, long arms, dangerous-looking teeth.

Swiveling, he clawed at his enemy, but struck only air.

Where was it?

Noah snapped his head around, expecting an attack. Instead, he heard an alarmed "cht-cht-cht" and spotted the dreadlock-haired gray monkey thing clinging to a ledge over the middle doorway, trembling, teeth chattering.

What do I do now?

If he picked one of the three openings he might get away from the...the...what? Monkey? Baboon? Or...? His mind locked up and spun around those questions. He had to call the creature something. Had to. But all he came up with was the sound that signaled the creature's return. "Uh-oh."

61

That didn't make any sense. It was like calling the creature "oops." But, stymied, he went with it, tried it out in his mind. *I'm trapped in a cavern in the middle of a mountain by an Uh-oh.*

And he *was* trapped. Bolting for a tunnel meant turning his back on the Uh-oh. The beast could pounce on him as he passed. But returning the way he came was out of the question. That tunnel led to that crazy old dude's lair and his wild talk about quests and stones and skins and—

The creature sprang from the overhang and landed with a plop in front of Noah.

"Yikes!" Noah flinched and backpedaled. Then adrenaline pumped through him again and he bent his knees, ready to spring.

The gray thing shook its curls, fluffed them out around its head and struck a familiar pose. It grinned at Noah, walked away from him and began to sashay back. Noah gaped at the Uh-oh which had captured the essence of his sister—her posture, the way she walked, even the crinkly smile was dead-on. As the Uh-oh drew near, it stopped, wrinkled his (her? its?) nose and emitted Abby's distinctive giggle. "Tee hee."

"That's Abby's laugh." Noah sprang at the creature. "Where is she?"

The creature dodged and scurried back to the ledge. Hunkering there, it put one hand over its eyes and swung its head back and forth, all the while pointing to the cavern floor.

"I don't have time for charades! Where's Abby?"

The creature somersaulted to the floor, and once again mimed Abby, an angry, combative, argumentative, and ultimately frustrated Abby.

"That's Abby in the cave, before we went to sl— You were spying on us!"

The animal recoiled a step, put a hand over the *O* of surprise it made with its lips, then shrugged his shoulders. "Of course," it seemed to be saying.

"Why? Where did you take Abby?" Noah clenched his hands into fists. "Tell me or I'll...I'll...stomp you."

Could he? He'd never fought anyone in his life.

The creature closed one eye and trained the other on Noah. Clasping its human-like hands behind its back, it stalked in a circle, stopping every now and then to extend a forefinger and scratch a spot in the middle of its dreadlocks. Thinking? Or impersonating someone thinking?

The Uh-oh stopped mid-stride and turned to repeat the single-eyeball gaze at Noah. A beaming smile filled its face and it held a finger in the air as if to signal "Aha! I've got it."

"Well? Tell me! Where's Abby? Why did those other creatures take her?"

Both of the animal's eyes opened wide and after scratching his head with a forefinger again, it shrugged. An apologetic frown replaced the smile and it dipped its head.

"You don't know why they took her? Or you don't know where she is?"

Another shrug, followed by a wrinkle of the creature's brow as the Uh-oh signaled upward with an extended finger.

"Up? They took her up. Up, where?"

The Uh-oh pantomimed walking up stairs, feigning exhaustion as it reached the top step. It used its hands to create the sense of a large chamber, an expansive room.

"So she's somewhere else in the mountain? Further up?"

The Uh-oh's lips curled briefly but its eyes conveyed sadness. It nodded.

Noah cast an eye at the openings in the rock wall. Going up would also bring him closer to the outside. "Do you know how to get there?"

The creature shrugged and went all thoughtful again, pacing the rocky chamber, a serious and determined look on its baboonish face.

Noah couldn't stand this pacing, and he couldn't stand thinking about how many creatures he might find with Abby, about the impossibility of freeing her. What he wanted was to get moving. Now. He pointed at the tunnels opening off the chamber. "Well? Which way do we go?"

The Uh-oh shrugged again and shook a clump of hairy ringlets out of its eyes. "Somewhere else," it warbled.

"What do you me—? Hey, I thought all you knew how to say was Uh-oh."

"Uh-oh," the creature echoed back.

"Can you talk, or do you just mimic?"

The Uh-oh shrugged.

"Do you understand everything I say?"

The Uh-oh shrugged again.

Noah considered for a moment. "Do you understand this? I'm going to get a rock and beat your head in if you don't run for your life."

The Uh-oh shrugged a third time and sat on an outcropping of rock.

Either it didn't understand me, or it doesn't think I would hurt it, Noah decided. He studied the creature as it huddled on the rock, picking at its knees with a long finger. It? Male or female, it had to be one or the other, didn't it? Male, Noah decided. The idea of being down here alone with a female thing that wasn't his sister made him a little nervous. Stupid. But still, that's how he felt.

Thinking about Abby brought an onslaught of guilt and fear and an ache for home, his own bed, his drums and...and...the refrigerator.

Noah's stomach growled. When had he eaten last? Not counting a few spoonfuls of that strange stew. Peeling the pack from his back, he dug through his extra clothes. His hand closed over the foil-wrapped leftover meatloaf he'd stowed. And then he found the orange, a little bruised from the fall. This was it. All the food he had. After that, starvation city. Unless he found his way out.

He thought of those frosted animal crackers Abby had in her pack. She loved those cookies. He fought back a sob. Would he ever see Abby again?

The creature cast longing eyes at Noah's provisions, but made no move toward them. He stood and walked to the three openings in the wall, poking his head into each one in turn and shrugging. After a while he seemed to give up and returned to the rock.

Noah held the meatloaf to his nose, trying to decide if the cold meat and onion aroma was tainted. He didn't know how long he'd been unconscious in the hermit's cave. It could have been days. It was cool down here, but food would still turn bad and the meatloaf could make him sick.

He started to set it aside, but hunger overruled caution and he took a little bite. It seemed okay so he wolfed down half, then picked up the orange.

The Uh-oh watched, like a dog begging at a dinner table, but made no move toward the food. A tear appeared in each of the creature's eyes.

"I must be nuts," Noah mumbled. Grasping the corners of the foil, he extended it toward the creature. "Take it."

The creature scuttled across the floor and seized the offering. Squatting, he pulled morsels from the foil with two fingers and popped them into his mouth.

Meanwhile Noah peeled the orange. The sharp-sweet aroma filled his senses, and for a moment he forgot the wet, earthy-metallic smell of the rock walls. He sectioned the fruit off and ate a segment, chewing slowly and licking his fingers afterward. When half the orange remained, he extended his arm and offered it to the Uh-oh. The creature blinked, smiled a little, then plucked it from Noah's palm. In perfect imitation, the animal chewed each segment, then stopped to lick its fingers. Noah smiled and the creature smiled back.

I think I've made a friend, Noah thought. "What's your name?"

This seemed to bewilder the dreadlocked creature and he tilted his head in puzzled-puppy fashion. Then, he unleashed a rapid-fire burst of syncopated cht-cht-cht sounds.

"No way I can pronounce that." Noah pointed at his former adversary. "Okay with you if I just call you Uh-oh?"

"Uh-oh?" the creature echoed, pointing at himself.

"That's right. You're Uh-oh." Noah curved his index finger back to point at himself. "And I'm Noah."

"Noo-ahh," the creature murmured. "Noo-ahh. Noo-ahhhhhh."

"Good. Now we have to figure out how to find Abby." He stood and walked to the first of the tunnels. "Should we go this way?"

Uh-oh shook his head.

Noah strode to the next tunnel. "This way?"

Uh-oh shrugged.

Noah marched to the final tunnel. "Then it's this way, right?"

Uh-oh mimicked flipping a coin, caught it on his forearm then peered at the result. Frowning, he extended his arms to either side, palms up in the classic "search me" gesture.

Noah swore under his breath. He'd have to try each tunnel in turn to see which one led upward. But what if he ran into cross-tunnels? He was lost and getting loster as Abby used to say when she was tiny.

He returned to his pack and threw himself down beside it. He should have brought a compass. Maybe he had some string. He dug through his pack again. Nothing but clothes, money, the picture of his mother, and his drumsticks. He pulled them out and flung them against the wall. What good were they here?

Uh-oh scuttled to retrieve the sticks. Noah tossed them away again. Once more Uh-oh ran after them.

"This isn't a game!" Noah shouted at the creature. "I don't want them. We can't eat them. They won't even make a decent fire. They're worthless." He gripped one in each hand.

Uh-oh cowered and backed away.

"It's okay," Noah lowered his voice. "I'm not going to hit you. I'm just going to show you. These are drumsticks. All you can do with them is this." He began to click the sticks against the surrounding rock, pounding out a rhythm of fear and frustration.

"This is bad. This is really bad," he muttered. "No way out. No way out," he mumbled, keeping time with the sticks.

Uh-oh bobbed his head, moving his lips as if trying to mimic the sounds.

Exhausted, discouraged, and tired of searching for answers where there were none, Noah let his mind go blank. As he did, he began to hear rhythms that weren't his own. The thudda thoomp, thudda thoomp originating deep at the core of the mountain reverberated through him as it had when he clung to the cliff. He drummed along with it and slowly, even over the sound of his sticks, he became aware of other sounds: water dripping onto rock, Uh-oh's soft breathing, his own heartbeat. Those sounds became counter-rhythms and punctuations.

Instinctually, he reached out with the sticks and tapped the wall, his pack, his legs, trying to recreate the sounds he heard.

Disconnected from the world, eyes clamped shut, hands flying, his spirit soared with the thunder of the tympanic creation rolling around him. As his fervor grew, and the speed and frenzy of his playing accelerated, he heard Uh-oh gasp. Noah opened his eyes to see that the light in the chamber had become liquid, rolling and flashing with his tempo changes, glowing in shifting shades of red, blue, and green.

"Cool," he mumbled.

The beat of the mountain speeded up. Noah kept pace. The sounds ratcheted up to a crescendo and he struck the sticks a final time against the floor, then sank back beside his pack. When the echo from his final blow died away, Uh-oh leaped to his feet, a look of undisguised admiration in his eyes. He drew his hands apart and brought them together with a soft pat. He repeated the gesture twice, a one-creature audience.

Grinning, Noah stood and bowed, then raised his arms, waving the sticks triumphantly in the glowing air.

Huh?

The light on ceiling was brighter than before. It was also lime green. And, unless he was hallucinating, the pattern of the lights formed an arrow pointing toward the left-hand opening.

Noah seized his pack, stashed the foil and orange peelings inside, and strode toward the tunnel, then stopped, wondering if this was a trick. He tried to think, tried to clear his head. What would Abby do? Would she go? Would she wait for more information? Or would she see something here that he didn't?

Noah decided it was definitely a trick. Well, he wouldn't fall for it. "I'm going," he told Uh-oh. The creature looked at the lights and then at Noah, but didn't move.

"All right, I'll go alone." Throwing his pack over his shoulders, he took a deep breath and, with much more confidence than he felt, entered the center tunnel. As he advanced, the light from the small cavern faded and he fought the urge to go back and take the left-hand tunnel.

He counted steps as his mind raced, going over the details of everything that had happened. A hundred steps, he left his house, two hundred, he met Old Hannah, three hundred, the creatures captured Abby, four hundred, the crazy hermit, the scrubbage stew, and his wild talk.

"Darn." He'd lost count, lost track of how far he'd gone. What if he had to find his way back? He looked behind him down the dim and empty tunnel, feeling exhaustion bowing his shoulders. "Five hundred and fifty," he guessed and made himself trudge on, step after slowing step, counting carefully.

He'd reached a thousand and forty-seven when he saw a glimmer of light. He increased his pace, desperate to emerge from the heavy gloom of the tunnel. "Eleven hundred and something," he muttered. Then a stench like rotting eggs, decaying meat, and garbage-bucket slime filled his nose.

He bent over, holding his stomach, and heard the low, bloodthirsty, back-of-the throat growl of an animal ready to pounce. Noah froze, remembering the cougar he'd seen at the zoo in Portland. This sounded bigger, nastier, scarier, hungrier.

He slid one foot behind him, preparing to pivot and run. His heel came down, not on rock, but on something soft.

"Uh-oh."

The creature had followed him. And now they were both prey for whatever lurked in the tunnel ahead.

The hungry growl filled the air around them. Closer.

Uh-oh gasped and Noah heard an uncanny reproduction of his own cracking teenage voice. "Bad, this is really bad. No way out. No way out."

CHAPTER 9

"Ooobaladoo, scoobaladoobaladoo fa-foom!" Chillout, Delacroix's goateed grungoid sidekick, flailed away at imaginary drums, while contributing his own vocal punctuation to the frenzied percussion climax thundering through the hidden speakers. Abby listened to the last notes ping-pong off the stone walls of the massive cavern, a crazy quilt of sound that seemed to take forever to dissipate. She glanced at Delacroix, who sat Buddha-like, staring into space through hooded eyes, his lips sagging in a melancholy frown.

Peering over her shoulder, Abby wondered if she should take this opportunity to run for it. The grungoid didn't seem to be paying any attention to her. She drank the last of her juice and considered. Which of the many openings in the rock wall of this cavern had they emerged from after leaving her cell? Before she tried to find her way out, she had to go back there and retrieve her backpack with her food and extra clothing.

But even if she got that far, could she outrun Chillout or his grody friends? They were lean and muscular, and they knew the tunnels well. All she had was memory tinged by fear and confusion.

71

Besides, what had Delacroix told her a few moments ago? About fate being her jailer, not him? What did he mean by that?

The analytical part of her brain overrode her rising panic. She'd stay, gather information, stockpile food, and try to locate Noah.

"Time for answers to some of your questions."

Delacroix's basso rumble startled her and she made an involuntary hiccup. She felt like he'd crawled inside her mind, reading her thoughts like a newspaper. Maybe he had that power. Well, she'd make some headlines for him. She concentrated on forming distinct words and displaying them on her brain: "Where's my brother? How can I find him? How do the mysterious lights sense when I'm awake or asleep and how do they read my moods?

A "gleeep!" escaped from her diaphragm, echoing in the airy chamber. OMG. What a messed-up time to get the hiccups.

"You have swallowed some air?" Delacroix's voice took on a tone of sympathy. "Try holding your breath for a count of ten."

"I know what to...'gleeep!'"...do," Abby gasped. But she obeyed, drawing a deep breath.

She'd counted to three in her mind when the next spasm caused her to exhale and hiccup at the same time. "Urkkip." The sound left her lips. "Gleep!" The juicy noise bounced back to her ears on the return trip off the stone walls. She felt herself blushing. A cool, in-control person did not hiccup like a baby. She covered her mouth with both hands, muffling the next spasm.

"Do not be embarrassed, Abby. We will fix it for you. Chillout, some moss-water if you will."

Abby didn't know if she wanted to drink anything called moss-water, but decided she'd wait until she saw it to turn it down. Besides if it, (urkkip-gleep) could end these (gleeep) hiccups, she'd try (urkkip-gleep) anything.

Delacroix studied her, a small smile tugging at the corners of his mouth. Finally, just when she was about to scream at him to stop staring, he spoke. "Another cure is to take your mind off the muscles. Perhaps you'd like to hear how you came to be here? And why Noah, your brother, is destined to engage in mortal combat with the forces of Spid, the evil one?"

"Spid? Urkkip-gleep! Mortal combat?" Noah wasn't a fighter. He ran from bullies. He didn't know anything about weapons and he certainly didn't have any with him. He had his drumsticks and maybe a little jackknife for peeling apples. She felt another spasm and tried to stifle it, but a loud gasp escaped from her throat and reverberated from the recesses of the room. "Oh, ex-urkkip-gleep-cuse me."

"Not to worry, Abby. It happens to all of us. I heard of a man who got the hiccups at about the age you are now and had them for forty-seven years."

"Thanks a urkkip-gleep lot," Abby snapped. "Uh, urkkip-gleep sorry." She didn't want to hear about the hiccup guy, but was afraid if she offended Delacroix he wouldn't tell her about Noah. "Did he ever get rid of them?"

"Yes, eventually he did. Do you know how?"

She cringed inwardly at the prospect of Chillout's return with the requested beverage. "Moss urkkip-gleep water?"

"No, although I do think the elixir will help you."

If I can make myself drink it.

"No, this man, after years of standing on his head, holding his breath, eating sugar, putting paper bags over his head, gave up. He determined to die, to pass to another life where he hoped there would be no hiccups."

73

She felt herself drawn into the story despite her preoccupation. "So what urkkip-gleep happened?"

"When it came the hour he had set for his demise, this man, though, he did not want to die. So he decided to embrace his malady. He coveted every 'hic" and every 'up" because it meant he still breathed, he still lived. No longer did he try to cover the sound in company. He refused to be embarrassed by the air bubbles and muscle spasms that lived within him and instead allowed himself to be as one with them. Instead of hiding away, he sought out people and carried on conversations, hiccups and all. He stopped thinking of the gulps and hics as invaders into his body and instead considered them part of what made him a unique creature, as punctuation for his thoughts, for his life."

"And then urkkip-gleep what? Did he wake up one morning and they were gone?"

"*Non.* One day, when he no longer worried about his hiccups and was totally at peace, one day when he was looking the other way, his wife snuck up behind him, stuck her fingers in his ribs, and screeched 'booga-boogah' at the top of her lungs." Delacroix chuckled. "*Voila*, no more hiccups."

Abby sighed. "That's probably the urkkip-gleep stupidest story I ever heard. Is there a urkkip-gleep moral or something?"

The growl-rasp of Chillout's voice announced the arrival of the promised moss-water. "Beverage boy here with your magic potion, little chickie. Scarf this down and those hiccups are gonesky."

He nodded toward a small glass on an oval tray inlaid with what looked like abalone shell and ivory. The concoction was a brackish green with bits of slime and moss-like stuff floating on it. It smelled like a wet cow pasture.

Abby felt her stomach lurch in apprehension. "Surely, you don't expect me to drink that glop? No way. I if you paid me all the—"

She noticed Delacroix's lips twist into a grin and heard Chillout giggle. Her hiccups had vanished.

"The moral of the story, *ma petite*, is that sometimes a little fear is good for what ails you. And, also, sometimes you can shrink your problems when you quit worrying about them."

"I'll drink to that, Lix."

Abby watched open-mouthed as Chillout snatched the glass, drew it to his mouth and poured the moss-water down his throat. "Ahhh." He smacked his lips. "Smooth, real smooth." With that, he turned on his heel and disappeared through another door that opened in what had appeared to be solid rock.

Abby squinted into the small tunnel before the rock sealed itself again. How many of these places were there? Places where the rock would open? Were they shortcuts or dead ends? Did Delacroix have a map stashed somewhere? "Where does all this...this...stuff come from?" She gestured at the glasses they'd been drinking from. "Does somebody go outside the mountain and bring it back?"

"Yes. And no." Delacroix's toes twitched. "We have a—how shall I say?—intermediary to the outside world. But..." Delacroix stopped and seemed to search for his next words. "This person provides only occasional treasures. Such as the Twinkie. You enjoyed it?"

"Uh, yeah. Sure. But where does the other stuff come from? Your pants, these pillows?"

He pondered that, scratching his chin with a big toe. "This might be perplexing if I try to explain. Let me, instead, take you there and show you, yes?"

Panic invaded Abby's calmed mind. Take her where?

75

Delacroix seemed to read her thoughts again. "It is only a short journey and I promise I will return you here safely. You and I and..." He began to pronounce the gargle-name of Chillout then coughed and corrected himself. "...the grungoid. Chillout. We will take you to the place of lost things."

That reminded her of Peter Pan and the lost boys, of the movies about Shangri-la and Brigadoon she'd watched with her mother. She felt small and alone, her confidence ebbing away. "Noah's lost. Will he be there?" She heard the quiver in her voice and blinked back a fresh set of tears. "I'm lost, too. When can we go home?"

"In a few short days, as you call them. Although, in the mountain, time is told in rhythms." Delacroix powered himself to his feet. "Come, *ma petite*. Do not waste time on tears. We will go to the place of mislaid plans, hopes, and desires. And on the way, perhaps you will learn a lesson, acquire knowledge that will help you assist your brother. With your help...our help, Noah will be armed with all he needs to defeat Spid."

Abby didn't move. In fact, she gripped the edges of her cushion. "What kind of a lesson? What kind of a challenge? Who's Spid? If you can go outside the mountain, why don't you get some real help to fight him? Get the sheriff. Get the army. We're just kids. What can we do?"

"Tut. We are all as children, little one. But you have been chosen. Noah too. He must do what I cannot. Now come."

"No." This all had to be some kind of twisted joke. A nightmare. "I won't go. I won't do it. I want to go home!"

The gigantic stub-armed man regarded her sadly. "Abby, if we do not defeat Spid, there will be no home. Not for you. Not for any of us. Never again."

CHAPTER 10

The cheer was supposed to go "two, four, six, eight, who do we appreciate? Spid! Spid! Spid!" But since most of the officers in Spid's army couldn't make any sounds outside of grunts, whistles, snorts, and growls, the echoing cacophony sounded more like feeding time at the zoo than an organized cheer. They hadn't even mastered the choreography, Spid noted, simple as it was.

Still, it's the thought that counts. He raised long and twisted arms, prying his green-nailed fingers into a victory salute.

They like me. They really like me.

Or perhaps they only feared him.

Close enough. When he took over the world of Above Skin, everyone would like him.

They'd have to.

If they didn't, they'd die.

The important thing, Spid concluded, was that when the time came, his forces would obey his orders. He twitched his thick lips into a predatory smile. No matter how bloodthirsty and unmerciful those orders were.

Contemplating that, Spid the Devious leaned back in the sculpted granite chair—hard as, well, rock—and looked out over the banquet tables. His fellow trolls, assorted ogres, flesh-shredding harpies, and other denizens of the land of Beneath gobbled down a traditional pre-apocalypse feast of roasted rock borer and fossilized fackus soup.

A shiver of joy ran down Spid's spine. A shiver of fear ran up it. He was the Grand Exalted Garboon.

Now.

These creatures had assembled at this banquet to honor his leadership and majesty. But if his troops failed in their effort or, worse yet, he never managed to break them through The Skin, he could be the entrée the next time they gathered at this table.

Rubbing the large wart growing from his cheek, he calmed himself. He couldn't lose. He had devised a perfect plan. Nothing could go wrong.

He picked up the braised stone-lizard on the table before him and chomped down on it. Grimacing at the acrid taste, he chewed the rubbery meat and reached for his flagon of deadly nightshade root wine. The red liquid wasn't much of an improvement, but it packed an alcoholic punch and cleared the palate like acid.

He set the wine goblet down, considered the stone-lizard steak again, then pushed his platter aside. When he took universal power, he'd get his own cook. Maybe one of those chefs on the cooking channel. Not that cute woman chef, though. He hated cute; just thinking about cute made him want to upchuck. But maybe that was the gross, leathery lizard. He wondered how a New York chef would prepare the noxious reptile. Infuse it with tangerine juice and slow roast it?

Spid sighed. Next to planning the grisly death of Delacroix and the residents of Above Skin, his favorite pastime was watching cooking programs on the Shadow Stone. He also dug those storage locker shows and the ones about the women who chased wild hogs.

Spid glanced at the smooth, black elongated crystal beside his place at the table. The Shadow Stone stood about two and half feet high, cast a cold glow, and never left Spid's side. Nor had his father ever let it out of his sight. When Spid slept, which was seldom and uneasily, he lashed the stone to his chest and clutched a sword in his hand. All power Below Skin in the realm of Beneath lay with the possessor of the stone.

Plus it got 238 pirated television channels.

He knew some of his historical antecedents, those who had held the stone and focused its power to marshal the forces of evil Below Skin, would frown upon using it as a satellite dish to tune in reality shows and cartoons. But he, Spid, was the Garboon now. The others had died centuries ago. Besides, even a leader of his importance, his magnitude, his girth, needed relaxation now and then.

Spid tapped the stone with his ring. "Shadow! Abraltos. Commenvarque. Find Noah Keene," he commanded.

The black pillar emitted a high, whistling tone. Its frequency increased and soared to an octave well out of Spid's hearing range. The gammits at the banquet table stopped gorging themselves and slapped their hands over their multiple ears. Too many ears and not enough hands. They shrieked as the sound burned into their brains.

Spid once again gave thanks that auditory excess was a recessive trait. Although gammits were able to pick up sounds originating miles away, they couldn't screen out near-by noises. Gammit females often pleaded headaches and gammit males usually wore dazed looks and thick hats made of gravel badger skin.

Spid's mother had seven ears at various locations on her head, his father two. His father's genes had prevailed and Spid's two ears were located in what he thought of as the correct place, on either side of his face. They had long and dangling lobes that he'd pierced and studded with dark and gleaming gems and metals from the mines of Below Skin.

A young gammit stood on the banquet table, spun in circles kicking food on those unlucky enough to be near him and screeched in anguish. Spid turned his eyes toward the Shadow Stone. Shards of light flashed within its ebony depths and a spinning irregular mass of murky jelly began a frenetic random journey within the stone. Spid bent closer, watching an image of the boy take shape.

Noah crouched in a dimly lit tunnel, rigid with fear, anticipation, even dread. Behind him, cowering near the boy's leg, a gray, dreadlocked creature trembled. As Spid watched, they advanced slowly, in tandem toward the tunnel's mouth.

The young gammit stopped howling and fell from the table, gasping and drooling.

Good, Spid thought, the whine has ceased, the stone is locked in. Leaning close, he heard the growl of a carnivorous creature rumbling from somewhere near the boy and his companion.

Beside him, the ogre who acted as his second-in-command hovered, as fascinated as Spid with the images within the black pillar. "Sounds like he's in a world of hurt, Boss."

"Good. Maybe whatever-it-is will devour the Keene brat and his sidekick. What kind of predatory creatures live in that part of the mountain, Yurk?"

"Dunno for sure, Boss." Yurk shifted from foot to foot, his curved nails scratching the stone floor. "Could be a burrowing throat weasel. Or maybe a razor-beaked Phlemus. We gotta watch out for those when we head topside, Boss. They can make confetti outa yuh in nothin' flat."

"If the boy becomes a heap of shredded flesh it certainly would eliminate any shred of doubt that we will prevail." Spid smiled at his own versatility with the language and his dexterity with adjectives. "Shredded. Shred. Get it?"

The ogre scratched his snout. "Uh, yeah. That's a real knee slapper, Boss. I get it. Funny stuff. Hilarious!"

Spid doubted Yurk's sincerity but decided to let it go. He'd promoted Yurk for his loyalty, not his brainpower. "Let us then root for the appearance of the Phlemus, shall we? And for its triumph."

"You got it, Boss. A cheer for the Phlemus." Yurk snorted mightily through his snout-like nose and turned to the assembled forces of darkness.

"Give me a *P*!" He roared.

"F'noorg." The beasts tried their best but couldn't manage a *P*.

Paying no mind, Yurk continued. "Give me an, uh, an *H*!"

"Fnooorg." The *H* was an audio twin to the *P*.

Spid sighed and turned back to the Shadow Stone. With the boy about to become subterranean supper for some roaming beast, all that stood between him and victory was the girl. She was smaller and weaker than her brother, but much smarter. Handling her would require finesse, not brute strength.

"Give me uh *L*!"

"Fnooorg."

Yes, Spid thought, he'd have to be much more careful with the female Keene. She thought things through logically and wouldn't impulsively plunge into danger like her brother. But he'd already devised a plan to use her brainpower to his advantage.

As he watched Noah and the gray animal advance, Spid smiled to himself. Perhaps, if he played his cards right, he could convince the girl to help him realize his dream. If not, she would die with the others.

"Give me uh *E*!"

"Fnoooorg."

CHAPTER 11

As he took one trembling step after another down the tunnel, Uh-oh scuttling close behind, images and ideas careened inside Noah's mind. Flashes of Abby being carried off by Uh-oh's companions, his father shaking a finger, Old Hannah dancing, his mother making dinner.

"Don't give up, Noah." He could almost hear Mom's voice.

Going back toward the crazy hermit would amount to giving up on the choice he'd made, the tunnel he'd picked. This passage continued upward—toward where his gray companion had pantomimed his sister was being held. He blanked his mind of everything but two thoughts: Keep going. Find Abby.

"Do you know what's making that noise?" He whispered to Uh-oh.

The creature shrugged, and Noah saw his gaze dart between the widening tunnel ahead and the way they'd come.

Maybe we *should* retreat, Noah thought. But they were so close to what seemed to be an opening and the other tunnels could be even worse. Plus they'd lose time backtracking. And this might be the only way out. Maybe this thing sounded worse than it was. The echo could magnify its growl. Maybe, Noah thought, like a skunk, this critter was small and depended on its eye-watering stench and its fearsome growl to force predators to back off.

Urging himself forward, a step at a time, was the hardest thing he ever did. The reek of the beast increased, and its low sputtering growl escalated as he and Uh-oh inched toward the glow of the opening. Maybe, he thought, as he visualized something huge with flesh-ripping claws and fangs, this thing wasn't planted right where the tunnel emptied into the chamber. Maybe they could skirt around it, perhaps scale the rock wall and stay above it. Of course, he thought, that's assuming this thing can't climb.

Too many unknowns. We're walking into a nightmare.

Cowering beside his left leg, Uh-oh moved with Noah, making faint, frightened noises. Several times, Noah caught him peering back down the tunnel longingly. Funny, Noah thought, he's going through the same thing I am. Fear. Indecision. I guess stuff like that is universal.

After what felt like hours, they emerged onto a ledge overlooking a deep depression inside an enormous high-ceilinged chamber. The chamber was so vast that the opposite wall vanished in the gloom, but it appeared that the cavern, like the tunnel they'd just traveled, sloped upward. With Uh-oh all but glued to his leg, he wavered on the narrow outcropping, searching for the best way through the cavern. The growling had ceased but the stench flooded Noah's senses, obliterating all other sensations.

To their left, the rocky ledge ended and Noah saw a sheer drop of several hundred feet onto the boulder-strewn chamber floor. And to the right? A narrow trail led down to a larger, flatter area. Halfway along that trail, a stumpy animal slid back and forth.

"What's that?"

Uh-oh scratched his head, then adopted his palms-up "beats me" posture.

Some help you are.

Noah scanned the cave for a more likely source of the putrid smell and frightening growls. He saw nothing. Maybe the noise came from some kind of huge lizard that blended into the rocky surface. Or maybe the beast, which had to be huge to produce this strong a smell, had moved on. The creature on the trail looked smallish, slow and stupid. He could probably jump over it with a running start.

He took a dozen quick steps down the trail.

"Roawwwwrrrr!"

Noah froze. The throaty snarl sounded like it came from the quivering mound of fur a few yards ahead. Mouth breathing to keep from passing out from the stink, he eyeballed the thing and spotted nothing resembling a face. Vaguely round, with short fur or something fuzzy covering it, the animal bumped along. Its shape and lumpiness reminded Noah of a beanbag chair.

Another snarl, totally out of proportion to the creature, filled the cavern.

Noah retreated a few steps. The creature was definitely the source of the stink. Glancing over at Uh-oh he noticed his companion using a finger and thumb to pinch his nose. Apparently, he agreed. Although, to be honest, Uh-oh didn't smell like a bouquet of flowers, either. More like really grody gym socks.

Maybe he thinks I reek too.

Concentrate, Noah, concentrate, he scolded himself. You can survive the smell. Just figure out how to get past this thing.

Focused again, Noah watched the animal and tried to formulate a second plan. The trail widened out where the creature skittered back and forth. Maybe they could circle around. It didn't appear to be very agile. And when it roared, he hadn't seen any fangs or claws. "Okay," he said, with much more confidence than he felt, "let's start down."

"Okay. Start down," croaked Uh-oh. Then, almost under his breath. "Uh-oh."

Moving forward in a slow jog, Noah wondered again if his companion knew what he was saying or just mimicked what he heard.

As they drew closer, Noah decided the creature most resembled a big bag of goo—pudding, maybe—or a huge, fuzzy jellyfish. Instead of walking or crawling, it kind of oozed. What had looked like fur now resembled the mold that formed on left-too-long-overs at the back of the refrigerator.

The mold thing began to change shape, its fuzzy surface swirling and rippling as it morphed into a new but still random glump. Prune-sized dots that Noah guessed were the creature's eyes, danced along the surface, stopping to stare through the fuzz at the approaching intruders, then sliding away.

Okay, Noah thought, so it's weird and moldy and its eyes move around. That could be normal in this part of the mountain. He moved closer and shuffled his feet, looking for an opening. Should he hurdle the creature, or make a dash around it?

"Roooaaahhhrrr."

The mold-thing convulsed from top to bottom, shuddering as it rearranged its skin. An opening formed in the center of the lumpy body, an opening that expanded rapidly into a huge and gaping mouth. Noah froze, staring straight into the writhing purple belly of the beast. Slimy red stuff dripped from the upper rim of the mouth.

"Tssst." The red stuff spattered onto the ledge, sizzling, eating into the rock.

Noah crept backward. He couldn't turn. He couldn't tear his eyes from that horrible mouth.

And then, with a sort of squishing sound, the mouth closed on itself and disappeared.

Would it, like the eyes, appear again, somewhere else on the thing's body? What was this thing, this mold monster?

"Mold monster," came the echo from Uh-oh. "Not good."

Noah didn't remember speaking the words aloud. But he must have. Otherwise how would Uh-oh pick them up?

"You got any ideas on how to get around him?"

Uh-oh scrunched his face into a caricature of thoughtfulness, holding a forefinger in the air in front of him as if an idea was imminent. But then, as usual, he shrugged and shook his head.

"Well, it's not coming after us. I bet it's really slow." Noah forced himself to sound confident. "I bet if we get going we can run around it. We'll back up a few more steps and then sprint as fast as we can."

Uh-oh frowned but then nodded and they edged along the trail.

"Okay." Noah crouched. "Get ready."

The mold monster's oval eyes stopped darting around and locked in on Noah and Uh-oh. An eerie hissing sound intermingled with the low, burbly growl. The hiss grew in volume and the wavering growl became a short sharp snarl. A warning?

The mold monster's flesh vibrated and another mouth formed. As it did, the monster sprang, flying through the air in a blur, landing with a loud splat a yard front of them.

Noah's reflexes took over. He darted around the monster to the left. As he passed, something stung his leg, but he ran on. The stinging grew worse. His leg felt hot. The trail narrowed and ascended onto another rocky ledge. Pausing there, he looked at his pant leg. A glob of some kind of red yucky stuff stuck to the denim. He felt it burning. He smelled scorched flesh.

"Ooowww," he moaned, hopping on his good leg. He wanted to get the red slime off, but if he grabbed it with his fingers it would burn them too. Reaching into his backpack he groped for something to protect his hands and found a pair of spare underpants. Using the cloth as protection he grabbed at the glob of gunk, trapped it between layers of cloth and pulled it loose.

"Sssstt." The stuff made an angry sound as it came away.

Noah flung it from the ledge and peered through the hole in his jeans. A red and charred spot the size of a half dollar glowed on his skin. Small wisps of smoke curled from it, but he couldn't see any more of the red goo. He touched the spot gingerly and shrank from the pain.

"Big trouble. We got big trouble." Uh-oh's panicked impression of Noah's voice came somewhere behind him. In his pain and desperation to peel the fiery glob from his leg he'd forgotten about the mold monster. He looked around frantically. Where was it?

He spotted Uh-oh, fifty feet away, perched on a narrow outcropping a few feet above the main ledge. Yes, get higher, Noah thought. Get off the trail. Maybe it won't be able to follow. He tried to scrabble farther up the wall, but there were no handholds and his efforts only led to a shower of small stones.

"Rooahhr."

Noah looked down. The mold monster waited below Uh-oh, its fuzzy flesh rippling in expectation. Although

Noah couldn't see its mouth from where he stood, he could have sworn he heard the thing smack its lips.

If Uh-oh falls, he'll plummet right into its stomach.

His mind raced. What could he do?

A part of him said, "Just run, jump to the next ledge, get away and let Uh-oh fend for himself. After all, it was his creepy little friends who started this whole thing when they kidnapped Abby."

As if he could read Noah's mind, Uh-oh moaned. "Uh-oh. Bad trouble."

Impulsively, Noah picked up a baseball-sized stone and hurled it at the mold monster. It struck with a resounding splat-thump. The hissing and growling stopped. A rusty squeal replaced it.

"No!" Noah commanded, his voice quavering with fear and doubt. "Leave my friend alone. Get away. Shoo."

Shoo? Noah grimaced. He could almost hear Abby's taunt: "Brilliant, No-way, Shoo. Exactly the right word to terrify a mold monster. It will probably shiver the whole time it eats you."

The fuzz on the creature vibrated again, and the hissing returned, low and threatening. The acrid smell of the beast flooded Noah's senses. He bent over, gagging.

The mold monster spun and leaped, whirling upward and forward. It landed with another loud splat in front of Noah, gaping mouth dripping red ooze, protruding black eyes glued on its prey.

The stench alone nearly slammed Noah against the wall, but he no longer felt paralyzed by fear. He couldn't leap to the next ledge now; he'd reached the end of the road. Nowhere to run. Slimed to death by a mold monster. Resigned and somehow ready, he braced for the mouth to engulf him, for red goo to burn him to death. He hoped it wouldn't hurt for too long.

Then a rock embedded itself in the creature's soft back. The mold monster squealed and its eyes migrated toward Uh-oh who'd descended from his perch and now prepared to fling another tennis-ball-sized stone. The monster opened its massive mouth again and roared at the coil-haired gray figure. One eye traveled back toward Noah.

It's confused. It can't decide which of us to attack first.

That's when Noah got the brainstorm. Reaching around into his pack he groped through the jumble of clothes. Where was it? Had it fallen out? Had the hermit taken it?

A hissing sound drew his attention back to the mold-monster. It seemed to have made up its mind. Eat the kid within easy reach first, then move on to the annoying little gray thing.

Uh-oh slung another rock, but drew only a warning hiss. The mold monster's bulging black orbs trained themselves on Noah. The mouth gaped open farther and Noah felt hot, putrid breath on his face. He saw orange wormy things, wiggling in the monster's stomach, waiting for their feast.

Then his hand closed around the plastic bag of salt water taffy. He yanked it from his pack and threw it into the cavernous mouth. The lips closed. The flesh quivered.

Life's too short, eat dessert first. He remembered his mom's giggle when she'd read the words on a sign in a restaurant in Coos Bay.

Laugh it up, Noah. You're about to die.

With grim fascination, he watched the creature. Flesh bunched and released, twisted and relaxed. Noah heard a cross between munching and squishing.

Uh-oh hefted another rock, a bigger one.

90

The monster reared up. It snarled. But the sound came out muffled. "Grymmph."

Uh-oh raised the small boulder over his head with both hands. Noah backed away as far as he could. When the rock hit, the monster would react.

But Uh-oh paused, up on tiptoe, peering at his adversary. As Noah stared, the monster's gyrations increased, its mouth opened, closed and twisted, then spread into a weird grimace. Its fuzzy surface rippled. The mouth appeared, but opened only an inch, just enough for Noah to see a gummy mess of taffy and waxed paper wrappings.

The monster spun around, slamming itself against a boulder.

Noah raised one hand slowly and motioned for Uh-oh to put down the rock. Then, as the mold monster's mouth closed, he swung his pack at it. Reflexively, the monster rolled away from the blow, skittering to the lip of the ledge. It teetered there, convulsing, trying to balance. Failing, it tumbled.

"Uh-oh," said Uh-oh, but with a mocking tinge in his voice.

"Run," Noah shouted.

He raced to the far edge of the outcropping and leaped to the next ledge, Uh-oh right on his heels. In a few minutes they paused and looked down.

The mold monster lay in a heap on the floor of the cavern far below. Noah almost felt sorry for it. He blinked and reminded himself that the thing had nearly eaten him. Now it appeared to be digesting itself. As they watched, its body became a puddle of steaming red ooze.

"Whew," said Uh-oh. "Close call."

Noah grinned over at his sidekick. He didn't remember ever saying "close call," out loud. But he'd definitely thought it.

Great. My sidekick is a psychic, rock-throwing mime.

But he had a warm feeling about Uh-oh. The dreadlocked creature was courageous and, for some reason, loyal to him.

Uh-oh scratched his head with a thin, gray finger and pointed along the steadily rising trail toward the far side of the cavern. Noah nodded and followed. He hoped they'd find something to eat or drink soon. He had a little water left in his canteen. They could share that the next time they rested.

And that needed to happen soon.

His head swirled and his legs juddered. Something bitter-tasting had worked its way up from his stomach to his mouth. And he was tired. So tired.

It will pass in a few minutes, he told himself. But as they trudged on the sick feeling didn't go away. He began to sweat and his leg throbbed and stung. He looked down and saw the spot where the red goo burned him had turned greenish yellow and was swelling.

"I...I...need to take a break." Noah stumbled to a halt and leaned against a rock.

Uh-oh glanced back. "Uh-oh," he intoned training his gaze on the swollen leg.

"It's nothing," Noah said. "Just a burn. The swelling will go down in a little bit." If only he had some ice. And aspirin. He felt his forehead with the back of his wrist the way his mother used to do. Warm. Was he running a fever? Was his leg infected? Couldn't be. Not yet. Or could it? Things were different down here.

Noah slid to the ground and closed his eyes. The dizziness passed and he sat up and peered along the rocky path toward what appeared to be a lush, green valley. Stranger yet, even though they were inside a mountain, he was certain he saw a forest. If they could make it to the woods, they might find water. He pulled himself to his feet. "Let's get to the woods."

Hot green nausea clawed at his stomach and his eyes swam out of focus. He dropped to his knees. Maybe if he rested a little longer.

Uh-oh's face hovered just inches away, his dark eyes moist.

Noah's head seemed to balloon with heat. Sharp pains ripped at his gut. A dark wave washed over his mind and shut it down.

CHAPTER 12

They clambered up a path so steep that Abby found herself gasping by the time they reached the top. Delacroix, the Grand Exalted Pettifog of the Upper World, led her into a small, rounded chamber about the size of a bathroom and waited for her to catch her breath. Chillout stood close by and Abby caught a whiff of his gamy body odor. It didn't seem to bother her as much as it had at first.

Delacroix bent at the waist and peered into her eyes. "Faith, you know, is a very important thing to have," he said quietly.

What was he talking about? Faith like in church, with miracles and prayers? "I don't—"

"Understand?" He finished her sentence and continued in his lilting patois. "Ahh, but that is the crux of the matter, yes, that is what faith is—believing without understanding. Sometimes, suspend our disbelief, we must."

The idea didn't appeal to her. Understanding, knowing, that was everything. Reasoning, gathering evidence, then using her mind to generate logical conclusions. Faith, on the other hand, felt like leaping off a cliff.

Delacroix's voice hummed in her ear, almost trance-like. "Having faith begins in very small ways. *C'est vrai.* To begin, you must place faith in me, little one. Faith in the ways of the mountain. You must believe I would not do anything to cause you pain, that I would put my life down to protect yours. Can you believe what I say?"

Could she? Fear jangled her nerves and her heart pumped double-speed. How could she trust someone she just met, who had her kidnapped and brought to the inside of this mountain? She wanted to scream, for Noah, for Dad. But that was pointless.

She forced herself to take a deep breath and think logically. If Delacroix intended any harm, he could have attacked her by now. But would he give his life for hers? "I'm...not sure what you mean."

"You will know when you know," Delacroix assured her.

"Let's make the scene Lix, she's like copasetic." Chillout's hipster growl wheedled and he stepped closer. She was glad to have him near, even glad about his scent. He was warm and funny and...safe, even though he'd held her captive. "Time to play between the notes, baby," Chillout told Delacroix.

"Shhh, Chillout. Not yet. The vibrations are not yet exactly right. Listen."

The grungoid sucked in a deep breath and held it, cocking his head. In the sudden calm, Abby heard the faint heartbeat of the mountain again, distant and reassuring. "Thrum-thrum, thrum-thrum, thrum-thrum." As she listened, she felt herself disconnect and drift.

"Thrum-thrum, thrum-thrum, thrum-thrum."

She looked up and saw a beatific smile on Delacroix's large, brown face. Chillout, too, seemed blissed out. She put a hand up to her face and felt her own lips drawn up in a wide smile.

"Thrum-thrum, thrum-thrum, thrum-thrum."

In her dream-like state, she heard Delacroix's words almost as if they were spoken through water. His head turned toward the ceiling of the chamber and he began to chant something over and over.

"Alameezos gravititos," she thought she heard.

"Thrum-thrum, thrum-thrum, thrum-thrum," answered the mountain.

Delacroix chanted again. Maybe he was saying "Gravuhmeezos Alamitos."

Abby felt her heart answer the mountain. "Thrum-thrum, thrum-thrum, thrum-thrum." She tilted her head and saw the pinpoints of light on the ceiling swirl and blink with the increasing intensity of Delacroix's chant, which now sounded like an indistinct mumble, mumble, mumble.

Beneath her feet, the surface of the rock shifted, swayed, and jiggled. She looked down to see the floor dissolving at the edges of the chamber. She seized Chillout's hand, his skin and hair rough beneath her fingers. The grungoid smiled at her, then gazed at Delacroix who continued to chant.

Abby cast her gaze to the floor again. The solid rock on which they'd stood was now a small island in a lake of liquid. Her stomach churned and a scream rose in her throat.

"Faith, little chickie," Chillout whispered.

Faith? Faith won't let me walk on molten rock!

She tried to tear her hand from Chillout's. Maybe she could leap over the lava or magma or— Wait a minute! Rock melted at a thousand degrees centigrade, maybe more. And yet, it was cool in this cavern, almost chilly. So the melting floor was an illusion. An illusion couldn't hurt her. Could it?

She relaxed, concentrating on the "thrum-thrum, thrum-thrum, thrum-thrum" and Delacroix's repetitive chant. Then she had a horrible thought. Everything was different down here; maybe rock could melt without heating up. She felt a wave of panic and tried to pull away from Chillout again.

"Faith," he whispered again. "Let go. Believe."

Let go? But how? How do you just decide to believe?

Blind panic swept through her brain like a tsunami and she gripped Chillout's hand tighter. They'd fall together. Down, down, deep into the mountain. She closed her eyes. She couldn't look. The chanting and thrumming became an ocean-like roar in her mind, the rock beneath her feet oscillated with the mountain's beat. She felt herself swaying and realized there was nothing beneath her.

She twisted, dancing like a kite in a gentle breeze. But she wasn't falling!

She opened her eyes a little at a time and saw Delacroix and Chillout smiling. The Pettifog looked up at the ceiling once more and nodded. The grungoid extended a long gray finger downward. Abby could have sworn she heard him say something like "Cowabunga." Or maybe it was "Wobucanga."

Then the bottom fell out.

She heard a sharp sucking sound, as if a giant was drawing a milkshake through an enormous drinking straw. "Voorrrvvvv."

She felt herself plummeting downward, going faster than she'd ever moved, even in Dad's car on the freeway.

Her heart dropped into her stomach. Cold air rushed by. Rock walls flashed past. Everything was a blur, including two other figures that may or may not have been Delacroix and the grungoid.

"Hellllpppp!" Abby shrieked. The sound, torn from her lips by the buffeting air, faded in an instant.

Closing her eyes, she thought about faith. Was faith generated by mind-numbing fear the same as faith you accepted when life was calmer? She concentrated on believing she wouldn't crash into whatever was beneath, that she wouldn't die, that somehow something would break her fall. As if from a long distance, she heard the beating of her heart. Or the mountain? Did it matter? She locked onto it, chanting, "Safe landing. Safe landing. Safe landing."

Time telescoped and then another sound seeped into her consciousness—a far-away sighing. It swelled, becoming a steady roar that eclipsed the beat of her heart and the thump of the mountain. The pitch of the roar changed. It grew deeper, slower.

Abby opened her eyes to see the walls of the rock tube come into focus. After a moment she saw the faces of Delacroix and Chillout where before there had been only smudges of high-speed color. The sharp suction that had drawn them like water down a long drain became a gentle exhale. They drifted, then touched solid ground.

"Oh." Abby stumbled and put out a hand. Chillout steadied her. "Your first trip on the Vorv," he told her. "Far-out, right on, and mega-cool, huh?"

The Vorv? She looked up, but saw only a rock ceiling, no open shaft, no sign of where they'd fallen from. "Where are we?"

"A special place," Delacroix answered. "A place very near where you will help your brother repel Spid."

"Noah? Is he here? Can I see him now?"

Delacroix's voice took on a note of deep sadness. "Not yet, Abby. Soon. Many obstacles, he must still overcome.

He will face danger, but others will help him. Allies. Loyal friends, yes?" With this he cast an eye at Chillout and then back to her. "You, *cherie*, you must use the time well. Prepare yourself to play your part. As it is written."

"Written? Written where?" Panic niggled at her again. "What is my part?"

"Shhh." He raised a stump and Abby imagined the missing forearm. Muscular, she bet, with strong, supple hand. She visualized a finger raised to his lips. "You will look and you will learn, no? And when you have gathered the evidence, then you will move. Just like in chess."

"But what will—?"

Delacroix ignored her and strode ahead down a narrow footpath. Chillout, scuttling to keep pace with his master, stayed right behind. Abby, still quivering from the long fall, trailed, her mind racing. What was that thing they'd fallen down? An elevator shaft? An air flume?

Ever since she and Noah came to Humbug Mountain she'd observed things she would have never believed existed, things that weren't logical. At least, she corrected herself, not logical based on her previous perceptions, on the solid, unshakeable facts that ruled the world she knew before.

She noticed Delacroix and Chillout had disappeared around one of the twists and turns in the passageway. Picking up her pace, she caught sight of them outside the entrance to another chamber.

"Welcome to Cave-Mart. little chickie," rasped Chillout, pointing up at a crudely lettered sign over the opening in the rock wall.

"Cave-Mart?" She glanced at the sign. The letters spelled a phrase in some kind of foreign language. Greek? Latin? *Thela stpla ceyo ulo ok*

Not Greek. Not Latin. What people, or creatures had written these words? Had other humans lived down her, centuries ago? "What does the sign say?"

"It says what it says, little one," Delacroix answered with a shrug. "You will soon decipher the words and gain their meaning. Or not."

As usual, his philosophy infuriated her. "All you do is talk in riddles. It drives me crazy. Say something that makes sense for once."

Delacroix beamed at her, then shook his head slowly. "Could I, would I, Abby. But, I can only do what I can do. I can only tell you what I can tell you. What the sign says is your conundrum, your first challenge. For us to push Spid back to his dark hole, you must discover the path. I cannot, the brush clear from your way, you see?"

Abby seethed. "Spid. Spid. Spid. I don't even know who he is. How can I help defeat something if I don't know what it is?"

"Oh," Delacroix's smile faded to a grim-lipped frown. "Spid will appear to you soon enough, *ma petite*. Too soon, I fear. Now inside, shall we go?" He ducked through the doorway and Chillout followed. Abby, still angry and frustrated, took a last look at the sign, memorizing the order of the letters and the spacing so she could try to decipher them later.

She entered a huge chamber, large enough to accommodate ten or more of the one where Delacroix lived and held court, and her eyes widened in amazement. Everywhere she looked were stacks and stacks of what she could only describe as...stuff. Everything imaginable. She walked around gaping at hundred-foot-high stacks of men's wallets, a virtual mountain of car keys, a matching peak constructed of eyeglasses. She fingered one of thousands of woolen mittens. "What is this place? Where did all of this come from?"

"Pretty trippy, huh?" Chillout chortled. "It's everything-o-rama."

Delacroix's frown loosened. He waved a stump at a creeping avalanche of paperback books. "You see Abby, this is where what is lost ends up. Have you never misplaced something? You could swear it disappeared into thin air, no?"

Organized as she was, Abby remembered a homework assignment she mislaid and never found. She looked for days, took an incomplete rather than do it over because that would have been admitting she was fallible. "Um, once. But you can't mean that everything that gets lost—"

"—ends up here?" Delacroix shrugged. "Impossible, no? But your eyes tell you what your mind wants to deny. Look around you. Is it not fantastic?

Abby had to admit it was. Thousands, no millions or maybe even billions of...of...things. She saw paths that led up the wall of the cavern and openings that hinted at other tunnels, other caverns, even more stuff.

She strolled around, checking out stack after stack. Sure enough, against one wall was a huge hillock of papers. She pulled a few loose and found bills, report cards, stock reports, contracts and what looked like homework assignments. She wondered how long it would take to find hers. A part of her wanted to try, but as she studied the pile she realized she might spend the rest of her life waist deep in paper. Still, just to set the record straight...

Delacroix chuckled. She swiveled her head and he winked, as if he knew her secret. Embarrassed, she walked on, watching Chillout scramble from pile to pile, chortling. The grungoid yanked a Seattle Mariners' baseball cap from a heap of hats, yarmulkes, and wigs and jammed it on his head with the bill pointing to the rear. Smirking, he bolted on toward a stack of cellular phones.

She wandered farther into the chamber and found an enormous pile of socks of all colors. Just past the socks, she found a similar-sized pile of unmatched shoes. She turned to Delacroix and again he seemed to read her mind. "Did you not ever puzzle, Abby, why the single shoes you always see along the highway?" Delacroix waggled his eyebrows and shrugged. "Where did the other shoe go? Before you, you see the answer. They are all right here."

An amazing array of things was crammed into every available space inside the huge rocky chamber. There was even a pile of musical instruments, saxophones, French horns, clarinets, flutes, and drums. Abby saw a pile of discarded drumsticks near the mound of instruments. She thought about picking up a couple for Noah and that made her want to cry. Would either of them ever escape from this crazy-mirror world? Would they ever see Dad again, walk on the beach, or go to school?

She fought the panic rising in her chest. Faith, she reminded herself. She had to believe that she would find Noah and they would go home again.

"It is sad, no?" Delacroix mused. "A whole world of music never created because the means to make it was lost." He touched a drumstick with his toe. "Come, we must ride the Vorv back."

They circled the back of the chamber, past baby clothes and beach towels, scissors, yarn, and needles, and turned back toward the entrance. "Why did you bring me here?"

"Because the prophecy said I must."

"The prophecy?"

"The story as it is being told."

"You're doing riddles again." Abby stamped her feet in anger. "Talk so I can understand you."

He sighed. "I know you are frustrated. But I am only a guide, you see. What you seek will be revealed in time, Abby. And by your own ingenuity, yes?"

She scowled at him and he shook his head mournfully. "Soon, you will know more. This promise, I can make."

Give it up, the logical side of her brain told her. If he doesn't know, he doesn't know. And if he won't tell, you can't make him. She sighed and followed him past stacks of alarm clocks and radios and a huge pile of dolls and other toys. Farther along, they found another opening in the rock. After traveling a hundred yards or so down the tunnel, they arrived at a doorway with an actual wooden door. Over it, a sign read *Tak emyw ifepl ease.*

"What's in there?"

"Open it and find out." Delacroix suggested.

Nervously, Abby reached for the shiny brass doorknob and turned it slowly. The door opened without a sound, revealing a chamber shrouded in darkness. She peered into the gloom, waiting for the tiny ceiling lights to come on, as they always did. Somewhere in the distance one person began to laugh. The lonely sound echoed off the walls.

"Who's there?" Abby called. "Come out where I can see you."

The laughter continued, and, in a moment, another voice joined in. Then another. Soon she was surrounded by the eerie disembodied laughter of hundreds of men, women, and children. They chuckled and chortled, giggled and guffawed. It sounded like the laugh track from one of those unfunny sitcoms, but multiplied by a thousand. Spooked, Abby slammed the door.

"Are there people trapped in there? Lost people?"

"No," Delacroix said. "But something, they have lost. Something you must be careful to hang onto, Abby, even to the very end."

Chillout mimed the posture of a stand-up comedian holding an imaginary microphone in front of his mouth. "And then the parrot said, that'll be two bucks lady. And next time skip the birdseed. Thudaboom-chick. But seriously folks, take my wife..."

Abby giggled at the impersonation. "I see now. That room was filled with lost senses of humor. Laughter sure sounds weird all by itself."

"Yes," Delacroix agreed. "You need the smile to make the mirth real."

As they left the chamber, Abby again studied the sign over the door of the storehouse of lost things.

Thela stpla ceyo ulo ok

Hard as she tried, she couldn't figure out why the letters looked familiar. Some kind of code or cipher? A language from before Greek or Latin?

The trip back to the top was a reverse duplicate of the trip down. But Abby was so preoccupied with her riddle, she barely flinched as they leaped toward the hole that appeared in the ceiling of the chamber and hurtled upward, riding the Vorv.

After a dinner of nuts, rootburgers, and orange soda, she laid down on the gel-bed. But, tired as her body was, her mind wouldn't turn off. The letters kept sliding behind her eyes. *Thela stpla ceyo ulo ok, Thela stpla ceyo ulo ok.*

She tried reading the phrase back to front. She tried counting the number of each distinct letters. If you knew which letters were most common in a language, it helped crack a code. But nineteen letters didn't provide a decent sample. She tried substituting other letters for the ones in the phrase, hoping it might be a cipher. But it wasn't. Or at least not one she recognized.

She got up, went to her backpack and dug out a pen and small steno pad. As she did, her fingers touched the translucent ball she plucked from the surf. She pulled it out, rubbed her hands over its smooth cool surface, then set it down on a stone ledge. Flopping on the bed, she opened the pad and began playing with the letters. She filled three pages then, exhausted and frustrated, flung the pen and pad to the floor and drifted into a fitful sleep.

CHAPTER 13

The burning wound on his leg sent out tentacles of heat, scalding Noah's entire body. Wild images jumped and jangled through his mind. Nonsensical but grim mental pictures flickered and danced like nightmare cartoons, lingering only long enough to register before the next flash crowded them out.

He saw a terrified Abby chased across a barren landscape by a leering thing with five immense arms. The hermit appeared, his forefinger imitating a windshield wiper as he scolded Noah. A cool cloth settled on his forehead, then he was dancing a wild and frenzied jig with Old Hannah. "Don't forget the steps, Noah, don't forget the steps," she cried, then was gone. Another picture flicker materialized and he saw Dad, holding hands with Mrs. Ramsden. He heard himself sob. The image faded.

Sounds and sensations mixed with the visuals. The stench of the mold monster. The earthy taste of scrubbage stew. And penetrating that was the fire, licking at his leg, heat radiating to his entire body. Sweating, then freezing, then sweating again.

Through it all, he felt his hands moving, in sympathetic rhythm with a beat coming from somewhere inside the mountain or inside himself. Snare rim and high-hat cymbal. Ta-ta-ta-ta ching ta ta...ta ta ta...da-ding ta.

Other hands pushed his arms to his sides and he heard a woman saying "go back to sleep, Noah, it'll be all right." Mom? He tried to open his eyes, but his lids felt enormous, thick and heavy.

At one point his stuttering mind generated an image of himself, clutching Uh-oh's leg, and falling, falling, falling. He flung an arm out to try to break the fall, but couldn't. A different female voice, higher pitched and anxious broke through the wall of fever. "Will he make it?"

Then the first voice again. No, not Mom. A woman, calm and reassuring. "Yes, of course he will. He must. He's needed."

Finally the waves of fever ebbed. The sensation of falling ended and Noah felt as if he were floating on a cool sea. He raised an arm, just to see if he could, then moved the back of his hand up to rub his eyes. His dry and gritty eyelids scratched and grated and then opened to a blur of light. He blinked and blinked again. A small room. Not rock like the hermit's chamber. Some other kind of material. Brown and reedy. A massive carved wooden chair stood beside the arched doorway.

Lights twinkled on the ceiling, growing brighter as his vision cleared. He plucked at the soft quilt that lay across his legs and realized someone was sitting on the bed beside him. No one he knew. A young woman, a girl really, about his age.

She regarded him with raised eyebrows. "You're back." She peeled a warm damp rag from his forehead and replaced it with a cool fresh one.

He managed a croak. "I...uh...guess so."

"Shhh." She put a finger to her lips. "Don't try to talk. Here, swallow a little of this." She turned to a small table beside the bed, dipped a wooden spoon into a bowl and brought it to his lips. The pungent aroma of the stuff reached him before he felt the warm liquid against his cracked lips and swollen tongue. He tasted a familiar, organic flavor, but, as he sucked at the second spoonful, other flavors crowded out the first. They were unlike anything he'd sampled or even imagined. Sweet and bitter at the same time, with a zest that made him tingle. "Scrub...scrubbage?"

"Yes." She put her finger to her lips again. "With some monga root and violet toadstool. One of mother's most potent recipes. It will put you on your feet in no time. Which is good, because you're behind schedule. You took the wrong tunnel."

Wrong tunnel? He remembered his decision to ignore the lighted arrow because it could have been a trap.

"Of course it could have," the girl said. Noah flinched. Could she read his mind like Uh-oh? Or had he spoken the words aloud. He couldn't tell. "We'll get you to The Skin on time, don't worry."

The Skin? On time? For what?

Noah shook his head. Everyone he encountered, starting with Old Hannah on the beach, knew where he was supposed to be and when and what he was supposed to be doing, but he didn't have a clue. He felt like he already lost a battle without getting to the battlefield.

Exhausted by emotional turmoil, he accepted another spoonful of the thick broth and studied the young woman. No, not yet a woman, but well on her way. She had smooth skin the color of an oatmeal cookie, and short hair a strange shade of brown that reminded him of the beach at first light. Large expressive hazel eyes, a strong nose and a generous mouth that always seemed turned upward in mild amusement. All that made for a face that was not beautiful, but definitely interesting. She wore some kind of khaki coveralls, with a long-sleeved flannel shirt underneath.

"Who are you?" This time the words didn't hurt as much coming out.

"Deidre," she murmured, as if it didn't really matter. "Here, eat another spoonful. Then you need to sleep."

"Where am I? How did I get here?"

She ignored the first question, but answered the second as she spooned another dollop of stew into his mouth. "Your little gray friend." She stood, putting the utensil beside the bowl on the small table. "He must care about you a lot. He carried you a long way after you escaped from the Skeezbo's lair."

Skeezbo? The mold monster?

Noah shuddered, remembering the gaping mouth, the writhing things in the stomach. He'd thrown a rock, hadn't he? And then Uh-oh pelted the beast and he found the taffy and— "Is that thing, the mold monster, is it dead?"

"Mold monster." Her eyes twinkled and her lips curled. "Yes, very dead."

Noah remembered his moment of pity for the beast as the taffy turned its stomach against it. But he also felt great relief. He'd survived.

"We call those things Skeezbos around here," Deidre told him. "Nasty things. Anyway, you're a local hero. You and the little gray guy."

"He really carried me?" Noah tried to imagine Uh-oh, with a hundred and fifty pounds draped across his shoulders, struggling down the rocky pathway.

"Well, I think he kind of dragged you most of the way. You're a lot bigger than he is. But he's a determined little creature. Good to have on your side."

Amazing. Why hadn't Uh-oh just left him there? After all, he'd had no idea how far he'd have to drag his burden before he found help, or even whether he'd find help at all.

Friend. Deidre had called him that and Noah decided she was right. He and Uh-oh were friends. Friends by fate more than by choice, but friends nevertheless. And friends helped friends.

"I've got to go now," Deidre said. "You take a nap, okay?"

The lights on the ceiling dimmed. Noah nodded, but didn't close his eyes. Watching Deidre stride across the room, he realized she stood an inch or two short of his own six feet. At the chair by the door, she picked up something and strapped it on. A scabbard. She slid a kind of two-pronged sword into it and settled the belt on her slim hips.

"Why do you need a sword?" His words were slurred with sleep.

"Spid," she mumbled.

"Who's Spid?"

Her hand fell to the hilt of her sword. "You'll know soon enough. And you'll wish you didn't."

CHAPTER 14

"The last place you look!" Abby sat up, wide awake and marveling at the answer delivered by her subconscious mind. Of course! *Thela stpla ceyo ulo ok. The last place you look.*

Smiling, she sank back against her pillow, remembering other times when she blurted stuff out loud and jerked herself awake in the middle of the night. Sometimes, only a few words ejected themselves from her sleeping mind, but often she'd recite a complex string of numbers or words in multiple languages. Mom and Dad would race into her bedroom, certain she was traumatized by some gruesome nightmare. After she explained that she just figured out the value of X in some complex algebraic equation, or finally understood how to use the conditional tense in Spanish, they'd stumble back to their bedroom, shaking their heads.

The pinpoint assemblage of lights above her danced and twinkled into a bright white glow, as if they shared her excitement. She beamed up at them. They must be what Delacroix referred to as the Darksuckers. But what were they? She thought again about standing on her bed and trying to take a closer look, but decided to wait until morning.

She smiled again. That implied this was night. Night as she knew it, defined as the opposite of day, the time when the sun shone on the other side of the earth. Those definitions carried no meaning inside the mountain. Or perhaps they had new meanings. Having faith, she realized, could still mean believing in order and structure—just a different kind of order and structure.

Thela stpla ceyo ulo ok. It was so simple. So obvious. You just took the whole thing, squished it together, *Thelastplaceyoulook,* then broke it up another way. *The last place you look.*

People always said that when you were searching for something. "You'll find it in the last place you look." Kind of a "well duh," if you thought about it, since nobody kept looking *after* they found something. You were always going to find it in the last place you looked. Or you wouldn't find it at all. And it would end up piled on a stack of lost things in the storeroom down below.

Would she end up there? Would Noah?

Faith trickled away. She felt small and afraid.

The lights flickered and the gel bed rocked beneath her.

Abby felt a finger of fear jab her stomach. Earthquake? Were the tectonic plates off the coast shifting as one slid beneath the other? Would the rock walls and ceilings collapse?

She peered around, searching for somewhere safe. Couldn't crawl under the gel bed. The rickety table where her pack sat wouldn't protect her from rain, let alone falling rock. Weren't you supposed to stand in a doorway? She started to get up, but spotted something that froze her in place.

Over on the stone ledge opposite her bed, the orb Delacroix called the Chameleon Stone was throbbing with color, strobing streams of red, blue, green, and bright white across the walls. Soon the colors ran together, darkened and formed a midnight black pool. A funnel of dark blue beamed from the stone. Above her, the twinkling lights, the Darksuckers, seemed to flee toward her, leaving the ceiling above the orb in darkness.

The bed quivered again. The orb strobed faster, the beam rotating, swirling into a vortex. Stunned with fear, Abby couldn't tear her gaze from it as a figure materialized. The Darksuckers fled to the wall behind her, thrusting her shadow out to meet the intruder. Abby shrank back, terrified and fascinated.

This person, this thing, was huge. An enormous head with eyes like black holes and ears that dangled to its chin emerged from the neck of a gray business suit. The arms hung past the creature's knees and where the trousers ended, instead of polished shoes, were bare...well, Abby guessed they were feet, although they were nothing like human feet. These were reptilian, with webs between the toes and folds of loose skin.

She swept her eyes upward and gaped at the creature's grotesque face, at skin like wet, hairy leather that had been left to dry in the sun, skin that was kind of purple-colored. A major wart protruded from one cheek, wiggling around almost like it had a mind of its own. In contrast, the thing (was it a he?), sported neatly-combed dark hair that looked like it had been professionally cut. Dangling from the long-lobed ears were dozens of earrings and studs, ornate, jeweled and jangly.

Abby squealed and shrank farther into the corner.

"A most predictable and understandable reaction, Miss Keene. But lamentable. You have nothing to fear. I am Spid The Devious, the Grand Exalted Garboon of the land Below Skin, the land of Beneath, transmitted to you tonight through the Shadow Stone."

The precise, effete, slightly bombastic tone of the voice surprised her. It sounded out of place, practiced, as much a façade as the suit. The Darksuckers glittered, making her shadow twitch like a broken marionette. Her voice quavered. "They, uh, they warned me about you."

"Warned?" Spid's voice grew in volume, but remained falsely smooth. "Warned? Why would they warn you, my dear? And why would you listen to their lies? All I intend to do is apply my superior intellect, logic, and highly evolved moral certainty to set things right with the world."

He puffed out his chest, straining the buttons on the vest, and thrust one lizard-like hand high into the air. "Only I have the answers to mankind's profound dilemma. Only I can provide the ethical center from which all good things will spring."

"Dittos, Boss. You're right, as usual," a growl-gargled voice agreed.

An even uglier figure materialized beside Spid. This one was shorter, with a red scaly body and beady, leering eyes. He wore a military type uniform with epaulets and braid. As he stared up at Spid adoringly, Abby saw some kind of green gunk bubbling from his lips.

"Yurk," Spid informed her by way of introduction. "My assistant and leader of my armed forces."

He lowered his voice and leaned toward Abby as if confiding in her. "Not too bright, but loyal, like most of my followers who have found themselves converted by my unmatchable oratorical style and inarguable rightness. Am I correct, Yurk?"

"You duh troll, Boss. You duh troll." Yurk wiped a potentially monumental green booger away from his nose with the back of his hand.

Spid grimaced, then sighed. "It's good to be Garboon."

"You're a troll?" Abby forgot her fear for an instant and leaned forward. "A real, like, troll like in...like in that billy goat story?" From this new angle, she realized she could see the wall behind Spid, and concluded that she wasn't looking at flesh-and-blood creatures, but lifelike holograms created by the dark light funneling through the Chameleon Stone. Could the Shadow Stone that Spid referred to have somehow linked with the orb she found in the surf?

"Vicious rumors and gossip spread by—" Spid stopped and swiveled his head back and forth as if looking for enemies. Finally he sputtered.

"—Delacroix. That's who, and him an outsider who wasn't even born in the mountain. And the hermit and the Shroomers and all kinds of other wackos. Scaring everybody with stories about how evil I am and how much destruction I'll wreak and..."

"You go, Boss, you go." Yurk, the ogre chimed in. "Say hallelujah! Go tell it in the mountain!"

"They'll stop at nothing to prevent my ascension." The troll paced, hands clasped behind his back. Then, almost as an aside, he muttered, "My people haven't lived under bridges and eaten children for hundreds of years."

"Really?" Now that she knew he was only a hologram, wasn't actually here with her, Abby's fear subsided, giving way to scientific interest.

"Not since the Dark Ages. We were...misunderstood, you see? And so we were all banished to Beneath. All of us. Ogres too." He gestured at Yurk, who tried to make a deep sweeping bow and promptly fell on his keester.

Spid shook his head and continued, "Banshees, gronnks, skrees, gammits and—" Here a sly smile crept onto his face. "Well, you'll meet them all soon enough. How long, Yurk?"

115

The ogre consulted what looked like a kind of crude wristwatch on his arm. "Uh, let's see now, carry the seven, divide by two, subtract eight..."

The troll rolled his eyes, folded his massive arms, and tapped his foot.

"Move the decimal over...uh... a little less than five days, Boss."

Abby cringed as Spid drew back a scaly arm and prepared to backhand the stubby ogre. At the last minute, he caught his downward motion with the other hand, took a deep breath and intoned calmly. "Use the correct tool next time, Yurk. The watch appears to be...defective."

"Oh...oh...kay, Boss. Next time for sure." The ogre ducked out of range.

"In...something less than five days, my dedicated army of creatures from the land of Beneath will pour through The Skin and I will lead us in the glorious conquest of the land Above Skin. Soon, The United States of America will become known as the Unified Spid Amalgamation. No point in changing all the letters. That's inefficient. Think of all the stationery and signs and websites we'd have to change. Washington already wastes enough money."

Abby calculated. If a day here equaled a day on the outside, the attack he bragged about would happen on the solstice.

"First we'll capture everyone inside Humbug Mountain and then we'll fan out. We have the men, uh creatures, and the tools, and of course," he tapped his chest, "the leadership."

"Except Noah will stop you," Abby blurted. "And I'll help him."

"Noah? Noah? Don't make me laugh! That whelp is no match for the awesome power of Spid The Devious," the troll thundered.

"All praise Spid the municipal!" Yurk bellowed, striking a threatening pose, his mottled face a bright crimson.

"That's munificent, Yurk." Spid elbowed his cohort to the rear, "Not municipal—mew-niff-ih-cent. As in generous and caring."

The troll turned to Abby, lowering his voice to a soft, courtly, almost apologetic rumble. "Noah's only a boy. And you, Abby, should know better than anyone that he's not a very, shall we say, focused kind of boy. Is he?"

"He's a real airhead, Boss," Yurk burbled. "You could outwit him with one lobe of your brain tied behind your back."

Like you're a rocket scientist! Abby bit back the words. As much as it irked her, she decided to play along with Spid and Captain Ugly, to figuratively send out a pawn to gauge their strategy. She'd see if she could learn anything that would help her and, ultimately, Noah. "Noah tends to be a little scattered," she admitted.

"Scattered would be an excellent way to describe him." The troll smiled. Abby supposed he was trying to infuse some warmth into the conversation, but he succeeded only in making his face lopsided. "And soon he will face the challenge of his life. If indeed, he lives to make it to The Skin in time."

"He'll make it." Abby heard her voice ring off the rock. Behind her, the Darksuckers glowed like tiny suns.

"Ah, loyalty. And love for your brother. Admirable qualities, Abby. Truly. You are a paragon. I have, in my own way revered you from afar, you know."

"You have?" This sounded ominous. Creepy even. Could he have, through his Shadow Stone, watched her at home? While she slept and ate or even...a shiver of revulsion ran down her spine...while she took a bath?

117

"Yes." Spid rubbed his webbed hands together. "I've observed since you began the fulfillment of the prophecy by plucking the Chameleon Stone from the surf."

She shuddered and pulled the blanket around her, relieved but still repulsed. "That's disgusting. And it's an invasion of privacy." The Darksuckers gathered closer, laying more light across her shoulders.

Spid put a hand on his chest and took a step back. "Miss Keene, I am appalled that you think I would take advantage of the magical link between my Shadow Stone and the orb which you possess for any other than the most noble of motives." He offered a sly smile and raised one bushy eyebrow. It reminded her of John Belushi in *Animal House*. "You can be assured that I always closed my eyes at the, um, indelicate moments."

"Peeping Tom," Abby mumbled. "Pervert."

"What was that?" Spid's voice held a tone of menace. "Speak up." He took two steps toward her.

Even though the image was only a projection, Abby felt a cold chill of fear. "I, uh said, 'Chameleon Stone, you subverted it.'"

Spid stared hard at her and scratched his head with one claw.

"Uppity little thing, ain't she, Boss?" The ogre licked his lips and wiped another green gob from his nose.

"She is indeed, Yurk. But she'll learn to respect my superior powers soon enough."

"Dittos, Boss. Mega dittos."

Anger overrode the last of Abby's fear. "So what are you doing here now? Did you just come to gloat?"

Spid raised one eyebrow again and put an even softer, more wheedling tone into his voice. "Gloat? No, indeed. I came to propose a battle of wits. I have observed your sharp powers of logic and deduction, your extensive vocabulary, your outstanding visualization skills."

118

Abby forced herself to ignore his flattery. "So?"

"Yurk! Bring out the board."

"Coming right up, Boss." The squat figure of Spid's hench-beast faded into the blue light.

"Do you like word games, Abby?"

She thought about it for a moment. Was this some kind of a trick question? "You mean like unscrambling words? Like in the sign over the door of the storehouse?"

"You mean *Thela stpla ceyo ulo ok*?" Spid's voice took on a puzzled tone and he rubbed his chin.

"Yes, *The Last Place You Look*."

Spid's jaw dropped. "What?"

"If you squash it together and put in spaces the right places, it spells *The Last Place You Look*."

Spid's finger wrote imaginary words in the air. She heard him mumble, "*The Last Place You Look*."

"Pretty simple, isn't it?" The Darksuckers twinkled around her, making her shadow dance.

Spid sniffed. "Of course. I just wanted to make sure you really knew."

Abby felt a sudden jolt of confidence. Maybe Spid's belief in his brainpower was his fatal flaw. Plus, he hadn't overheard her when she discovered what the words meant; that meant he wasn't watching or listening every minute.

With a loud popping sound, Yurk's image reappeared from the blue funnel, clutching a large game board to his chest.

"Ah, yes, here we are." Spid rubbed his hands together.

The ogre set the board up on a sort of tripod arrangement and produced a large leather bag, cinched closed with a drawstring. The bag made a clacking sound when he shook it.

Curiosity got the best of Abby and she edged closer to the two grotesque figures. "Why, that looks like Scrab—"

"No, don't say it!" Spid interrupted.

"Why not?" Puzzled, Abby glanced at the board again. "It does. It looks just like Scrab—"

"No! Do not say that word!" Spid made a chopping motion with his hand. "Spid the Devious, the Grand Exalted Garboon of Beneath, the all-seeing and all-knowing ruler of the armies of darkness and soon to be the conqueror of all of Above Skin quakes at only one thing."

What thing? Abby stepped closer. This could be the way to help Noah.

"Lawsuits. Right, Boss?" Yurk croaked.

"Absolutely, my churlish one. I don't want to get into copyright infringement litigation."

"But it sure looks a lot like—"

"Superficially," Spid interrupted hurriedly, "perhaps, but there are major differences, innovations I have personally added to provide more depth to the game, to make it more challenging to my indescribable mental skills."

Abby sighed, tugged the quilt from the bed and wrapped it around her. If he played like he talked, they could be here all night. "So if you don't call this game Scra—"

"Put a sock in it, kid," Yurk growled.

"Anyway, if you don't call it that, what do you call it?"

Spid took a step forward and made an imaginary frame with his fingers. "The game's name is every bit as original and descriptive as the play is fast-moving and intriguing. Which is understandable, since it was I, Spid, who developed it."

Abby rolled her eyes.

120

"Soon," Spid continued, "every day, every man woman and child in the world, when they're not paying homage to me, will be playing—" he paused dramatically "—Spiddle."

"Spiddle?" Abby asked, trying to keep a straight face. It sounded like something a puppy would do on a sheet of newspaper. "And you think every man, woman and child in the world will *want* to play a game called Spiddle?"

"If they don't want to die screaming they will," Yurk croaked.

"Well, of course the game *will* be mentioned in the decree of martial law," Spid confirmed. "So, would you like to play?"

Abby perused the board once again. "Uh, I guess. What are the rules?"

"The rules? Oh, don't worry about those. I'll tell you as we go along." Spid's voice reeked with false heartiness. "Okay?"

The Darksuckers behind her flickered. A warning? But it was only a game. And Spid was only a hologram. "Um, okay."

"Good." He attempted another smile, making the wart on his cheek jiggle. "Only one thing remains to be decided."

"What's that?"

Spid narrowed his eyes and rubbed his hands together once more. "What shall we play for?"

CHAPTER 15

This sleep was deep, dreamless, and restful. Noah emerged by degrees, shrinking from the gentle but persistent hand that shook his shoulder and the soothing woman's voice that drew him toward consciousness, toward responsibility.

"Time to wake up, Noah." The voice reminded him again of his mother. Honey sweet, but insistent.

"Just five minutes more. Then I'll get up," he mumbled.

"No, Noah. Now. Your friend is waiting. And time is very short."

He dragged his eyelids up, noting that this time they didn't scrape and his vision was clear and sharp. He looked up into the twinkling eyes of a woman with silver-streaked blonde hair and a reassuring smile.

"Up and at 'em now," the woman coaxed. "How do you feel?"

Noah took stock. Actually he felt much better, a little stiff, but no longer feverish. He slid a hand down his leg and ran his fingers along the spot where the mold monster's spit burned him. Other than a rough bumpiness, the wound had disappeared. He couldn't detect any swelling or soreness either. How long had he been here? "I'm, uh, okay."

"Good," the woman continued in a no-nonsense tone. "I made you some breakfast. After you eat, you can walk down to the water and bathe. You've gotten a little whiffy." She said this with a tone of amusement. "When you crawl out of bed, chuck your drawers in the corner so I can wash them along with everything else. She gestured to a robe that hung from a hook by the door. "Throw that on and come on out for breakfast. After your bath, Deidre will join us and chart your course."

"Deidre?" The girl with the two-pronged sword?

"My headstrong and fearless daughter," the woman said in a voice both proud and wistful. "She's decided to accompany you on the next leg of your journey. To the Temple of Cheltnor—a dangerous trek, and your next test."

Noah sat up and ran his hand through egg-beatered hair. "Listen, everyone keeps talking about some kind of a journey. I don't want to go, okay? I just want to find my sister and get out of here."

"And you will." The woman stood, unblinking, seeming to turn inward and focus on a landscape that existed only in her mind. "If all goes as I hope." She smiled at him, warm and encouraging and shook out her long quilted skirt. "But you will need an ally. The prophecy allows for you to take another companion and Deidre insists she must travel at your side. And when Deidre insists, you might as well argue with a shitake tree."

"A what? That's a kind of mushroom. Mushrooms don't grow on trees."

She laughed. "Not where you come from, no. But here, inside the mountain, things are much different." She turned to gather the half-empty bowl of cold stew from the table beside the bed and said, "You'll find out what I mean when Deidre leads you through the forest."

Noah felt like a massive weight rested on his shoulders. Too much information. Too much uncertainty ahead. Everything he already faced seemed like a distant dream, unreal and shrouded by mist. Surely, with all the twists and turns he'd made, he couldn't be that far from home. This woman got in here somehow. So did Deidre. Why couldn't he just leave the same way? Without going on a journey. Without meeting strange creatures like—"Uh-Oh! Is he all right?"

"Quite exhausted, I'm afraid." The woman raised her eyebrows. "But I think, with another dose of distilled wormroot and freemish blossom we'll have him on his feet and ready for your departure this afternoon." She snapped her fingers three times. "Now, hurry."

Noah waited until he was certain she'd left before he flexed his legs and arms, stumbled from the bed, pulled on the robe, belted it tightly and then stepped out of his undershorts. He sniffed. Deidre's mother got that part right. He smelled like Uh-oh.

She fed him a huge breakfast, featuring blue pancakes with lumps of some strange kind of nut or grain, a mound of scrambled eggs with cheese, and a delicious juice that reminded him of a cross between apple and strawberry. His polished off five pancakes and three glasses of juice.

"Not to rush you, but..." she handed him clean clothes, his pack, a rough-weave towel and a bar of what looked like homemade soap. It was green and gray and smelled like freshly cut grass. Smiling, she pushed him toward the door of what he realized was a house constructed of cubes of densely packed dirt. Sod? Down here? Another mystery.

"Just take the left fork of the path, walk about a quarter mile and turn right at the oatmeal tree," she told him. "Careful, the slope to the wish pool is pretty steep."

Noah's head swam. "Oatmeal tree? Wish pool?"

"When you take your bath, make a wish. As for the oatmeal tree, you'll see when you get there. But don't eat any. It's poisonous until it's cooked."

"Thanks for the warning." He turned to go, then stopped. "Thank you. For everything."

"You're quite welcome. I ask only one favor in return."

"What is it?"

"Later. When you meet with trouble, keep an eye on Deidre. She's very very brave and very very able and," her frown betrayed her concern, "sometimes a little impetuous."

Noah pushed doubt aside and said what she wanted to hear. "I'll do my best."

"I know you will." Her eyes locked on his and he felt a sizzle, like electricity, in the back of his head. He remembered the sensation from his encounter with old Hannah. Maybe they were both psychic. Or something.

He nodded, started for the door again, then turned back. "You saved my life and I haven't even asked your name."

"Names can shift like the breeze," she laughed. "But I'm called Eve."

"Just Eve?"

"Just Eve."

"How did you get here? Why do you stay underground? Why don't you go," he pointed toward a wall, "out into the other world."

Her eyes locked on something in the distance he couldn't see. "I'm in many worlds, Noah. This is just the one I occupy at the moment."

"Huh?"

"You see, Noah," she locked her eyes on his again and he felt the sizzle, now at the top of his head. "There are those who will tell you I am a witch."

125

Noah stood at the edge of the pool and looked in every direction.

No one around. I'm all alone.

Still, he blushed as he peeled the robe away and stepped into the water. "Brrr uhrrr uhrrr." Teeth chattering, he forced himself to take three more steps into the deep blue pool, until the water lapped at his bellybutton. Rubbing the soap against his body, he lathered up, wishing all the while that the water was warmer. As he scrubbed his arms, the surface glimmered and swirled, then steamed. In a moment it was almost too hot.

"The wishing pool, huh? I wonder if I wished for Abby and I to be out of Humbug Mountain and back home if it would grant that wish?" He stopped scrubbing and concentrated, fixing a picture of Abby and himself walking down the driveway to their house, Dad hurtling off the porch to greet them.

"It only grants small wishes." Deidre's voice echoed around him.

Aware of his nakedness, Noah dropped the soap and splayed his fingers across his groin.

"Warmer water, a candy bar, your favorite song," Deidre continued. "If you want something major, you've got to make it happen yourself."

Noah glanced behind him to see her standing on an overhanging rock a few yards away. He squatted, duck-walking into deeper water. His feet slipped and he went under.

"Oh, get over yourself, Noah," Deidre told him when he emerged flailing at the surface. "I'm not trying to scope you out."

Angry, Noah didn't answer. He treaded water, both hands anchored again over his groin.

"How's the water?"

Ignore her. She'll get tired of tormenting you and go away.

He kicked harder, gasping for breath, and turned his back on her.

"Hey, I could use a bath too. Maybe I'll jump in. Here goes my shirt!"

Heat flooded up Noah's neck and onto his face. He told himself he wouldn't, then peeked over his shoulder.

"Made you look." Deidre threw her head back and laughed.

"Very funny," Noah panted. His tired legs felt like blocks of granite.

She stopped laughing and fixed a steady gaze on him. "You need to lighten up, Noah. Laugh while you can. Laugh now. Because there's lots of serious stuff on the way. Life and death stuff." With that she spun on her heel, jumped from the rock, and started up the slope toward the cottage.

"I'll laugh when something's funny," he yelled after her.

"Fy-ine." Noah heard her trill. "By the way, nice buns, Noah."

Fuming, Noah waited until her throaty giggle faded completely, then retrieved the soap and finished his bath. He'd get even. He'd nail her when she least expected it. Meanwhile, he'd pretend this never happened.

The thought of revenge pumped him up. After drying off, he pulled on fresh underwear, clean jeans, a T-shirt, and white socks. He even hauled his toothbrush out of his pack, found the toothpaste, and brushed his teeth. As Abby would put it, he "scrubbed the moss off his chompers." He'd find his sister soon. The witch said he would. Witches knew stuff like that, didn't they? They could read the future with crystal balls. Or was it gypsies that did that? Whatever.

He combed his hair, tied his tennis shoes and set off for Eve's cottage, whistling a little syncopated tune. He stopped to catch his breath at the oatmeal tree, a tall, broad, wide-limbed growth that did, indeed have the texture of a huge stack of raw breakfast cereal. He was careful not to touch it.

When he arrived at the small sod house, he found Eve waiting in front. His gray, stumpy friend leaned against the wall beside her. Uh-oh's eyes were sunk in his head and his dreadlocks hung like tired black worms.

Noah felt like hugging Uh-oh, but decided that might look a little geeky. He grasped his hand instead. "Thank you, Uh-oh. Thank you for throwing the rock at the mold monster. Thank you for carrying me here."

"You're welcome, Noah," Uh-oh rasped. Something resembling a smile crossed his face.

"So you *can* talk." Noah felt his heart leap with excitement. "You understand what I'm saying and you can answer me?"

"You're welcome, Noah." Uh-oh repeated. "Welcome, Noah."

Noah sighed, defeated again. Uh-oh must just pick up bits and pieces, he decided. Or else he's holding back. Maybe he doesn't trust me yet.

As he mulled that over, Deidre strode around the corner of the house. She now wore an outfit that resembled lightweight armor: loose-fitting pants, covered in what looked like tortoise shell platelets and a top made of the same material. Her sword hung from a belt, prongs up, and she carried a pair of leather and metal harnesses and a second two-tined sword in a scabbard.

Eve raised her eyebrows, kissed her daughter on the forehead, and went to the door. "Play nice, Deidre. I'll put your provisions together."

"Thanks, Mom." Deidre handed the long-handled twin-headed weapon and a harness to Noah. "This is a sonic sword, also called a battle fork."

"What, do you do with it? Hit people or stab them or what?"

Deidre made a "you're too dumb to live," face at him as he examined the sword, feeling its heft and balance. The shaft seemed made out of some kind of light metal with a leather strip wrapped around its center. The prongs were metal too, not sharp-edged, each a different color, one kind of brass-like and the other more bluish.

"This is how you wear the decibelt." Deidre strapped on her harness so the circular metal plate protected her chest. "Come on, hustle up. We don't have time to waste."

With Uh-oh's assistance, Noah strapped on the harness, pulling the leather straps tight across his chest and shoulders.

"The sonic sword, Noah, is a gigantic, highly sensitive tuning fork."

She thrust the blunt end of the shaft against her metal breastplate with a clang. Noah heard a low, escalating hum emanate from her weapon. Copying her, he activated his own battle fork. It began to vibrate and he struggled to hold it upright. Uh-oh's eyes widened and he scuttled out of harm's way.

"Alright, pay attention, Drum Boy." Deidre stabbed at the air with the sonic sword. "And I'll show you how to knock down a charging wormonocerous. If you learn the right moves."

Noah gripped the sonic sword, his arms thrumming. *I'll learn them, Soldier Girl. And then I'll use them to kick your butt.*

CHAPTER 16

"What do I get if I win?" Abby's voice quavered. "Can Noah and I go home?"

"Ah, if I but had the power, I would do that, Abby. Win or lose." Spid smiled in a way that made his face look like an evil prune with ears. "I would send you home in a trice, if I could. Half a trice even. But fate has decreed the challenge must be met before the assembled multitudes at The Skin. So there you have it."

There I have what? Abby stared at the hologram, trying to make sense of the words. He'd let us go if he could, but he can't until the challenge is met. And what part would Noah play in this challenge at The Skin? What could he possibly do? His only talent was drumming. "So why should I play Scrab—"

"Spiddle!" Spid shrieked. "It's Spiddle." Then he seemed to gather himself and asked, "Are you worried about Noah?"

Beyond worried, Abby thought. Semi-frantic. But I won't let this ugly troll see that. "I'm...concerned."

The troll's smirk told her he wasn't buying her nonchalance. "If you win the game, then, using the powers of both the Shadow Stone and your Chameleon Orb, I can allow you to see your brother, to reassure yourself that he is indeed alive and well and, as ill-conceived as it might be, following the path to our final confrontation."

Tears stung Abby's eyes. If she could see Noah, figure out where he was, maybe she could devise a plan to get them out of this madhouse.

"Unfortunately, you cannot speak with him, you understand, just observe him." The troll sighed heavily. "He's in a spotty reception area."

"Magical stones have reception problems?"

Spid sniffed in disgust. "How little you mere humans know. Magical stones are not unlike cell phones."

Abby nodded. She still had to take her shot. "And if I lose the game?"

"You could fill a small employment need. I've had, er, recruiting problems. I need someone to act as a..." he paused and stroked his chin as he thought, "...researcher. Yes, that's it. A researcher."

He sounded like somebody trying to sell her something she didn't want. "Researcher?"

"Exactly." He rubbed his hands together. "Let me explain. By now, you have surely noticed that the light around us," he gestured to the roof of the cavern, "is provided by living creatures."

She nodded. "I suspected."

"Indeed. They are called the Zezzue. Or, in your language, Darksuckers."

Zezzue. The troll pronounced their name like says-you. Abby practiced it in her mind. "Why are they called Darksuckers?"

"Because that is literally what they do. You have probably learned in your school that darkness is the absence of light, am I correct?"

"Yes, although the nature of light is one of science's continuing mysteries." She almost giggled. She sounded so serious and scholarly.

"Your experts are in error," Spid declared. "Darkness is, in and of itself, an entity, a living presence. It exists in nature in varying quantities."

The concept boggled Abby's mind. "You mean...?"

"Precisely. Certain things can literally destroy areas of the darkness. Fire, electric lights, the sun, the moon. But as soon as light is extinguished, darkness reproduces and reclaims its territory."

Could Spid be correct? "And the Zezzue?"

"Can inhale many, many times their own body weight in darkness."

Abby looked up at the light on the wall and ceiling around her. It glowed a sort of amber color, then shifted to a more reddish tint. She wished she could see the pinpoint light creatures through a microscope—watch them in action. "Where do they exhale it? The darkness?"

An eyebrow went up. Spid cleared his throat. "An excellent question. One, I am hoping you can determine through, er, um, research. There is reputed to be an immense catacomb of chambers, a maze somewhere in the mountain. According to legend, the Zezzue, at regular intervals, fly in and expel their accumulated darkness."

All that darkness. Abby shivered and thought of the tulip-shaped nightlight Mom bought for her second birthday. She still used it every night.

Again, it felt like Spid intercepted her inner thoughts, probed her mind. "You are not alone in your fear of darkness, Miss Keene. It is shared by many living creatures." He gnawed at the tip of one green fingernail. "And, in the Realm of Exponential Darkness, if indeed that exists, what the Zezzue exhale is compressed a million billion times. It is darkness so intense it swallows all the other senses. In its presence, it is reputed, you cannot hear yourself breathe, feel your heartbeat, or smell your own fear."

"Yegggh," Yurk growled. "Stop it, Boss, you're scaring me."

Spid ignored his toady. "And there you have it, Miss Keene, the reason I need your, er, assistance. I don't want my troops wandering into the Realm of Exponential Darkness by accident. They would suffer great er, um...discomfort and apprehension. Plus it would disrupt the Zezzue. They are critical to my future plans."

"So you want me to watch where the Darksuckers go? Spy on them?"

"Never!" Spid took a step back. "Merely observe and report, that is all. The Zezzue communicate with Delacroix. And with the hermit."

"The hermit? The hermit is real?"

"To my misfortune, yes. At any rate, the Zezzue may decide to convey information to you. And should you lose the Spiddle game—"

"You'll want to know everything they tell me." Abby finished his sentence. "Well I won't have anything to do with your evil plans for the world. I won't help you defeat Noah, and open The Skin and conquer the earth and make everyone play Spiddle. I won't!" She stomped her foot.

Spid sighed again. "Naturally. Of course you won't. Your ideals and loyalty prevent that. But," his fleshy lips pushed in and out, "I really don't require your assistance for my triumph. That situation is totally under control. All I ask is research data about the Zezzue. When you lose the game."

"Spying." She insisted. "*If* I lose the game."

"If you must, then spying it is." Spid shared an oily smile. "But only for the best motives. For the good of the world. Trust me."

As if. Her mind raced. Did this grotesque egomaniac really have the resources to conquer the world? Could he read her mind? Could he tell if she lied? It was worth a gamble. If she lost the game. "Just the Zezzue? Where they go to exhale darkness? That's all?"

"Correct."

She crossed her fingers behind her back. "All right then, fine, I'll do it."

Spid smiled. Okay, he hadn't read her mind that time, didn't know she had lied, had no intention of helping him. "Let's play Scra—"

"Shhhhh!" Spid held a thick finger to his lips. "Remember. The lawyers."

"Oh, right. Spiddle. How do we start the game?"

"Yurk!" Spid howled for his hench-monster.

The ogre stepped forward with the canvas sack, cleared his throat and began to growl the rules. "Each player draws nineteen letters. The value of each letter is written on the tile. After you have put a word down on the board, the mystery spaces beneath the letters will light up with bonus values and your score will appear on the automatic scoreboard." Yurk gestured at an oblong black area that had appeared with their names written in glowing script at the top of two columns. "After you play, you draw letters to bring you back up to the original nineteen. When the bag is empty and one player uses all of his or her tiles, the game ends. The player with tiles remaining must subtract the total from his or her score."

"Very good, Yurk. Shall we begin, Miss Keene?" Spid took the bag from the ogre and offered it to Abby.

She reached for it, then realized she couldn't touch it because it was merely a projection. "How can I...?"

"Just say the word 'draw'," Spid smiled. Your letters will appear."

"Draw."

The bag unbunched at the top and nineteen tiles flashed onto a three-dimensional tray that appeared in front of her. It was a motley assortment of letters, evenly divided between vowels and consonants. The most striking difference she noticed between this and a conventional Scrab—that other game—was the value of the tiles. For example the *U* counted as seven points instead of one. And the *Z* was only two. *P*s apparently were highly thought of, with a value of seventeen points. She had several *E*s, ranging in value from four to eight points. Confused, she studied her letters while Spid commanded "draw" and got his own set.

"I'm sure you've noted that you are unable to rearrange the letters by hand because they aren't physically in the same space you occupy," Spid said. "All you need do is point at one and then at the new spot you want it to go. When you're ready to lay them down, just visualize the word and the place on the board and *voila!*"

Spid pronounced the French word Vo-ill-uh instead of Vwoy-lah'. Abby considered correcting him but checked herself. No need to irritate him; not if she wanted to see Noah. Following his instructions, she tried rearranging the letters to form possible words. Finally, she decided on one. "Who goes first?"

"Ladies, Miss Keene." The troll gestured toward the board. "Fire at will."

"Does it matter where I set the first one down?"

"Not in the slightest."

Visualizing the word *P-E-R-A-D-V-E-N-T-U-R-E*, she examined the board. This was a tough game. Not only were there more letters from which to make words, but you didn't know what bonus the board would award until after you laid down your letters. The squares on this board were all the same gray color, unlike the other game where colored squares announced the availability of extra points.

The board was immense, possibly ten times larger than the board from the game she'd played before. Finally, she made her choice. To her amazement, the letters flew from her tray in single file formation and plopped down on the exact spot she'd pictured.

Both Spid and Yurk twisted their heads down to examine the word. Yurk used a sausage-sized finger to scratch his forehead.

Lights lit up beneath three of the letters and numbers rolled up on the scoreboard—347 points for her word. She got two triple word scores and one sextuple letter score on the *D*, which already had a nine-point value.

The troll hissed in annoyance. Yurk produced a thick book and began to thumb frantically through the pages.

"Is that a dictionary? Are you going to challenge?" Abby hadn't heard Yurk mention challenges. Were they allowed?

"Ahem, well, I was considering..." Spid paused and appeared to be deep in thought. Finally, he decided. "I think not. Not this time. But I should have Yurk explain the rule about challenges."

"Oh boy. Oh boy, oh boy," the ogre growled. "Good move, Boss. Peradventure *is* a word. It means," he pointed down at the page, "perhaps, maybe, a possibility."

"Of course." With a self-satisfied smirk, Spid prodded Yurk to continue. "I knew that. The challenge rule, Yurk."

"Right, Boss." Yurk took a step forward and droned. "Each player shall have one challenge of the other player's played word without penalty. After that, an unsuccessful challenge shall lead to the challenger having their choice of being immediately thrown into the river of molten mildew, or being eaten alive by giant loamsters." The ogre drew in a deep breath and then rapidly and in a very small voice, tacked on a disclaimer. "Unless aforementioned challenger is Spid, the Grand Exalted Garboon of Beneath."

Abby gasped. "But that's not fair!"

"Fair?" Spid did the Belushi eyebrow thing at her again and shrugged. "All right. To show you how flexible I am," he paused and squinted at her word again. "I will waive the death penalty and instead, stipulate that the second unsuccessful challenge, whether by you, an ordinary, if somewhat advanced mortal girl, or by me, the Grand Exalted Garboon of the..." Spid drew a deep breath. "...You get the idea. At any rate, that wrongly made second challenge will result in immediate victory by the party whose honesty and intellect was assaulted. Is that fair enough?"

Sure, thought Abby. If you considered any game where one of the participants could change the rules as the game went along fair. "I suppose. Your turn."

She looked at the bag and said, "Draw." New letters flew from the bag. This time she got a *Z* which scored four points, not two like the previous *Z*, and three *V*'s which ranged from two to eighteen points. Very strange.

Spid studied the board for a moment, pointing his finger at different letters and shuffling them around on his tray. Finally, he nodded and a river of letters flowed onto the board. Using the *V* from her word Peradventure, the troll had laid out a perpendicular word that looked like utter garble to Abby. *G-V-L-E-E-X-B-M-A-O-G-R-N-T-H*. Fifteen letters in all. She looked at the board and saw six spaces light up under various letters. The scoreboard blinked and brought up Spid's score. 789 points. He'd hit two sextuple letters, three double words and the eleven-point value of the *X* had been squared.

"Horsehockey!" She yelled her father's favorite word. "That's not a word."

"So, then Abby, is this a," he paused and gave her an evil leer, "challenge?"

"Of course it is. Everybody knows that can't possibly be a word." Even as she said it, a weevil of a premonition gnawed at her brain. She heard her mother's voice. "Impulsiveness almost always leads to trouble, Abby."

"Yurk!" Spid thundered. "The dictionary."

The Ogre quickly flipped through the pages and found the *G*'s. "Here it is, Boss. You spelled it exactly right *G-V-L-E-E-X-B-M-A-O-G-R-N-T-H*. A sound made by a charging Vorkal as it steps on a slippery mound of Rimosaurus droppings."

"Just as I suspected," Spid smirked again and examined his fingernails.

"If you'd added *L-Y* you could have made it an adverb, Boss," Yurk noted solemnly. He turned to Abby and scrunched his face into a smile. "That's one."

"What kind of dictionary is that?" Abby snapped.

Yurk turned the cover of the book toward her. It read *Spid and Wagnall's Unabridged Dictionary of Modern English and Beneathese.*

"Beneathese? We're allowing words in this other language?"

"It's the language the whole world will be speaking very soon, Miss Keene. Our language. Right, Yurk?"

"Vrgamisptk, Boss." This appeared to be some kind of private joke. Both Spid and his ogre sidekick slapped their thighs and laughed uproariously.

To Abby, Yurk's comment sounded like someone talking with a mouth full of oatmeal. She fought back her anger, reminding herself she hadn't expected Spid to play fair, not for a minute. "All right, I've used my challenge. By the way, how do you pronounce that word?" She pointed at the board.

Yurk consulted the dictionary again. "It's pronounced geks-moh-rith."

"In other words, just like it's spelled, eh, Yurk?" Spid smirked and the two of them fell into a third fit of laughter. "Our language can be a bit tricky, Miss Keene. Some letters are not always pronounced. And others are pronounced differently than you might think. Draw." Letters flew from the bag to his tray.

Abby felt her hopes of winning at Spiddle diminish. But she had to continue. What other choice did she have? And so they played on, for a very long while. Abby had no way of telling how long, but it felt like several hours. As she'd feared, despite her valiant efforts, Spid built a huge lead. Several times, he used all of his letters, a move Yurk notified her paid off with a thousand-point bonus. She searched the far corners of her mind for long words, but found out they didn't always score big. It all depended on which bonus lights came on.

Biting her tongue, Abby fought off the urge to shout "horsehockey" again. Often, it seemed that Spid was just throwing letters down at random, knowing she feared Yurk's next trip to the dictionary. Second challenge and it's over, she thought. I spy on the Darksuckers for a power-mad troll.

Surprisingly, despite having mostly ignored her plays, Spid did challenge her once, when she laid down the word *H-E-G-E-M-O-N-I-U-S* and earned herself a nice 6,000 points. The *M* had been a seventeen-point tile and it fell on a value cubed square. The 6,000 drew her closer to Spid, within 500 points, and she felt a glimmer of hope. The troll had squirmed and picked at his nose with one long green fingernail. Finally, in a loud and confident voice, he challenged. Yurk looked up the word and shrank back as he told Spid the bad news.

"Are you positive, Yurk?" Spid roared at the hapless ogre. "Are you saying that The Grand Exalted Garboon of the Imperial Kingdom of Beneath, a personage who controls your fate, can decide whether you will be allowed to live or die, that I, Spid, the son of Glaub the Wrathful and Dismalia the queen of the gammits, have challenged incorrectly?"

"It, uh, appears so, Boss." Yurk looked as though he might bolt into the dark cone and disappear as Spid loomed over him, his breathing sounding like an over-stoked steam engine. "It says here that it means leadership or dominance, especially in a nation or—"

"Zip it, Yurk!" Spid bellowed.

"Pronounced hedge-uh-moe-nee-us," Yurk babbled. "Maybe the dictionary is wrong, Boss."

"The-dictionary-is-not-wrong," Spid muttered from between clenched teeth. "I wrote it. I should know."

He stomped to the back of the hologram and Abby wondered if he would end their game, return to his lair in Beneath, and rob her of a chance to see Noah.

"Listen," she offered, "I could put down a different word if—"

"No. No, of course not." Spid huffed as he drew near again. "I wouldn't think of it. I knew hegemonious was a word. I just thought perhaps there was a *D* in it. I, um, thought it only gentlemanly and sportsmanlike to even the challenge count to make a game out of it."

"Humor him," a little voice in her brain counseled. "Oooh-kay, thanks. It's your play."

They played on. Spid threw down tiles in exceedingly odd sequences to score major points. But she didn't dare challenge. Finally, Abby saw the bag fold itself up after he'd drawn his letters.

This is it, she thought. If I can find a word that uses all nineteen of my tiles, I can end the game and he'll have to

140

deduct his letters. She peeked at the scoreboard and her heart fell. She'd fallen more than 9,000 points behind. 97,384 to 106,415. The game was as good as over. She wouldn't get to see Noah. She'd have to spy for Spid. Tears filled her eyes.

Once again Spid seemed to know exactly what she was thinking. Or maybe he was just rubbing it in. "You've played well, Miss Keene. There is no shame in losing to the finest mind on the planet."

Finest mind!

She'd almost been ready to consider throwing herself on his mercy and begging to see Noah even though she'd lost. But Spid's smirking face made her clench her fists. She would finish the game, play it all the way out. Nobody could say Abby Keene was a quitter.

She studied the letters, working them back and forth in her mind, but fourteen letters was the maximum she could arrange into a valid combination. She lifted her eyes toward Spid and Yurk who had bent toward each other, carrying on a hushed conversation in the Beneathese language that sounded like words chopped up in a food processor. The light in the room dimmed and flickered. Abby rubbed her eyes. The lights fluttered again. Spid and Yurk, rapt in their discussion didn't seem to notice.

Tipping her head, she stared at the ceiling directly above her. Then she rubbed her eyes again. The Zezzue had swirled into letters—the exact same letters, in the same order that Abby had on her virtual tray. The lights switched and shuffled moving the letters around. Then they stopped, forming a word that resembled the strange combinations Spid had been laying down.

She smiled at the lights, then slid her eyes to the board, Her tray didn't contain an *X* which occupied a spot halfway through the Darksuckers' gift word, but she spotted an open *X* left by Spid on his last play.

Still, she hesitated, tilting her head to gaze up at the Zezzue. They were trying to help, she was certain of that. But this strange clump of letters couldn't possibly spell a word, could it?

The lights twinkled.

The letters they formed flashed.

She made her decision.

Pointing at the tiles on her rack, she moved them around until they took on the exact order written by the lights. As soon as she arranged them correctly, the lights twinkled again, then scattered. Spid and Yurk were still in a huddle.

"Here goes," she whispered. She visualized the location on the board and the tiles played follow-the-leader, dropping into their proper places.

The scoreboard flashed and the numbers rolled. Spid and Yurk looked up from their conversation and down at the Abby's word.

T-I-R-K-D-E-S-C-X-O-S-L-K-N-U-R-P-L-V.

Abby felt a little less confident as the mystery squares lit up and her score blinked under her name. She'd done pretty well, with three triple words, a cubed eleven-point *K* and a quadruple seventeen for the third *Z*. Her final score flashed on the screen. 106,381. Abby did some quick subtraction. If she trapped Spid with more than thirty-four points on his rack, she would win.

"Challenge." Spid hissed, pointing down at Abby's word. "Most obviously the last gasp of a desperate player. I challenge."

Abby felt her stomach clench as Yurk flipped dictionary pages at high speed, looking for the word. Spid leered, rubbing his hands together.

The ogre stabbed at a listing in the huge book, pulled his hand back, rubbed his eyes vigorously, then found the place again. His tiny beady eyes darted from the page to

Spid and back to the page. Perspiration dribbled down his forehead and across the bridge of his mashed-potato nose.

"Well, Yurk!" Spid ordered. "Tell this girl her bluff has failed and let's get on with it. I have things to do, ogres to see, torture to supervise."

"Errr." Yurk's usual growl was reduced to a distant rumble. "Uhhh."

Spid turned his attention to Abby. "Now when Delacroix is talking to the Zezzue, you—"

"It's a word, Boss." The ogre whispered. "It's from the old days and now it gets broke up into a bunch of littler words, but it's still in the dictionary."

Above Abby, the lights twinkled at high speed.

"—pretend you..." Spid turned and stared at his hench-beast. His jaw dropped open, his eyes widened in amazement and Abby heard him draw a ragged breath. "Ridiculous! It can't be."

"I know, Boss. But it's in the book. Right here." He pushed the book toward Spid, who snatched it and scanned the page. His complexion changed, first to an ash white, then mottling with a reddish tinge.

Abby scurried to her bed and shrank into the far corner, watching Spid grow angrier and angrier, looking as though he might explode at any minute.

"Look here, Boss." Yurk pointed to Spid's letters, trying to make sure he wouldn't be the target. "If you wouldnta challenged, you would have beat her."

"Don't you ever tell me I'm wrong!" Spid thumped Yurk alongside his head, then became a raging volcano, spewing what must have been dirty words in his language, and backhanding Yurk so hard he fell out of the hologram. Abby pulled her quilt around her, grateful that Spid wasn't really in the room. Tears welled in her eyes. She'd never get to see Noah now.

143

Finally, after what seemed like an eternity, Spid stopped shouting. "So, Miss Keene," he intoned. "It seems you have won a battle. Just a skirmish, really, the war is yet to come, but still..." He put both arms out to the side, palms up in a gesture of acceptance.

I should apologize. Maybe then he'll let me see my brother. "I—"

"No!" Spid pointed at her. "You will not speak. The time for words has passed. You won at Spiddle and you will be able to observe your brother as I promised. There." He gestured to the Chameleon Stone. "But mark my words, Miss Keene. We will meet again in—" He snapped his fingers at Yurk who had crawled back into the frame and was gingerly rubbing his head. Scowling, Yurk pulled out his calculator.

"Four days, nine hours, twenty-two minutes and fourteen seconds, Boss," he muttered.

"And, Miss Keene, the next time we meet it will be face-to-face." Spid's voice dripped menace. "And I will hold the three stones, your Chameleon, my Shadow and of course, the Methuselah, which your brother has been sent to procure. With their combined power, I will rule absolutely and with no mercy. Then, and only then, will we speak of winners and losers."

Abby watched the troll and the ogre dissolve and the black shadow draw into itself and finally disappear. She crouched on the bed, cold fear bumps erupting on her skin. With teeth chattering she wobbled over to the Chameleon Stone. As she peered into it, colors swirled and melded until finally an image appeared.

"Noah!" She reached a hand toward the glassy surface as if she could touch him. Her brother stood in a green area, grasping some kind of strange spear-like thing. Like one of those tridents that Neptune carried in the mythology books except with only two prongs.

As Abby watched, Noah leaped toward a dark-skinned girl decked out in some kind of crude armor and holding a two-pronged weapon of her own.

The girl raised her weapon.

Noah fell to the ground.

Abby screamed.

The picture within the Chameleon Stone winked out.

CHAPTER 17

"Attack me," Deidre commanded.

"With this?" Noah swung the humming sonic sword in a wide arc, fascinated by the Doppler Effect the motion created.

"No, with your shoe," the feisty girl taunted, thrusting her own battle fork toward him.

Noah heard a sharp sizzle. Then a sound wave passed inches from his head, as loud as a small jet plane.

"Of course with that." She crouched, holding the sonic sword slantwise to her body. "Come and get me Bun-boy!"

Noah felt a blast of heat blaze up his neck and scorch his face. "What did you call me?"

"Bun-boy," she smirked. "Too formal for you? Would you prefer just Buns? Ummm. Maybe Bunny Buns. How about that?"

Something snapped in Noah. "Yaaahhhh!" He charged headlong at Deidre, sonic sword extended like a lance.

He was nearly on top of her when something slammed into his chest with a roar of sound. His feet left the ground. He catapulted backwards, spinning around and landing hard on his stomach in a bed of moss.

"Pfoooooooo." He felt all the air rush from his lungs. A bolt of pain shot along his spine and into his head. He tried to heave in another breath, but his diaphragm seemed paralyzed. Panicked, he rolled onto his back, wheezing. Tears of fear and rage streamed from his eyes.

A hand grasped his harness, tugging him upright.

"Just knocked the air out of you," Deidre said. "You'll be fine in a minute." She pulled him to a sitting position and held him there. "Try little breaths. It'll come."

He gasped and shuddered, gasped again and heard himself moan.

Deidre bit her lower lip. "Sorry. I didn't mean to hit you that hard."

Geez, how humiliating. I'm glad Abby couldn't see this; she'd rag me like crazy.

Noah sucked air again. This time it went down easier.

Frowning, Deidre looked like she wanted to say something then walked away, stopping a few yards down the path. As he concentrated on breathing that until a minute ago had been purely automatic, he watched her pace in a tight circle, muttering to herself. Noah strained his ears and above his labored breathing he caught one word: "Hopeless."

Heat rose from the tight center of his chest. Rolling over and pushing with quavering arms, he got his feet under him. He'd show her.

He spotted the battle fork a few yards away, stumbled to it and hoisted it. Banging the butt end against the metal plate on his decibelt, he set it humming and turned to face Deidre. "Again," he demanded. "Let's go again."

She stopped pacing, a bemused smile pulling the corners of her mouth up. "You sure? You were flopping like a gutted cave fish."

"You just winged me. C'mon, let's rumble." He amazed himself a reckless show of bravado. Let's rumble? Where had that come from?

"All right!" Deidre banged her sonic sword against the decibelt plate and Noah heard it vibrate with a high-pitched whine. She grinned. "If you've got the heart to fight, the moves will follow. Now, hold your hands like I've got mine and bend your knees. Stay loose, but stay ready." She circled him. "I'm going to shoot a bolt. You've got to block it."

For the next several hours they skirmished. Noah felt jolts of energy replacing his exhaustion as he learned the moves that could save his life or slay an enemy. He discovered that each tine hummed at a different frequency. The bluish one was used to attack and the other, brass-colored, to block sound waves from another battle fork or deflect more conventional weapons.

Within an hour, he grew adept enough to force Deidre to give ground when he attacked. He began to anticipate her moves and turn aside her offensive waves. After one particularly heated exchange of blows, blocks, and counter blows, they collapsed beside each other on the mossy ground.

"Much...foof...better." Deidre wheezed. "You're starting to...huff...get it."

Gulping air, Noah nodded. Finally, he found enough breath to respond. "I...gasp...feel like maybe I am. But you're not...puff...going full speed."

"About seventy-five percent," she conceded. "Fyooo. But you're still not doing that...whew...bad."

A gray hand reached out with a mug of pale yellow liquid and he looked up to see Uh-oh standing over him. Eve handed a similar drink to Deidre and watched them take long swallows. The flavor, a mix of sweet carrot and a kind of citrus, refreshed Noah instantly. He drained the mug and stood.

"Time for lunch," Eve said. "And then you need to set off." She took the mug from her daughter and a look of misgiving passed between them.

Deidre squared her shoulders and fumbled with her decibelt harness and Noah felt strong pangs of jealousy and loss. He didn't have a mother. In fact, since he and Abby got separated, he didn't have a family at all. No one to care about him. Unless you counted a strange gray creature that smelled bad and mimicked everything, a warrior-girl who teased him about his rear end, and her mother the witch. An all-American normal-as-apple-pie group. It sounded like something from a cable reality show. *The Real Humbugians.*

Smiling a little, he followed Eve and Uh-oh into the hut where they lunched on thick slabs of earthy brown bread, cheese, fruit, and some kind of vegetable Noah couldn't identify. He dug in, voracious after the violent exercise. As he finished his fourth slice of bread and cheese, he remembered how his mother would tease him, saying they would need to take out a second mortgage on the house to pay their grocery bills. He wondered what people used for money in the Mushroom Forest and if they had mortgages.

"Time to stop stuffing your face and hit the road, BB."

Ignoring Deidre's taunt, he turned to thank Eve. The chair at the head of the table was empty. "Where's your mom? I didn't see her leave."

The girl pushed back her chair and picked up a provision-stuffed pack from beside the door. "She does that. She always has. Just goes off. Kind of blinks out like a light. I think she didn't want to watch us go. She's worried."

"Where does she go?"

Deidre shrugged. "When I ask she just smiles and says 'out.'"

Noah felt a spark of hope bloom in his chest. "Out of the mountain?"

"Out of the mountain?" Deidre stared. "You're raving again, Bun-boy. Why would she want to go out there?"

Noah considered her answer. "What do you know about out there?"

"I know there *is* an out there. That's all I need to know."

"You've always lived in here? And your mom, she always lived here, too?"

"I...uh...don't really know."

"Did you ever ask her?" Noah thought of the stories his mother used to tell, stories about the Nebraska town where she grew up.

"One time."

"And?"

"She said she didn't know. She just woke up one day and was a grownup already. The people who live on the other side of the Mushroom Forest found her, wandering all alone, just before I was born."

"Wow, that's really weird. She wasn't with your father."

"She wasn't with anybody. And she doesn't remember getting married or anything. It used to bother me, not knowing where we came from, but it doesn't now. It won't change who I am."

"Good point." Noah swung his pack to his back, shaking it to settle and balance the contents. Eve had even provided Uh-oh with a small knapsack and the gray creature slung it over his shoulders while peering down the path that twisted out of sight.

Noah hefted his sonic sword and remembered Eve's request that he watch out for Deidre. What if they got into major trouble? Sure, he'd improved with the battle fork, but he couldn't fight at her level. And he didn't have any other weapons. Only his drumsticks. What could he do with them? Poke an enemy's eye out? Ha. The old feeling of hopelessness flooded through him.

Deidre tousled his hair. "Everything will be fine. I guarantee it."

"Yeah? Are you offering a money-back guarantee?"

She flashed a smile. "Don't be silly. If we screw up, we all die. I won't be able to pay and you won't be able to collect. But look at it this way, if we're dead, we won't need money, right?" With that, she strode off down the trail.

Noah hitched his backpack up another couple of inches and started after her with Uh-oh on his heels. As they scrambled down the dirt path through the towering brown and white fungi of the mushroom forest, he heard an approximation of his own voice enunciating his doubt from over his shoulder. "We're following a crazy girl, Noah. Big trouble ahead. Big trouble."

"Shut up," Noah growled at his companion. "Save your breath. You may end up dragging me again before this trip is over."

Far above the narrow trail leading into the dense woods, two figures stood on a rocky ledge. Cool, dank air streamed from an opening in the rock behind them as they watched the quick-stepping girl, the thin blond boy, and the gray creature called Uh-oh.

"Well rested, he looks. Ready for the next challenge, no?" The muscular, armless brown man nodded at the figures passing below.

151

The disheveled and stooped rag-tag fellow beside him grunted and tapped a sturdy walking stick against the rock. "They will sleep for the night among friends and then ascend to the unholy river.

The large figure turned his eyes skyward and watching the fluxing glow of the Zezzue. The hermit grunted again, snuffled into his sleeve and tilted his head. The billions of pinpoint lights glowed and faded and glowed again in a slow, syncopated rhythm. Around them, the soft thud of the mountain's rhythm beat in counterpoint to the Darksuckers' ebb and flow. "Thuh-duh-rum-puh, thuh-duh-rum-puh, thuh-duh-rum-puh."

"And if they cross the fire, they will encounter the Temple of Cheltnor and its guardians. Will he find the correct stone?" Delacroix studied the roof of the huge cavern. "What do the Zezzue say?"

"The Zezzue do not reveal their thoughts about the matter, Pettifog," the Hermit growled. "You should know that. They are enigma."

"True." Delacroix watched the figures on the path below grow smaller and smaller and disappear around a bend. "Their role they will play in the end game. As will we. But only they know what that may be, yes?"

The hermit grunted and snuffled agreement. Delacroix continued, "The Zezzue allow us to use them, for light, for guidance, to communicate with one another. But they are truly, how you would say, the wild card?"

"We can't command them," The hermit agreed.

"*C'est vrai*. We must hope the boy can retrieve the third stone quickly. Time is short. The moment approaches."

The hermit ran his hands through unkempt, greasy hair. "What of the girl? The little one?"

Delacroix chuckled. "She has sent Old Spid and his grotesque sidekick back to Below Skin with their tails between their legs. Beaten him at his own game, if you will."

"Will she be ready?"

"I think so, yes. She has a most formidable mind. Questions upon questions. Her curiosity will help her untangle the most important riddles."

"All right then," gruffed the hermit. "I'm going. Anything you need from the outside? Records, maybe? Some more of those snack cakes?"

"Not now, my friend. I can think of nothing but the solstice and our fated meeting with Spid and his horde. But for the asking, I thank you."

"Welcome. We rendezvous again at The Skin?"

"*Oui*," Delacroix nodded and watched the decrepit codger shuffle along a trail that seemed to appear before him and disappear behind. "It will all play out at The Skin." With that, he walked through the opening in the rock, and disappeared into the mountain.

CHAPTER 18

Abby sprawled on the gel bed for a good long time, gnawing on her fingernails and trying not to freak out over what she'd seen in the Chameleon Stone before the transmission faded to black. The warrior girl might have wounded Noah or even... Despair overtook her. Nothing she could do. Nothing.

Her only consolations were that Noah appeared taller and more sure of himself and that he wielded a weapon identical to that of his nemesis. Before he advanced on the girl, he banged the end of his forky thing against a metallic disk that hung from a harness across his chest. His arms vibrated as he raised the two-tined spear. Sound waves? That had to be it.

Satisfied with her analysis, Abby recreated her memory of the girl. Dark-skinned and curly haired, she looked intent, but not angry or vindictive. In fact, it seemed that her lips were about to flex into a smile.

Abby pounded her fists against the bed and felt the gel shimmy under her assault. It was so frustrating. What happened?

She paused, panting, and flopped onto her back. If Noah hadn't survived, maybe she should try to escape and save herself. The break-through-the-skin-conquer-the-world thing with Spid wasn't her battle.

Or was it?

She recalled the troll's gloating remarks about what he had planned when he broke through. "There will be no mercy," he'd roared.

No mercy. That meant when he and his evil minions took over, he might kill them all. Noah, Delacroix, Chillout, and all the other grungoids. "And me."

She pulled the quilt tight around her shoulders. After that, Spid and his minions would surge out of the mountain. They'd overrun Port Anvil. Kill her father. Kill everyone.

She rolled into a tight ball and surrendered to fear and grief, sobbing. What on earth could she possibly do? She was just a girl, barely a teenager.

Around her, the Darksuckers glowed brighter. On its shelf, the Chameleon Stone throbbed with a pale green light. She sensed the Zezzue swirl, flicker, and swirl again. A little voice nagged at her. "Stop it, Abby. Stop the pity party."

Abby sat up, knuckled away the tears, and stared at the color-shifting orb on the shelf. Spid would have to capture the Chameleon Stone to consolidate his power. That's what he said, that he would link it to his Shadow Stone and to the stone Noah would bring back, the Methuselah Stone. The oldest stone in the world, Delacroix had called it. Maybe even older than the world. Where would Noah find it? What would it look like?

Above her, the Darksuckers stopped swirling and twinkled in microscopic flashes of red and green. Like Christmas lights. She smiled. "Thank you for helping me win the game. Thank you for helping me beat Spid."

The lights blinked out, then fell around her in a burst of gold and blue and silver, like the cascading sparks that follow the explosion of fireworks on the Fourth of July. She couldn't see these tiny creatures, couldn't touch them, but now, surrounded by them, she felt she wasn't alone.

Despite her pessimism, Abby grinned. Maybe she could turn Spid's towering ego and overconfidence against him. Clearly the troll didn't take Noah seriously and he hadn't worried that Abby might outwit him at Spiddle. Not that she could have pulled it off without the Darksuckers, but still, Spid clearly over-estimated his own knowledge and skill. If he fell into the same trap again, she should be prepared to take advantage of that.

She sat up, reached for her backpack, and dug around for the small notebook with the ballpoint pen clipped to it. In neat block letters she inscribed the word the Zezzue had given her. *T-I-R-K-D-E-S-C-X-O-S-L-K-N-U-R-P-L-V.*

She stared at it for a few moments, making sure she had the right letters in the right order. What could it possibly mean? How did you pronounce it? Yurk had said it was an old word, now broken into smaller ones. Kinda like The Last Place You Look. She took a stab at dividing it. "Turk-desk-exosall-knurp-love," she mumbled and then tried repeating it faster and faster.

It sounded like somebody trying to talk with an entire cheeseburger stuffed in his mouth and made no sense. But then, as Spid pointed out during the Spiddle game, in Beneathese some of the letters didn't get pronounced. And some were pronounced totally differently than in English.

Abby played with the word, dividing it different ways. Nothing. Frustrated, she returned to nibbling at her fingernails.

"Hola, little chickie. Like, what's the haps?"

She looked up to find Chillout standing in the doorway of her room, appraising her over the tops of his sunglasses.

156

"Oh. Hello. I was just," Abby gestured at the pad, "trying to figure—"

"I can dig it, baby. What a flipped out cat that Spid, huh? A real fream. Like double bummer to the ninth power."

"Huh?" Her mind scrambled to sift this new information. The grungoid knew about her visit from the troll. Did he know about the Spiddle game? And Spid trying to turn her into a spy? Had the grungoids bugged her bedroom? Or had the Darksuckers told Delacroix?

Chillout acted as if she hadn't spoken. "Lix requests your presence. You're playin' the big room."

Abby nodded and followed the gray creature to the immense chamber. There, Chillout wound her around a couple of boulders and back to a corner of the cavern where they found the massive armless man lying on his back in front of a strange apparatus.

Some kind of leather-like material was stretched between two columns of rock about twenty feet tall and twenty feet apart. Elevating his legs, stomach muscles rippling, the Grand Exalted Pettifog swiveled his hips back and forth and up and down, drumming out a series of complex rhythms with his feet on the huge makeshift drumhead.

Ta-boom-ta-tee-tee-bum bum? Delacroix's left foot beat out the musical question. The right foot answered. Tee-dee-bum-tee-dee-bum-tee-dee-bummity-bum.

As Delacroix played, the patterns grew more rapid and more complex. At times, Abby saw his legs only as a blur. Fascinated, she leaned against a nearby rock and watched.

Finally, increasing the speed to a level she wouldn't have dreamed possible, he finished with a flourish. Ta-dibbity-dum-dum-dibbity-boom-boom-bummity-bum.

Panting, sweat rolling from his chest, he lowered trembling legs.

"Some crazy groove," Chillout rasped. "I brought the chickie. I got to be fadin' now. Hasta." The grungoid swiveled on his heel and returned in the direction they'd come.

Delacroix wiped sweat from his eyes with the stump of his right arm, turned his head to look over at her and smiled. "Just an old drummer trying to learn new tricks, *ma cherie*. Practicing for my part of the ritual." He sat up and used his big toe to snag a nearby towel and blot perspiration from his body.

"Your part?"

"Counter rhythm little one. Backbeat, if you will. Noah will have to play the hard part, the rhythm that matches and challenges Spid's best drummer. That is the cadence that will keep The Skin from going liquid and the troll's nightmare army from riding roughshod over everyone up here.

Abby barely heard the last part. She'd fixed on her brother's name. "Noah? Is he all right? Have you heard anything?"

"He continues his quest for the Methuselah Stone."

Abby felt some relief. "So he's okay?"

"At last report. Let us hope he regains the time he has lost, because, if not, we are as they say in deep doo doo." He'd placed the emphasis on the second doo of doo doo. It took her a moment for Abby to decipher. Delacroix continued. "The prophecy says only Noah can drum against Spid's best."

Abby felt her heart leap and pumped a fist into the air. Spid was in big trouble. "Noah practices for hours every day. He plays really fast and loud."

"Ah, yes, fast and loud." Delacroix smiled. "I remember once, my ownself, thinking fast and loud and music were the same thing. But soon, I learn that sometimes you must play slow and soft. Or perhaps fast and soft. Or slow and loud. The drum, we must remember, began its existence as a way for people to talk over distance, to convey news, and plans, and emotions."

"So what song does Noah have to play to win? He's really good on 'Wipe Out'."

"Ah, the surf tune." Delacroix lay back on the stone floor and gazed at the ceiling. "It is not just the playing, little one. Noah must learn to listen. To release all he knows and hear the earth, the mountain, the ocean beyond." He gestured toward one of the walls of the mountain. "And he must tune in to his own heart, to let its beat join with the others. Only then, can his hands define the rhythms to keep darkness from us all."

Abby felt a chill pass through her. Could Noah learn to listen? To listen hard? Or would he argue the way he did with Dad? She could almost hear his defiant voice, the obstinate teenager bucking even small suggestions. "And me? What can I do?"

"What you do best. Seek knowledge, try to untangle the many puzzles. Look for strengths and weaknesses. Observe, organize, and strategize. But..." Delacroix raised the stump of an arm and Abby could almost see a phantom hand with a finger raised in warning.

"What?" Abby felt Delacroix's gaze lock onto her own.

"You must be careful, no? It can be possible to let your sense of logic and proportion and your skepticism dismiss the mysteries of the unexplainable. You too, Abby, must learn when to listen to your senses, your instinct, your heart. Not merely to your estimable brain."

"Why can't someone go for help?" She remembered she asked the question before and hadn't gotten an answer. "Why can't you tell the police about Spid? They have guns. They can kill him."

Delacroix laughed. "It is not easy to kill a troll, Abby. And who on the outside would believe in a troll, anyway? Or in his ogres and other horrific creatures? No, the prophecy says those of us who inhabit the mountain must fight this battle. And the prophecy will be as it will be."

"Maybe the prophecy is all messed up. I'm just a kid. So is Noah."

"And I have no arms." Delacroix shook his head. "But we must try. Not to try is to abandon hope. We cannot, we must not do that."

Abby nodded. She could try. She *would* try. "What should I do next?"

"That is the question, no? The prophecy only provides the outline and leaves for us the details." The drummer jerked himself onto his shoulders and the stumps of his arms and prepared to kick again. Looking over his shoulder he winked at her. "I believe you should explore, Abby, and consider what you know and what you don't. You are free to go wherever you want, follow any of the routes through the many openings in the cavern." His gaze shifted toward a narrow natural doorway in the rock. "In fact, you will find that one leads to the outside. A short walk and you are breathing the sweet clean air of Oregon. A short climb down and you walk the beach again. You are free to use that door, Abby. You would not be blamed if you chose to go home, little princess."

Home! Her own room. Her father's arms. Jennifer Ramsden's cookies. Far from this upside-down world and the terrifying prospect of the battle to come.

"No." She heard herself say the word and felt within her a steely determination she hadn't known she possessed. Spid could not win. Not if she could do anything to stop him.

"No," she repeated firmly. "I'm in. And I'll stay in until the end. Until we send Spid back where he belongs."

Delacroix thumped the drum-skin with his right foot, starting a steady thoomp, thoomp, thoomp rhythm. "Most excellent. Then explore and think your deep thoughts. Do not dismiss anything you discover. It could prove useful, yes?"

Using the tips of his toes on the left foot, Delacroix tapped light counter beats, adding another dimension to the sound. "As for me, I must work. The moment, it is coming." With that he launched into a series of complicated patterns, making each hit on the drum crisp and distinct, using contrasts between louder and softer beats to create different effects.

"Is there a map of the tunnels?"

Delacroix, without missing a beat, chided her. "A map will only take you where others have been, not where you may need to go. Sometimes the journey itself is the discovery you seek." Brown legs flashing, he shifted to a wild, exotically syncopated rhythm. The sound made her think of a warm beach with palm trees. "A map can only extinguish the curiosity, no?"

Abby wanted to scream, "Talk sense. How can a map keep anyone from finding the way? That's ridiculous."

Unless it was a very old map. Or badly drawn. Or the wrong map.

Delacroix smiled and Abby sighed. The point was, even if a map existed, he didn't intend to give it to her.

Ignoring the door to the outside, she picked an opening in the rock wall at random. Here goes. All alone, inside a gigantic mountain with no idea where I'm going or how things will come out. Like playing chess blindfolded. Perfect.

Taking a deep breath, Abby ducked into the dim tunnel. Cold damp air raised goose bumps on her arms as she tested the rock surface before she put each foot down. After a few hundred feet, the subterranean passage split into two branches. She stood for a moment and seemed to feel a pull to her left. She took that branch and, in a few yards, had three choices of directions, and then four. Each time, she stopped and tried to turn off her brain, turn on a connection to the mountain. She had no idea if the almost magnetic pull she felt was real or what she wanted to feel, but she kept on.

The relatively tight spaces and the twists, turns, descents and rises didn't bother her. Neither did the almost imperceptible light. She knew she could find her way back. She'd memorized each choice. All she needed to do was reverse her movements on the way back. Piece of cake.

She wondered what she might discover and thought about all the wonderful jewels that came from underground: diamonds and emeralds, sapphires and rubies. Was that what Delacroix meant when he said she should find what was there to be found? But no, her knowledge of geology told her she'd be unlikely to find any of those in this part of the world. Agates, yes. But no precious gems. At least not ones she knew about. Maybe there were dozens of types of precious jewels yet undiscovered.

She set that thought aside, pulled her jacket closer, and focused on keeping track of the twists and turns. But her mind drifted. She visualized the letters from the Spiddle game, Noah raising the strange spear to fend off a blow. What dark tunnel was he marching along now? And where was her father? Was he looking for them? Or had he given up? Did he think she and Noah were dead?

"Mom."

The cry name escaped her lips involuntarily. Surprised, she choked back tears and bit her lower lip, then leaned her head against the tunnel wall. "What should I do, Mom? How can I help Noah? It's so hard."

She listened, as Delacroix had instructed, knowing she wouldn't hear her mother's voice, but hoping she would feel something, some fleeting sense of reassurance. "Will I know it if I feel it?" Her whisper seemed to dissolve into the darkness, into a silence that made her feel even more alone.

The only things the tunnels seemed to lead to were other tunnels, more choices. A maze, a puzzle without any answer. She wanted to scream, to run, heard her heart pounding, her breath quickening.

Get a grip. Calm down, turn around, and reverse the directions.

She took a deep breath and took a right-hand tunnel, then one to the left. Feeling confident, she walked faster. Her legs grew tired and twice she stumbled on the uneven floor. The light dimmed and took on a dirty yellowish cast. Colder air lapped her ankles and she shivered in spite of her jacket. "Just around the next bend," she whispered several times. "Just along the next tunnel a little way. Just a few more steps."

But, even though she knew she'd memorized the order of turns and choices perfectly, she didn't emerge into Delacroix's chamber. Instead, she found herself in a smaller chamber with a rocky bench in the center. Four other tunnels opened from it. Nothing about the place was familiar.

Panicked, she stopped and tried to harness her twitching emotions. While she was daydreaming about jewels, she must have mentally misplaced one of the turns.

"Go over it again." She sat on the cold stone bench and retraced it in her mind. No, she hadn't forgotten a turn. The main chamber should be here. Right here.

But it wasn't.

But it had to be.

She stood. Maybe if she walked a little way down one of these new tunnels she'd find it. Okay then, she'd try the one to the right.

Fighting tears, she trudged into the tunnel and almost immediately arrived at another junction, a three-choice crossroad. That wasn't right. She went back the way she came and took the next tunnel in line. No good. She emerged into another unfamiliar room with five tunnel openings. The room was about the size of her bedchamber back at Delacroix's and its high ceiling loomed so far above her in the gloomy light that she couldn't see it.

Returning to the original chamber, Abby chose the third branch tunnel. Surely, this one had to be right. Her heart thudded in her throat and she wondered if Delacroix would send someone out to look for her. What if he was so intent on his drumming that he forgot for hours? For a day? Hunger gnawed in the pit of her stomach. How long did it take someone to starve to death?

The third tunnel emptied into the same high-ceilinged chamber with five entrances. A loop. Sweat ran off her forehead and into her eyes. She felt adrenaline pouring through her. Abby ran back and found the chamber with the bench again. Still on the dead run, she scrambled down the fourth tunnel, the only one she hadn't tried.

Or had she?

Lost!

The word filled her mind. If she was lost, she hadn't been smart enough, hadn't paid attention, hadn't marked the map in her mind correctly. Above all, being lost meant failure. She cried, sucking air in and choking on it. Blinded by tears, she bumped into the wall and banged her arm.

No. I can't be lost.

After what seemed like forever, she stumbled out of the tunnel and into a large room. Drying her eyes with her sleeve, she peered through reddened eyes at her surroundings. Her heart seemed to squeeze to a stop and she plopped to the floor. It wasn't possible. She'd taken another loop. She was back in that high-ceilinged chamber again. She was lost. Unmistakably, absolutely and irretrievably lost.

For the first time since the grungoids kidnapped her, she felt truly frightened.

CHAPTER 19

Noah craned his neck so often to check out the gigantic mushrooms towering around him that the muscles across his shoulders ached and twitched. But he couldn't stop to take off his pack and knead them. The long-striding Deidre set a killer pace and if he lagged, she taunted him. So he hustled, even jogging at times. Behind him, he heard Uh-oh panting and he worried that the little creature would collapse.

Could he carry his pack and his weapon and somehow drag his friend, too? Well, if he had to, he would. Uh-oh hadn't left him.

The trio had followed the wide path through the shade-darkened mushroom forest for nearly half an hour, and Noah saw no signs they were anywhere near the end. All around them fungi a hundred or more feet tall and up to twenty feet in diameter thrust upward from sodden, moss-covered ground. Above, bell-shaped caps spread out, blocking any view of the enormous cavern's ceiling. Smaller mushrooms, ranging is size from thirty feet tall, down to the grocery-store variety of Noah's experience, grew among the giants. Not all of them took the stem-and-bell shape. Some resembled real trees with thick reedy trunks and fuzzy green growth hanging from the limbs.

The dank, cloying perfume of decay filled the air, a reminder that the vital life of the enormous fungi depended on the death of other organisms. If he died here, would they feast on him?

"Are they edible?" Noah's voice sounded muffled, cushioned by the soft vegetation surrounding them. Deidre, about twenty yards ahead, paused and looked over her shoulder. He stopped, flexing his neck and shoulders, seizing a chance to rest. Uh-oh dropped to his knees, wheezing and holding his sides.

"Sure. Some of them," Deidre called. "Others will kill you within seconds. Trick is knowing which are which. Come on, let's go."

Hands on hips, she tapped one foot impatiently as Noah helped Uh-oh to his feet and angled for more rest time. "So, do you know? The poisonous ones from the others?"

"Some." She shrugged. "Some of them, though, even if they wouldn't kill you, you wouldn't want to eat them. Taste like mold. The big ones are too tough. Like eating wood. People build houses out of them. Others will turn you into a raving lunatic. But a lot are yummy. My Mom knows them all."

"It's pretty amazing." He peered up at the corrugated undersides of the mushrooms caps. Uh-oh slipped from his grip and sprawled on the ground again. Deidre looked at them with annoyance, but then her face softened and she walked back and plunked beside him. Relieved, but trying not to show it, Noah eased his pack off and dropped beside a mushroom that smelled like the compost bucket in his kitchen. There was even a hint of banana peel in the odor. The ground squished beneath him and he scuttled back to the graveled trail that cut its way, like a dry river, though the forest.

"Amazing? I guess they are," Deidre mused. "I've been around them all my life, so I kinda take this forest for granted, you know."

She pulled her canteen out, took a swallow and offered it to Noah. Grateful, he rinsed his mouth and passed it back. She handed it over to Uh-oh, who, opening one eyelid, then the other, accepted it and took a short pull.

"We can rest, I guess. We've made pretty good progress. We should arrive at Shroomtown way before dark."

"Shroomtown?" Noah laughed. "Are there, like, people living there?"

"Like people?" Deidre wrinkled her nose. "Like fer shurr."

Noah felt himself blush with annoyance. "I only meant—"

She grinned and punched his arm. "I know. I'm just yankin' your chain. Keeping in practice, like."

"Thanks a lot."

"You're welcome a lot." She punched him again, more of a tap.

A few minutes passed with only the sound of Uh-oh's slowing breaths, then Deidre said, "I spent a lot of time in Shroomtown when I was growing up. Mom would go off and leave me with Uncle Benny. You'll meet him and the others pretty soon."

Noah nodded and then something else she'd said struck him and he realized it had been puzzling him all along. "You said we'd get there before dark. We're inside the mountain, right? Sunlight doesn't reach in here, right? But there's light. And it's not sunlight. So how can it get dark?"

"When the Zezzue decide it's time," Deidre gestured upward, "it will get dark."

"The Zezzue?"

"The Darksuckers. Tiny creatures that inhale darkness and take it somewhere else."

"Huh?"

"They hang out on the ceilings." She waved toward the tops of the giant fungi.

Noah's mind clicked into gear and he flashed back to the hermit carrying on a conversation with the lights on the rock ceiling. He remembered how he ignored the arrow formed by the winking lights. That seemed so long ago. Years. He wondered what would have happened if he'd followed the Zezzue's directions. "The darkness. Where do the Zezzue take it?"

"Nobody knows for sure. Legend has it there is a place in the mountain where they, they, uh..." She struggled for the word. "Regurgitate it, I guess. Anyway, they say that place is darker than anything you could imagine."

Noah tried to wrap his mind around it and found he couldn't. It was like thinking about how empty space was and how far it was to a star. It made his brain fry. "Creepy."

"Yeah. They say it's so dark it swallows all your senses."

"Chhht...chhht...chhhht." Noah and Deidre turned to see Uh-oh on his feet and pointing up the path.

"Someone's coming." Deidre leaped up and pulled her sonic sword from its scabbard. Less gracefully, Noah clambered to his feet, drew his own weapon, and took a position in front of Uh-oh.

In a moment he heard hoof-beats and felt a strong vibration on the trail. It sounded like a small herd of horses or cattle, coming fast. Cattle in the mountain?

"Galloopapede." Deidre banged the battle fork against her decibelt, setting it humming. "Only one, I think."

"Galloopa-what?" Noah activated his fork and brandished it.

The sound of many legs hammering into the gravelly path filled the heavy air. Soon a form emerged around a bend. Noah stepped back, colliding with Uh-oh. Closing in was a creature about thirty feet long. Its long neck ended in a lizard-like face with floppy ears and a prominent beaky nose. Dozens of legs, a blur of motion, catapulted the beast along, spattering gravel.

"Be ready." Deidre raised her fork. "It could be bandits."

Bandits! Noah's heart thumped and his arms trembled. Raising his weapon higher, he waited, nerves jangling. He felt Uh-oh's warm breath against his back and heard his trademark "Uh-oh," drowned out by a loud bellow. "Pull up, Sznorspap. Pull up!"

Noah stared in amazement at a young man, probably not much older than himself, perched at the base of the beast's long neck, red hair streaming behind him. The rider yanked on what Noah at first assumed were ropy reins, then realized were the swept-back whiskers of the multi-haunched animal.

"Stop, damn your hide," roared the rider.

The Galloopapede, now less than twenty yards from them, showed no signs of slowing. Noah pressed himself between a pair of huge mushrooms and pulled Uh-oh in beside him.

Deidre lowered her fork and covered her mouth with one hand.

"Sznorspap, please. Stop!"

The rider's plea was almost drowned out by the thunder of what had to be a hundred legs and an echoing goat-like "waaankkk" from the charging animal. The

170

runaway Galloopapede pulled closer and Noah smelled it—a cross between dead crab and sewer gas.

As beast and rider swept past, Deidre called out a giggled greeting. "Halloo, Peitr. Goodbye Peitr."

"Hello, beautiful..." came the return call, fading even as it left the rider's mouth. By the time Noah heard the faint "I'll be right baaaaack!" the Galloopapede had stormed out of sight.

"You know him?" Noah returned his battle fork to its scabbard.

"I grew up with him. You'll like him. If he, uh..." she broke into a whole-hearted laugh. "If he can ever get Sznorspap to turn around."

"Isn't riding that thing dangerous?"

"I broke my collarbone twice training him. But he's fine if you know how to talk to him." She smiled and gestured down the trail. "You'll see. Sznorspap will behave for me. He'll get us to Shroomtown in no time."

You'll get me up on that thing when clams tap dance, thought Noah. "No. No way I'm riding that Galloop-a...Gal..."

"Galoopapede." Deidre shrugged and examined her fingernails. "Fine, Bun-boy. Have it your way. You can ride atop Sznorspap half an hour, or walk by yourself for another three. Makes no never mind to me. I'll have a bath, eat dinner and be on my third truffle beer by the time you show up."

Noah had a nasty retort on his tongue when the Galloopapede and the freckled, lanky red-haired youth reined in beside them. The boy leapt from the creature's neck, took two steps, and gathered Deidre into a bear hug.

"Welcome home, little sister."

"Urrrfen mfrrrk bdnrk."

"Oh, sorry. You can't speak if you can't breathe." Peitr relaxed his hold and set her down.

171

She brushed at her tunic and straightened her belt. "It's good to see you, Peitr. How is Benny?"

"Good. Better, once he's seen your face." He turned to examine Noah and Uh-oh. "Who are your friends?"

Deidre pointed to Noah. "His name is Noah. He drums at The Skin when the sun marks the solstice and the mountain's heartbeat fails."

"He is the chosen one, then? The message the Zezzue delivered from your mother said he would come." There was no mistaking the disappointment in Peitr's voice. "I expected him to be—"

"He is the one," Deidre interrupted. "Old Spid will be sorry he tried to breech The Skin when we're done with him."

Deidre sounded confident, but how much of that was an act? Noah pictured her later, in the presence of her friends, confiding her doubts and qualms about his abilities. Not that he blamed her.

Peitr shrugged. "As you say. And the other one?"

Noah spoke up. "His name is Uh-oh. He saved my life back a ways."

"Then he will be a good soldier. As we all must be. The others of his kind will be glad to welcome him. Come. They are expecting us.

Shroomtown proved to be a small settlement with a couple of hundred residents. It sat against one wall of the immense cavern, hemmed in by the Mushroom Forest and a tumbling waterfall that veiled a tall cliff. People lived in shallow caves or in houses carved out of giant mushrooms or built of smaller fungi stacked up like logs. Where the meager township ended, a pathway led alongside the waterfall to a series of openings in the rock wall.

172

Riding high on the back of the Galloopapede which obeyed Deidre's every command, Noah observed clusters of people, men and women both, skirmishing with a variety of weapons. Some brandished sonic swords, much like the ones he and Deidre carried. Others held mock battles with more conventional swords or spears that looked like metal porcupines mounted at the ends of short poles.

They're preparing, Noah thought. In case I fail. Or getting ready for what will happen *when* I fail.

Peitr led them to his father, who watched over a group of about twenty people practicing hand-to-hand combat. Benny Vlavnosk, a burly man with wide shoulders whose hair color, eyes, and smile matched those of his son, waved a greeting. "Go wash up and get a little rest, Dee-dee. I'll catch up with you at dinner. Welcome, Noah. And your friend, too."

"All right, Uncle Benny." Deidre blushed as she hopped off the Galloopapede and helped Noah and Uh-oh down. Dee-Dee, Noah mused. Must be a name from when she was a baby. Something told Noah that Benny was the only one who called her that without risking a zap from her sonic sword. He filed the name away for the next time she started in with that Bun-boy routine.

Later, after cleaning up and napping on a spongy bed, they met for a communal dinner. As the lights dimmed overhead and the air cooled, Peitr and several others built a bonfire. Men, women and children sat around it, sharing food and talking into the night. The fire emitted a loamy-smelling smoke and Noah decided they were burning chunks of fungus he'd seen lying in the forest. Deadfalls, he guessed. Just like in a regular forest. A few days ago he would have dismissed the idea as impossible, but now he accepted the fact that somehow mushroom trees dried out enough to burn.

Noah enjoyed the food, a savory mushroom stew with other vegetables and some kind of meat. When he asked Deidre what it was, she rolled her eyes and told him he'd be better off not knowing. He put down his spoon, but then hunger overcame squeamishness and he emptied his bowl and asked for more.

Much to Uh-oh's delight, several dozen gray-skinned, dreadlocked creatures lived around Shroomtown. Uh-oh gravitated toward them and become the center of their attention. He seemed to be spinning out the tale of his journey with Noah, acting out the battle with the mold monster in between eating what looked like large insects. Something else, Noah decided, he was better off remaining ignorant about.

"So, Mr. Keene. You have an appointment with destiny at the Temple of Cheltnor, do you not?"

Benny Vlavnosk leaned toward Noah, one eyebrow raised. Up close, Noah saw his red hair was streaked with gray and his wide and bushy eyebrows seemed to have lives of their own.

"I...uh...guess so." The Temple of Cheltnor. The hermit had mumbled about that to the lights on the ceiling. The Zezzue..

Benny Vlavnosk smiled at him, eyebrows wriggling. "It seems that all roads lead here. Some just twist and turn more before depositing you."

"How long will it take to reach the temple?"

Benny stroked his beard and peered at the tunnel openings above them. "No one here has ever been to the temple. In fact we are not even sure it exists. All we have to go on is the prophecy that tells us to take the middle pathway up there." He elevated his chin an inch. "And that you must cross Pfhaaa, the river of fire." The name of the river sounded like a long, hot exhalation of air.

"River of fire?" Noah's voice squeaked and a ripple of laughter radiated around the circle. "What's that?"

"Despite what you might have learned in school, Humbug Mountain is volcanic still and melted rock flows through its interior." Benny threw another chunk of fungus onto the fire. Flames crackled and sparked, burning blue and silver. "Pfhaaa, the molten river, is wide and deep. Attempts to cross it have ended in tragedy. But the prophecy says that's the way you must go."

"You knew about this, didn't you?" Noah flung the accusation at Deidre. "A river of fire! How did you think we'd cross it?"

She offered a smile that seemed more of a wince. "I thought we'd cross that Pfhaaa when we got to it."

Her feeble attempt at a joke brought silence to the circle.

Noah glared at her, then turned away, freezing her out for the rest of the evening. Later, tossing and turning in his bedroll, he decided that being angry took energy better conserved for other things. After all, she was just going by the prophecy.

"Deidre?" he called softly.

"What?"

"Are you awake?"

"If I wasn't I couldn't answer you, could I?"

"Yeah, uh, listen, I'm sorry for getting mad at you."

A brief silence. "It's okay. I'm scared too."

This amazed Noah. "You are?"

Deidre leaned on her elbow, her eyes glowing in the dim light. "Anybody who says they're not afraid of what could happen in the next few days is either stupid or lying."

Noah thought about that. "Yeah. "Sorry again about yelling."

"That's okay. I probably would have done the same."

Deidre lay back and Noah sorted out his thoughts, following a thread of an idea, picking at a shred of memory, trying to polish a gleam of premonition. That faded, but he was left with a feeling of self-assurance—confidence like he'd never felt except when he was drumming.

"Forget about that river of fire thing. I've got it handled." The bravado in his voice amazed him.

Deidre didn't respond for a moment, and then he heard her giggle. "I admire your confidence, Noah Keene, but you are such a liar."

CHAPTER 20

Abby mentally retraced her route a dozen times—two dozen. How did she mess up? Even distracted as she'd been, how did she forget a tunnel connection? Her brain had let her down, left the lens cap on her photographic memory. And here she sat, cold and hungry.

She studied the mouths of the tunnels that converged in the high-ceilinged room. Two of them would lead her back to the room she'd stopped at before. But which two?

"Ohhhhh!" She clamped her hands to the sides of her head. "Think, Abby, think!" If only she'd brought something to mark her route, chalk or string or even pebbles like the kids dropped in that fairy tale with the wicked witch and the gingerbread house.

Gingerbread? Her stomach growled and she dropped her hands to clutch her middle. She could almost smell it. Her dry mouth filled with saliva and she swallowed. Her stomach growled again.

Don't think about food, she coached herself, think about how to find a way of here. Facts. She needed facts to make a smart decision. No matter what Delacroix said, no way could she just go wandering along, hoping she'd stumble on something. He'd told her to listen to her senses, her instinct, and her heart, not just her "estimable brain."

But how do you let go of what you've always relied on and grasp what you're not sure of? Abby moaned and rocked, the chill spreading through her body. She couldn't just stop thinking, could she? Just turn off her brain?

"I'm only a kid," she whispered.

So was the Dalai Lama, once.

The thought leaped into her brain. She'd seen him on television, a man without a country, but a man who radiated serenity, completeness, and self-fulfillment. She remembered reading how masters of meditation talked about focusing on one object or one sound, a mantra. They talked about breathing slowly and repeating the mantra, over and over again.

Maybe that would relax her or unlock some hidden memory about the tunnels.

Abby eyed the openings in the rock wall and realized she couldn't even remember which one she'd come out of. Not only was she lost, but her mind felt all snarled up and fuzzy, like tangled yarn left out in the rain.

This whole thing was No-way's fault. Why couldn't her bonzo-brained brother have stayed home and talked it out with Dad? But noooo. He had to run away and dance with some old crone on the beach and—

She leaped to her feet and screamed at the top of her lungs. "Darn you, Noah!"

The words echoed eerily back at her, toneless but somehow taunting. "Darn you Noah, arn you Noah, you Noah, u Noah, Noah, oah, ah." The words ran together, then dissipated, like swirling smoke in a breeze.

She yelled again. "Darn you, Noah!" The words echoed, chasing each other, colliding, but somehow cleansing her mind. Feeling foolish, Abby clenched her eyes shut and chanted the words over and over, melding them together. "DarnyouNoah, DarnyouNoah, DarnyouNoah, DarnyouNoah."

As she chanted she tried to breathe in and out as slowly as she could. Folding her legs into an approximation of a lotus position, she repeated the words until they became a continuous string without beginning or end. Gradually, she felt a warm glow tingle up her arms and legs and center itself somewhere between her eyes.

As she chanted faster and faster, the "darn" fell away. She knew she was saying it, but all she heard back in her ears, or maybe just in her mind, was "you-Noah, you-Noah, you-Noah, you-know-uh, you-know-uh."

"You know-uh how to find your way."

The voice was a quiver in the air, a faint wisp of sound.

Abby opened her eyes to find herself floating near the ceiling of the chamber. Below her she saw a girl sitting in the lotus position on a large rock and mumbling, Youknowuh, youknowuh, youknowuh, youknowuh."

She studied the girl with detached interest and realized with no surprise that it was herself.

I can't be there and here, too.

"Why not?" The hum of sound filled her head.

"Why not?" She whispered to the voice and rolled onto her back in mid-air. Above her, the ceiling glowed with a strange tint of violet. The Zezzue. She was talking to them. Or perhaps just listening. More words appeared in her head. "You know-uh the way, Abby."

"I thought I did," she whispered. "But I got lost."

"You have the map in your soul. Trace the route with your finger. Then use your finger to lead your body."

Above her, the lights danced and swirled. She watched a map appear, saw a series of tunnels linked by larger chambers. Turning her head, she saw herself, still sitting cross-legged on the stone, still chanting at high speed. "Youknowuh, youknowuh, youknowuh, youknowuh."

Facing the Zezzue again, she extended her arm and let her forefinger circle the map, then touch a spot, a chamber with multiple entrances. The lights flashed a bright blue and she smiled. "You know-uh the way."

Dreamily, she dragged the finger along the simulated tunnels until she touched a huge cavern. The lights flashed again.

"I know," she whispered proudly. "I know the way."

With a heart-wrenching jolt, she found herself inside her body, arms tingling, legs cramping, feet numb. She continued to chant, almost afraid what would happen when she stopped. "Youknowuh, youknowuh, youNoah, youNoah, arnyouNoah, darnyouNoah."

Then, without her brain commanding it, she stood, opened her eyes, flung out her arms, and screamed again. "Darn you Noah."

The words echoed back at her once, then all sound died. She nodded. No longer afraid, she stretched, yawned, and stomped circulation into her feet. Time to go. She jumped from the rock and took six confident steps toward a tunnel entrance, then froze.

Was that the right one? She looked at the tunnel beside it. Maybe that one? Yes, it looked right. Or did it? She felt a wave of panic and returned to her rock, breath coming in long, shuddering gulps. How could she have forgotten already?

"You must keep your eyes, closed, Abby." The vibrato murmur from overhead seemed to swell inside her head. "Close your eyes and walk."

"But won't I run into stuff?"

"Your eyes deceived you. Now trust your other senses. Follow your finger."

"Follow my finger?" She held up her right index finger and studied it.

"You'll get even more lost," an angry voice inside her brain shouted. "You're just dreaming those lights and voices. Use your brain. Think your way out of here."

"No! I can't think! I have to know!" She closed her eyes and breathed slowly. In a moment, she opened her mouth, freeing the words she knew would realign her consciousness. "I know the way. I know the way. Iknow theway. Iknowtheway. Iknowtheway. Iknowtheway. Knowtheway. Knowtheway."

Extending her right arm, Abby let her finger drift in a slow circle. When it stopped, she swallowed her fear and moved in the direction it pointed. She stopped whispering and concentrated on keeping her mind empty except for the words, concentrated on seeing in other ways. She heard her shoes brush and pat against the rock, heard the fabric of her jacket whiffle as she moved her arms, tasted metallic air on her tongue as she filled her lungs.

After a while, she noticed that her feet moved faster, that she'd stopped testing each step before she put her weight down. Once, she felt her arm swing fast to the left, moving like a water witcher's wand. Her body followed and she felt the air tighten around her. As she went on, it felt warmer, too, and smelled different, like growth and decay. She wanted to open her eyes, but forced herself to keep the lids squeezed shut and her left arm at her side. A little farther along her knees bent without her brain sending them a command. Something brushed against her hair and she realized she'd ducked to enter a low-ceilinged chamber or passage.

Again and again she heard the faint voice of her intellect. "You'll clunk your head and knock yourself out! What if there's some ferocious animal just ahead? What if the ground opens up and you fall?"

She blanketed those fears with her mantra, chanting faster.

"Knowthewayknowthewayknowtheway."

Something like a cobweb brushed her forehead. An image flashed across her brain—cascades of diamonds, rubies and emeralds. Had she walked through the energy of her previous thoughts? Was that possible? Was this the place where she daydreamed about finding precious gems? If it was, her journey was nearly over.

Her knees pumped and her feet lifted higher with each step. She ran, her breath rising and falling with the effort—now at a full sprint—faster than she ever ran before, with her eyes still squeezed shut. Her mantra matched the rhythm of her pounding feet, became an endless string of sound with no beginning or end, like the Mobius strips they made out of paper in school. Like the symbol for infinity. Her right arm bent and she took a sharp corner full out, felt a warm wind current pass over her body, smelled vanilla, cinnamon, and hot grease and heard the raspy voice of Chillout. "Whoa, little chickie."

She stumbled and stopped, bent double, gasping for breath.

"Cool your jets, baby. You were really goin' flat out. Almost made this cat get floor parallel, you dig?"

Opening her eyes, she shrank back from what felt like an automobile headlight pointed squarely into her face. She blinked furiously and the bright glare became the normal, Zezzue-generated light of Delacroix's huge cavern.

"What's the haps, Abster? Where's the fire? I was, just like, you know hangin' here, minding my own biz, when you accessed my personal space."

"Oh. Sorry. I'm really here?"

Chillout cocked his head. "Far as I know. Everybody got to be somewhere. You hungry? Almost time to tie on the feedbag."

Abby's stomach answered before she could, delivering a rumbling growl. "Excuse me. Yes. I'm very hungry. Where is Dela...the Pettifog?"

"He'll be boppin' in momentarily if not sooner. Could you scarf down a heapin' helpin' of chicken fingers and cinnamon buns?"

"Sure. Great." Fleetingly she wondered again about items that clearly came from outside the mountain. They must have a regular supply train. But what did they use for money? What could they barter for chicken fingers and cinnamon buns?

"Me, I don't mind what happened to the wheat and sugar cane," Chillout interrupted her thoughts, "but I feel kinda bummed out that some chicken's not gonna get a shot at playing the piano."

Abby groaned at his silly joke.

The grungoid shrugged his shoulders, gestured for her to follow, and walked to the other end of the chamber.

Before she joined him, Abby tipped her face to the haze of lights on the ceiling and mouthed the words "thank you."

The lights flickered. A rainbow wave of colors passed across them and broke with shower of gold sparks. She heard the tremolo whisper a final time. "You knew the way."

CHAPTER 21

Deidre stopped five yards ahead on the rocky trail. "Pfhaaa. Hear it?"

Uh-oh, his baboon-like face creased with worry and exhaustion, shook back his hair, his once tightly-bunched dreadlocks now a mound of unwinding and unruly clumps. Noah shuffled to a standstill, listening for the sound of the River of Fire, his plan for crossing it still just a glimmer of hope and possibility.

Straining his ears, he heard only the hollow silence of the immense cavern. But then, he picked up the faint undercurrent of sound—like steam escaping from a kettle, interspersed with whip-crack snaps and pops and a nasty rolling gurgle. The river's audible signature created an instant understanding of why someone gave it the name Pfhaaa.

He wished he was back in his bedroll in Shroomtown. Or, better yet, back home where the worst that could happen was falling off his bike or having Dad ground him. All the problems of BHM—before Humbug Mountain— seemed as insignificant as mosquito bites.

He rubbed his eyes and tried to remember if he'd slept at all last night. Maybe a little, at the very end. His brain wouldn't turn off, and the harder he labored to extract embedded information from his memory, the more elusive the mental nuggets became. His traveling companions hadn't rested well either. Deidre's usually glimmering hazel eyes looked like red-rimmed dark marbles and Uh-oh's usually nimble pigeon-toed scuttle was a syncopated scraping of hairy feet across rock.

Noah nodded to Deidre. "I hear it."

She pursed her lips and held his gaze for a moment. She said nothing, but her body language asked the question: "Have you thought of a way across?"

Noah bent and fiddled with his shoelaces, then drew in a deep breath, swallowed the panic rising in his throat and forced his mouth into a tight smile. "Let's get down there," he gruffed. "I'll get us across."

Deidre nodded, hitched at her pack and started off ahead of him.

"You're such a liar Noah, such a liar." Noah heard Deidre's voice from behind him.

The rangy warrior girl spun, eyes darting. "Who said that?"

Noah stepped aside so she could see Uh-oh, frozen in a perfect Deidre pose, hands on hips, head held defiantly high, eyes steely. The gray creature's lip curled in a sneer. "You're clueless, Noah, clueless." He stalked back and forth, aping the girl's muscular, arm-swinging gait.

Noah felt a laugh erupt from his throat.

Deidre frowned for a moment, then giggled. "I...oh...er." Unable to contain it, she fell into a laughing fit, pointing at Uh-oh. As if someone hit a switch, Uh-oh's face reformed into its normal, lost-in-space expression.

"How did he learn how to do that? Did you teach him?"

"No. He does me too. Imitates how I sound and look." Tears of laughter streamed down Noah's face and he

185

coughed, fighting for control. "He must have heard us talking last night."

Deidre thumbed her nose at the smallest member of the trio. Uh-oh responded by shrugging and waggling his thin eyebrows. "It's good we laughed now," she told Noah in a serious tone. "It might be our last chance. Ever." She turned and walked down the trail.

Noah followed, trying to keep his mind empty—leave space for life-saving ideas to slide in. Within a few hundred yards, the hissing, snapping, and crackling melded into a steady roar, echoing through the immense chamber. The rotten-egg reek of sulfur triggered a gag reflex and he fought the nausea twisting his stomach. The stench grew stronger as they walked, mingling with the odor of hot metal. Waves of heat undulated over him and the air grew thicker, harder to breathe. His throat felt raw, his eyes watered. As they crested a small rise, Noah saw the angry orange glow of the river.

"Maybe a half mile more to the edge," Deidre shouted. "Are you all right?"

Wiping sweat from his forehead with the back of his wrist, Noah nodded and forced himself to put one foot in front of the other. Glancing back, he saw Uh-oh plodding twenty yards behind, huffing and stumbling, sweat dripping from the ends of his snarled curls. Noah waited for his friend to catch up and offered his arm for Uh-oh to lean on. "Don't look at Pfhaaa," he advised. "Just take it one step at a time."

The creature gave no signal that he heard or understood, but kept moving. When they halted on an overhang fifty yards shy of the molten flow, Noah cupped his hands over his nose, trying to shield it from the intense heat and the venomous stench of liquid rock, straining to draw a normal breath into his scorching lungs. A mixture of sweat and tears flooded his eyes and he fought the impulse to turn and run. Not only did he not know how they would cross the river gurgling through the deep cut in the earth below, but he wondered how long before his blood boiled and his brain exploded and blew his head apart. His skin already glowed scarlet and the hair on his forearms smoked.

Then, above the unending roar and the pounding vibration of the rock on which he stood, he imagined he heard Abby's voice. "Be logical. Use that thing on top of your neck, No-way." It carried the chiding tone she used when they played chess. "Think, big brother. Look at the board. See what I'll do after you've made your move. Better yet, try to think a couple of moves ahead."

Okay, I'll think. But this isn't chess.

He narrowed his burning eyes and tried to focus on the molten river. There didn't appear to be any way around it. To his left, it flowed for what looked like miles, twisting and bending, conforming to the sheer rock face of the chamber. To the right, not far from where they stood, the gurgling, spitting, hissing flow ran over a ledge, creating a waterfall of fire. The crash and crackle escalated the noise level to a painful threshold. If there truly was a hell, this could be what it looked like.

He felt a gentle tap on his shoulder. Turning, he saw Deidre, her face glowing with sweat, her ears as red as flames, her hair wild with static electricity. He felt a sharp tug on his pants leg and looked down to see Uh-oh clinging to him, struggling for air.

He looked to the left again. Not that way. They'd be worn out before they reached the edge of the horizon, and there might be no crossing when they arrived. Maybe the right? Perhaps they could climb the rocky face beside the waterfall and edge their way over the molten lava upstream. No. The rock wall was slick and without many footholds. Even trained climbers would struggle. Two

187

exhausted kids and a whatever-kind-of-creature didn't have a prayer.

Blinking his eyes to clear the sweat, he peered directly across the flow. Was he imagining it, or did the river narrow there? And was that a kind of rocky beach on the other side? He rubbed his eyes and squinted hard, trying to block out the waves of shimmering heat rising from the river. Yes, it was a beach. And beyond it he saw a tunnel cut into the rock wall.

Certainty filled him. They had to cross Pfhaaa there. And soon.

A crackling boom erupted and a finger of fire shot fifty feet into the air. Globs of molten rock spun free, swirled and arced, then crashed back into the flow with a prolonged "Tsssssssssst."

The memory he'd dug for flashed across Noah's mind. A fire. The beach. The bedraggled old woman. Music. And the sound of the mountain. He could hear it now, even over the rushing torrent of fire. "Thoomp Thoomp. Thoomp Thoomp. Thudda-Thoomp."

Noah reached into his pack, groping through clothes and bundles of food until he found the drumsticks. Grasping them, he looked around for a likely rock. There. He balanced the sticks in his fingers.

Deidre's hand dropped to his shoulder again, this time an insistent grip, pulling him to face her. She put her mouth next to his ear and snarled. "What are you doing, Noah? We're about to become crispy critters and you're—"

He whirled, found a flat place on the rock and beat time to the music churning through his mind. Hannah. The strange dance on the beach. Moving with her to the music playing on the boom box. The scene filled his mind, crowding out other thoughts.

The sticks seemed to move by themselves as his memory took control of his arms and hands. On the movie screen that filled his brain, he watched himself spin and backpedal and lunge and retreat in the fandango on the sand.

He closed his eyes tighter, then opened them wide and saw Deidre, a panicked scowl on her face. She pointed to the river and shouted something he couldn't hear. What he heard was Old Hannah and the words she'd left him with. "Don't ever be afraid to dance, Noah. Remember the steps."

Crazy. How is dancing going to get us across a river of lava?

He thought of the mold monster, brought down by a bag of candy. Impossible. But it happened. Could impossible happen twice?

He jammed the drumsticks into his pack, shoved past Deidre, and started down the path toward the river. "C'mon. Follow me," he bellowed over his shoulder.

Deidre didn't move. Uh-oh, on hands and knees, continued his battle to draw breath.

"Trust me," Noah yelled, knowing as he walked on that he could never explain the insane idea that drove him. Would his companions have enough faith to follow his lead?

His sonic sword shimmered an eerie orange, the hair on his arms scorched, his fingers swelled like broiling hot dogs, and the sulfurous smell bent him nearly double with each breath. Across the river, shadows flickered and danced as flames spit from the molten flow of rock. At the edge of the current he turned to see Deidre half carrying Uh-oh.

They came. They believe in me. They trust me.

He felt himself crest a wave of elation and slide into a trough of despair. What if this didn't work? He turned to Deidre. She tightened her cracking lips and shook her head. Uh-oh turned his back and crawled away from the river.

Noah spread his arms over the roiling lava and hummed the music of Old Hannah's dance.

Within seconds, flat, round, metallic blue stones, about the size of large dinner plates appeared. Each surfaced for a few seconds, floated until another popped up nearby, then slid beneath the surface with a sharp "tssssssssst."

Shielding his eyes against the relentless heat, Noah watched them rise and sink. Random. No rhyme or reason at all.

Humming louder, he peeled off his pack and ran to Uh-oh, his lungs screaming with the effort, his legs trembling. "Climb on my back," he yelled, working the words into the music.

Uh-oh shook his head and tried to scuttle away, but Noah seized him and tossed him over his shoulder as easily as if the creature had been one of Abby's dolls. Uh-oh instinctively flung his arms around Noah's neck and squeezed his legs around Noah's waist. Noah retrieved his pack and slung the straps over his right shoulder. He no longer seemed to feel heat, thirst, or exhaustion. He advanced on Deidre, humming louder, put his right hand around her waist and grasped her right hand with his left.

Was that the way he'd danced with Hannah? Was that where he'd put his hands? He hoped it didn't matter if he didn't get this part exactly right.

Deidre recoiled and struggled to pull away, but with strength he didn't realize he had, he clamped his hand around hers and pulled her close against his chest. He stepped to the edge of the river and eyed the surfacing rocks. Uh-oh's breath steamed in his ear. Deidre's frightened eyes stared up at him. He hummed the song from the beginning again, the sound a mere whisper over the roar of the molten torrent at his feet.

"This is crazy," Deidre shrieked. "What are you doing? We can't—"

Noah spun her around once and backed them onto a blue rock as it surfaced inches from the bank.

CHAPTER 22

"Once Bravo Company completes the pincers movement, cutting off the supply line to Delacroix's force, we'll march toward Shroomtown and perform a flanking operation on their defenses." Spid, the Grand Exalted Garboon of Beneath, used a long pointer to indicate broad red *X*'s marked on the huge map held by two small gammits squatting on the oval stone table.

"Brilliant, Boss. Patton couldna' come up with a better plan." Spid's second-in-command, the simpering ogre Yurk, growled the anticipated compliment.

Spid beamed and blinked through the acrid haze of the oil-lamp-lit chamber to see if the gathered generals of the combined Beneath forces agreed with that appraisal.

Freghzpad, the gammit commander, sat staring into his mug of mud-colored coffee, multiple wrinkles of confusion writhing across his broad, leathery face. His assistant, Stozalg had crammed three of his fingers into a like number of ears on the right side of his face. He seemed intent on digging something of substantial size out of them.

Farther down the table, Krellep, the massive skree who led the air forces, hunkered with his head tucked beneath one huge wing, apparently nibbling on some tidbit. Spid felt his stomach tilt and roll and wondered how the flying flesh-shredder could stand being that close to his own armpit. But, he decided, the raunchy aroma unleashed by the skrees as they flapped their wings could tilt the odds in their favor. If he, Spid, could barely stomach it, imagine how the odor would affect the Above Skin defenses.

He puckered and smiled, then turned his gaze to a trio of ogres, Yurk's field commanders, who drooled on the table and themselves. Their slack-jawed, glassy-eyed expressions betrayed their nearly non-existent attention spans. But once the killing started, Spid knew they'd acquit themselves well. He'd seen Yurk's forces in action before, hundreds of years before, at the great conflict in the coal beds where the ogres had triumphed over the gronnks and cemented the forced alliance that stood to this very day.

"Could I offer you a scone?" A four-armed gronnk appeared beside Spid's right shoulder, bearing a tray stacked with flaky, dark brown pastries.

"Scones?" Spid studied the plate suspiciously even as his stomach rumbled and saliva pooled beneath his tongue. He cocked his head at Yurk. "Scones?"

"Sure, Boss, you told me to come up with some goodies for this here final planning meeting, so I had Glemmis whip up something special."

"I hope they're better than the cappuccino, Yurk. That tasted like whipped muck."

The ogre's small beady eyes darted back and forth, meeting the gronnk's for a moment. The multi-limbed creature shrugged and used one of the arms not balancing the tray to hand two scones to the suddenly uncertain ogre. Yurk set them on the table and cleared his throat twice. "It, uh, *was* muck, Boss. We don't have real coffee down here."

"Delightful." Spid stared at the liquid in the cup at his right hand. He couldn't wait to get Above Skin, couldn't wait to march up to one of those ubiquitous espresso stands and demand a latte with a dusting of nutmeg and a cookie with real chocolate chips, not chunks of coal.

"Uh, try a scone, Boss." Yurk nodded toward the tray. "And could you, uh, try not to hurt Glemmis' feelings? She spent all day in the kitchen."

Spid sighed and took a pastry, forcing himself to smile into the pointed face of the gronnk. The scone felt grainy and heavy. He sniffed it tentatively. It didn't smell half bad. At least, not compared to the armpit of a skree.

Beside him Yurk munched energetically on a substantial chunk. Lifting the scone to his mouth, Spid bit off a small section. For a moment, the sensation was pure texture, a not-unpleasant biscuit-like flakiness that ground between his teeth. And then the full impact of the flavor assaulted Spid's tongue, rocketed to his brain, and exploded.

"Pffffutuuuui!" Spid spat out the wad of masticated dough. The globby projectile caught one of the ogre generals flush in the face. The squat, ugly creature reached up with a two thick fingers and scraped the goo off his hamburger-like face. He jerked a knife from his belt, bared his teeth at Spid and growled a warning.

The troll was too busy blowing the remaining fragments out of his mouth and onto the rock floor to acknowledge the threat. "Pfuii, pflagh, pfuii."

He slammed the uneaten portion of the scone to the table and gargled with the remains of his mud coffee in a vain effort to clear his palate and salve his taste buds. "Yurk," he gasped, pointing at the scone. Before he could say more, the horrible taste made another assault on his taste buds.

His second-in-command chewed contentedly on the final portion of his own pastry with a look of innocence and delight. He wiped his mouth on his sleeve and pointed to the remains of Spid's scone. "So, you're not going to finish that?" Without waiting for an answer, he reached over, snatched it and stuffed it into his mouth.

Spid coughed and spat, considering the plusses and minuses of ripping his own tongue out of his mouth to end the distress messages streaming to his brain. "What in the devil did she put in that...that...scone, Yurk?" Spid thought his voice sounded charred and wondered if the damage was permanent. "It tasted like dried Stegalope droppings."

A wail of despair erupted from Glemmis, the scone-serving gronnk. She dropped the tray with the remaining scones and Yurk's generals dove for the pastries in a blaze of knives, battle clubs, and spiked brass knuckles. Glaring at Spid and muttering incoherently, Glemmis stalked from the chamber. Just before she disappeared through the entryway, she used all four hands to flip him a rude gesture.

"Aw, Boss, you gave away her secret ingredient. And you insulted her food. Now she'll never cook for us again." Yurk looked with obvious distress at the few crumbs remaining on the table, then licked them up.

Spid heard a grumble of annoyance swell from the assembled ogres, skrees, gammits, gronnks, and trolls. He'd broken one of the few rules of protocol in the land Below Skin. He'd have to act quickly or his leadership would be undermined and the alliance would disintegrate. "Yurk!"

"Yeff, Boff?" Tongue scraping the table, the ogre turned one eye toward Spid, then snapped to attention.

Spid swallowed and forced what was left of his voice to sound calm and reasonable. It wouldn't do to show the least sign of weakness. He had to appear totally in control. "When we have finished our strategizing, Yurk, I want you to find Glemmis for me."

"I'll make a note, Boss." The ogre pulled out a piece of slate and a sharpened bit of charcoal and began scribbling. His strokes made a grating sound and several gammits moaned and covered their multiple ears with their arms. "Find Glemmis. Got it." He licked the charcoal.

"If you would, please apologize to her and tell her I meant no offense."

"No offense." Yurk wrote on the slate. "I like that, Boss. Nice touch. It takes a big man, uh troll, to admit when he's wrong. That's what makes you such a great leader. Your humility."

The rumble from the other end of the table swelled. Spid thought he heard a small giggle from one of the gammits. He ignored it and concentrated on controlling his breathing and resuscitating his damaged voice. "Would you also please remind her that my show of disrespect was inappropriate, but that hers was more so. Seeing that I am the Grand Exalted...well you know. Tell her I would appreciate it if she would not repeat that at any point in the future."

"At any point in the..." Yurk turned the slate over. "...future."

"And one thing further. After you've gotten her solemn promise..."

"Solemn promise." Yurk scratched the word onto the slate

"Then have her—" Spid leaned back in his chair and took a deep breath before his roaring, venomous voice, almost as strong as it ever had been, filled the chamber with his uncontrolled rage. "—THROWN FROM MY THRONE ONTO THE PLAIN OF MISERY!!!"

A gasp rose from the assembled generals. The ogres sat up straight and cut looks at each other from the corners of their eyes. Even the skree withdrew his head and eyed Spid with a look that might have been respect. Yurk gulped and dropped his slate. "Do what, Boss?"

Spid swallowed painfully and lowered his voice to a calm purr. "You heard me, Yurk. Now obey!"

Yurk gulped, saluted, and tucked his slate and charcoal back in a pocket of his blousy field jacket. "Y...Y...yes, Boss. I'll get right on it."

"Good." Spid smiled at his minions. He continued in a controlled, almost salesman-like oily tone. "And, Yurk."

"Yes, Boss."

"I'll want to know exactly how many times she bounces."

A second gasp rose from the assembled generals, assuring Spid he made his point. The skree blinked its reptilian eyes. "Yes, Boss," Yurk mumbled.

"And have what's left of her strung up over the main archway as a reminder to those who might consider any form of rebellion."

Yurk pulled out the slate and charcoal again and made a note. "Any form of rebel...rebel? Two *L*'s in rebellion, Boss?"

"Yes, Yurk, two *L*'s." Spid smiled at his commanders. They were with him again, he could feel it. "Now then, gentlemen," he tapped the pointer on the battle map. "If I could have your attention, we'll proceed."

Practically stampeding over one another to get to the front of the room, Spid's commanders formed a half circle around the young gammits who held the map. They straightened their stilt-like legs and gripped the edges with clawed hands the color of phlegm.

197

Spid tapped the pointer against a large green area on the hand-drawn representation of the world Above Skin. "I'll need your forces here, Freghzpad, to create a diversion while Krellep and his skrees provide air cover for a blitzkrieg by Monghelk and the first platoon of ogres. When the enemy begins to fall back, I'll want..."

After nearly an hour of discourse, Spid stopped and fingered his prodigious wart, rolling it between his fingers. No doubt about it, he was a military genius. In millenniums to come, young trolls would read about how he deployed his troops, the way he anticipated each feint and flanking turn by his enemies. "I think we're all on the same page, now, are we not?" He tipped his head toward Yurk and the ogre took his cue.

"Brilliant, Boss. You are Napoleon, Genghis Khan, and Alexander the Great all rolled into one."

"True as it may be, Yurk, thank you for saying it. Are there any questions?"

Freghzpad raised a timid paw and Spid pointed at him. "Yes, my friend?"

In a series of grunts, squeaks, groans, and sputters the gammit framed some kind of question. Spid of course, could not make heads or tails of it, even though his mother had spoken gammit. The language, filled as it was with glottal stops, triple negatives, idioms, and constantly-changing slang, was difficult to master. Not that he, Spid, had time to try. "What did he say Yurk?"

"Well, er, uh..." The ogre chewed at a lower lip that reminded Spid of a picture he'd seen of bratwurst.

"What?" Spid prompted. "Out with it."

"Well, says he likes your plan. It's a great plan. The best battle plan he's ever seen. But, um, well, he was just wondering if, instead of going through all the maneuvering and coordinating and stuff, could they just rush in and kill everything in front of them?"

Spid felt angry blood rush to his brain. "Weren't they listening? Don't they understand why I've spent years on this plan? Everything depends on split-second timing, on teamwork, on knowing the signs and signals! They can't just rush in and..."

He eyed motley gathering—the gronnks and gammits alternately scratching themselves and picking lice from their bodies with their teeth, the ogres staring open-mouthed at the ceilings, walls, and each other. He, Spid the Devious, the Grand Exalted Garboon, deserved better than this.

He sighed heavily, plucked the battle map from the young gammits' hands, and rolled it up. He'd be better off concentrating on training the mutant five-armed gronnk who would drum the way through The Skin and into the land of Above.

"Tell them that will be satisfactory. But ask them not to harm that brat, Abby. She's mine."

CHAPTER 23

As their feet settled on the first stone, it sank slightly. Deidre gasped and dug her fingers into his shoulder.

Noah ignored her. Half closing his eyes, he focused only on the music, the memory of the steps, how quick and how slow each one had been, how long and short each stride or shuffle. Uh-oh snuffled into the collar of his shirt and clung like a tick. Heat radiated from the boiling magma scant inches from their toes and the pungent skanky-egg smell mixed with the rank odor of their fear. White-hot rock popped and exploded, sending red and orange contrails into the air.

Planting his right foot, he pressed Deidre tighter against his chest, pivoted and placed his left foot where he hoped the second stone would be. For a fraction of a second, he felt only blistering heat, then, with a slap, his shoe struck a solid surface. It felt almost cool. "Yes," he breathed into Deidre's hair.

He hesitated for a half second, then stepped backward onto another surfacing rock. Glancing over Deidre's shoulder, he saw the stone they'd just left sinking into the bubbling orange liquid. Uh-oh's grip tightened.

For one desperate short moment, Noah's attention wavered. He stopped humming. He forgot the steps.

The stone beneath them begin to sink.

His toes felt like they were on fire. He started to scream and then was overtaken by a cool silence within which he heard only the old woman's voice commanding him: "Dance, Noah, dance. The steps. Remember the steps."

The stone beneath them wobbled and tilted. He wondered if he'd have time to scream before the heat seared the skin off his body.

"Don't look," he shouted to his friends. "Hold on tight. It's gonna get hairy." Humming again, he swiveled them all to the left, pushed off, and guided them through three long steps, a stutter, a spin and another three backward steps. During the sequence their feet touched seven different stones. Each sank just after they danced to the next.

Faster and faster the stones rose and fell. Louder and louder grew the roar of the river and the explosions of rocks split by the heat. Noah could barely hear himself hum. He knew that if they stopped now, for even a second, they'd sink into the roiling inferno. He swung his friends to another stone and another, dancing faster, dipping and swaying, feeling the jolt in his spine each time his feet struck a surfacing stone.

Noah glanced back at the shore they'd left, then toward their destination. The advance and retreat of the dance had carried them only a quarter of the way across Pfhaaa. His back ached. Sweat stung his eyes. He blinked frantically to clear them and gasped for oxygen in the roasting air. No way would they make it. He wasn't strong enough.

"Promise me you'll never give up, Noah." His mother's voice. As clear as if she were standing beside him. "I'm with you, Noah. Dance. Dance."

A sort of mental mist clouded his surroundings and he no longer felt the heat of the river or tasted the acrid sulfur smoke. His entire being, every molecule, focused only on the music filling his mind.

He straightened, took a deep breath, dipped, and stepped. Deidre, as if she sensed his transformation, seemed to meld into him, to become one with him, and even anticipate his next series of movements. Even the burden of Uh-oh seemed as insignificant as the weight of his shirt.

They glided on across the molten river, dancing for their lives. Inside Noah's head the music built, the beats like hail. As the melody swirled toward a crescendo, the river of fire melded into an orange blur and he felt seasick, dizzy. A cold emptiness balled up in the pit of his stomach and he glimpsed the darkness creeping in around the edges.

"Hang on," he told himself. "Just a little more." The song inside his head climaxed with crashing cymbals and blaring horns. His field of vision narrowed and crimped. He felt himself sway, his center of balance shift. The putrefying smell of sulfur assaulted him.

I'm going into the river and I'm taking Deidre and Uh-oh with me.

"Don't give up," he croaked through cracked and parched lips. His field of vision narrowed to a pinpoint, then went black. He fell, burning.

"Hey, get off me."

Deidre's yell sent Noah swimming to the edge of consciousness.

"Come on, Noah, move it!"

Hands pushed at his chest. Others pulled at his shoulders. He opened his eyes to see Deidre pinned beneath him a few yards from the tumbling, hissing Pfhaaa. The rock beneath him felt cool. Or at least less hot. He felt Uh-oh's long fingers clamp around his shoulders again, trying to lift him.

We made it!

"Noah, c'mon, you're heavy for a scrawny little goof. Move it," Deidre yelled and pushed once more at his chest.

He tried to obey, but his body took forever to respond. Finally, he managed to roll away, sending Uh-oh sprawling. The gray creature, now streaked with soot and with half his hair singed off, tried to stand, but his legs wobbled and he plopped on his rear end with a groan.

"We got to drink some water," Deidre gasped as she sat up. "We're dehydrated." She clawed at the canteen on her belt and twisted the cap. It opened with a hiss and a puff of steam shot out. She put the canteen to her lips, then jerked it away. "Too hot. Come on, we need to hit the road. Now!"

Noah's socks and shoes were little more than blackened scraps of fabric and melted rubber. Inside them his feet throbbed. The hair on his arms was black and crispy and broke at a touch. Another huge wave of dizziness assaulted him and he fell. "Can't."

"Can!" Deidre shouted.

She lurched to her feet, steadied herself, and stumbled to Uh-oh. The gray creature clung to her arm, trembling, and together they tottered to Noah. "Come on, Bun-boy. On your feet."

"I can't," Noah moaned.

How much more did he have to endure before they let him go home? Why had he ever left in the first place? It all seemed so trivial now.

"Get up or you'll die here." Deidre seized his hand. "Get up or I'll drag you. Do you want to be dragged around by a girl? What will your friends say?"

"Don't have any," Noah muttered.

But that wasn't true. He had at least three: Abby, Uh-oh, and Deidre. He shook off her hand, heaved himself up and reeled after her, panting.

With each slow step away from the molten river, the air and ground cooled. Before them, the tunnel they spotted from the other side loomed. The air rushing from it seemed almost frigid, and they inhaled deeply and gratefully and drank now-tepid water from their canteens. Noah peeled off his shoes and socks and tossed them aside. The rock beneath his burning feet felt marvelously cold and soothing.

"You might need your shoes later." Deidre started to retrieve them. "I can carry them."

Noah shook his head. "They're worthless." He glanced at Deidre's feet. Her sturdy boots, although scorched, seemed to have survived intact. "We don't need the extra weight. Besides," he pointed at Uh-oh, "he's been barefoot all along."

Deidre opened her mouth as if to argue, then changed her mind and nodded. As they hiked into the dim tunnel, Noah heard her whisper. "That was fun. Let's do it again sometime."

Noah grinned, found her hand and squeezed it. "Next time we'll make it a slow dance."

He noticed that she didn't pull her hand away. He also noticed that he couldn't stop smiling.

An hour or so later, they emerged into a smallish chamber. A stream of water slid from a crevice in the ceiling and pooled in a natural basin in the wall before overflowing into a crack in the floor. They flopped down, opened their charred packs and dug out the sandwiches Eve packed. Noah bit into his and marveled that the heat from the river hadn't spoiled it. The ingredients between the slabs of a rough-crusted wheat bread had melted together into a tasty filling, almost as if that's what Deidre's mother intended. He swallowed the first few bites quickly, then chewed more slowly, detecting some kind of mushroom, onions, tomatoes, and a green that resembled lettuce but probably wasn't. The mushroom had an almost meat-like salty flavor, reminding Noah of bacon. After they demolished the sandwiches, they ate cookies made with what tasted like molasses and carrot.

Uh-oh fell asleep clutching his second cookie. Deidre fought a yawn and looked over at Noah. "So, Fred Astaire. Nice moves out there."

Noah blinked. How could she know about Fred Astaire? Where would she have seen the graceful, thin, tuxedoed man with the slicked-back hair. "You weren't half bad yourself, Ginger."

She giggled. "Thanks. I never danced much before. They have some kinda half-baked dances in Shroomtown. Mostly klunky boys stepping on your toes and everybody kind of doing their own thing. Not real dancing."

Noah nodded. "Sounds like junior high back home." The thought of home sobered him. Home was where he'd seen Fred Astaire in old black and white movies on late-night TV. His mother had loved watching the dancer's effortless movements. "Hey, how do you know about—?"

"Fred Astaire? Mom has an old magazine. About movies and people who were in them. It's kinda ragged and tattered. It's been lying around our place for as long as I can remember. I asked her about it once, where it came from, but she didn't know; she had it with her when the Shroomers found her."

They both sensed movement and turned to see Uh-oh, up from his catnap and on his feet, clutching an imaginary dance partner. He advanced and retreated, twirled and high stepped. Flinging his remaining curls back, he spun his invisible partner out and away from him, then brought her back with a flick of his wrist. Bending her over backward, Uh-oh posed, face tilted toward the imaginary applause from an audience. Noah and Deidre rewarded him by clapping enthusiastically. Uh-oh bowed deeply, spun in place and plopped back on the ground, grabbing his cookie as he landed. Munching and letting the crumbs dribble down his chin, he waggled his eyebrows and growled one word. "Tadah!"

"What a clown." Deidre rolled her eyes.

"He really is pretty amazing," Noah agreed.

"So are you. I gotta tell you, I was pretty freaked out when you grabbed me and stepped out on that rock. Where did you get the idea to dance across?"

Noah stretched out on his back and closed his eyes, enjoying the feel of cool and solid rock against his spine. "Something happened. Earlier. Before I came to Humbug Mountain." He turned to gaze at her.

Deidre asked "and?" with her eyes and he told her the story of Old Hannah and the music on the beach, how Abby was kidnapped, and how he and Uh-oh fell into the ocean and woke up in the hermit's cavern.

"I've seen him. The hermit," Deidre told him. "At a distance. Up on some of the high ledges above the main caverns. I asked Mom about him and she said he was just another lost soul down here. Like the ones in Shroomtown."

Noah realized he hadn't wondered about where the Shroomtown residents came from. "Huh?"

"They're all descendants of people who disappeared. You know, lost hikers, children who vanished on their way home from school, people who never returned from vacation."

"That's what we all are down here. Lost souls." Deidre lay back and closed her eyes. Neither of them spoke for a time and Noah had nearly drifted into sleep when she broke the silence. "Noah?"

"Yeah?"

"What's it like? Out there?"

Out there. Home. Abby. Dad. His room. His drums. The smell of the ocean and the forest. Port Anvil, with its little stores selling junk to the tourists. The Clam Shack with the best chowder anywhere. The cars zooming by on Highway 101 headed for Gold Beach and Brookings and California. The mall in Coos Bay.

None of that seemed to be right to describe "out there." Where should he begin? "Well, in here you go only so far and you run into a wall. Out there it's...open...with no boundaries."

Her jaw dropped and her mouth formed an oval. "Really?"

"I can sit at night, on the bluff by the lighthouse, and look up at the sky and see a billion stars."

"Stars?" He saw her face scrinch as she reached for understanding and failed. "What are those?"

"They're huge balls of burning gas that are trillions and trillions of miles away, so they only look like little pinpoints of light in the sky."

She punched his arm. "You're making this up."

"No. I wouldn't lie to you." Friends didn't lie to friends.

She looked at the roof of the cave illuminated by the Zezzue. "What's the sky?"

"It's...well, it's miles and miles of air, going up and up and up." Noah put a hand up and pointed. "And one of those burning balls of gas isn't that far away from us and

207

our whole planet circles around it, spinning while it does, so that sometimes it's dark outside and sometimes it's light. Dark and light. In a regular pattern. And when it's dark we turn on electric lights."

"Get out of here. Really?" Deidre's eyes opened wide. "So you don't have any Darksuckers out there?"

"Not that I know of." But he didn't know what Darksuckers were before he came here. For all he knew they were everywhere, responsible for all light and darkness. "Um, we get light from the distant stars, the close one we call the sun, and the moon."

"What's the moon?"

"It's a big dead chunk of rock that reflects light from the sun as it circles around earth. The earth is the planet we're all on. The moon glows at night, kind of silvery or orange or yellow. Some nights you can see all of the moon and sometimes only part."

Noah heard Deidre draw in a long breath. "Will you show me some day? When all this is over?"

He felt himself blush. "Sure. Definitely. Yeah. I'll show you the moon and we'll watch a Fred Astaire movie and eat popcorn and I'll even let you tease my little sister."

And all I've got to do first is figure out how to keep some evil thing called Spid from killing us.

As tired and played out as Noah felt, he forced himself to his feet. "Maybe we'd better get started again."

"In a second," Deidre mumbled. "Is there evil out there? Like Spid? Like the nasty things that live Beneath?"

Noah took a moment to think before he answered. "Yeah. Of course there is. There are bad people, or even regular people who sometimes do bad things. And sometimes..." He felt his eyes mist up. "...really bad things happen to really good people. Like my Mom."

"Oh."

That was all she said, but Noah didn't need any prompting. He wanted to tell her. "My mom died. A little more than a year ago. She had cancer. Evil stuff that grows inside your body and hurts you and kills you."

"I'm so sorry. But...at least you had her for a while. You had both of your parents. I never had a father."

The words hung in the air between them. Slowly, Noah let go of his anger and when Deidre lifted her hand he took it and helped her to her feet.

"Time to hit the road," she said. "The Temple of Cheltnor can't be much farther."

"Hope not."

"You got a vision for what we do there?"

"I'll think of something," he answered with false confidence. His mind felt empty, as if all ability to think had been fried out of it by the heat from the river. Maybe something else that passed between him and Old Hannah would surface. He'd think about it while they walked. Or maybe he shouldn't think.

Deidre helped Uh-oh to his feet and turned to stride ahead into the tunnel. "I've got bad vibes about marching into Cheltnor and carrying the Methuselah out of the temple. Somebody's not gonna be cool with that. And you're probably not going to dazzle them with footwork."

CHAPTER 24

Lix Delacroix picked up a chicken finger from the platter in the middle of the table by trapping it between his big toe and the next one. He paused to dunk it in a container of sweet and sour sauce, lifted it to his mouth, and devoured it in one bite.

Abby forced herself not to gawk and nibbled at a yeasty cinnamon bun running with butter. Eating with your feet? What would Mom say? Actually, Abby thought, she probably would have gotten a kick out of it. And Delacroix's feet were clean. She watched him wash them in a basin before dinner. Chillout appeared at her elbow, refilled her mug of lemonade, then moved to his own spot at the table.

Abby felt a wave of heavy homesickness press down on her. Before Mom got sick, Dad would often stop for take-out food on his way from work. The four of them would sit around the dining room table, munching burgers or tacos or sharing orange chicken and pork-fried rice from little white boxes. They'd talk about their days, news of the community, and plans for the weekend.

Mom would often tell a funny story about one of her customers at the supermarket. Dad and Noah would talk about music. Sometimes, after they helped Mom clean up, they'd wander out to the garage and jam together.

Gosh, she'd completely forgotten how close they'd been. She and Mom would play chess or two-handed pinochle and listen to the wail of Dad's alto saxophone over the rhythmic thunder of Noah's drums. After that, they might crowd onto the couch together and watch a movie, passing a bowl of buttery popcorn back and forth. It felt so real, so close, that Abby wanted to cry out at the injustice of it all. But she couldn't lose it; she had to stay strong so she could help Noah when he returned with the Methuselah Stone.

Where are you, Noah? What are you doing? I hope you're all right.

She wiped a drop of butter off her chin and guessed that patience was another lesson she needed to learn. Only a few days remained until Spid would try to break through The Skin. Delacroix insisted that he and Noah had to practice together before they faced Spid's drummer. If Noah didn't turn up soon, they were sunk. All of them.

While they ate, several visitors approached Delacroix and carried on hushed conversations in languages that sounded like word whirlpools. Some were human or humanoid and some were grungoids. But there were also creatures she'd never seen, or even imagined before. One of them resembled a large, brown anteater with two eyes on either side of its triangular face. Another towered over the table, a hair-covered bear-man at least seven feet tall with glowing orange eyes and furry feet so large they would make ten of hers.

Even though Abby understood none of the words exchanged during these whispered confabs, the tone was all about war. The occupants of the Above part of Humbug mountain were gearing up to fend off an invasion. They would fight in the caverns and cubbyholes and tunnels. They would fight to the last man, woman, or creature.

She nibbled at one of the fried chicken chunks, no longer tasting it, and watched as Delacroix extended his leg and wiggled his toes over the platter, preparing to help himself to another portion.

"Don't you ever miss them? Your arms?" Abby slapped both hands over her mouth, as if she could stuff the rude question back in.

Delacroix plucked another morsel, dipped it, popped it into his mouth, and dabbed his lips with a napkin he captured with the other foot. Smiling, he set the napkin down and arranged his legs into a lotus position. "Of course, I miss them. They are, or were, a part of me, after all."

"But it's as if you never had them," she marveled. "You do everything with your feet. You're amazing."

"*Merci*," he acknowledged. "But of course, for some things, nothing can replace your hands and arms."

Abby nodded. "The drumming of course."

"But many other things too, Abby. I miss having my elbow to lean on and my hand to hold my chin when I daydream. I miss doing the spider-on-a-mirror thing with my fingertips when I am trying to solve a particularly perplexing problem, you know? And..." His face took on a wistful expression. "I especially miss the hugging."

Abby felt a lump constrict her throat. Mom had loved hugging people. Dad too, until— She couldn't stop her next question. "Did you lose them in the plane crash?"

Delacroix sighed and raised his foot to scratch his ear. "You don't want to hear this story. It is a sad one and it can change nothing."

Chillout stood and made a faint chhht, chhht, chhht sound. Perhaps he had something to say that he didn't want her to understand.

When Delacroix didn't respond, Chillout gathered up the remainder of the dinner and disappeared, leaving a long silence behind.

Finally, Delacroix cleared his throat. "There once was a musician, a young man who learned to play drums on his native island in the Caribbean, by listening to the rhythms of the world around him. There, on that green, green island in that blue, blue sea, he listened to the surf, to the breezes in the trees, to the beating of birds' wings, and the rush and rumble of streams after a rain."

Abby could almost see it. She gathered her legs beneath her in imitation of his lotus position and watched his eyes as he spoke.

"He came to America and found success, this boy, this man, no? Other musicians, they liked his sound, and they invited him to play with dem. He recorded his music and people bought it and he made a great deal of money. Before he knew it, he had the fame, you see?"

"How old were you then?"

"By the time I bought and learned to fly the aeroplane I had passed my twenty-seventh birthday, *ma petite*. Always, I had desired to fly." His voice dropped and she heard bitterness in the next words. "To soar with the birds."

"How old are you now?" Another question blurted out.

A bemused smile drew his lips back. "I am not sure, not knowing how much time has passed. There are no clocks here, and the sun does not rise and set. Probably the downhill side of forty, I am guessing. But then I was returning from my honeymoon. With Melanie."

"Noah told me she was an actress."

"*Oui.* A very fine young character actress, she appeared in plays in New York. She was to begin work on her first movie when we—" He choked and dabbed at his eyes with the napkin.

213

Crashed. Abby mentally filled in the missing word. Silence once again filled the chamber and she shifted her legs. A part of her, a very large part, wanted to get up and go to him, to give him a hug and tell him everything was all right. But, while she considered that, his low, rumbling, musical voice picked up the thread again, telling the story as if it were happening that very moment.

"We are to fly from Portland to San Francisco. About four hours. An easy flight. But suddenly, we find ourselves, how you say, in the middle of a thunderstorm. The wind, it howls. My little plane, she is punched and pummeled. I pull her up, to try to climb above the evil black clouds, but the swirling wind is stronger than my engine. It slaps us down like you might slap a fly. The rain, it falls so hard we are flying blind."

Abby shivered as she visualized Delacroix and his pretty young bride huddled together in terror. She felt like she should say something, anything, to ease his pain. But all she could do was nod.

"I see the mountain. I pull the nose up so we will not strike head-on. I aim for what looks like a clear spot. And then it is like nothing I have imagined. Big trees. A grinding collision. A bright flash. And pain. So much pain."

Abby shivered. "How awful."

He went on in a rush, as if, now that he had begun, he was compelled to complete the tale. "After that, I have no memory until I awaken in the middle of the wreckage. Rain falls and wind blows and my body hurts in ways I did not know it could hurt. In the darkness, I feel beside me for Melanie and find her seat empty. When the morning comes I see the blood."

Abby gnawed at her knuckles watching Delacroix's eyes grow distant, lost. If he reached for Melanie, she thought, he still had his arms.

"I think maybe she stumbled into the woods, among those enormous trees, trying to walk down the mountain searching for help. I crawl out and drag myself through the brush. Inch by inch. The sun grows hotter. I call her name until my voice it is lost, no?

And then, just when I think I can go no farther, I hear a rustling in the brush behind me. Melanie! My heart leaps."

"Was she all right?" Abby leaned forward, feeling her eyes widen.

Delacroix shook his head. "Alas. I do not know. The rustling in the brush, it is made by a large creature, a creature that stalks me. A cat. I hear it snarl. A big cat who thinks he has found his dinner. I am large enough, he could have invited friends, no?"

The dark humor made Abby smile despite herself. "What happened? How did you get away?"

"I climb to my feet and shout with all of the power I can gather." He threw his head back and boomed the words across the cavern. "You go away, *Monsieur le Chat*. I am not ready yet for to be your dinner."

Abby giggled. "And did it work?"

"I am alive today."

"But...your arms?"

"Yes." He held out the stumps that ended above his elbows. "My arms. I do not know how long I search for my Melanie. But then the rain comes. I crawl into a cave, thinking perhaps she sought shelter. The cave it is dark, very dark. The ground gives way beneath my feet. I slide, down, down, down. My head hits rock and everything is darkness. And when I wake up, I have no arms."

Abby couldn't imagine how someone could fall down and wake up without arms. "Were they torn off when you fell?"

"No. Melacherub removed them. To save my life."

215

"Melacherub?" Abby swiveled her head to see if Chillout had re-entered the chamber. He hadn't. "You mean one of the grungoids operated on you?"

"No, *cherie*, Melacherub was not a..." He used the ancient name for grungoids that sounded like gargling. "Melacherub was a very old, very wise wizard. He was, before me, the Grand Imperial Pettifog."

"A wizard?" Abby scoffed. "With a long beard and a magic wand?"

"You don't believe in the magic?"

She shook her head. "What I've seen is all sleight of hand and misdirection."

He laughed. "Ah, my little scientist. How do you explain how we fell down that air shaft, the Vorv, and remained uninjured? How then do you explain how you found your way here from the maze?"

He had her there. That magic wasn't rabbits-out-of-a-hat stuff. It was...was...what? Abby remembered the sensation she felt while chanting and threading her way through the labyrinth with her eyes squeezed shut.

"Melacherub was short and bald." Delacroix continued. "He reminded me of the man I hired to watch after my money in New York. To count the beans, as they say. A what you call it...?"

"Accountant?"

"Yes, accountant. But he could summon the magic, of that there is no doubt."

"So he cut off your arms?"

"While I was unconscious. Without anesthetic."

Abby flinched.

"I did not feel it, *ma petite*."

"But couldn't he save them?"

"He tried, but the gangrene spread. He could not cure it with potions or spells. So he took my arms from me. But not with a knife. He used only his mind." He held out the

216

stumps. "There are no scars, no marks from stitches. It is as if my skin it grew that way when I was inside my mother."

Abby reeled at the concept. A wizard. Psychic amputation. Impossible. And yet... Another question popped into her brain and immediately to her mouth. "After you healed. Why didn't you go back out? Into the world?"

Delacroix flexed his legs and rose smoothly to his feet. Abby attempted the same move and toppled over.

Delacroix grinned. "Getting up with no hands is like anything else, little one. It takes the practice."

Scrambling to her feet, she asked the question again. "Why have you stayed here? All of these years."

"Because, I..." He sighed. "My sweetness, my Melanie, must have perished up there," Delacroix lifted his gaze toward the ceiling, "on the mountain. "She could not have survived. And..." He shrugged. "I could not leave her."

Love? Guilt? A combination of both?

The giant shrugged. "Without my arms, I did not have the music, I could not play. So I decided I would live my life here, alone. Except, I found I was not alone."

Surrounded by weirdness, Abby thought, but not alone.

"The others accepted me. Eventually, after I learned the ways of Humbug and its inhabitants, Melacherub moved on. I became the Pettifog."

"Where did Melacherub go?"

"Some think he went somewhere to die by himself. Others think he lives on. No one for certain knows." Delacroix turned to go, then stopped and looked back. "Have I satisfied your appetite? Have you asked me every question generated by your hungry mind?"

Abby bowed her head. "I'm sorry. I didn't mean to pry."

Delacroix smiled warmly and chuckled. "Your curiosity is a blessing and a curse, is it not? But on balance, I think it serves you well. Do not stop questing, Abby."

"One more question, please. Do you ever miss it? The outside."

Smoothly lifting one foot to scratch his chin while balancing effortlessly on the other, Delacroix considered for a moment. "Not so much. Perhaps a little, at odd times. You have noticed, have you not, the food. Eating the grubs and worms and tiny bugs like Chillout and the others has limited appeal, no?"

"Definitely," Abby agreed with a shudder.

"Truth be told, I think Chillout has become addicted to *cuisine le refuse* also. He especially loves the onion rings and milkshakes. I have ruined him. But other things I do sometimes miss. Birds. Train whistles in the middle of the night. The smell of the plantains frying at the stalls in the marketplace in my country. The exquisite green-blue water of that warm sea."

"Do you ever think about going back?"

"Sometimes. But then I realize that life there, without my Melanie, would not be complete. And I remind myself that I belong to Humbug Mountain." With that he turned, ducked his head to enter a passageway, and walked away.

After a moment, Abby strolled to the other side of the chamber and entered her own room. Notebook in hand, she propped herself up on the bed and began again to try to untangle the word the Zezzue gave her at the end of the Spiddle game. *T-I-R-K-D-E-S-C-X-O-S-L-K-N-U-R-P-L-V.*

But her mind wandered to Delacroix's story, to Noah and the upcoming battle with Spid. All of them seemed to be missing something, she realized. Delacroix missed Melanie and, of course, his arms. Noah missed Mom and the tight connectedness they enjoyed before she died. Abby missed her mother, too, but had shoved her feelings into the background because Noah mourned so deeply and openly. And Spid? Was Spid missing something? Besides a realistic self-image?

Chuckling, she sat up and stared at the word that had won her the game, then tossed her pencil aside and flopped back on her pillows. Maybe, instead of thinking about what was missing, she should concentrate on what she had and how to use it.

What she had was letters that spelled no word she could recognize. No way to know how to use that. But she also had her brain, her heart, and the friendship of Felix Delacroix, the Grand Imperial Pettifog of Above Skin and his bebop man Friday, Chillout. "And I have a wonderful, talented brother who cares about me."

T-I-R-K-D-E-S-C-X-O-S-L-K-N-U-R-P-L-V

She examined the bizarre word again, letting it bounce around inside her mind without running into the walls and corners thrown up by her logical self. Remembering the floating, out-of-body state she reached traipsing blindly through the tunnels, she closed her eyes and mouthed the words: "Youknowuh, youknowuh, youknowuh,youknowuh."

She kept it up for at least half an hour, but felt no transformation, no shift in her consciousness, no emergence of an alternate self to guide her. Finally, frustrated and sleepy, she wrapped herself in her quilt. The Zezzue dimmed themselves and she thought she heard them hum as she yawned and rolled over and hovered between wakefulness and the edge of sleep.

"You know the way," the Zezzue whispered. "Follow your heart."

She tried to pull herself out of the spiraling darkness, tried to ask them what they meant, but she couldn't.

When she woke up, the tiny lights seemed cold and distant and she wondered if she might have dreamed it.

CHAPTER 25

By the time they caught sight of the Temple of Cheltnor, Noah's bruised and blistered feet ooozed blood and every step triggered a wince. For an hour Deidre set a merciless pace through twisting, turning passageways that eventually opened onto a rock shelf overlooking a broad plain strewn with immense boulders. In the distance, Noah saw a wide crack in the earth with a vivid violet glow rising from it.

"Cheltnor," Deidre declared. "And the Methuselah Stone will be there. Or so the prophecy says." She didn't sound convinced.

Uh-oh extended a bony forefinger toward the radiance flowing up through the far-away fissure, made a nervous chhht...chhht...chhht sound, and scuttled behind Noah.

Deidre smiled, but her eyes revealed the unspoken question that hung between them like a cobweb: What's the plan?

You'd be better off asking Uh-oh, Noah thought. Or one of those boulders down there. I am major clueless to the forty-second power. Crossing Pfhaaa? A fluke—beginner's luck.

"Bout half an hour more." Deidre glanced back the way they came.

221

"Uh huh," he grunted, wondering how she knew how long half an hour was. She didn't carry a watch. In fact he hadn't spotted anything that kept time since he woke up in the Hermit's quarters.

He started to walk again, each step sending needles of fire up his legs to his brain. Maybe he should have kept his burned shoes. Any protection would help. He gritted his teeth as they picked their way through the boulder field, weaving between the massive rocks. Jagged splinters of stone nicked his feet, opening new cuts.

Uh-oh checked back over his shoulder from time to time, as if afraid somebody pursued them. Noah wondered if the creature had seen or heard something or if he just had a bad case of jangly nerves.

By Noah's internal clock, it took twice as long as Deidre predicted to arrive at the rim of the crevasse and look down on the temple that hulked on the far side of the rocky floor of the rift. The temple itself was broad and stood several stories high. It appeared someone had carved it right into the rock wall that defined the other side of the narrow canyon. Its surface sparkled jewel-like, catching glimmering light and spinning it in different directions. The aura was largely violet, but Noah saw twinkles of orange and green and blue and practically every color he could imagine.

"It's beautiful," Deidre gasped.

"Sure is," Noah agreed. And scary. Like those pretty flowers that snap their jaws around unsuspecting insects. He studied the crevasse. Only a few hundred yards long, but several hundred feet deep. "How will we get down?"

"Very carefully." Deidre peeled her pack from her back. "We'll leave these here. They'll just slow us down on the climb back up."

"Makes sense."

"I've got some rope." She produced it from a deep pocket of her pack. "We'll tie ourselves together in case—" She didn't finish the sentence, but the implication hung in the air. Noah dropped his pack and Uh-oh followed suit. His dreadlocks shook as he trembled, glancing between the temple and Noah.

Deidre roped them together, looping the sturdy cord through their belts and knotting it around Uh-oh's waist, leaving about twenty feet of slack between them. "One of us must always act as the anchor," she said. "In case the others lose their footing."

Uh-oh tilted his head, peered at long drop, and shuddered.

"You'll be good at this," Noah told him. "Remember the day we met? You fell only because I grabbed you. I'm depending on you to help me."

Uh-oh nodded and took a deep breath.

"Let's do it." Deidre led the way over the edge, finding handgrips and footholds with little difficulty.

The girl must be part mountain goat, Noah decided. So agile and sure-footed. He started after her and was surprised to find that, if he studied the rock and didn't look down, it was relatively easy. But thirty yards from the bottom they ran into trouble—a wide slide of loose rock that funneled to the floor of the basin. Noah shaded his eyes against the violet glow and peered at a boulder off to his left. "Can we get around it?"

Deidre studied the slide. "Not unless we go back up and find another spot. We're in a layer of shale. It fractures easily, that's why this sheared away. But maybe it's finished shifting.

She took a few tentative steps as Noah anchored her. "Feels firm," she called.

He followed her onto the slide and Uh-oh trailed him, lagging at the full length of the rope.

"It's getting looser," Deidre called after they'd gone a few yards. "Careful. I'm going to move toward the edge."

Noah nodded and took a few more baby steps. Then his ear picked up a soft cracking sound above him. He halted and all was quiet for a few seconds, then he heard the grating of shifting rock.

Uh-oh, arms flailing, dug with his feet at a stream of stones.

"Deidre. Look out."

Uh-oh tumbled backwards and shot toward Noah, hands clutching for a purchase. Noah tried to plant his feet, but the shale slid beneath them.

No way! No way can I stop him.

Uh-oh bounced and skidded past, his eyes dark with fear. Noah leaned back into the slope, gripping the rope. It played out between them as fast as a striking snake, then snapped taut.

Rock rasped beneath him and for a moment Noah teetered. Then Uh-oh's momentum propelled him down the slope like a water skier on a gravel lake.

"Aaaaaagh. I can't stop."

He tried to dig his heels in, but only managed to lose his balance and fall onto his side.

"Get ready to grab me," Deidre screamed as Uh-oh careened past just out of her reach. She flopped down on the slide and flung out one arm. "Now."

Their forearms slapped together. Noah's fingers grasped at empty air. Then her hand clamped around his wrist. Through rising dust, he saw her face contort as she strained to hold him. He dug in his toes, trying to swim against the stone-fall. Why hadn't he kept his shoes?

He heard Uh-oh squeal and turned his head to see the rope snap across the lip of an overhang. Uh-oh dropped out of sight.

The rope tightened around his waist and Noah heard another squeal. His own.

For a moment, Deidre supported all of them. Sweat beaded across her forehead and her face turned a mottled purple with strain. Then Noah's bare foot found a solid spot beneath shifting rock shards and his slide stopped.

"Bad news, Noah," Uh-oh's voice rose from the end of the rope. "Very bad."

"Hold on, Uh-oh," he hollered down. "We'll pull you back up." He torqued his neck and looked up at Deidre. "Won't we?"

She nodded, chest heaving as she drew in a series of breaths and called down the slope. "Uh-oh, stay as still as you can. Don't try to climb. We'll rescue you, but it'll take time."

Without waiting for a response, she addressed Noah. "Have you got a good hold? Can you support Uh-oh for a bit?"

"I think so." He dug his free hand and both feet into the rockslide, ignoring fragments of stone that sliced his fingers and toes.

"Let's find out." Noah felt her grasp on his arm loosen. He slid half an inch. An inch. Two inches. Then the motion ceased.

"There's a ledge just below you and to your right." Deidre said. "Turn your head slowly. Don't make any sudden movements."

"I see it." He loosened one foot from the grasp of the slide. "I'll—

Her voice cracked like a whip. "Shut up and listen."

Uh-oh whimpered. Noah forced himself to stay still. "Shutting up now."

"Good. You hold Uh-oh. That's your job, your only job. Got it?"

"Got it," he agreed.

"Okay. I'm going to work my way over to that ledge. Looks like I've got to go up a few feet first, and then I think I can pick my way."

Noah thought she sounded less confident than when she told him to shut up. "Is that plan A?"

"Right."

"What's plan B?"

"We all fall and hurt ourselves."

He forced himself to grin, remembering a scene toward the end of *Ghostbusters* where the team decides to do what they'd concluded earlier was too dangerous to try. "I'm wild about plan A."

"I thought you would be. Soon as I get to the ledge, I'll help you scramble over and we'll double-team Uh-oh. Okay?"

He forced bravado he didn't feel. "Piece of cake. Take it slow."

She released his arm and he dug the freed hand into the slide as a spray of loose gravel rained down on him. If Deidre fell, he couldn't stop her, not while holding Uh-oh on the end of the rope like a puppet.

Don't think about it.

Deidre grunted. "I'm okay. I found a handhold."

Out of the corner of his eye, he saw her clamber to a position about ten feet above the ledge. He heard her mutter something unintelligible, then she hurtled past.

He turned his face into the rockslide and prepared for the sudden yank on the rope that would signal the start of the skin-ripping slide before the fall to the canyon floor.

"Oof." Deidre grunted.

Noah heard the slap of leather on rock, risked a look, and saw her crumple on the ledge below him. "Deidre! Are you hurt?"

It seemed an eternity before she answered. "Just shook up a little. Let's get you over here."

226

Deidre helped Noah slide down to the ledge. From there they could see that Uh-oh dangled thirty feet above the rocky floor of the crevasse. "It will be easier to lower him than haul him up," Deidre decided.

"You've got the lead in this dance," Noah said.

When they'd eased Uh-oh safely to a flat spot below him, they adjusted the tangled ropes and inched down the rest of the slide without incident. At the bottom, they rested, sipped from their canteens and took stock. Noah's pants and shirt were shredded and his feet and hands rubbed raw. Uh-oh had a number of deep oozing scrapes and Deidre had twisted her ankle. Lucky, Noah thought. We were lucky.

Five minutes later, they stood at the ornate entrance to the Temple of Cheltnor. This close, the colored light reflecting from the surface created a glare that made Noah hood his eyes with his hands. Squinting, he saw the walls were comprised of thousands and thousands of crystals like the chunks of amethyst in Port Anvil gift shops.

Inside, they found themselves in a long, high-ceilinged room with smooth and polished walls. The air grew colder and the echoes of Deidre's footsteps seemed to hang in it as she strode across the gleaming translucent floor. At the far end of the great hall, four stone statues depicted figures seemingly flash-frozen while in action. Made of red-tinged stone, they ranged in height from twenty to thirty feet. They're kinda crude, Noah thought, like what little kids make out of clay.

One stone character, a boy or man, with some kind of sticks in his hand, beat on an imaginary surface. The second statue was that of a girl, one hand covering her eyes, the other reaching upward.

Noah and Deidre turned their heads at the same time to examine the third statue. He saw her shiver and he felt a companion chill run down his own spine. This creature was short and squat and boasted five arms, each grasping a stick. He, too, seemed to strike out at a flat surface. The final stone figure, the tallest, loomed over the other three. Noah felt violence radiate from the smirking countenance.

"Troll," said Uh-oh in a voice they'd never heard before. It sounded like that of a very young child. "Maybe Spid, maybe not Spid."

"Is this what a troll looks like? What Spid looks like?" Noah asked.

The gray creature shrugged and hugged himself.

"If it's not Spid, it's one of his ancestors," Deidre confirmed.

"You've seen Spid?"

"Kind of. For quite a while now, he's been appearing at different places. But it's not really him. It's kind of a ghost of him or something. It moves and talks, but you can put your hand right through it."

"Like a hologram?"

"I don't know what that is."

"It's a projection, like a shadow, only with color."

"Huh. Well, when he appears, he says we must obey him or die." Deidre scowled and spit on the ground. "He also says that those who join him will become wealthy beyond their wildest dreams and possess all that they want."

"That's some incentive. How many have joined him?"

She looked at him in amazement. "No one. No one here would join Spid. Especially not for wealth. That means nothing inside the mountain. We have all we need, and we share all we have."

"That's the way it should be," Noah said. But he wondered how Deidre's view of what she needed might change if she spent a few hours watching one of the television shopping channels while thumbing through a fashion magazine.

He looked up at the statues again and saw something he hadn't noticed before. Perched on the shoulders of the troll were other creatures huddled with wings folded, beady eyes surveying the room. Their faces were wrinkled and deformed, and they had pointed ears, webbed feet and talons for hands. Human, birdlike, and reptilian. They emanated pure evil.

He sensed he'd seen them somewhere else—in a book, a movie, or a nightmare. What they were called? As he cast about for the word, another image popped into his mind, a fuzzy memory that focused instantly. He knew he had to take on this portion of the quest alone. The girl warrior wouldn't like it, but he couldn't risk her life again. Couldn't risk Uh-oh's life, either.

Deidre pointed to the menacing creatures. "Ugly suckers, aren't they? Good thing they're just stone."

Noah nodded numbly. In a moment he'd tell her his decision, then fend off an avalanche of protests.

She peered into a dark opening between the statues. "There's a set of steps. Pretty narrow. I'll go first." She pulled her sonic sword from its scabbard.

"No you won't."

"We'll spread out when we get to the—" She turned. "What?"

"I've got to go down alone."

She shook her head. "Bad idea, Bun-boy. Vetoed."

"Vetoed," Uh-oh echoed.

He brushed aside Deidre's anger. "Remember when I told you about dancing with the old woman at the beach, and how she sent a bunch of stuff into my head, pictures and words and...and...I don't know like feelings?"

"Yeah. So?"

"So I remember now that I saw this place. I saw you and Uh-oh and the statues and all of it."

Deidre blew air between her lips. "So?"

"So I saw myself walking down those steps." Noah pointed at the opening in the floor. "Alone."

Deidre smacked the butt of her sword against her breastplate. "Well I don't care about that craziness. I'm going with you."

Frustration buzzed in his head. Eve had warned him how obstinate Deidre could be. No way she'd give in. Unless she had to. "Sonic swords to settle this."

"What?" An amused smile formed on her lips. "You're loopy, Bunster. You can't carry my lunch." She leveled her weapon at him.

"Probably not." Noah pulled his own fork from the scabbard, banged the butt against the metal plate on his decibelt and started it humming. Deidre charged hers once more and they stood, ten feet apart, weapons and nerves vibrating. Uh-oh, muttering his usual refrain, took refuge behind a statue.

"Before we start, we need to lay down the rules." Noah lowered his fork and took a step toward her.

"Rules?" Deidre scowled and dropped her fork to waist level. "There aren't any rules in a fork—"

Kuh-zap.

Noah caught her a glancing blow with the attack wave and sent her sprawling, her weapon clattering across the floor. "Oops. You're right, Deidre. There aren't any rules in a fork fight."

Stunned, Deidre stared up at him through glassy eyes. That was really awful to pull that trick Paul Newman did in that Butch Cassidy movie, Noah thought, but I couldn't let her come. "Keep an eye on her Uh-oh. I'll be back in a flash with the Methuselah Stone."

"I'm going to kick your fanny, Noah," Uh-oh mimicked Deidre's voice.

"I'm sure she will, Uh-oh." Chuckling, Noah headed for the stairs, sonic sword held before him.

His laughter died before he descended more than ten steps. The air hung about him like a steaming towel and sweat dribbled down his face. Every so often, he arrived at a short landing which sent the stairs in another direction as they twisted ever downward. Crude drawings were inked onto the walls and he strained to see them in the dim dust-flecked light.

In one, the boy represented by the statue in the chamber above stood with a group of other beings, flailing with his stick at some kind of immense upright circular structure. On the other side, the character Deidre had identified as Spid stood behind the five-armed creature; the artist had created a sense of a flurry of motion at the ends of each of his appendages. An assortment of ugly beasts stood behind Spid, watching the drumming.

Noah gulped. Was he that boy? Would he have to compete against a creature with a three-arm advantage?

Another portion of the wall depicted a girl holding an object from which rays emanated. She seemed to be calling out to a figure racing up a narrow path to a smaller, circular object. Very strange. The crude drawings didn't really look like him and Abby, but deep in his brain a little voice, sounding much like Deidre (or possible Uh-oh imitating her) mocked him. "Of course it's you. Why else are you here?" Weak kneed, Noah hurried down the next flight.

At a final landing, he found himself in a stuffy, cobwebbed chamber about the size of the inside of his house, except with much higher ceilings. As he paused to catch his breath, the mountain's rhythm vibrated through him, muffled, bassy. "Thoomp-thoomp, thooomp-thoomp, thoomp-thoomp." Noah felt his heart flutter, find the cadence, and match it.

Three carved stone arms protruded from the floor at the center of the chamber. Each extended arm had a hand holding a stone as if offering it to Noah. Edging closer, he heard the mountain, or his own heart in his ears. "Thoomp-thoomp, thoomp-thoomp, thoomp-thoomp." His eyes shifted sideways, taking in stone creatures squatting on thick pedestals on both sides of the array of arms and hands. He'd seen creatures like them in a book on mythology.

"Gargoyles."

The sound of his own whisper made him start. These carved stone monstrosities loomed larger and more detailed than the ones perched on the shoulders of the troll statue in the upper temple. Hewn from smooth, green-gray rock, they scowled at him, wings half-folded and talons fully displayed. A gruesome picture appeared in his mind. Razor sharp claws ripping at his skin.

"Stupid, Noah. They're just stone. Lighten up." Deidre's voice in his head again. Thinking of her made him feel better, not quite alone. He pictured her fuming, waiting to launch into him when he returned. Smiling, he advanced to examine the carved hands and their stones.

The first hand held a dazzling, clear, multi-faceted rock about the size of a tangerine. Diamond? It would be worth millions. Maybe billions. Out there.

"Put it in your pocket," a gravelly and greedy voice urged from the back of his mind. "If it's not the Methuselah Stone, you can sell it. You'll be rich."

He stretched out his hand and heard Deidre telling him: "We have all we need." He'd smiled at the unworldly innocence of her outlook, but now, staring at the diamond, he admitted that wealth couldn't bring back his mother and heal his family. Besides, wealth wouldn't mean squat if Spid triumphed.

Moving to the next hand, he examined what lay in its palm. This stone resembled an inverted flask, wide at the top, narrow at the bottom. At the bottom, the pure green neck of the flask melded into another stone, a brilliant red, with dancing light playing across its surface. Noah couldn't relate it to anything he'd seen or even imagined.

The final stone, propped on the palm of the third hand, resembled a sickly cantaloupe-colored rock replica of a human brain. It didn't glow. It didn't sparkle. It just sat there.

Which one is the Methuselah Stone?

He examined all three again. Maybe the diamond. Diamonds were very old. They'd once been coal. And before that, what? The plants dinosaurs ate?

What about the green and red one? Maybe its shape signified something.

And then there was the brain stone.

His head throbbed. Abby, he thought, where are your little gray cells when I need them?

Maybe he should take all three.

But no, the prophecy said the Methuselah Stone. One stone.

He tried to remember where he'd heard the word Methuselah before. The Bible. That was it. Methuselah lived like nine-hundred something years.

He knew then. Age. Wisdom. Brains. That had to be it. Didn't it?

Stuffing his sonic sword in its scabbard, he snatched the brain stone from the upturned hand, tucked it under his arm like a football, and took the stairs two at a time.

"Noah." Deidre's angry voice echoed down the twisting passageway.

He grinned. When she saw he had the stone, she'd cool off. His aching bare feet slapped on the warm stone steps, but he didn't mind the pain. He had the stone. The mountain and his own heart beat in his ears.

And then he heard other sounds—scuffling and snuffling and growling.

Just as he hit the next landing he felt hot breath on the back of his neck, smelled a putrid odor, worse than rotting garbage, more pungent than dead fish, as foul as burning tires. Behind him, something scrabbled and scratched at the stone steps.

Run! Don't look back.

He forced his tortured feet to move faster, felt his heart pump harder.

Near the top of the next long flight of steps, something sharp raked at the back of his leg, ripping his tattered jeans, snagging on the hem.

He tore the cloth loose without slowing his pace, but he couldn't stop himself from risking a glance over his shoulder. What he saw petrified him.

Two living, grunting and snorting gargoyles crouched below him, ready to spring.

CHAPTER 26

"Have they ripped the flesh off of his body yet, Boss?" Yurk entered the smoky chamber, rubbing his hammy hands together in glee.

"Momentarily, my impatient friend." Spid pointed to the Shadow Stone and the miniature version of Noah's desperate situation projected onto the tabletop. "When he turns to run again they'll have him."

Chortling low in his throat, he pulled out the chair beside his own. "Come in, Yurk. Make yourself comfortable. In a moment they will pick young master Keene's bones clean and proceed to his misguided friends to further quench their thirst for blood."

"It's a good day, huh, Boss?" Yurk sidled toward the table.

"Indeed, Yurk, indeed."

"I brought him, Boss." The ogre extended a hand to someone behind him. "The gronnk. Your drummer. From the depths of Colongurg."

"Thrndur?" Spid leaped to his feet and peered beyond Yurk, to the figure whose face was obscured by shadows thrown from the sputtering oil lanterns. "Step forward, so we can see you. Your peerless leader has spoken."

Obediently, the creature trundled into the room. "My lord," he intoned, his voice a gruff but sly whine. The gronnk bowed from the waist and flourished four of his five arms. The fifth, the one growing from his forehead, slapped the stone floor.

When he straightened again, Spid saw that he stood almost a head and a half above average for a gronnk, nearly six feet tall. He remembered that some said Thrndur's mother had been pure gronnk, but his father had run with the Abysswolves. No one ever said that to Thrndur's face, but Spid noted the lupine features in the long nose and prominent front teeth. The fifth arm, Spid decided, must be a mutation. But what a great asset for the challenge ahead.

"At your service," the gronnk rasped.

"Ah, yes, Thrndur." Spid tipped his upper body a few centimeters in an imperial bow. "You have been chosen, to stand at The Skin when the sun touches the northern sky. You will drum the rhythms that will open the way for my hordes. You are the key to upholding the honor of Beneath and extending our lofty goals to the slacker creatures of Above, to harnessing the power of the Darksuckers for the greater good of..."

Spid hesitated, wondering if he should blush. He decided not to. "Well to be quite honest, for the greater good of me, Spid. But I will be most generous in sharing the wealth. When and if that becomes convenient, of course, and after the auditors have been through my books, naturally. I welcome you and thank you for volunteering your services."

Thrndur grunted, scratched his head with two of his hands and looked down at Yurk. The ogre shrugged and said in a stage whisper that Spid couldn't avoid hearing. "You've been well paid. Just play along."

Thrndur nodded, satisfied. "For my lord Spid, the Grand Exalted Garboon of Beneath, I take up my weapons willingly, to give my all for the cause." He reached into a long, narrow skin bag hanging from his waist and extracted ten drumsticks. They were white, polished, and unmistakably the bones of some unfortunate creature. Taking two in each of his five hands, he began to twirl and juggle them, slowly at first and then at lightning speed, passing them from hand to hand to hand, spinning them behind his back and through his legs, tossing them high into the air.

After a few moments, he set five of the sticks aside and began beating out rhythms on the walls, tabletop, and other surfaces, creating different tones and different levels of rhythm with each hand. The stone vibrated with sound and Spid felt a renewed sense of confidence, of purpose, of destiny.

As he watched Thrndur, he caught flashes of movement from the projected images thrown by the Shadow Stone. But he no longer cared whether the guardians of the Temple of Cheltnor devoured Noah Keene. Even if he somehow survived to team with that armless, ineffectual, dark-skinned buffoon from Above in defending The Skin, the boy was doomed. He, Spid, would deploy the ultimate drumming machine. The Skin would open before you could say Vlorspak Morkphoy. All those who dared oppose would pay the ultimate price. The world would soon realize the talents, the towering intellect, and, of course, the modesty of Spid the magnificent.

As if sensing his mood, Thrndur stopped the manic, multi-handed drumming and set down all but two of the drumsticks. Bowing his head in a posture of solemnity, he began a slow, funereal roll on the surface of a chest.

"Thuhdutdutdutdutdutdutdutdut." Individual drum hits soon became a continuous mournful drone. Spid smiled as he recognized what they symbolized. The walk of the condemned to face the blade of the executioner.

CHAPTER 27

"Noooooah!" Deidre's voice floated down the stairway toward Noah.

He wanted to call out, but he couldn't speak, couldn't move, couldn't think.

On the step below a gargoyle crouched, poised to strike, its lizard-like eyes glaring, its mouth twisted into a cruel leer. Beyond it, a second gargoyle hunkered. Poisonous orange drool dripped from the corner of its mouth.

Noah's heart slammed against his chest triple-time. The rest of his body seemed frozen solid. He couldn't feel his feet or the stone beneath them.

The gargoyles held as still as he did. Their eyes seemed to burn into his.

He drew in a fluttering breath, felt himself shudder.

The gargoyles didn't move. Their eyes didn't flicker.

He drew in another breath, all the way to the bottom of his lungs.

The air, or maybe simply the motion of breathing it, seemed to trigger his survival instinct. He kicked out with his right foot, catching the first gargoyle square in the forehead.

It teetered and tipped back into its companion, knocking it off balance.

Noah didn't wait to see how far they rolled. Clutching the Methuselah Stone under his arm, he ran, screaming. "Deeeeeeidre!"

When the echoes died, he heard a heavy thump, thump, thump.

Don't look. Get to the next landing. Draw your sword.

But even as he made his plan, a voice within told him they were too big and too powerful for him to fight alone.

So he ran on, ragged sobs of breaths exploding from his lips, blood-curdling, shrieking hisses of pure rage and hatred surging around him. Feet clawed at the steps behind him and the powerful stench filled his nose and made his eyes water as he leaped to the last landing. Why did all the monsters down here have to smell so bad?

"Faster," Deidre screamed, "they're right behind you."

Her sonic sword clanged against her decibelt. "C'mon, c'mon."

His right knee slammed into the edge of the fourth step from the top.

Pain shot up his leg and he nearly lost his grip on the Methuselah Stone. A gurgling growl filled his ears and a sharp talon ripped his shirt from neck to waist. Then he felt a bolt from Deidre's battle fork pass an inch above his head.

"Hggnnn." The beast behind him growled and claws raked against rock.

Noah stretched out his arm and felt the heat and strength of Deidre's hand closing around his. With a single yank she pulled him up into the temple.

"Draw your sword, Noah. We'll make a stand here." Deidre waved the two-pronged weapon, creating a warped ringing sound in the close air.

Noah secured the Methuselah Stone under his shirt, anchoring it between his belt and breastplate, then drew his weapon and banged the butt against his decibelt to give it a fresh charge. Bracing his feet, he waited for the two hellish creatures to emerge from the hole. The mountain's heartbeat matched perfectly the hammer thumping against his chest. "Thoodah-thump, thoodah-thump, thoodah-thump."

He glanced at Deidre. "Where's Uh-oh?"

"Dunno. He was here a second ago."

Noah turned his head away from the opening in the floor, scanning the temple for their companion. Claws scrabbled against the stone steps. He barely heard Deidre's scream over the snarling, screeching, and hissing of the approaching gargoyles.

"Fooof! Fooof!" Expulsions of rancid gargoyle breath seemed to suck the oxygen from the temple.

Jerking himself around, Noah spotted the fearsome creatures catapulting through the air, claws extended from scaly green arms. "Rrrrggghhh!"

"Take the one on the left!" Deidre's voice cracked with the command as she turned her fork to the right.

Noah raised his weapon. But before he could fire, the two gargoyles fell with loud and solid thuds.

One beast sprawled on its belly, a fearsome snarl frozen on its face. The other teetered for a second on its hind legs, then crashed to the floor.

Deidre let out a long breath. "What the...?" She prodded one with her sonic sword. It didn't move.

"Got me," Noah whispered. "They're statues again. Stone. Like when I first saw them in the bottom chamber. And when I was on the stairs."

"Why? How?" Deidre tapped her knuckles against one and then the other.

Noah shook his head. "No clue."

241

From the corner of his eye, he spotted Uh-oh edging out of the shadows. I don't blame you for hiding, little pal, he thought. I'd like to hide, too, like to put my head under my pillow and wake up to discover this is a horrendous nightmare, that these stone statues couldn't come back to life at any moment and tear me into bloody hunks.

Statues.

The word reverberated in his memory. The game. The one they played in elementary school. Statues. All of the kids but one would line up at the end of the schoolyard. The "it" person would stand at the other end, back to them. The other kids would start creeping toward her. Some would even run, trying to get there before she opened her eyes and yelled "freeze." That's when everyone had to pretend to be a statue. Anyone caught moving was out.

Was it possible they were playing a deadly version of that same game?

"Deidre. Uh-oh." The authority in his voice amazed him. "Listen."

"What?"

Uh-oh gave a nervous "chhht-chhht-chhht," then mimicked Deidre. "What?"

"I want to try something. Both of you turn away for a moment. Don't look at the gargoyles."

"Are you nuts!" The voices of the girl-warrior and the gray creature came as one.

"Maybe, but do it anyway." He raised his sword. "I'll guard us."

From the corner of his eye he saw Deidre wrinkle her nose and roll her eyes, but she backed away from the gargoyles and nodded to Uh-oh. They swiveled and looked the other way.

Noah clanked his battle fork against his decibelt again. He'd need all the power it had if he was wrong.

But he wasn't.

The horrifying beasts remained statues.

"Okay, turn back around." Noah grinned and gave Deidre a thumbs-up sign. "They didn't move. I'm it."

"What are you talking about?"

"Statues. They're statues, like in the game. They only come back to life if I don't look at them."

Deidre shook her head. "That's absurd. It can't be that simple."

"I think it is, but let's try another experiment. Get your battle fork ready."

She shrugged and recharged her weapon.

"Let's move back a little for this." Keeping his eyes trained on the gargoyles, Noah backed toward the outer door. Deidre and Uh-oh followed his lead, stopping about thirty yards from the stone creatures.

"Okay, be ready, here goes." He squeezed his eyes shut. Instantly, he heard a screeching, hissing growl from the statues. Clawed feet scrabbled at stone. He heard Deidre gasp but forced himself to keep his eyes closed.

"Uh-oh. Uh-oh, Uh-oh." The gray creature mimicked Noah's panicked inner voice.

"I believe you," Deidre cried. "They're getting close. Open your eyes."

Noah heard the beasts talking to one another in a guttural gargle-growl-chant. Claws scrabbled harder, faster. Rancid breath made his head ache.

"Noah! Open your eyes! Noah! Now!"

He stretched his lids open wide. One gargoyle froze just a few feet away, its hind legs flexed, front legs clawing the air. The other, farther back, was bent over, apparently scratching an itch in an embarrassing place.

Uh-oh laughed and pointed at the beast.

243

"It works." Deidre breathed a sigh of relief. "Well, let's just back on out of here." Battle fork at the ready, she retreated.

"Backing now." Noah followed. "I wonder if it works because I have the Methuselah?" He patted his midsection and felt the reassuring hardness of the brain-shaped stone. Once they got away, he'd stow it in the center of his pack. It would definitely be the pits to go through all this then lose the stone or drop it and crack it. "Guide me on the steps so I can keep my eyes on them."

"What about when we go out the door and you can't see them anymore? Or what if they split up and you can't watch them both at once?"

"Hmmm." He hadn't thought about that. But then, fifteen minutes ago, he hadn't thought statues could come to life. "I guess if we get out of sight we'll turn and run like hell until they're right behind us, and then I'll freeze them again. And if they split up, I'll turn my head back and forth real fast."

"Good," Deidre said sarcastically. "For a minute there I thought you didn't have a plan." Facing away, she linked their left arms. "Uh-oh, take his other side. We'll go faster."

With his friends leading him, Noah backed across the huge room, keeping his eyes trained on the stone gargoyles. Finally they passed through the archway. "Run," he ordered.

He turned, leaped down the stairs and sprinted behind his companions toward the canyon wall. Within seconds he heard pounding, growling, and hissing close behind. He ran a few more yards, snapped his head around and halted the creatures in mid leap. Again they clattered to the ground.

Noah stared at them, feeling a new emotion—pride. He, Noah Keene had the ability to turn these creatures to stone or back into living creatures. He felt bigger, stronger, smarter.

As he backed away from the statues again, a wicked idea popped into Noah's head. He would test his new power, use it to get something he wanted.

"Deidre?"

"Um-huh?"

"Did I mention how tired I'm getting of being called Bun-boy?"

"It's just a nickname, Noah. Get over yourself."

"I'm not going to have to get over it, Deidre. Because if you don't stop using it, I'll do this." He squeezed his eyes shut and instantly heard the stirrings of the gargoyles.

"Noah!" Her voice was shrill. "Open your eyes."

"Not yet." Heavy feet thudded toward them.

"All right. All right. No more Bun-boy."

"Promise?" He opened his eyes and froze the gargoyles fifty feet away.

"Yes." Deidre punched his arm. "But grow up. This isn't a game."

"Hmmm, I don't think I heard the 'I promise' part of that promise." He squeezed his eyes shut again. A hissing screech rose from the gargoyles. Noah could almost hear Deidre grinding her teeth. This was great.

"Oh, all right, I promise," she snapped. "No more Bun-boy."

"Thank you Deidre." He opened his eyes and halted the gargoyles at twenty feet.

"You're welcome," she said. Then, under her breath, "creep."

"Creep I can live with," he grinned. "C'mon, let's get out of here."

As he backed to the edge of the rockslide, Noah felt a twinge of regret for what he'd just done. What if he'd taken it too far? What if the gargoyles moved faster than

245

before and hurt Deidre or Uh-oh? He could never forgive himself. Or, worse yet, what if there were only a certain number of times he could freeze them and he exceeded that limit?

He felt a chill and realized he'd learned something about power. It shouldn't be used to manipulate people or abused for amusement.

When they arrived at the beginning of the long, steep slope, Noah cut his eyes toward rocky slide. This could get real ugly, real fast. They almost fell to their death on the way down and now he had to climb backwards.

As if she read his mind, Deidre sheathed her battle fork. "Here's what we'll have to do." The snap of authority was back in her voice. "We'll move over there." She pointed at a spot ten yards to their left. "Looks like the footing's better."

He felt fear overtaking him, much as the gargoyles had. "But how's this gonna work, Deidre? I've got to go up backward so—"

"Right." She ignored him, directing her comments to Uh-oh. "Since his lordship has to keep staring at those ugly muthahs, we're going to have to drag his cute little buns up the hill."

She directed a smirk at Noah. "Notice I didn't violate our agreement."

Noah made a face, taking care not to pull his eyes completely off the frozen gargoyles.

Deidre unfastened the looped rope from her belt and ran it under the straps of Noah's decibelt where they crossed in the middle of his back. She secured one end around her waist and the other around Uh-oh's. "Okay, Uh-oh, you'll climb a little ahead because you're shorter. We'll stay about fifteen feet apart. Noah, you'll be the point of the triangle. Keep your eyes trained on those things and help us climb with your heels and hands when you can. It'll be slow going, but we'll make it."

She was right. It took nearly two hours for them to inch their way up the slope. The route she picked proved easier than the one they'd taken down, but much of the time she and Uh-oh had to literally pull Noah up as he struggled to keep his eyes locked on the gargoyles.

At the top, they hurried to where they left their packs and collapsed. Noah's thigh, shin, and calf muscles burned as if someone had set fire to them and the breastplate had bruised his chest when he'd hung suspended between his friends. He guzzled water from his canteen and poured some on his bleeding feet.

"Noah?" Deidre set her canteen down and stared at the rim of the canyon, her eyes wide with fright. "Noah. You stopped looking at them! Those suckers had wings!"

Fatigue forgotten, both of them leapt to their feet and snatched their sonic swords from their scabbards. In unison, they banged the weapons against their decibelts and scrambled to the edge of the canyon.

Far below, Noah saw two distant dots scuttling back across the dusty plain toward the open maw of the Temple of Cheltnor. He felt relief flood his veins. Either the creatures couldn't follow, or else they wouldn't. Beside him he heard Deidre sigh and deactivate her battle fork and he did the same.

Deidre returned her sword to its scabbard, then dug nuts and fruit from her pack and passed them to Uh-oh and Noah. "Can we see the Methuselah Stone?"

Noah untucked his frayed shirt, pulled the stone from beneath it, and passed it to Deidre. She turned it over and over in her hands, examining it from all angles. Uh-oh, moved near to get a look and scratched his head. "Kinda underwhelming," Deidre commented.

"Really, really, underwhelming." Deidre's voice again, this time originating from Uh-oh.

"Are you sure it's the right one Bun—" she caught herself and handed the stone back. "I mean, Noah."

"Well, I was in kind of a hurry, and it was pretty dark, and there weren't any nameplates or anything under the three I had to pick from but," he put the stone back into his pack, "yeah, I'm pretty sure, this is it. Seemed to get those 'goyles pretty fired up when I snatched it."

"True. But they might have come to life whichever one you took."

Self-doubt eroded Noah's temporary feeling of confidence. "Yeah, could be. But this is the Methuselah. I'm sure." He hoped she didn't realize he wasn't. "Now we've just got to figure out where to take it."

"The Skin." Deidre told him. "And soon."

"You know the way?"

"Maybe." She looked flustered. "Kinda." Her face scrunched into a grimace. "No, not really."

"Great!" Noah threw a nut at a rock. "Just great. I'm getting tired of wandering around down here. Don't you have a map or something?"

She shook her head. "No. There's only up and down and across. You have to remember where you've been and what people say about where you're going. But, I think I can get us to the chamber of the Grand Imperial Pettifog."

"The who?"

"Pettifog. He's like a...a...kind of wizard or something. I've never met him. But people talk about him. He's part of the prophecy."

"What part?"

"He's supposed to help you drum to repel Spid."

"Well then," Noah climbed to his feet. Uh-oh sighed and pushed himself upright. "The Pettifog it is." Perhaps, if he really was a wizard, he could find Abby. "Which way?"

Deidre pointed with her finger. "Up."

"Up? Can you be a little more specific? How far up? Which way up?"

The dark copper of her skin glowed with a reddish tint. "I just told you. All I know is up. But I bet you don't have a better idea."

He didn't. That was a fact.

"So, we'll go up." Deidre got to her feet and brushed herself off, avoiding his eyes. "That way." She pointed around the crevasse to the right and to a cliff thrusting from the plain. "Try to keep up, okay?"

Noah grunted and stretched. He felt aches and pains in places he didn't even know existed. And his clothes were in tatters. But it seemed pointless to put on something fresh until they reached the chamber of the Pettifog.

"And another thing." Deidre's defiance took on an angry edge as she shouldered her pack. "I owe you for that trick in the temple. As soon as we handle this little Spid problem, I've got serious plans to knock you on your keester. Repeatedly."

"Yeah?" Noah replied belligerently. "You and whose army?"

"I won't need an army. Write it on your calendar, Drummer Dude."

"I will!" Noah found himself suddenly grinning. Why worry about whether she could beat him up? Spid's army would probably cut them to shreds when they broke through The Skin, anyway.

"What's the silly grin about?"

"Tell you later," Noah chuckled. "Let's go. Up." He laughed, throwing his head back. As he did, he saw movement on a shelf of rock across the crevasse. He blinked hard, trying to focus. Either he was imagining things, or there was that raggedy hermit. As he watched, the figure turned and, leaning on a walking stick, started along a path that angled upward from the ledge.

Noah tapped Deidre on the shoulder and pointed.

She craned her neck. "What?"

"Didn't you see him?"

"See who?"

"The hermit. He was up on a trail. There."

Deidre scanned the upper reaches of the cavern. "You're hallucinating, Noah. I don't see a trail."

But Noah felt the same sure sensation he experienced dancing across the river of fire. Running from the hermit had been a big mistake. He wouldn't make it again. "It's there. It's where we need to be."

Without waiting to see what she'd do, he strode off.

CHAPTER 28

In Abby's dream, she saw herself at five years old, drowsy and cocooned in a fluffy blanket. Mom sat beside her on the bed, reading her a story from a huge book filled with colorful pictures and paragraphs that began with immense first words. She felt warm and secure, lulled by her mother's voice, her clean, apple-soap smell, her light touch as she stroked Abby's hair. "Which story would you like to hear next?"

"One about Noah. A happy story." Her voice had a lost-tooth lisp.

Mom beamed and pulled another book from a shelf beside the bed.

"This is the story of Noah and the troll," Mom read, shifting to a trilling, high-pitched, "story lady" voice very unlike her own.

"No, Mom, I don't want that story," the five-year-old Abby protested. "I want a different story. I don't like the way that one ends."

"Now, Abby, you know this story has a happy ending. For me, that is."

The soft, loving smile of Abby's mother dissolved to reveal an evil leer on the broad-nosed, blotchy-skinned, wart-encrusted face of Spid. Little-girl Abby clapped her

251

hands over her eyes, but the vision of Spid didn't go away. He opened a thick, blood-red, leather-bound book and extended a long, pointed fingernail at a figure on the stiff parchment. "Look here." Spid's voice oozed oily smarminess. "Look what's happening to your big brother now."

Curiosity won out over fear and revulsion. Peeping between her fingers, the little girl saw colorful inked drawings spring to life on the page: gigantic ferocious flying dinosaur things; ugly, squat four-armed monsters; ax-wielding ogres; and Spid himself, chasing a cartoon of Noah across the parchment.

"Run, Noah, run," she screamed.

The story-telling Spid laughed low in his throat with fiendish pleasure and turned page after page. Each featured different nightmare creatures chasing Noah toward the margins of the paper. From time to time, the drawing of Noah would stop and drum on a flat surface and the inked creatures would pause and watch, then chase him again.

"Help him, Mom. Help Noah," the dream girl cried.

"Your mother cannot help you, Miss Keene. She's gone. Noah is living out his destiny." Spid's voice dripped with malice. "And mine."

"Can I change things?" five-year-old Abby asked the troll.

Spid reached a claw-fingered hand toward the dream-Abby's face. She cringed and shrank back, squeezing her eyes shut so hard she saw white light.

Soft fingertips stroked her cheek. "Of course, dear." Abby felt Mom's hand cup her chin and heard the reassuring smile in her voice. "You know the way, don't you?"

"I...I...think so. But I'm so sleepy." The girl in the dream pulled the covers around her.

"Don't worry, baby," Mom began to sing an old Beach Boys song she used as a lullaby when Abby and Noah were small.

Fighting sleep, the five-year-old's eyelids drooped. She couldn't see Mom now, but she heard her smiling voice. She yawned again and Mom's singing faded and melded into a musical hum that grew louder and louder. It filled Abby's ears, filled her head, filled the entire room.

Abby snapped from the dream world and sat up. The humming saturated her body now, making her ribs and teeth vibrate. A rainbow splash of color panned across her face and then continued around the room. Her eyes followed the color burst to its source—the Chameleon Stone. It spun on its natural shelf, throwing off shafts of multi-colored light and emitting a drone that grew louder and louder.

Abby slapped her hands over her ears but couldn't shut out the maddening noise. Surely Chillout or the other grungoids would hear it soon and come to check. Maybe they'd know why the stone was humming, and how to make it stop. Or maybe the walls muffled the sound. Perhaps she could turn it off herself. Or take it to Delacroix and have him look at it. Were there geeks who fixed magic crystals like the geeks who repaired computers?

Abby eased back the covers and stood. As she did, the orb changed color, from rosy pink to a honey-spun gold. Looking up, she noticed the Zezzue had adjusted themselves to the exact tint as the globe. The humming grew louder, deeper. Her whole body vibrated and the rock beneath her feet shook. She fought her rising panic. What was happening?

As if answering her question, the Chameleon Stone levitated and spun across the room. Wide-eyed, Abby watched it orbit around her, then hover above the chair where she laid her neatly folded clothes before going to bed.

"You want me to dress?" She felt foolish talking to a rock but, to her surprise, it bobbed up and down and zipped into another orbit around her head.

"I'm thinking that means yes."

Abby put aside her self-consciousness and yanked off her nightgown, slipped on her jeans and shirt, then sat to pull on her socks and tennis shoes. The moment she finished, the rotating Chameleon Stone orbited her a final time, then spun through the doorway.

Abby tied hasty double knots in her shoelaces, grabbed her jacket, and ran into the main chamber. The stone, now sapphire-colored, hovered near Delacroix's practice drum. The Zezzue emitted only minimal light, and she heard nothing except the humming of the floating stone. The cavernous room was deserted. Abby opened her mouth to call Chillout's name when another sound penetrated the hum.

"Thuddah-thoom, thuddah-thoom, thuddah-thoom." The heartbeat of the mountain filled the cavern, drowning out the Chameleon Stone's buzz. As she neared the crystal, it bobbed once, then darted toward the entrance to a tunnel.

"Thuddah-thoom, Thuddah-thoom, Thuddah-thoom." The heartbeat throbbed, a constant presence accompanying Abby as she stumbled up the dark pathway behind the now translucent turquoise orb. Once again, as she reached out to touch it, the stone darted away, disappearing into the tunnel.

Abby filled her lungs, forced herself to exhale slowly, then followed. In front of her, the Zezzue lit the tunnel with a soft orange glow. "Thank you," she told the tiny lights. They flickered and increased the intensity of their illumination.

She followed the narrow tunnel for about a hundred feet before it ended in a small, bathroom-sized chamber resembling the one that transported her, Delacroix, and Chillout to The Last Place You Look. Another Vorv. Faith elevator, Abby had taken to calling it.

The Chameleon Stone drifted to the center of the chamber, spinning in place as if waiting for her to enter.

"Where are you taking me?" The fluttering sound of her own voice echoed back to her. Once again, she felt utterly ridiculous, talking to a chunk of rock. The Chameleon Stone didn't answer. Not that she had expected it to.

Abby felt her nerves jangle and her stomach quiver at the memory of her experience riding the sucking air at warp speed plus. Maybe she shouldn't follow the Chameleon Stone. Maybe Spid had control of it.

She backpedaled and stood trembling in the doorway. Above her, the Zezzue glowed brighter, pale blue now, like the sky she hadn't seen since the day she and Noah ran away. She felt tears burn the rims of her eyes and rubbed them away. What should she do?

"Thrum-thrum, thrum-thrum, thrum-thrum," the mountain answered—the beat growing in intensity. A low murmur of a voice synched itself with the rhythm. "You know the way, Abby."

"Thrum-thrum, thrum-thrum, thrum-thrum."

"Youknow,youknow,youknowtheway,theway,theway."

She took three tentative steps, positioned herself beneath the Chameleon Stone and looked up into the spinning orb. Colors swam in a milky ocean, darting across its diameter, swirling along its edges. She felt her mind emptying, her muscles relaxing, her senses blunting, and her essence borne along by some cosmic tide into a trance-like state. With one tiny functioning corner of her mind, she searched for the words Delacroix had called out to make the rock melt beneath their feet. Alameezos gravititos? Or maybe Gravameezos Alvitos? Or even Alvagravos Meezotos?

Abby forced herself to blank her entire mind, open her mouth and let the words tumble across her tongue. "Alameezos gravitos," she intoned. "Alameezos gravitos." Louder now. "Alameezos gravitos. Alameezos gravitos." Over and over she repeated it, until the words stuck together and melted into one another.

She clenched her eyes shut and didn't watch the rocks dissolve from the edges in. The chamber shuddered and she heard the mountain beating in synch with her chant. Don't think, she told herself just chant.

"Alameezos gravitos. Alameezos gravitos." The words came in a rush. "Alameezos gravitos."

"Voorrrrrvvvvv!"

Air blasted over her and she plummeted down the shaft that opened at her feet. The air pushed under her eyelids, forcing them open, and she scrunched her face to clamp them closed. She fell and fell and fell, hoping every second to hear the growing roar that would drown both her hammering heartbeat and the percussion of Humbug Mountain, the signal that she had almost touched bottom.

After what felt like hours a low-pitched rumble became a thunderous warping warble. She glided to a stop and her stomach twitched. She blinked away blurriness and saw the walls swirl for a few seconds. Then the nausea passed and she looked around.

A tunnel stretched ahead, an oval of light promising only a short walk to a larger chamber. Abby wobbled a few steps, then halted. The Chameleon Stone. Where was it? She craned her neck, but knew before she looked that it wasn't hovering overhead. No hum tickled her ears, no splashings of color lit the walls. Her heart sank. She'd lost the orb.

She felt sick with dread. Delacroix had told her the Chameleon Stone would play a critical role when they met Spid at The Skin. Maybe the troll had lured her into the elevator so he could steal it.

No. Not possible. Spid couldn't physically inhabit the world of Above. Not yet, anyway. And she hadn't spotted anyone else around. Except the Zezzue, and they wouldn't cooperate with the troll. Not if they had a choice.

So where had the Chameleon Stone gone? Had it arrived before her and spun on its own along the tunnel ahead of her?

It only took her a few moments to emerge from the passageway into a high-ceilinged cavern. The sloping floor went on for half a mile or more and was littered with rocks and boulders and crisscrossed by crevices. No sign of the Chameleon Stone.

Abby plopped down on a rock, scanning the broken landscape. Was she meant to cross this cavern? And if so, for what purpose? She looked to the Zezzue for advice, but the lights were far away, spread out along the distant ceiling. She couldn't tell if they flickered an answer.

A warm breeze lifted her bangs. She licked her forefinger and held it up. Wind. Definitely. Except for in the Vorv, this was the first time she'd felt this strong and steady an air current inside the mountain. Was this chamber so huge that varying pressures created a draft that rose along the slope of the plain? Or did the wind originate outside and funnel its way in through a passageway? Was something or somebody trying to show her a way out of Humbug Mountain—a way home? Who stood to gain if she left?

She knew the answer that. Spid.

Standing, squinting across the plain, she searched for a shaft of light, then shook her head. No. She wouldn't go.

She started to turn toward the tunnel, but something caught her eye. At the bottom of the cavern, a dark dot of movement danced into her vision.

The Chameleon Stone?

No, she could never have spotted it at this distance. And it wouldn't appear dark, would it?

Clambering to the top of a boulder, she rubbed her eyes and concentrated on the dot. It zigged and zagged, then disappeared behind a ridge of rock. When it emerged she saw three distinct dots, not one. As she narrowed her eyes and peered down at them, the dots grew heads and arms and legs. Two of them were people. Humans. The third looked shorter, grayish. Like Chillout and the other grungoids.

Who were they? Friends coming to confer with Delacroix? Or enemies? Should she greet them? Or hide?

She settled for climbing down off the rock and crouching beside it. Had they seen her? How fast could she scramble back to the air elevator if they weren't friendly? And how fast could she activate the Vorv?

Abby's rational brain flashed *danger-danger-danger,* and urged her to run now and find out more later, but something kept her hunkering beside the rock, eyes glued to the steadily-growing figures picking their way across the plain.

A tall, muscular, cappuccino-colored girl clad in some kind of armor led the way. Abby thought she resembled the young woman she'd seen in the Chameleon Stone after the Spiddle game. A boy limped just behind her, his clothes in tatters, his tangled hair across his forehead, his head bent with the weight of his pack. The grungoid scrambled to keep up, dreadlocks bobbing.

Abby studied the boy again. Could it be Noah?

No. This boy, despite his limp and obvious exhaustion, appeared taller, surer and stronger than her brother. This boy, who matched the Amazon-like girl stride for stride even though he wore no shoes, couldn't be the sulking young-for-his-age brother who lived so deep within himself. This boy, even with his head down, radiated power, and determination.

He looked up and their eyes met.

Abby's heart jumped in her chest. "Noooooooooah."

Recognition flashed across her brother's face. He raised his arm to wave, said something to the girl, and broke into a hobbling trot. "Abbbbby."

Running, screaming, and laughing at the same time, Abby collided with him, wrapped her arms around him and squeezed.

"Oof." He recoiled. "Take it easy, Abby. I'm kinda sore."

"Too bad," she squeezed harder, sobbing against the metal plate harnessed to his chest. "I'm sorta-kinda glad you're alive."

"I'm sorta-kinda glad too, Abby. Extremely sorta-kinda glad." Noah chuckled and returned the hug.

That's different, too, she thought. Noah didn't hug like that. Not since Mom died.

She released him and knuckled away tears. "Where have you been? Who's the girl? And the grungoid? Are you hungry?"

She took a step back and noticed his blistered and bleeding feet, the rips in his pants and shirt that revealed bruised skin, his blow-torched eyebrows. "Noah. You're hurt."

"It's nothing, Abby. I'm okay." Noah put a hand to his sooty face and ran his fingers over a couple of healing scrapes.

"Yeah, he just cut himself shaving. With his sword," the brown-skinned girl said with a laugh. She looked like a gladiator, but she was pretty, Abby decided. Not beautiful, but naturally attractive, with strong features and an aura of energy. She, too, looked bruised and beat up.

Noah chuckled and turned to smile at the girl and she grinned back.

"Well, Bunny-buns are you going to introduce me to your sister or what?"

The girl's lips hadn't moved. She and Noah exchanged glances and she laughed, pointing to the grungoid who stood, hands on hips, tight curls brushed back from his forehead. The girl shrugged and tipped her head at Noah. "Hey, I promised *I* wouldn't call you that. Can't help what Uh-oh does."

"You put him up to it."

"Me? Would I do that?" She turned from Noah and stuck her hand out. "Doesn't look like he's going to get to it, so... Hi, Abby, I'm Deidre."

"Deidre." Abby repeated as she took her hand. The grip was firm but warm. "Pleased to meet you. What happened to you guys?"

Deidre opened her mouth, but Noah interrupted. "No time to explain. I've got to get to The Skin."

"I know."

"You do? How?"

"Hello-oh. Brains of the operation here." She tapped her forehead. "Leetle gray cells at work. You're not the only one with a story to tell."

"Yeah?" Noah raised what was left of his eyebrows. "Well, we'll catch up later. Do you know the way to The Skin?"

"No. But I can take you to somebody who does, somebody who's been waiting for you."

A few minutes later they stood in the semi-circular chamber at the end of the short tunnel. "Ready to rock and roll?" Abby grinned at her brother.

Noah touched the walls and the solid ceiling. "Rock and roll to where? We're kinda dead-ended here."

"Wrong. It's the Vorv." Abby couldn't wait to see Noah's reaction when the air current swept them aloft. "Everybody hold hands."

Deidre clamped her hands together. "Not until I know what the Vorv is." The grungoid made a soft chattering sound and inched toward the door.

"Trust me." Abby patted her brother on the shoulder and felt him flinch. She must have hit another tender spot. "Sorry."

"It's all right." He smiled but clenched his teeth, then touched the walls again and exchanged a glance and a shrug with Deidre.

"It's like an elevator. It's how I got down here. Join hands."

Deidre grabbed onto Uh-oh and Noah. "Can't be as crazy as dancing across the river of fire."

"River of fire?" Abby asked.

"Later. Let's do this," Noah gripped Abby's hand and nodded for Uh-oh to take her other one.

"Close your eyes and take a deep breath. As deep as you can," Abby instructed. "Clear your mind, then breathe in again. And hang on."

"Alameezos gravitos," she chanted, closing her eyes. The words ran end-over-end-over-end, fusing into a pulsing hum. She felt the lightheadedness of the trance-state and in a matter of seconds the ground began to vibrate.

She heard a collective gasp from the others and knew they'd peeked and seen the rock above their heads dissolving. She smiled, concentrating despite Uh-oh's panicked chhht, chhht, chhht, Deidre's small squeal of anticipation, Noah's whooshing exhalation and the distinctive "Vorv" sound that signaled the beginning of the pneumatic ride. She felt the wind peel her from the floor and they were sucked upward, riding air to the chamber near Delacroix's cavern.

When the Vorv's braking mechanism deposited them, Deidre took a single step and fell to her knees, Uh-oh careened into a wall, and Noah gripped Abby's shoulder.

"The twirly tummy will pass. Take a few more deep breaths and I'll lead you to Mr. Delacroix, the Grand Exalted Pettifog."

"Delacroix?" Noah cocked his head.

"Step right this way and meet your hero." Grinning, Abby trotted along the short tunnel that led to the drumming practice area where Delacroix lay on his back thumping rhythms on the stretched surface. At the end of the tunnel she stepped aside and motioned Noah forward. As he passed, she saw his jaw drop and his eyes bug out.

"Y...y...y...you're Delix, Feelacroix...I mean Fecroix Dela-lix, but-but-but I thought you were d...d...d...dead, I mean how could you... Wh...wh...wh...what happened to...uh, I mean..." He leaned against the wall, shaking his head.

Delacroix continued thumping out the steady beat but turned his head, grinned, and winked. "I'll 'splain it all, my man. Now get out your sticks. We got lots of work to do if we gonna ruin old Spid's party."

Chillout piped in. "Crazy, man. It'll be like stereophonic."

He snapped his fingers to Delacroix's rhythm, then spotted Uh-oh, who'd emerged from behind Noah. A rapid exchange transpired in grungoid-speak with a series of rapid clicks, gargles, and chatters. Finally, Chillout took Uh-oh by the arm and led him away from the group. "This cat needs nourishment, dig? Wants to lay on some tale about dancing on fire. Now that's entertainment."

Noah advanced toward the practice skin, fumbling with his pack.

"Hungry?" Abby asked Deidre.

"I could definitely eat something. Like a large animal or a small building. And I wouldn't mind a bath."

"Let's go to my room." Abby put a hand on Deidre's arm and guided her toward the outer chambers. "I'll show you where you can bathe."

Abby noticed Deidre had to duck her head a little to enter the sleeping chamber. The bed had been made and a table set for two was laden with dishes filled with potato chips, some kind of smoked fish and oatmeal cookies. The prophecy? Had Delacroix known she'd return with Noah and his friends?

Another surprise. The Chameleon Stone glowed on its shelf, glimmering a muted shade of ocean blue.

Abby stared at it, feeling awash in guilt. In the excitement of finding Noah, she'd forgotten all about the orb and her fear she had lost it. But somehow it had found its way back. She heard the beat of drumming from the other chamber. Things would work out. They'd find a way to defeat Spid at The Skin. She didn't have a clue how, but as Delacroix often said, it was all a matter of faith.

CHAPTER 29

"I know the way out of Humbug Mountain. At least I think I do." Abby volunteered. "If you want to, we could go home."

Noah frowned, sniffed and bit into the strange fruit Chillout had delivered for breakfast. It tasted a little like pineapple but crunched like an apple. The grungoid had also provided thick slabs of brown bread like the kind he ate at Deidre's mother's house. Everybody down here must make it, he thought. Probably the flour comes from some root or something that grows underground, maybe even from mushrooms.

He contemplated the night in Shroomtown, the talk of the battle ahead. He hated to admit it, but he was scared. And part of him resented being thrust into this fight because of some crazy prophecy. Still, he'd come this far, he knew what was at stake, and he was committed. But Abby? No way should he let her stay here and get hurt. And she would, if Spid broke through The Skin.

He took another bite and recognized the flaw in getting her out of the mountain. If Spid's army of trolls, ogres, and other unspeakable beasts broke through and overran the tunnels and caverns, everyone on earth was doomed.

And of course Abby knew that. She'd witnessed Spid's wrath, or at least the wrath of his image, when she beat him at...what had she called it? Spiddle? And the troll would want revenge against her first if he got through The Skin. If she got out now, she'd have at least a little more time to live.

"Well?" Lost in his thoughts he hadn't noticed Abby put down the notepad filled with strange letters and lean toward him. She gripped his wrist and prevented another hunk of fruit from reaching his mouth. "Do you want to try to leave Humbug Mountain?"

"No. But you go home and be with Dad." He played the guilt card. "Dad loves you, Abby. He needs you."

"He needs you, too."

Noah sighed, but decided not to argue that point. "I have to stay."

"So do I." She released his wrist. "The prophecy says so. And I feel it. There's something I have to do. I just don't know what it is yet." She took a bite of her fruit and said between chews. "But it's something I don't have to practice for. Speaking of which, you better go."

Their eyes met. Noah felt his chest constrict. He wanted to tell her what a great little sister she was and how much he loved and admired her. But the words wouldn't come. Finally, stood and rubbed the top of her head with his knuckles. "See you later."

"Right." She swatted at his hand. "Later."

Walking to the practice area, he marveled at how memories of his house, his room and even the drum set in the garage had fuzzed over in his mind. So much had happened since the hermit rescued him that it was like his head no longer had room for older memories. One thing he did remember was the conflict with his father. But he couldn't waste energy on that now. If he survived, he'd be a different person. Maybe his father would be, too.

He found Lix Delacroix, Grand Exalted Pettifog of Above, on his back, feet spanking a syncopated series of rhythms on the tight surface of the practice skin. Noah stood for a moment listening, watching, marveling at the perfection of the sequences, the seemingly effortless shifts from one time signature to another. Even without hands, Felix Delacroix still rocked. The greatest drummer ever, no question.

At first, Noah was in total awe of his skill, unable to lift his sticks. But Delacroix put him at ease in the language they both understood, the beat. They talked using taps, thumps, clicks, bops, and booms.

Noah's wooden drumsticks had suffered on the journey. The dance across the licking flames of Pfhaaa scorched them and he chewed the tips ups drumming on rocks. But they were what he had and he hoped they would be worthy of the rhythms Delacroix created.

As he took his place beside the practice skin, Delacroix patted out a beat with his left foot, adding accents with his right. "Call and answer. I am thinking Spid's drummer will lead with something like this. What should we respond?"

Starting with one stick, Noah picked up the beat, then slid into a counter rhythm with the other. Call and answer. What you played had to duplicate what was laid down by the other drummer or team. Then, using their original rhythm, you spun it into an improvisation of your own. Then they had to answer you while you listened to the rhythms and hoped your arms remembered. After a while, it seemed the beat bypassed his brain. It came from somewhere else. His heart, maybe? His dreams?

Depending on the fluctuations in the rhythm, and who had the upper hand, The Skin would either soften or grow more rigid. Delacroix knew from the prophecy that if they fell behind, some of Spid's forces could push their way through the soft spot. If Noah and Delacroix failed entirely, The Skin would disintegrate and evil would rampage through the world.

Noah stopped drumming and set the sticks aside. "What is The Skin made of?"

"We do not know." Delacroix didn't miss a beat. "No one has seen it for hundreds of years. Since the last time."

"Oh." Noah's dread grew. What would it feel like to strike it? What would the beat sound like?

"I believe it is more an energy than a solid thing, you know? A portal between worlds. Made of the stuff of the universe."

Noah let his head bob to Delacroix's rhythms, his fingers starting to twitch, to itch to hold the sticks. When he could stand it no more, he picked them up. "We could try this." Doubling the rhythm his left hand played, he worked a three-hit attack in between beats.

"Good." Delacroix shifted effortlessly to put a bottom beat under Noah's lead. "And then to the 12/8 beat I think. That would be a fat groove." Shifting gears he slid into a wildly syncopated bass pattern, his legs and feet moving so fast they seemed like a total blur.

"I got it." Noah moved faster to parallel Delacroix's acceleration. "And then maybe a slide-hop here."

"Ah. Yes!" Delacroix grinned, his teeth a flash of white against his glistening skin.

They practiced until Noah's right hand cramped and he dropped his stick. As if he'd been waiting for that cue, Chillout appeared with a tray of lemonade and a plate piled high with chocolate chip cookies. He also brought a couple of towels to dry the sweat that ran in rivulets from their bodies.

It was a moment, Noah decided, he would remember for the rest of his life. The lemonade tasted sharp and tangy, the cookies sweet and crunchy. The air he gulped in was clean and cool. Despite his exhaustion, he felt content, satisfied with himself, at peace.

If I die tomorrow, I will have played with my hero. And he doesn't treat me like a kid, an amateur. Me and Lix Delacroix. Amazing.

Delacroix flexed the stumps of his arms, easing his back. "You must promise me you will remember something, *mon ami*, remember it when at The Skin we attempt to send Spid back into the depths."

Noah took another sip of lemonade. "What is it, Mr. Delacroix?"

"Please, no. Lix is what you should call me. We are partners."

Partners. And he wants me to call him Lix.

Awed and uneasy, Noah took him at his word. "All right. Lix? What do I need to remember?"

"Although we practice many of the variations that the other drummer may play, he can choose from millions of others. Is that not true?"

"Yes." The thought sobered Noah. "True."

"There is no way, in the time we have, we can practice even a tiny percent, no?"

"Yes. I mean no. We can't." His elation of a moment ago crumbled like dry beach sand. All this practice might be a complete waste. So many things could go wrong. He could drop a stick, lose the beat, play too fast or too slow, work into an improvisation that drove them down a rhythmic dead end.

"So." Delacroix stood and stretched to his full height, tilting his head upward and raising the stubs of his arms toward the sky. "We must, both of us, listen. We must hear completely. We must take the sound of the other drummer into us, and let it saturate every pore in our bodies. And then we must let the energy flow into our hands." He grinned, raised his leg and wiggled his big toe at Noah. "And into our feet."

"Concentration." Noah nodded. He wondered if Abby told Delacroix that his mind tended to wander. He felt a flash of anger. What did she know? His mind never wandered while he drummed. Never.

"No!" Delacroix's adamant denial rang from the walls of the chamber. "Not concentration. Surrender. Total submission. What we must not do, my friend, is let our brains speak louder than our hearts. The drumming, it is not about thinking. The drumming, she is pure feeling. Pure emotion."

Noah hoped he understood what Delacroix meant, hoped the passion he felt duplicated what the armless man experienced. "Yes," was all he managed to say.

Delacroix nodded. "You have already proven your bravery several times over. All anyone can ask is that you do your best."

"I'll try. I will."

"I know. As I too, will try my best. And if we should fail..." He shrugged his shoulders and lowered himself into position in front of the practice skin.

This might be his last full day on earth. Or under the earth. "Are you afraid?" Noah picked up his drumsticks, rolling them between his hands.

"Afraid to die?"

"Um, yeah." Noah bent his head and beat a slow rhythm.

Delacroix sighed and then flutter kicked the drum with his left foot. "Of course. Not of what comes or does not come after we have ended this gig, you know." He rolled his head, as if to get a long last look at the cavern where he lived. "But only that I may not be as strong as I want to be, that I may not bear the pain as well as I hope. But..."

The word hung for a moment. "But what?" Noah asked in a quiet voice.

"Something I am more afraid of than death."

"More than death?"

"*Oui*. To die knowing I have not truly lived."

CHAPTER 30

Abby sprawled on her bed and squinted at the Spiddle word for the thousandth time. She hated admitting defeat like in that moment at chess when you had to tip over your king and concede that your opponent had maneuvered you into a hopeless position. It didn't happen to her much—she hardly ever lost. But now she might as well admit she couldn't win. Without an English to Beneathese dictionary to refer to, she'd never figure out what the Spiddle word meant, or even how to pronounce it.

She closed her eyes, remembering the troll's reaction when she laid the word on the board. Spid's instantaneous challenge. The first stunned, then enraged expression on his face when Yurk told him he found the word in the very reference book, which he, Spid had compiled, that it was ancient, but still a viable word choice for the game.

Neither of them pronounced it, nor had they told her what it meant. In fact, she remembered Spid clamping his hand over Yurk's mouth. So it must be important. Even dangerous. But why? What was its function?

The jumble of consonants with a few vowels sprinkled in looked like alphabet soup spilled on a tabletop. She felt like crying. But she wouldn't let herself. Not now. It was too late for tears. Or perhaps too soon.

Frustrated and angry, she climbed off her bed and roamed out to the massive outer cavern. At the far edge of the arena-sized room, she saw Noah and Delacroix at their practice. Even at that great distance, she heard the throbbing beat vibrate through her body. Once again, she noticed how confident Noah appeared. She felt a burst of pride that he'd been chosen.

Toward the center of the cavern, on a broad level area, Deidre and several of her friends from Shroomtown scrimmaged with battle forks. Fascinated, Abby listened to the sizzle and warp of the weapons as the combatants circled each other, thrusting and blocking, ducking and attacking. She considered asking if Deidre could train her, give her a fork to use against Spid, but decided she couldn't learn enough in a few hours to be any more than a fleeting nuisance to the troll.

In another corner of the immense room, Abby found Uh-oh with a cluster of grungoids gathered around him. Although they only communicated in grunts, whistles, and the almost snake-like chhht, chhht, chhht, sound, she got the impression he was lecturing them.

Abby wandered the chamber, gathering a wave from the boy Deidre said was named Peitr as he practiced fighting imaginary attackers from the back of his many-legged Galloopapede. A little further along, Benny Vlavnosk talked earnestly to a group of men and women about the tactics of tunnel fighting.

Finally, she circled back to the practice skin to watch the drumming. Noah and Lix Delacroix had toiled almost non-stop since she found her brother. Sweat rolled off both of them as they drummed with an intensity that surpassed any level Noah reached in his garage-haven at home. Amazing, she thought, they've almost melded into one drummer.

Noah, his hair flying like cooked spaghetti around his head, darted from place to place, striking his sticks on different areas of the taut practice skin, creating a universe of sounds. His eyes were clamped shut in concentration and his lips pushed in and out with the rhythm. He seemed to be speaking a musical language with his drumsticks, drawing the words and phrases from another place, a place where no one else could go.

Delacroix nodded his head, keeping time with the bass beat that anchored the bottom of the controlled fury Noah delivered to the quivering drum. "Here Noah," he said. "You must take this moment and fly."

Abby couldn't believe it. Her brother, already drumming at a superhuman speed, dialed it up another notch. He hammered the practice skin with a ferocity that sent a crackle of electric excitement up her backbone. He hammered harder, faster, sending cascades of rapid-fire rhythm resonating through the chamber.

"Kuhrack. Kuhrack."

Not one, but both of Noah's drumsticks snapped in half.

The rounded tip ends flew in different directions. One whizzed by Abby's head, thunked into the wall behind her, and shattered into splinters. The other went straight up like a bullet. Noah, eyes and mouth wide, watched it. Delacroix stopped drumming. The projectile hesitated, began to fall. It seemed to take an hour to spin past and land, making a tink, tink, tink sound as it bounced on the cavern floor.

The jagged edges of Noah's drumsticks protruded from his clenched hands. Delacroix furrowed his brow, tapped the drum twice more with half-hearted kicks, then arched his back and snapped to his feet in one motion.

"The sticks. They could not take the stress. You have another pair, yes?"

Noah shook his head. "Just these." He opened his hands. The fragmented wood clattered to the floor.

Abby saw his face crumple and turned to Delacroix. "Don't you have...?"

Even before he raised his eyebrows and the stubs of his arms, Abby realized how silly the question was. "No, I guess not. But can't somebody make a pair? How hard could it be?"

"It is a long way to find the right wood, *ma petite*. And no proper tools to carve the sticks with."

"I...I...could play with my hands." The quivering in Noah's voice betrayed his fear and uncertainty.

Something tickled at Abby's brain. A memory. A picture. Drumsticks. But where? Ah! "Wait!" Abby shouted, her voice bouncing off the cavern walls. "I know. I know where there are drumsticks. Lots of drumsticks."

Delacroix arched himself to his feet. "Where, Abby? I will send someone to retrieve them, quick like the wink."

"They're in The Last Place You Look," she said smugly. "A whole bunch of them."

"Huh?" Noah stared at his sister. "The last what?"

"Place you look." Delacroix raised an arm stub and pantomimed striking his forehead with his palm, then laughed at himself. "*Alors*! I am so into the drumming, I forgot all about it. It's the place where all lost things go," he told Noah. "It's at the bottom of the Vorv."

"The Vorv we rode up in?"

"No, another one. There are many Vorvs. Or perhaps the same Vorv many times. They are a mystery onto themselves." Delacroix turned his attention back to Abby. "Tell me where you saw the sticks and I will send Chillout for them."

Abby tried to visualize where, in the massive piles of luggage, car keys, school books, wallets, wristwatches, socks and everything else, she'd spotted the drumsticks. Near the mittens, or on the other side, next to the bracelets? She made a rapid decision. "I can't really describe where they are, and Chillout's busy scavenging provisions. I'll go. I like riding the Vorv and I bet I can walk right to the drumsticks. I'll be back in a few minutes."

"You can't go alone," Noah insisted. "It's dangerous."

"I've been there before," Abby said defiantly. "I know the way. You get something to eat. Take a nap."

"She is a stubborn one, your sister." Delacroix laughed. "But she is right. It is perfectly safe. The monsters are all behind The Skin still."

Abby stuck her tongue out at her Noah. "If I'm not back in an hour, send out a search party."

Before Noah could argue, she spun on her heel and headed for the tunnel that led to the first Vorv she'd ridden with Delacroix and Chillout. Even before she stepped into the semi-circular room, she started chanting and, in a matter of seconds, felt herself spinning down the airshaft. Within seconds after landing she shook off her dizziness and scuttled beneath the sign that read *Thela stpla ceyo ulo ok.*

Inside, she scanned the chamber, trying to get her bearings. She remembered Chillout cadging a pair of sunglasses toward the back of the room, remembered all the instruments. She walked quickly, telling herself to ignore the books, video games, and cell phones. Still, she stopped and picked one up, wondering if she could use it to call her father. In a moment, she tossed it back. "You can't make a call through solid rock."

Trudging on, she found saxophones, trumpets, guitars, drums, harmonicas, and flutes piled in stacks three times as high as her head. She ran her finger across the cool brass of a Sousaphone. How could somebody lose something that big? And then she remembered reading about a cellist who accidentally left his three-hundred-year-old instrument in the back of a taxi. People lost things. All kinds of things.

She spotted a smaller mound of drumsticks, tangled like the sticks in that game she played in grade school. Which ones should she take? Did it matter?

The logical part of her brain told her it didn't. Drumsticks were drumsticks. The important thing was to grab two sticks, or maybe four or six in case another broke, and hurry back. She reached down, grasped several sticks, and yanked them from the pile.

"Fate is not random. Fate is the way."

The eerie humming whispered voice of the Zezzue startled her. The sticks clattered to the floor.

"You know the way, Abby," the Darksuckers whispered.

She looked up to see the tiny creatures had formed a soft swirling nebula of violet and golden light. Were they trying to tell her that the drumsticks she took *did* matter?

Maybe this whole adventure, everything she and Noah had experienced, was like putting together a giant jigsaw puzzle. The Chameleon Stone was one piece. The drumming was another. Noah had brought a segment of the puzzle back with the Methuselah Stone, and she'd found another in the word game against Spid. She didn't know where that fit yet, but she knew that there was only one right place or the picture wouldn't make sense.

She gazed at the pile of drumsticks. What made one pair special, different? Some were lighter and some were darker, some had patterns painted on them, and some were worn and splintered. How could she decide which were the right ones?

A laugh almost snuck out. How had she discovered anything inside this mountain? By not looking with her eyes, that's how.

She sat beside the pile, closing her eyes, breathing slowly. In the darkness inside her mind, she searched for that calm sensation that led her out of the tunnel maze. A picture formed, Noah, his hair flying about his head as he hunted for the rhythm, the perfect rhythm.

"Thrum,thrum, thuddahthrum, thrumthrum." Abby heard the beat. It vibrated all around her, but she couldn't tell whether the sound was real or existed only in her mind.

"Thrum-fadit-ditthrum.   Ticketytick-thrumthrum. Thrum,diddah-boom, ticketytick thrumthrum."

Inside her mind Noah played a duet with the mountain, flailing at The Skin ever faster, more insistently. She felt her arms raise, her hands roll at the wrists, her fingers matching his movements.

 Clackety, clack, clack, clack, clackety, clack.

She opened her eyes to see an amazing sight. The drumsticks, hundreds, if not thousands of them, were moving, shifting, spreading out on the floor, rolling against each other, spinning, tumbling. The golden light from the Zezzue beamed down on them like a spotlight. The sticks levitated.

Abby gasped, jumped to her feet, and backed away to give them room.

Spinning end over end, the sticks formed a huge spiral that drew in tighter and tighter until it seemed a solid disk. The center of the disk sank and the sticks formed a swirling cone. They clacked against each other, the sounds overlapping, swelling to a rumble. The cone lengthened, the top broadening, the base tapering like a tornado.

Faster and faster it spun, closer and closer. Abby held her breath, held her ground. The tornado hovered a few feet in front of her, then rose until the narrow base was level with her shoulders. The swirling drumsticks were a blur, except for the two on which the cyclone balanced.

Were those the ones?

She peered at them, saw something gleam, and forgot all fear and uncertainty. These were the sticks she needed. But how could she pull them from this spinning galaxy of drumsticks without mangling her fingers or bringing the whole thing down on her head?

You're over-thinking once again. Give your brain a rest.

Abby closed her eyes, took another long breath, extended her arm, and chanted. "Iknowtheway, Iknowtheway, Iknowtheway," faster and faster and faster until the words dissolved into a single entity, a hum that melded with the high-pitched whine of the wooden maelstrom.

She opened her hand.

Smack.

The drumsticks slapped against her palm.

She closed her fingers over them and opened her eyes. The whirling mass toppled away from her and caved in upon itself. Drumsticks clattered to the stone floor.

"I know the way," Abby crowed, staring at the sticks in her hand. They were made of pure white wood. Inlaid in mother-of-pearl on the butt end of each of them were the letters LD.

"Lix Delacroix?" she marveled. "Not possible."

But the last few days had shifted her ideas about what was possible and what wasn't. Had the Grand Exalted Pettifog lost them in the plane crash? After all, he'd had something more important to look for—Melanie. And when he lost his arms, what was the point of searching for his sticks?

No time to wonder now. Noah needed them. And he wouldn't need any spares. This pair would endure. She tucked them in her back pocket.

"Most impressive Miss Keene. You really have honed your mental acuity to a new level. I applaud you."

Spid's three-dimensional image blocked the way to the Vorv. He was decked out in polished black armor, a hatchet-like club hanging from his wide leather belt. Applauding with the tips of his horny-skinned hands, he produced a light, echoing thuff, thuff, thuff. "You are of course, still not at the pinnacle of thinking I have attained but..."

Abby shivered and shrank back, then reminded herself he was only a hologram.

"You can say that again, Boss. Dittos. Mega-double-uber-dittos." Yurk appeared beside his troll commander with a soft pop, saluting, bowing and scraping, and all but kissing Spid's ring. He carried a long sharp spear, and a spiky hammer.

What a suck-up, Yurk is, Abby thought. What an awful way to go through life, playing toady to a troll. The thought distracted her from fear and she threw her shoulders back. "I don't have time to talk to you. I've got to—"

"Deliver the drumsticks to your brother. Yes, yes," Spid said with a smirk. "I know all about it. And I must say, Abby, that your scrawny older sibling has also astounded me. He has demonstrated a great deal of determination and courage crossing the river of fire and outsmarting the gargoyles." The troll pushed his lips in and out. "But, I'm sure you know he cannot win."

"The little geek's in a heap of trouble, isn't he, Boss?" Yurk chortled.

"I would not have phrased it in exactly that manner, Yurk, but yes, sadly... Spid adopted a mock sympathetic tone, oily and unctuous. "...he and the accursed Pettifog will face a humiliating lesson in drumming delivered by Thrndur. Followed immediately by a painful and agonizing death."

"And then the cocktail hour, right?" Yurk chortled.

"Right, witless one. The slaughter and celebration will proceed on schedule, unless—"

"Unless what?" Abby snapped, her anger boiling over. "Unless I throw in with you?"

"The terms have not changed since our last meeting."

"Very generous of you, Boss."

"Thank you Yurk. And, Miss Keene, the offer extends to your brother. He could prove useful in the future. But it does not extend to Delacroix. The brown wizard is an annoyance that I wish to remove."

Abby almost blurted out something she'd heard her father tell a late-night telephone salesman: "not only no, but hell no." But as she opened her mouth, a thought occurred to her. It filled out, and became a plan. Possibly a futile plan, but a plan, nonetheless. To enact it she needed to stay on Spid's good side—or at least not openly antagonize him.

"I really don't want to die." The truth of the statement lent credibility to her acting. "But I can't speak for Noah. And I won't betray him."

"Ah, yes, devotion. Another fine quality, Miss Keene. One I encourage my many subjects to develop. As least as it pertains to me. Well then, let me frame my offer in practical terms."

Abby felt her skin crawl. "Practical terms?"

"Yes," Spid smirked. "In fact, you might call them terminally practical. You will have one final chance to join me. At The Skin. There, when the portal is breeched and my actual physical magnificence breaks through, I will accept your abject apology for opposing me."

Dude's a serious megalomaniac, Abby thought, biting her tongue to keep from blurting out: "So, who's going through The Skin first? You or your ego? You both won't fit at the same time."

"Am I clear?" The threat in Spid's voice and his poisonous dagger-like glare vanquished all thoughts of making a flip remark.

"Yes," Abby said petulantly. "Can I go now?"

"Of course. Give my best to the boys. *Ciao!*"

Ciao? OMG but Spid was pretentious. Abby swiveled and started across the cavern. She was nearly to the door when Spid's purring, smirking voice halted her.

"One little thing further, Miss Keene."

She turned. "What now?"

"Until you join me, you represent a threat to my success. Granted, the chance you'll ruin my plans is miniscule, but I can't risk it. Remember when we played Spiddle and I told you I had devised the most masterful and fair rules?"

Abby swallowed a comment about his twisted idea of fairness.

"Well, I dictate the rules for this game too. The larger game." He sidestepped to expose the image of the Shadow Stone on a pedestal beside him and rubbed a spot on the gem. "Maculostis Astigmaneesus," Spid commanded and pointed a long green fingernail at Abby's face.

A beam of dark light sprang from the stone and lanced into her eyes. Spid's image exploded in a bright flash within her brain.

She shrieked and fell to her knees.

Pain broke over her, then receded like a wave on the sand. When she opened her eyes she couldn't see Spid. She couldn't see the mounds of misplaced stuff. She could make out only faint shapes behind a wall of blackness. "No," she moaned.

"Yes," Spid laughed. "You are as good as blind, Abby. I hated to do it, but it was a necessity. When you present yourself to me and, in your abject humility admit defeat, we will talk of bringing light back into your eyes."

Abby summoned anger to sustain her. "I'd rather die."

Spid guffawed cruelly. "That, too, can be arranged."

Abby heard a sharp pop and sensed Spid's image had disappeared. She was alone. Tears dribbled down her cheeks and her teeth chattered. In the absence of sight, other sensations sharpened. She felt a faint current of air wisp across her face. The always-present rhythm of the mountain amplified. "Thrumm, thrumm, thrumm, thrumm,thrumm, thrummm." She smelled the lemony soap she'd washed her face with that morning and the unique tang of the oil that lubricated the pads and joints of the brass instruments on the stack near her.

Blind, she mourned. Maybe for the rest of her life. Which, if Spid got through The Skin, might not be all that long.

Oddly, her dark joke squelched her temptation to give up. Stop it, she scolded herself. Self pity sucks. She blotted her face with the sleeve of her sweatshirt and tried to clear her mind.

She had to take the drumsticks to Noah. Unless she accomplished that, nothing else mattered.

I can do this. I know the way. Heck, I could find my way back to the Vorv with my eyes closed.

Which, thanks to Spid, was exactly what she'd have to do.

She wouldn't even need to chant, just use her memory and common sense. Piece of cake.

She touched the drumsticks to make sure they were secure in her pocket, then walked into the current of air, arms extended, feet shuffling so she wouldn't trip.

Ten steps. Piece of cake. She should be alongside the pile of hair dryers. Turn right. Another eight steps to the mound of barrettes. Ten steps or so to the small mountain of papers. Homework assignments mostly. Must be the ones the dog didn't eat. She grinned.

Another twist and another turn into the air current and she stood in front of what felt like a doorway. A strange sound emanated from it, a kind of low level buzz. Some kind of energy radiated by the Zezzue, maybe.

She stepped through, already planning the rest of her route to the Vorv. About twenty yards, a right turn, and then into the tunnel. No prob.

Frazzzz! Abby's hair crackled and stood on end. Her skin prickled as she passed through some kind of energy curtain.

Fzlooorp! The sound of the force field was replaced by something else.

Laughter.

"What the...?" A cascade of chuckles, chortles, giggles, guffaws, snorts, sniggers, and haw-haws reverberated around her. The hilarity of hundreds of men, women, children, and what she could have sworn was a small pack of hyenas, created an eerie and sinister cacophony.

She slapped her hands over her ears. She must be in the room where lost senses of humor went. The one with the sign that read: *Tak emyw ifepl ease.*

But that was impossible. She'd been so sure of her route. And besides, when she came here before, there was a weird wooden door. How could this be?

As she wrestled with the problem, the volume and intensity of the laughter grew, creeping her out, making it harder and harder to think. "I must have come in another door," she yelled. She could barely hear the words. "I'll go out the same way."

She took two steps. Her hand struck rock.

Don't panic, she told herself. You spun around when you first heard the laughter.

She made a quarter turn, walked another two steps and found another a solid surface. As if hearing the punch line to a particularly funny joke, the laughter swelled and roared. The panic she'd fought overtook her in a dizzying flood. She darted left and right, sliding her hand along the wall, searching for an opening.

Nothing. Around her, laughter rang out, louder and louder.

Nooooo! Her head swam. Her thoughts seemed to break loose inside her brain, they flitted like light-drunk flies dive-bombing a glowing bulb, they collided and crashed.

Stumbling, tears streaming down her face, Abby groped at the cold rock wall. "Stop laughing!" she shrieked at her disembodied tormentors.

The hilarity grew more manic, a waterfall of mirth crashing around her.

She forced herself to stop, to take slow deep breaths. She heard herself panting like a thirsty dog.

Chant, she thought. Chant Abby, chant. "Iknowtheway,Iknowthe way,Iknowthe..." She couldn't hear herself. Laughter clogged her mind, her throat. Her lips stopped moving. She clutched the drumsticks to her chest.

I screwed up, Noah. I'm so sorry.

She tried not to think what would happen at The Skin, but the vision crowded everything else out of her mind— Spid and Yurk, flailing at her brother with their weapons, laughing, laughing, laughing.

Something brushed against her upper arm. She flinched. A spider?

It brushed her again. Not a spider web. Fingers. Hairy fingers. She opened her mouth to scream. A hand clamped down on her shoulder.

CHAPTER 31

Noah knew he needed down time to gather strength for the coming challenge, but he couldn't shut his brain off long enough for any real slumber. If the sandman had shoveled tons of sleep-dust under his eyelids it wouldn't have mattered; he was too worried about Abby to relax.

After she departed to find the sticks, he and Delacroix resumed their practice. Noah tried slapping the practice skin with his hands, using his fingertips and the heel of his palm to achieve different sounds. It felt futile, and sounded like mere noise, but he'd kept at it until Chillout appeared. "Uh, Lix? The little chickie is like major latesky. You want I should check?"

"Abby?" Noah had leaped to Chillout's side. "She's not back? I'll go, too."

Lix had arched his back and snapped to his feet. "Not a good idea. You are needing the rest. We are only a few hours from meeting Spid."

"But..."

"Chillout will locate her. And you will go to your bedchamber and rest."

Before Noah could protest again, Chillout dashed away.

That seemed like hours ago. Noah flopped to the other side of the sleeping mat and closed his eyes again. Images flickered through his brain, the river of fire, the gargoyles, the scraggly hermit talking to the Zezzue. He saw Mom, Dad, Abby, his bedroom. The fluffy pillows on his bed beckoned, and he sank his head into them. Maybe he would sleep, really sleep, just for a minute.

"Wake up, brother monster. Time to spring into action."

"In a minute, Ab-normal. I'll get up in a minute."

"No, doof." A hand shook his shoulder. "Now. Put on a clean shirt and let's go kick some serious troll tush."

He opened his eyes to see his grinning sister. "Hey. You're back."

"Terrific grasp of the obvious, bro."

"Chillout found you?"

"Not before he scared the whoosymajoosey out of me, but yep, our favorite beatnik grungoid turned up in the nick of time."

Noah sat up, nerve endings jangling. "What does that mean?"

"Nothing." Abby backed away, hands sweeping the air behind her.

Standing, he took a tentative step toward her. "What's wrong?"

"Nothing." She tucked her chin. "C'mon. Hustle up."

In two long leaps, Noah closed the space between them and locked his hands around her forearms. "Abby, look at me," he commanded.

She sighed, then raised her head, and he saw what looked like inkblots blanketing the irises and pupils of her eyes. "What happened? Are you blind?"

"Politically incorrect, bro. I'm visually challenged. A lovely parting gift from our friend, Spid."

"Spid? But he can't get into this world."

"He can't. Yet. His hologram cast a spell on me with the Shadow Stone."

Noah pulled her against his chest. "Abby. I'm so sorry. If I'd stayed home, or if I'd taken you back, we wouldn't be here."

"Know what, big bro? I think we'd be here even if you weren't a dork. Abby pulled away and her voice sounded almost cheerful. "And even with this," she brought her hand up to touch her eyes, "and being scared half out of my mind three or four times, I wouldn't change a thing. It's been amazing, hasn't it? The stuff we've seen. The things we've done. No one will ever believe it."

For the first time, Noah thought about that. If they returned to the world out there, they'd have to keep all this to themselves or their father would have them talking to psychiatrists for the rest of their lives. "Well yeah, but..."

"Shush." Abby put a finger to her lips. "Let's go finish it. Here." she reached into her back pocket and drew out a pair of slim, ghostly white drumsticks, "If you can't beat Spid with these, then you ought to take up the kazoo. Check out the monogram."

Noah took the sticks and twirled them between his fingers. Perfect. He spotted the letters LD. Lix Delacroix. "But how?"

"Found 'em, downstairs. Or maybe they found me," she amended with a grin. "Just when you thought things couldn't get stranger, huh?"

Noah stared at the sticks for a moment, then flipped them between his fingers again. "Tell Lix I'll be right out."

CHAPTER 32

The earlier ride up in the Vorv, Noah thought, was nothing compared to the ride down to The Skin. It felt like they were being sucked into the very core of the earth. The force of the descent splayed the flesh on his face and he couldn't prevent drool from escaping his loosened lips. Then, as suddenly as the ride began, it ended with an emphatic "Vorv." An updraft lowered them to the ground like a feather drifting to earth.

"Ungggh." Noah attempted a tentative step. His stomach somersaulted and he lurched to the wall and bent over, trying to regain his equilibrium.

"Offer you a barf bag, my man?" Chillout put a hand on his back.

Is he kidding? Noah felt blood rush into his head and decided that, from what he'd seen of the hipster grungoid's foraging ability, he just might produce an air-sickness sack. Holding up a hand to decline, Noah straightened and felt his stomach settle and his head clear.

"Quite a ride, huh?" Abby waggled her eyebrows and, on her second try, patted his shoulder.

"In-tense," he agreed.

They walked down a short tunnel in silence, but as they drew nearer to the opening at the far end, Noah heard the steady pulsating of Humbug Mountain. "Thrum-thrum, thrum-thrum, thrum-thrum." The insistent throb vibrated through his cells. "Thrum-thrum, thrum-thrum, thrum-thrum." They were, he knew, very close to the source. Emerging from the tunnel and onto a balcony hewn into the rocky wall of the drumming chamber, he halted, open-mouthed.

"Describe it to me." Abby groped for his hand.

"Huh?"

Her fingers dug into his palm. "Earth to Noah. Little sister. Visually impaired. Hell-oh-oh."

A flush of embarrassment and guilt warmed his face. "Abby. I'm sor—" He noted the "cut the pity" grimace on her face and laid it out for her "We're standing on a wide ledge about two-thirds of the way down into a really tall, tubular chamber. It's maybe fifty yards across at the bottom."

She cocked her head. "I hear other people, I think."

Noah confirmed it. "There's kind of a spiral trail that runs up the walls and there are tunnels every so often. And there are people and creatures. Shroomers, and grungoids and some kinds of animals I've never seen before. They're all on the ledges, looking down at The Skin."

Delacroix added. "My friend Chillout goes to join them. As with the others, he protects his home."

Noah glanced around. The gray, dreadlocked creature with the Ray Charles shades had vanished. Delacroix continued his explanation. "If we fail, they will defend Above from Spid and the darkness on the other side. They will fight in the tunnels and caverns until Spid is vanquished or until..."

They fell silent. Abby turned her face up and swept a hand through the air. "What's above us?"

"The shaft narrows," Noah answered. "I can't," he craned his neck, "really see where it ends."

"Somewhere up there," Delacroix said, "they say there is a portal to the Realm of Exponential Darkness."

"Where the Zezzue go," Abby said, reverence in her voice. "To purge themselves of the darkness they inhale to give us light."

"According to the legend," Delacroix added, "the Zezzue have regurgitated darkness in that place since the very beginning of our universe. If it were to be released it could extinguish the sun."

"Like a black hole," Abby agreed.

Noah shuddered and dropped his gaze to the figures watching from the natural balconies around the chamber.

"Thudda-thoom, thuddah-thoom, thuddah-thoom." The sound echoed around him, and he looked down at a rock platform that rose from the floor. At the rear of it was The Skin, a taut and almost diaphanous oval membrane. Light strobed across its surface, green and blue and red, casting an unearthly glow on three figures standing before it. From her upright, combative posture there was no mistaking that one was Deidre. The small gray figure beside her had to be Uh-oh. Noah felt a twinge of joy and love. The grungoid had stuck with him through thick and thin. A brother. A small, weird, and smelly one, but a brother nonetheless.

Even though Noah had met him only briefly, he recognized the third figure as the Hermit of Humbug Mountain, disheveled and leaning on a staff, here to fulfill the prophecy. A tingle of anticipation skittered along Noah's spine. This time, he almost welcomed fear. It wouldn't stop him. In fact it would drive him. He knew how to use it, how to work through it.

"We must go, Noah," Delacroix said. "We must begin to drum as the sun approaches the solstice. There will be a moment when the moon and all planets align, when the seas stop their ceaseless movement, when all will synchronize and reset. The mountain's beat will falter. That is when The Skin will open. Unless we succeed."

Noah felt the chill hand of the inevitable grasp his heart as they followed the trail along the perimeter of the spiral chamber, descending toward The Skin. To distract himself, he took a deep breath and described what he saw to Abby. "The drum is huge. Maybe fifty feet across. There are steps in the rock on both sides of it. Deidre's standing next to it on a huge platform with Uh-oh and the hermit I told you about. From this distance, they look like toys."

"What color is The Skin?"

"Hard to say, it's several— Wait a minute there's something...whuh-what's that?" Noah turned toward Delacroix and pointed to a swirling tubular dark cloud forming near the front edge of the platform. "It looks like a tor—"

"Spid." Abby clutched her brother's arm. "I can feel him."

The dark funnel of light and shadows glimmered; the enormous armor-clad troll materialized. Beside him stood a squat, ugly figure with a globule of green drool escaping from one corner of his mouth. Yurk, thought Noah, just as Abby described him. Only a faint aura and their translucency betrayed them as holographic images.

Noah heard a collective gasp from the defenders of Above. Deidre drew her battle-fork and set it humming. "Get me down there," Abby cried.

"No. Stay here."

"Noah!" Abby clutched at his T-shirt. "You must take me down there."

"Yes," Delacroix said. "She's right. We must all meet our destinies."

Noah opened his mouth to argue, then gritted his teeth and led Abby down the trail to the platform.

The intimidating images of the troll and his grotesque second-in-command snapped into focus. Spid looked out over the arena, cleared his throat, and spoke. His voice was a round-toned, self-important, drone—a combination of boring teacher and oily politician. "We have gathered here—"

"Tell em, Boss. Lay it on thick," Yurk bleated.

"To witness..." Spid let the word ring. "To witness the demise of the ill-conceived, illogical, and quite possibly illegal regime of Felix Delacroix, the pusillanimous Pettifog of the astoundingly under-achieving land of Above."

"You go, Boss. You duh troll."

"Horsehockey," Abby hissed, fingers digging into Noah's arm.

"You might reflect," Spid continued, "all of you gathered here, as you live out the final moments of your lives, how you transgressed against the all-wise, all-seeing, all-knowing, soon-to-be ruler of the reunited realms of Above and Beneath..." He paused, looking expectantly at Yurk.

The ogre looked puzzled for a moment then blurted out, "Uh, that would be you? Right, Boss?"

Spid cast a narrowed-eyed poisonous glance at his hench-beast then continued. "Yes. I, Spid the devious." He raised his hands and paused again.

No one moved. No one spoke. Yurk jumped into the yawning silence. "C'mon, let's give it up for the big guy." He slapped his ham-like hands together. Thungh-thungh-thungh.

"Major-league suck-up," Abby whispered.

Noah put a hand over her mouth, but Spid swiveled his head toward them. Noah saw the glint of his eyes, felt them searching for weakness. He forced himself to return the stare without blinking.

Spid smiled. "Well, I see, the victims, uh, I mean our worthy opponents, have arrived."

"Ignore him," Delacroix ordered. He took the steps to the platform with Noah guiding Abby right behind him.

The troll sniffed. "There is no cause for rudeness. Especially since you will be begging for my most munificent mercy in a matter of mere moments."

Man, Noah thought, this guy really loves the sound of his own voice.

The Skin shimmered and the lights of the chamber dimmed. The surface of the enormous drumhead turned a burnished orange and quivered as if someone had thunked it with a giantic forefinger.

"Ah, the solstice approaches." Spid gestured to The Skin. "Soon we will know without question whose power will prevail." His image went static, as if he'd removed himself from it.

For the first time, Noah noticed a large recessed stone face carved into the rock wall beside The Skin. It glowered at him, mouth pulled into a tight grimace, empty cavities for eye-sockets. A scooped out area above the forehead formed a narrow shelf. Delacroix nodded at the visage. "The stones," he said.

Noah withdrew the brain-stone, the Methuselah, from his backpack.

"And Abby, you have with you the Chameleon Orb, no?"

"Right here." She drew the translucent stone, now glowing the same orange as The Skin, from her own backpack.

Noah took her by the arm and led her to the primitive face. They knew what they had to do. Delacroix had told them.

Noah helped Abby up the steps and placed her hand on the right-hand eye socket of the carved face. She studied it with her fingers, then set the stone inside. Noah helped her down, then climbed and placed the Methuselah in the second eye socket. Reaching into his backpack again, he drew out the picture of his mother. He touched her smiling face, then set the picture on the shelf made for the Shadow Stone.

"I'll do my best, Mom," Noah told the photograph, then led Abby back.

Once at the bottom, he locked onto the piercing gaze of Spid whose image had reanimated. Abby seemed to sense it. "Spid's scary, huh?"

"Yeah." He felt his stomach muscles jitter and pulled in a deep breath. "Reminds me of Mr. Trangle." The mention of the high school football coach and gym teacher made Abby giggle and Noah knuckled her head. "I'm glad you're here with me."

"Where else would I be doofus?"

Deidre appeared at his elbow. "Noah," she said softly, "you ready?"

"Hi, Deed," he grinned. "No problem. I have a plan."

"Then there's no reason to worry." She smiled with trembling lips, then kissed the corner of his mouth. He felt his breath catch in his throat.

"You'll try your hardest, I know. And I'll be right here." She backed away and rejoined Uh-oh and the hermit who stood, arms folded, eyes on The Skin.

Boooom!

A single bass drum beat exploded the stillness.

"Noah." Delacroix tilted his head toward The Skin. "It is showtime."

CHAPTER 33

Noah gave him one thumb up, then peeled off backpack and fished out the drumsticks. Delacroix stared at them in disbelief. "Where did you—?"

Bah-Booooom!

The second drumbeat reverberated through the chamber. The figures of Spid and Yurk, nearly transparent now, hovered at the front of the platform.

Noah rubbed the drumsticks between his palms. "Abby found them."

"Ah, Abby. As always, she astounds, does she not? But we must hurry." Delacroix folded himself to the ground, rolled unto his back, and raised his feet. Noah grasped the sticks, head spinning, nerve endings sparking, heart pounding. Totally unreal. A few days ago he was just another kid finishing his sophomore year in high school. And now he was fighting for his life. And Abby's. And the world.

Bah-Boooooom!

A thick column of light shot down and surrounded him in a yellow glow. He stepped to The Skin and through its now nearly transparent surface saw, for the first time, their opponent.

Bizarre. Weird. Grotesque.

Even those words weren't enough to describe the jowly face with clumps of black hair sprinkled across its cheeks and the wolfish snout. The creature pulled broad lips into a profane leer, exposing four sharp fangs. Noah willed himself not to flinch, but what he saw next made his confidence plummet even though he'd seen the statue in the Temple of Cheltnor and guessed what his rival would look like. Protruding from a body covered with armor-like platelets were five arms. Two sprouted from each side. The fifth unfurled from a bushy growth of hair on the creature's forehead. Each of the hands clutched a jet-black drumstick.

"You're in way over your head, kid." The growled taunt came from the other side of The Skin.

"Play, Noah. Nothing can be done about what you see on the other side. Let your heart guide your hands." Delacroix patted his feet against The Skin, laying down a steady pattern. "Play."

Noah tore his eyes from the creature and focused on gripping the sticks once held by the greatest drummer on earth.

The greatest drummer anywhere.

He stepped to The Skin and beat out an easy pattern, a place to jump from—three hits with the left hand, two with the right, three more with the left. Repeating the three-two-three, he accelerated into a kind of early Ringo Starr style.

The five-armed creature raised his drumsticks and sent a volley back from his side of the portal. Using his forehead-arm and one lower one to mimic Delacroix's bass beat, he picked up Noah's lead with the other lower arm and one of the top ones. With the remaining arm, the beast played a series of short, sharp rolls, sliding them perfectly into the main beat.

297

Noah answered, keeping a steady 5/4 going with the left hand and doing roll, punch, roll, with the right. Delacroix picked up the change, spinning the bottom end to a new counter rhythm.

The Skin appeared to thicken.

A low cheer rose from the watchers on the ledges. The creature on the other side faltered for a moment, then plunged into a volley of higher-pitched strikes, segueing into a Ginger Baker style attack with two of the other hands. Noah took a second to react and The Skin grew more transparent.

The creature smirked. Gritting his teeth, Noah picked up the challenge, playing a syncopated 6/8.

The surface of The Skin turned a milky hue.

It senses what's happening, Noah realized. The Skin knows who's ahead and who's lost the beat.

He drummed faster. The Skin grew milkier. He grinned.

The sound of chimes tinkled through the chamber.

Chimes?

The Skin pulsed and shimmered. Noah saw his opponent as if nothing stood between them. The surface of The Skin slackened. The creature leered.

"Think it," Delacroix commanded. "Think what you would play."

Chimes. Chimes. Chimes.

Noah struck The Skin and heard the silvery notes. He followed the creature's lead. The Skin tightened.

Congas.

Before the second syllable formed in his mind, he heard the hollow wood and leather thudding. Wow!

The creature picked up the rhythms and added his own.

Chimes and snare.

Noah heard the sound of chimes, jingling and tingling from the stick in his left hand, the staccato rattle of the snare from his right. The Skin's surface grew milky again.

Bells and tympani, tom-tom and rim.

Noah's hands fluttered and flew. His feet and legs flew, too, up and down the stairs, deepening and raising the tone of the beat. Back and forth, up and down, faster, slower, rolls, chatters, slides, and slaps.

His focus narrowed to a pinpoint, his concentration absolute. He no longer felt the heat of the light that poured onto the stage. No longer could he hear the gasps and applause of those gathered above the stage watching him, their fate in his hands. As it had been many times in his garage, everything else blurred, faded into nothingness. The rhythmic structure filled his entire being. He lost track of time and his fatigue disappeared. His cloud of self-doubt burned away, incinerated by the heat of the beat, the beat, the beat.

The five-armed drumming dynamo across The Skin became only a smudge of color in his consciousness, Delacroix only a brown blur as he pump-shifted his legs to lay the solid bottom behind Noah's machine-gun improvisation.

The Skin hardened and softened. It changed color, shifting with the tempo and emotion of the drumming. Red, blues, greens, oranges, and yellows, flashed by Noah's eyes, but he barely noticed. The sweat-mop of his hair flopped into his eyes and he flipped his head to fling it away. Nothing mattered, nothing could shift his attention from the beat.

He found himself in a combination he first learned by hearing Felix Delacroix play it on his *Live at Carnegie Hall* album. He took the core of it and moved it to another level, mixing in right hand hits as he thought of a steel drum. Across The Skin, he felt the other drummer hesitate. The Skin stiffened. Maybe. Maybe he could turn this into an advantage that would—

Clack. Clack.

Noah stared in horror as his sticks collided when he tried to pump up the tempo. He'd let himself get distracted.

The Skin radiated yellow light, slackened, and moved toward clear. The five-armed wolf-pig thing sneered, as if to say "thanks, sucker," riffed back into the correct rhythm, then shifted into an amazing combination of his own, Dopplering a tympani and conga crosscurrent that made Noah's head swim.

The Skin softened, wobbled like jelly, glowed with grayish tint. A fusillade of snare hits cascaded from the other side.

"Noah!" Abby screamed. "Play. Play!"

"Now!" Delacroix commanded. Inserting a six-note downbeat over the top of the other drummer's cluster, he cued Noah in with an emphatic nod.

Noah's hands reacted automatically. He echoed the back-and-forth syncopation created by his opponent, then inserted a muted tambourine counterpoint. The Skin glowed a faint turquoise and firmed a little. He felt the breath rush from his lungs and realized he'd been holding it.

He nearly lost it all. For everyone. He drew in another breath and picked up the tempo.

For what might have been hours, it went on and on. He and the demonic drummer took musical ground and gave it back again. Whenever Noah wanted to go on the attack, Lix anticipated him perfectly, helping him create seamless segues. But, though he tried to ignore them, the limitations of his body began to erode his wall of concentration again: a quick pang of pain when he raised his arm to hit a high counter-beat, neck muscles tightening, lungs straining as he raced to the top of the steps.

As exhaustion overtook him, Noah knew he had to make a move, gamble, and try to end it. Like the decision to backpedal onto the burning river, this one was born of non-existent choices.

With uncanny timing, Delacroix swung into a low, rumbling tympanic roll. He nodded at Noah, and winked. *Here we go.*

When they talked about this final flurry that would determine victory or defeat, Delacroix had called it the musical equivalent of playing chicken in speeding jalopies racing for the edge of a cliff.

Snare drum.

Noah issued the official challenge with three sharp strokes. The hits rang out like gunshots. Bang! Bang! Bang!

In the quick silence between strokes, Noah sensed the spectators again. He heard their mumbles, heard a distant clatter of unsheathed weapons. At the edge of his vision he saw Abby, her sightless eyes staring off into space, her lips moving in and out as they did when she worked on a chess problem or her physics homework. Deidre, battle fork at the ready, raised her chin. Behind her, the hermit smiled at Noah and tucked his arms into the sleeves of his burlap robe. Across the nearly-transparent Skin, Spid and Yurk hulked behind their drummer, muscles bunched in anticipation.

Three whip crack beats came back from the other side of The Skin. Challenge accepted!

The membrane quivered and changed color from red to orange to yellow. It flashed yellow a second time. Delacroix nodded three times. After the third yellow The Skin would green light the final challenge.

Noah forced himself to breathe in as deep as he could and exhale in a long stream through his pursed lips. He moved the rounded tips of the sticks over the area he intended to strike first.

So much at stake. And it's all on me.

But a strange peace settled over him. Win or lose, at least he tried. He did his best. And he didn't give up.

CHAPTER 34

"Thudddddaaaa....thooommmp. Thudddddaaaaaa...thoomp."

Abby felt the mountain's pulse slowing. The spaces between the beats stretched and stretched until she feared each beat might be the last. She dug her fingers into Deidre's arm and blinked her nearly sightless eyes. "What's happening? Tell me what's happening! Why isn't Noah playing?"

"He's about to." Deidre slung an arm around her shoulders. "He's holding his sticks ready. He's really tired. And The Skin, it's gone totally clear. It's vibrating like you wouldn't believe."

"Where's Spid?" Abby stood on tiptoe, then dropped back to her heels shaking her head. That didn't help. Neither did squinting. She might never see again. She might spend the rest of her life asking people to tell her what they saw, and trying to remember the faces, shapes, and colors she once saw for herself. "Can you see Spid?"

"He's right behind the other drummer, ready to burst through. He's even uglier in person." Abby felt Deidre's arm muscles ripple as the warrior-girl flexed them. "And that squatty-body ogre is disgusting."

"That's Yurk," Abby said. "He's dumb, but dangerous."

The snarling rattle of a snare drum sliced the air. "Noah." Deidre released Abby and clapped her hands. "Wow. He doesn't sound tired at all."

But Abby, who had listened to her brother drum all her life, knew better. She heard almost imperceptible hesitations, not-quite-as-crisp-as-usual attacks and combinations.

"Listen." She tugged on Deidre's arm and shouted over the ever-building thumping and crashing. "I may have to take radical action." With her free hand, Abby felt the rolled parchment in her back pocket, the parchment she'd had Deidre write on. "And you gotta trust me."

Even though I'm not sure I trust myself.

The snap-bang of a particularly violent exchange of drumstick gunfire drowned out Deidre's response, but Abby felt the older girl's hand squeeze her shoulder. When the thunder ebbed for a moment, Abby shouted, "How far from here to The Skin?"

"About thirty feet." Deidre's hands gripped Abby's forearms, turning her slightly to her left. "Straight ahead the way you're facing now."

Abby nodded. Thirty feet. Fifteen long steps. More or less.

Another drum volley began, this one notching up the intensity to a level Abby would have thought impossible before today. This time the volley didn't ebb or dampen to allow time to gain momentum for a new skirmish of drum hits, cymbal rolls, bell glissandos, or bass thumps. This time it just built and built and built and built. She no longer felt the mountain's pulse. Had it had shut down as the prophecy forecast?

The pace increased and the pitch climbed, stretching Abby's nerves. She tried to visualize Noah, his hair stringy with sweat, eyes clamped shut, hands flying faster than hummingbird wings.

A series of cymbal explosions punctuated every third beat and kicked the high-geared din up to another, louder, faster level of compressed fury.

Thututut, kuhrash, thututut, kuhrash, thututut, kuhrash.

If Noah played any faster he would incinerate. She felt her eyes well up. She was so proud of him.

Again she felt the parchment. What if she'd calculated wrong? What if, instead of fitting the last fragment into the puzzle, she was forcing in a piece that didn't belong? What then?

Simple answer. She would die. And so would Noah.

Her knees wobbled and she leaned against Deidre and screamed at where she thought the warrior-girl's ear would be. "Has The Skin changed?"

"No," Deidre yelled back. "Exactly the same. Clear. But solid."

The drumming, seven hands and two feet already at supernatural velocity, shifted up another impossible notch. The last burst.

Thutcrashthutcrashthutcrashthutcrashthutcrash.

The wall of percussion built and built, drumbeats as ammunition, drumsticks and feet as firing pins. Abby's ears ached and she felt her teeth grinding together. How much more could Noah take? How long before Delacroix's leg muscles cramped or one of them missed a beat?

Crashthutcrashthutcrashthutcrashthut.

The air pressed against her skin, thick, dense with sound waves and ripe with the smell of fear and adrenaline. She felt Deidre tense and her instincts told her the end had come.

As if by prearranged signal, the drummers on both sides of The Skin trip-hammered one more rapid run up the ladder. Thutututututututututut. Then they crashed to a close. Kuh-woooom. Kuhrash.

The sound reverberated in Abby's ears for what seemed like hours. Just as the last echo, she heard Deidre yelp.

"It's Spid. He's trying to push through."

Deidre pulled away and Abby heard a ringing whack as the warrior-girl activated her battle fork against the decibelt.

If Spid gets through, I have no choice.

"Whew," Deidre sighed. "He just stretched the surface of The Skin. It's rubbery. But it's holding."

"Thudddaa."

The mountain's pulse throbbed weakly beneath Abby's feet. Trembling, she touched Deidre's arm again. "Where's Spid? Where's Noah?"

"Spid's on his knees. His drummer's collapsed. The troll's trying to pull him up. Noah's on the ground, too, lying next to Delacroix. He's panting. And now there's a—Oh! It's beautiful."

"What? What's beautiful?"

"There's a drum. No, two drums, one on each side of The Skin. They're on high ledges near the top of the chamber. And there's light, like inside of them. The drums are glowing like they're made of gold."

"Thoomppp."

Humbug Mountain's heartbeat sent images swirling through Abby's head. The golden drum. The prophecy.

"Noah's on his feet," Deidre told her. He can barely stand." Abby felt the warrior girl pull away. "I'll help him."

"Thud...da."

"No." Abby grabbed at Deidre's arm. "He has to climb alone. Noah told me about the drawings on the temple wall. High ledges. Two drums. A boy scaling a cliff."

Abby heard Delacroix's urgent instructions. "The rhythm, Noah. Three beats, then four, then five. Once again. Strike it three times and then four."

"Uh-heff, huff-huhn."

"Not too fast. Let each one ring out."

"Whoo, heff. Uh-huhn."

"Then return for three final strokes on The Skin to bring this battle to an end."

"Noah!" Deidre screamed. "The five-armed drummer. He's up."

"Thoom..."

"Run, Noah! Run!" Abby screamed.

She heard his damp feet slap the platform. "Tell me," she commanded Deidre.

"I can't see the five-armed creature. He's too high." Deidre's voice was tight. "Noah's on the first tier of rock."

Abby nodded. "Climb, Noah, climb," she whispered into the hushed silence that gripped the chamber after the thunderstorm of drum beats. A pebble clattered off a rock and she gasped. "Careful, Noah."

"Thud."

The mountain's heartbeat sounded even weaker than before.

Deidre stiffened, then darted away. The "wooorp" of the sonic fork whistled through the air. "Get back. Get back." She punctuated her shrill demand with another shot that brought an enraged snarl of pain and rage.

Spid. He must have tried to push through again.

"The Skin, it is...huff...very soft, ma...whuff...*cherie*." Delacroix laid a trembling hand on Abby's shoulder. "I do not...phew...know if hold it will." He gulped air like a drowning man. "But Noah nears the top. He climbs straight up now. Very steep."

"The other one." Abby touched the stump of Delacroix's arm. His skin seemed to steam. "Where is the other one?"

"Thooo...wump."

The mountain's heartbeat was little more than a whisper.

She felt Delacroix twist and his body sag. "Impossible, Abby. I cannot see far enough."

Wooorrpp.

Abby heard the sound wave from Deidre's weapon and another roar of pain. Spid's venomous threat followed, clear even through The Skin. "You will die first, fork-wielder. Prepare to perish."

"I prepare only to drive you back to the depths," Deidre shouted back.

Abby felt tears of pride burn her blinded eyes.

"Good girl," Delacroix whispered. "Strong girl."

"Thd."

The mountain's beat flickered.

"Where's Noah?"

"He is nearly there. He is climbing up over the—"

Faint and far, a drum beat sounded.

Thump, thump, thump.

"The other drummer," Abby gasped. "He'll start the mountain's heart and it will beat for Spid, for evil."

The demon's drum sounded again.

Thump, thump, thump, thump.

"Hurry, Noah," Abby cried. Huddled against Delacroix, she heard another wave from Deidre's sword, another roar of rage from Spid, then five hits on the distant drum.

Before the echoes dissolved, Abby heard the sound of Noah's first strikes.

Thump, thump, thump.

"Get back!" Deidre shrieked.

Abby heard a long stretching sound followed by an explosive pop, then the sickening crunch of something heavy and solid striking flesh.

"Deidre!" Delacroix cried. "She's hurt. Stay here, Abby."

Deidre whimpered. Metal rang against rock. Spid roared with triumph, a roar not muffled by The Skin, a roar that rattled Abby's ribs.

"Now you will experience my supreme power in action." the troll snarled. "The wrath of Spid will send you all into oblivion."

The echoes of the five-armed drummer's next-to-last three-beat stanza and the louder sound of Noah's second strike, four beats, punctuated the troll's threat.

Noah will never make it. He'll never beat the demon drummer back to The Skin. Unless...

Thirty feet, Abby reminded herself. Screening out the shouts of those swarming down from the tunnels, she strode toward the sound of Spid's voice. Six steps. Eight. Ten. She knelt. A blast of fetid breath burned her eyes and nose, the odor of concentrated evil. Her knees touched the cold rock and she heard Spid's oily purr.

"Ahhh. Miss Keene. So you've seen the light? So to speak." He laughed and trailed a scaly finger down her cheek. "You've come to kiss the ring of your new master?"

Abby forced herself not to flinch. The final beats reverberated from Spid's drummer. He'll start down the cliff now, she thought. With his five arms, he'll move faster than Noah. He'll arrive at The Skin first. How can he not?

She heard the thump of Noah's five beat midpoint. Deidre moaned and Delacroix launched a curse in some kind of island dialect as a ripping, rending noise came from The Skin. Was Yurk thrashing his way through to his master?

"Pleasedon'tkillme," she blurted, running her words together in a gurgling, lisping, scared-little-girl string. "I'llfollowyouanddowhateveryouwant!"

Spid chuckled. "Well, I don't know, Abby. This comes at rather the last moment." Noah's three beats sounded from above. "A more cynical sort than I might judge you insincere."

Abby heard the malicious pleasure in his taunting voice. Where was the demon drummer?

"This will prove my sincerity." Abby reached into her back pocket, pulled out the parchment, and thrust it toward Spid. "Delacroix's plan to defend the tunnels from your troops after the breakthrough. I stole it."

She felt the reptilian hand pluck the parchment from her. "I see. A token of your profound esteem and fear of unpleasant death, eh?"

This is it. She crossed her fingers. What if he didn't read it out loud? What if I didn't divide it right? But it had to be. It had to.

"Let's see now. Thuh-dur?"

Good. *T-I-R*. Thuh-dur. He's doing it.

She heard Noah's final four beats and wondered if he heard the other drummer and realized how far he'd fallen behind.

"Kuh-neh?" Continued the Troll. What is..."Kuh-neh?"

Abby would have never guessed *K-D-E-S*, was pronounced "Kuh-neh."

"Ess-shull?" A small note of suspicion crept into Spid's voice as he read the *C-X-O-S-L*. "What kind of battle plan is this?"

"I don't know." Abby answered. Pleasepleasepleaseplease. The next two words. Say them. *K-N-U* and *R-P-L-V*. Say them. Say them!

"Nut-Prr? Revale? Gibberish. All of it." She heard Spid crumple the parchment. "This is worthless."

Not to me.

The wheels whirred in Abby's head. Thuh-dur. Kuh-neh. Esshul. Nutpur. Revale. She threw the whole thing together into one long string in her mind, then redivided it. At first it eluded her. But then she made the connection from the last two words. Nut-pur-re-vale. Not prevail. The rest came in a flash.

Leaping to her feet, she threw her head back and screamed at the top of her lungs. "The darkness shall not prevail."

A vicious buzz, like a million angry hornets, sliced the air above her.

Abby turned and stumbled. Hairy fingers gripped hers and a small voice said "Uh-oh." She heard Deidre's sonic sword hiss and a great roar from Spid.

The buzzing grew louder and louder. Uh-oh towed her backwards.

The buzzing swelled to a horrendous level.

Zzeeezpop.

Silence.

Uh-oh whispered his name again, and Yurk howled. "Hey, what's the big idea, Boss, who turned out the lights?"

"Yes!" Abby pumped her fist into the air.

But now came the really hard part. Noah had to believe, had to trust her. And there was no time for lessons, no time to experiment like she had. He had to have instant faith.

"Jump, Noah! Jump to The Skin. Now. Do it. Jump!"

Her shrieked commands echoed back to her. The final word repeated over and over again as if from a record stuck on the last groove. "Jump. Jump. Jump."

CHAPTER 35

"Jump, ump, ump, ump, ump."

The trailing echo of Abby's insistent voice reached Noah as he clung to a narrow jut of rock below the ledge where he'd pounded the glowing drum.

Jump? That's crazy!

But this whole adventure was crazy. Dancing across molten rock, riding the Galloopapede, battling gargoyles, zipping at mind-bending speed up and down in the Vorv. Crazy, just plain crazy. So if Abby, the personification of logic, told him to jump, then why not jump? It was no crazier than anything else. And the other drummer was far ahead.

He turned one foot and then the other, pivoting to face out into the chamber. At least it was so dark he couldn't see the platform, couldn't anticipate the moment he'd splatter like a bug on a windshield.

Relaxing his grip, Noah jerked his drumsticks from his belt and launched himself, swan diving into the inky abyss. All his exhaustion, all the tension accumulated over the course of his strange journey, funneled into a wild yell. "Ah-yooooooo!"

He spread his arms wider to embrace the air and fell into thunderous stillness, cool air rushing by, his damp hair trailing behind him, his shirt fluttering.

Then a low murmur hummed in his ears. A glowing cloud of hazy green light overtook him with a deepening buzz, rippled beneath him, and disappeared.

Down, down, down he sailed.

How fast did falling objects fall? Abby would know the equation to compute that. Not that there was any point. Tears formed in the corners of his eyes and were swept away by the quiet wind.

Brighter now, the green cloud billowed below him.

I'm going to hit it!

And he did.

The buzzing glow enveloped him. He felt heat and something else—a force? Life? Thought?

Yes, within the profound buzz, he heard the distinct murmuring of individual voices. He couldn't extract words, but it felt like they were comforting him, reassuring him.

The downward rush slowed. The humming cloud cocooned him. His fall stopped. His feet swung beneath him, his toes brushed the platform.

The buzzing ebbed and he recognized it for what it was—the sound of millions, no billions, of microscopic wings beating. The Zezzue. Somehow Abby had harnessed their power. Or perhaps Abby had merely requested their help and they had consented to give it.

No time to think about that now. Where's Spid?

As he pounded the golden drum, Noah had seen Spid break through and Deidre lash out and then fall under the troll's ax.

The Darksucker cloud cast a dim light, so dim he couldn't see how far he was from The Skin or who stood between him and the place he must strike three times. Would Spid cut him to shreds before he got there?

The green cloud released him.

His feet hit the platform.

A slender beam of light fell on one edge of The Skin.

Noah ran, drumsticks clutched in his outstretched hands. The green cloud swept along ahead of him, a mirage of dim light in a desert of darkness.

As he pulled back his stick to strike the first blow, he saw a shadowy figure on the other side of The Skin, one of its five arms cocked.

Noah snapped his right arm forward and struck the drum.

"Kuhboom."

The sound rang out in the darkness.

"Kuhboom."

The twin sound came so close behind the air shimmered.

Whose stick hit first?

Noah didn't know.

But he knew he had to concentrate on the ritual. The three beats that began the challenge came five seconds apart. The final beats couldn't vary.

Light bloomed around him as he counted it out in his head. He glanced over his shoulder and saw Spid, lips pulled back from teeth like spikes, hands gripping a five-bladed ax. The troll strode toward him. Yurk, wielding a long spear, trotted after his master.

"One thousand five." Noah kept his eyes on Spid as he brought his stick down on the flaccid surface of The Skin.

The other hand, the other stick, hit the other side of The Skin.

K..K..Uh..Uh..Buh..B..Boom.

Noah heard a definite lag between strikes. But, with his attention riveted on the advancing troll, he still had no sense of who hit first.

"One thousand one."

His muscles tightened as Spid raised the ax.

"One thousand two."

He wouldn't move. He couldn't. Everything depended on him. If Spid cut off his right arm, he'd drum with his left.

"One thousand three."

Maybe he could duck, take a glancing blow and—

Something hurtled through the air. A pair of large brown feet kicked Spid full in the chest.

"Oof."

The troll crashed to the platform. The far edge of The Skin convulsed and three more fierce creatures squeezed through the rubbery surface with a series of ripping pops.

"One thousand four."

Delacroix rebounded to his feet.

Voorp.

The sound wave from Deidre's sonic sword walloped Yurk. The ogre yelped and scuttled away.

Spid roared. He stood. He charged.

Crunch.

Spid's ax found flesh. Delacroix fell.

Time.

Noah struck The Skin.

CHAPTER 36

Kuh-Kuh-Boom-Boom.

The drum strokes sounded like rolling thunder, thunder that followed a thousand-mile-long lightning bolt.

And this time Noah heard a definite separation of the beats. Perhaps an eighth of a second.

Had he struck first? Or had his five-armed foe?

The Skin knew.

It throbbed, quivered and glowed. Rainbows of color swirled across it, racing and chasing each other.

Noah's flesh tingled and he felt the hair on his arms ripple and prickle. Swiveling his head, he saw everyone locked in place, frozen like the gargoyles under his gaze. All eyes turned toward the stone face where he and Abby had placed the two orbs. The stones, too, glowed. Color radiated in synch with the flashing strobe of The Skin.

Bands of rippling color flew around the cavern, flashing across the faces of all of those gathered on the platform. Faster and faster and faster the colors twirled until Noah could no longer make out individual tints and they blended into unearthly blinding whiteness. Only Abby didn't squint or shade her eyes.

The light compressed, forming a thin beam that connected the orbs and the center of The Skin. The beam arched high above the platform. An image formed, a translucent figure, reed thin, with a flowing robe.

"The convergent solstice has passed." A high, wavering voice, flat and expressionless delivered the information. "The drums have spoken. The prophecy is fulfilled. Humbug Mountain lives. You have satisfied destiny."

"Melacherub," Delacroix said in a pain-tinged whisper.

Melacherub. That was good, right?

Noah held his breath. Every muscle in his body quivered as the image of the departed wizard surveyed them, its eyes without judgment.

"The Skin is now healed." The apparition pointed and spoke again. "Let those from Above and those from Beneath remain apart until the next alignment of the myriad components of our universe."

Then, as suddenly as it had appeared, the figure shrank into itself and vanished. The beams of light streamed back into the two orbs and The Skin. The electric crackle that filled the air sputtered and died.

Noah put his hand out and touched The Skin. It felt like smooth wet leather. He tapped it gently with a drumstick and got only a dull "thung."

"You haven't won yet!" Spid roared.

Noah whirled. Spid, Yurk, and three of the troll's grotesque soldiers raised their terrible weapons. Footsteps pounded on the narrow trails and ledges high above; the tunnel defenders rushing to their aid.

"Noah. Catch." Deidre, blood running down her side, banged a sonic sword against her decibelt and flung the vibrating weapon toward him butt-end first.

317

He plucked it from the air. His sword. He hadn't seen her bring it. He raised it to the ready position and scanned the platform.

Spid advanced on Delacroix, who lay on his back, feet raised. Blood welled from one of his shoulders.

Yurk circled behind Abby, Uh-oh, and the hermit, his spear raised.

"I've got Captain Drool," Deidre called. She backed Yurk away with a sonic wave. "You take the three musty-teers behind you. Then we'll help the Pettifog."

Noah swung his battle fork at the four-armed reptilian soldiers. Warding off their blows, he blasted them down like dominoes.

"Piece of cake," he called out, and turned to take on Spid.

Too late.

The troll sprang at Delacroix, battle ax flashing.

Noah raised his sonic sword and loosed a bolt of sound. Spid howled, but raised his ax.

Lix rolled away from the first blow.

Spid's ax rang against the platform. Sparks and chips of stone flew.

Noah thrust with the sonic sword. The troll dodged the sound wave and raised the ax again. Delacroix flopped and rolled. A blade struck his thigh with a sickening crunch.

Noah released another wave.

The troll roared, yanked the ax loose, and came at Noah, blood dripping from the blade.

Deidre darted in and blasted Spid, turning him aside. Noah hit him with another bolt. Spid barely faltered.

Delacroix writhed, a red stream running from his leg, spreading across the platform.

Deidre raised her face to the ledges above where grungoids and humans, in single file on the tight trails, swarmed toward the platform. "Hurry."

She aimed the sonic sword. Voooooorrrrrpppp.

"I'm running out of juice." Deidre thumped the butt of the sonic sword against the decibelt. "It's not charging. I'll take Spid. Watch behind you!"

Noah spun to see Yurk and the staggering reptilian soldiers closing in. He swung the sonic sword and the squatty creatures fell. Yurk stumbled but kept coming.

"I'm running low, too!" Noah backed toward Deidre and checked the ledges. A few more seconds before help arrived.

"Despite my most considerable skills as a commanding general, and my infallible battle plan, it appears we are outnumbered." Spid's pretentious voice rang out.

Spid? Giving up?

The troll's evil leer dissolved into a jaw-drop.

"Throw down your weapons immediately and surrender to the Above-ite nearest you."

Blinking in confusion, Yurk stood firm, but the reptilian soldiers' weapons clattered to the platform.

The troll's lips hadn't moved.

"He did it again," Deidre crowed.

Noah turned to see Uh-oh, chest thrust out, chin imperiously jutted skyward. "I, the Grand Exalted Garboon, command you," Uh-oh roared in imitation of Spid.

A dozen men from Shroomtown, Benny and Peitr in the lead, hurtled up the steps and surrounded the reptilian soldiers. Chillout vaulted to the platform and raced toward Delacroix.

"You idiots!" Spid darted toward Uh-oh.

The grungoid zipped away, mimicking the cry. "You idiots."

"Yurk," Spid bellowed. "Do something."

"Uh, okay, Boss."

More of Deidre's compatriots, grungoids, and other members of the Above population swarmed to the platform, forming a bristling circle around Spid.

Noah lowered his failing sonic sword and turned toward Delacroix.

Something clattered behind him.

Deidre screamed.

Noah swiveled to see Yurk yanking her off balance with a grip on her braided hair. The ogre put the point of an obsidian knife to her throat. Deidre clamped her jaw, pure hatred in her eyes.

"Got her, Boss," Yurk drooled. "Want I should slice her up?"

"Perhaps that would be our best option, Yurk." Seemingly oblivious to the weapons that corralled him, Spid continued to pontificate. "An object lesson to these peasants to show them the futility of their opposition to the all-knowing and all seeing wisdom of my—"

"Noooooo!"

A dervish in brown robes flew at Yurk. The hermit brought the wooden staff down on his head.

Deidre twitched away from the knife, spun, and kneed the ogre in the stomach. Yurk doubled over, covering his head with his lengthy arms.

Again and again the hermit struck. His hat flew off, revealing a clump of matted, unruly gray hair.

"Noooooo!"

Noah stared. Was that a woman's voice coming from the hermit?

"Unnhh!" Yurk dropped his knife and groveled on the platform. "I give up! I give up! Don't hit me again!"

The hermit stepped back, panting, and leaned on the staff.

"Go to your master," Deidre commanded Yurk.

As the ogre belly-crawled toward Spid, Deidre tugged at the hermit's hair. "Mother?"

Noah blinked. "Eve?"

The gray wig tumbled to the ground and, yes, there was Eve's hair, pinned in a roll at the nape of her neck.

"Mother." Deidre wrapped her arms around Eve. "Thank you."

Eve smiled, kissed Deidre on the forehead, then disengaged her daughter's arms. "Mr. Delacroix needs me." She picked up Deidre's battle fork and handed it to her, then hurried to help Chillout tend to Delacroix.

"Give it up, Spid. You're done."

Noah turned to see Abby, inside the circle of Spid's captors, her finger leveled at the glowering troll.

"Ah, Miss Keene." Spid's tone swung back to the salesman-smooth tones of his pre-battle persona. "Come to bask in the glow of your victory, have you? Well, your celebration may be just a wee bit premature. As long as I possess the Shadow Stone, and can channel its power, I cannot be vanquished. I...uh...I..."

Spid frowned. Sliding both hands beneath his armor, he frisked himself. "Yurk!" he shouted at the ogre Deidre herded into the circle of captors. "The Shadow Stone, Yurk. Hand it to me. Now!"

The ogre's face twisted into a sickly grimace. "I don't have it, Boss."

"You don't have it?!? What do you mean you don't have it?"

"I mean you, uh, you left it." Yurk pointed toward The Skin "Over on the other side."

321

"You're quite mistaken, Yurk. I would never make a blunder such as that." Spid snapped his scaly fingers. "Hand over the stone."

"I can't, Boss. You said you'd go back for it after you killed everybody on the platform. You said once The Skin opened all the way up you—"

Spid's five-headed ax whistled through the air. The ogre ducked. "Cheez, Boss, careful with that thing. It's pointy and sharp."

Abby's voice, cocky, almost impudent, taunted the infuriated troll. "Like I said, Spid. It's over. Lose gracefully. Show some class."

"Class! Class! You impudent little pipsqueak of a girl. You won because you were lucky. Lucky!" The echoes from his roar careened through the cavern. "And we haven't lost. Not yet. We have the will, the courage, and the conviction. We will fight on and many of you will die."

He unsheathed a knife and handed it to the ogre. "It isn't easy to kill a troll. Or an ogre. "And we will fight to the death, right, Yurk?"

Yurk cleared his throat and confirmed in a sickly quaver of a voice. "Uh...dit...dittoes, Boss. To the...to the...death?"

"No!!! The darkness *shall not* prevail!" Abby's words rang out, not as a challenge but as undeniable fact.

Spid laughed. "No, you are wrong again, Miss Keene. The darkness most definitely *shall* prevail."

"Horsehockey," Abby muttered from the side of her mouth.

The lights in the chamber flickered. Noah tilted his eyes toward the roof and saw the Zezzue begin to roil.

Yurk tugged at Spid's robe. "Uh, Boss," the ogre pointed up at the ceiling, "I don't think—"

"The drumming hurt my ears, Mr. Spid." Abby cupped her hands at the sides of her head. "I didn't hear you."

As if he were a Shakespearean actor cued to start his soliloquy, Spid took a stride forward, thrust his chest out, jutted his chin and projected his voice to the furthest ledge. "The darkness *SHALL* prevail."

As the echoes died, Noah heard the distant whirr of Zezzue wings. He looked up to see the wild and vibrant colors of the agitated creatures strobing across the ceiling.

Spid raised his ax. "In a moment, you won't need your ears, you impudent little brat."

Benny stepped in front of Abby to intercept the blow, but before Spid could strike, the light in the chamber dimmed to near darkness.

"And you won't need *any* of *your* senses," Abby said.

A huge patch of white light burst from the blackness of the ceiling. Like a parachute, it dropped to a position directly over the troll and his second-in-command. The buzzing of the Darksuckers swelled as it fell.

"Wait," Spid commanded. "I was tricked. I didn't mean it. You cannot do this. As the Grand Exalted Garboon of the—"

Before he could say another word, Spid and Yurk were enveloped in a mass of furiously buzzing Darksuckers. The tiny creatures yanked the troll and the ogre off their feet and hovered for a moment, rotating like a funnel cloud, revealing a hand and then another, one encrusted with spots of green drool, the other bearing a thick ring.

"See yuh, Spid," Abby called. "Next time we play Spiddle, I'll spot you a couple thousand points."

The finger twitched. The ring clanged to the floor, rolled to Abby's feet, and spun to a stop.

Vuh-zooorp.

The undulating cloud of Zezzue shot upward, speeding toward the high reaches of the cavern. Noah watched them rotate into a narrow beam, then shoot through a tiny opening in the distant ceiling.

323

For a few seconds, total blackness encased them, then the Zezzue returned and blinked on.

Noah looked around, taking stock. Delacroix, wounds bandaged with strips from Eve's robe, lay with his head in her lap while Chillout massaged his feet. Deidre stood over them, staring at the armless drummer, her head cocked to one side, a finger against her chin. Uh-oh, following the Shroomtowners and the captive soldiers, marched toward the edge of the platform, scratching his stomach and pooching his lips in and out.

Abby stood alone in the center of the platform, her eyes clenched. Noah strode over and wrapped his arms around her. "Look at me, Abby. Don't be afraid."

She raised her face to his and opened her eyes. The dark screen across them had vanished.

"I knew the way, Noah. I really did know the way."

"Yes, you did, Abby." He kissed her forehead. "I love you, little sister."

CHAPTER 37

"That stuff she pours down us, it tastes vile." Delacroix sat propped against several pillows in a bed carved into the rock of his chamber.

Even the mention of the root, fungus, and scrubbage concoction Eve fed them made Noah's taste buds shrivel. Mokblag, she called it. It tasted as ugly as it sounded. "Yeah. Nasty to the max," he answered, scrunching down into a beanbag chair Chillout hauled up from The Last Place You Look. "But I feel stronger. How about you?"

"*Oui.* It is true," the big man conceded.

Exhausted, dehydrated, and in general shredded from his ordeal, Noah regained most of his strength within a day. Delacroix, who many feared would not survive the fearsome wounds inflicted by Spid, bounced back in three.

What was it Eve told him? "Some people say I'm a witch?" Well, Noah didn't know about that, but Delacroix was living proof she knew how to heal.

Abby and Deidre had gone off for a last ride in the Vorv. Since the battle, the two of them did everything together. And he and Deidre were...well, he didn't really know but he had hopes. His lips tingled with the memory of her pre-battle kiss. The smile that crept onto his face must have betrayed his thoughts because the amusement in Lix's voice was unmistakable.

"She is quite a girl, my daughter?"

"No. Uh, I mean yes, she is. I like her a lot."

"And I know she thinks much of you, my friend. She has told me."

"Really?"

Delacroix winked. "But do not say that I told you so. She would forgive me not."

"Sure. Of course. Lix?" Noah still had trouble using the legendary drummer's nickname.

"Yes?"

"When did you know? That Eve was really Melanie?"

"Before I knew she was Eve."

"Huh?"

"As I lay bleeding on the ground, visions appeared to me. I could not distinguish what was real and what was not. It was like..." He paused, searching for words. "Did you ever see one of those little books that when you flipped the pages very fast it made for a cartoon?"

"I think so." Noah vaguely remembered his dad making something like that for him years ago.

"It was like that. Except the little pictures were all different. Memories, hallucinations, real events. I could not tell."

"You were close to death."

"Yes. Very close. And one of those pictures was my Melanie. And I did not know if it was only a memory. But then she smiled. That wonderful smile. And she told me everything would be all right. And I knew I had found her. Or perhaps she had found me."

"But you must have suspected...I mean, Deidre is..."

"She is beautiful, yes? A brown like coffee and cream. Yes. But I did never see her closely, Noah, until we were at the skin. And then you and I were drumming and there was no time to wonder."

"She told me she knew you were her father the minute she saw you up close. She said it was like looking into a mirror."

Delacroix shrugged. "Most unfortunate she has not gotten less of me and more of her mother." He grew a little misty-eyed. "She came to me, my girl, and called me father and told me I must get well because there were many things she needed yet to tell me—and for me to tell her. So, I do as I am told. I drink Melanie's evil brew and I sleep. And now I am nearly healed."

"Did Melanie tell you how she became Eve? And the hermit?"

"There are many gaps yet in her memory, you know? She can recall only preparing herself for the crash." A faraway look filled Delacroix's face. "A blinding flash of light and then pain. Awakening, she crawls. A great distance she crawls and then there is nothing. And she awakens again to find herself inside the mountain. With the people of Shroomtown. She needs a name. They call her Eve. Miraculously, the baby in her is not harmed. And so Deidre arrives."

"Why did Eve, uh, I mean Melanie, call her Deidre?"

"My love's best friend, her bridesmaid, was called Deidre. Without knowing, she linked to her past. The human mind it is a strange thing, no?"

"No. I mean yes." Noah heard the slap of shoes on stone and turned to see Abby and Deidre. He scrambled out of the chair. "Here they are now."

As they drew nearer, talking and laughing, he marveled at how comfortable they were with each other. Almost like sisters.

"So, it's decided? You'll come stay with us?" Abby asked.

Deidre smiled. "Yes. First I need to get to know my dad. But then I would like to see the world. The other world. Out there."

"I can't wait. You can help me keep No-way from messing up."

"But what will you tell your father? How will you explain who I am?" Deidre stretched out a hand and touched Noah's hair with her fingertips. It sent a tingle down his spine.

Abby shrugged. "Noah will think of something, won't you, brother?"

Noah felt himself blush. "Uh, sure. I'll come up with a plan."

"He'll come up with a plan." Deidre and Abby looked at each other, then broke out in giggles.

Noah scowled at them. "You're ganging up on me."

Deidre grinned, bent over Delacroix, and adjusted the bandage on his thigh. "Did you eat your mokblag, Papa?" Noah noticed she had picked up a little of the lilt of Delacroix's speech patterns.

Delacroix gave a loud mock groan. "The cure is worse than the sickness."

Deidre rubbed his bald head then planted a kiss on his cheek. "Suck it up or when mother gets back she'll double your dosage."

"Suck it up?" Delacroix wrinkled his brow. "Such language from a young lady, Deidre."

"Hey, I'm entitled." She touched the bandage on her shoulder that covered the healing ax wound. "I had to eat it too."

"Misery, she loves the company. Does Melanie return soon?" Delacroix's voice took on a tone of fond wistfulness.

"Don't know. Said she had to pick up a few things. You know how she is." Deidre smiled. "Maybe she'll bring you some of those little snack cakes."

"All of that time," clucked Delacroix. "The hermit would bring me things from the outside. And I did not know it was Melanie. Could not see her beneath the grit and the grime and the scowling."

Noah could relate. He hadn't made the connection either. Or recognized that Eve and old Hannah were the same person.

Delacroix betrayed his pride. "She plays the part well, yes? She tricks the audience. And with her amnesia, she did not recognize me. Except maybe faintly, in her heart." He touched his chest with the stump of one arm.

Noah and Abby exchanged glances. Time for them to go. "Here. These are yours." Noah pulled the monogrammed drumsticks from his belt.

Delacroix shook his head emphatically. "No. No. Of this, I will not hear. You must keep them, use them. Of what use are they to an armless drummer?"

"But—"

Delacroix cut him off. "It is destiny, Noah. Remember. We play our parts as they are written. Mine is to live here. With my family." He smiled at Deidre who put a hand against his cheek. "And yours is to share your gift with others. To feel and hear and play. The sticks must go with you."

The finality of his tone made Noah bite back further objection.

"Play that funky music, white boy." Noah heard Chillout's voice and turned expecting to see him. Instead, a sunglass-wearing Uh-oh slouched in the doorway with the ultra-casual hipster stance of the other grungoid. As the real Chillout appeared from a nearby tunnel, Uh-oh added. "It's been a stone gas working the big room with you, my main man. Slide back soon."

"Man, that cat is the eeriest." Chillout shook his head. "But she's cute, so I may let her hang with me a while."

She? Her?

If there had been a competition for synchronized double takes, Noah, Abby, Deidre, and Delacroix would have won hands-down.

All that time traveling with Uh-oh and he never knew. Noah's mind spun as he tried to remember if he undressed in front of her. Then he smiled. What did it matter now?

"Uh, little chickie." Chillout turned to Abby. "I got a, like, token of my esteem to drop on you. Kind of a going away thing, you dig?" The grungoid pulled out a velvet-covered ring box and presented it.

"For me? Why Chillout, you didn't need to..."

"Open it, *ma cherie*," Delacroix commanded.

Abby took the box from Chillout's outstretched hand and eased the lid open.

What Noah saw give him the shivers. The thick ring had been forged from what looked like polished iron. The stone, a gleaming eye of dark green, scattered light in all directions.

"Spid's ring," Abby exclaimed.

The lights in Delacroix's chamber dimmed and transformed to a brooding red. Noah felt apprehension tight in his chest.

Abby snapped the box shut. Instantly, the Darksuckers returned to a soft warm glow. "It...it's beautiful but kind of...of....I don't know, intimidating. I'm not sure I..."

Delacroix interrupted. "The ring itself is not evil. Not unless it lives on the finger of the evil one. Since the Chameleon Stone now must stay with us, we thought the ring might be for you, a what do you call it?"

"Souvenir?"

"Yes. A memento of what we have gone through together. You will keep it safe, no?"

Abby looked thoughtful. "Yes. I will keep it." She slid it into her pocket, walked to Delacroix's bed, and hugged him. Noah saw tears slide down her cheeks. "Thank you Lix. For showing me. For trusting me."

"Bye-bye, Noah." Uh-oh took two quick steps and hurled herself at Noah. Before he knew it, she'd wrapped herself around him and snared him in a tight embrace. "I'll miss you."

As fast as she sprang, she released her grip, dropped to the ground, and darted over to pick something from Chillout's skin. Examining it for a second, she popped it into her mouth.

Noah suppressed a gag. He'd never get used to that. "Goodbye, Uh-oh, I'll miss you, too. And you, Chillout." He put a hand on Delacroix's broad shoulder. "Goodbye, Lix. Can we drum together again sometime?"

"I would like that, Noah."

"Great. When I come I'll bring you some CDs for your collection."

Abby shifted from foot to foot. "We better get on it, brother."

"You guys go ahead." Deidre jogged off toward her sleeping chamber. "I'll meet you up at the tunnel."

CHAPTER 38

As they walked away, Noah felt a heavy sadness, a sensation not unlike the one he experienced when he hesitated at the door of his house before running away. He was leaving something behind, something special and unique. A family.

But now, it was time to try to repair the family he left. He felt his feet moving faster and heard Abby scrambling to keep up. He smiled despite the tears welling in his eyes.

Just as they arrived at the exit tunnel, Deidre caught up. In her hands she carried a pair of boots. "You're going to need these. You can't go out barefoot. Who knows how far you'll have to walk."

As Noah accepted her gift, his gaze met the warrior girl's and held. When she blinked, he grinned and admired the boots. They were much like the ones on her feet, made of some kind of plant fiber that felt like soft leather.

"And here," Deidre tossed him a pair of cloth socks. "Try them on."

Obeying, he sat on a nearby boulder, slid the socks over his feet, then slipped on the boots. They fit perfectly. "How did you...?"

"Abby knew your size. I had Mikkal cobble a rush order. He makes shoes for all the Shroomtowners."

Noah stood and walked back and forth, feeling the boots conform to his feet like another layer of skin. "Deed, they're amazing. Thank you. I...I..."

"C'mon for cripe's sake," Abby needled him. "Kiss her already. I'll wait in the tunnel." She stomped off, hooting with laughter.

Deidre blushed. "If you don't kiss me I'll have to take out my battle fork and give you a little jolt."

She pretended to draw the weapon she hadn't worn since they returned from The Skin. "And now that I think about it, I still owe you for that little incident at the Temple of Cheltnor."

Noah grinned. He took Deidre in his arms and pulled her close. He felt awkward and clumsy and warm and wonderful. "Deed, I..."

"Shhhh." She put a finger against his lips, then removed it and sealed his mouth with her own. Noah felt a tickling tingle and closed his eyes.

After a time, she pulled away, kissing the tip of his nose. "You'd better go," she said, in a voice even huskier than usual.

"Yeah," he choked. "I'll miss you Deidre."

"Knock, it off. Soldiers don't cry. Besides I'm coming out there. To your world. You said you'd take me to a movie. Remember?"

"I remember."

"Careful, Deidre, he hogs the popcorn." Abby called from the mouth of the tunnel.

The little sneak. She was watching the whole time.

"I'll remember that, Abby. And once I learn what popcorn is, I'll make sure I get my fair share." The warrior girl hugged Abby, gave Noah's hand a squeeze, then turned on her heel and jogged down the trail.

Noah looked after her until she turned and waved. He returned the gesture, wanting to run to her, but knowing he couldn't. "Let's go home, Ab-normal," he told his sister.

"Okay, No-way."

Laughing, they walked quickly along the tunnel. "Abby."

"What?"

"Remember what we talked about before the battle. We can't tell anybody, anything. About in here, right? Not even Dad."

"Who'd believe us, anyway? We'd be confined to Shrinksville getting our heads examined until the next century."

"Shrinksville?" Noah chuckled. "You sound like Chillout."

Abby said nothing for a moment, and then asked in a small voice. "What *are* we gonna tell Dad, Noah? About where we've been for—" He saw her glance at a delicate silver wristwatch she retrieved on a final scavenging trip to The Last Place You Look. It read 3:03 PM.

Noah glanced at his own watch, a waterproof model Uh-oh brought him from that same expedition. It read 10:27 AM. "How long do you think it's been?"

Abby shrugged. "A week? I don't know. Maybe, we could say we went to San Francisco and hung out with some people we met."

"Don't think that story would stand up to questioning, Ab-normal. You're the brain factory. You come up with something. Something that won't get us grounded until the next time we have to save the world."

"Save the world." Abby snorted and broke into a laugh.

Save the world. Noah chuckled. It sounded ludicrous. Even if it was the truth.

A sudden thought sobered him. What if Dad was just as inflexible when they got back? What if their disappearance made things worse?

Before long, the tunnel ended at a rock wall. "Grab your sticks, please," Abby commanded. "And sync with the beat."

Noah pulled his drumsticks out of the backpack and listened for the heartbeat of Humbug Mountain.

"Thrum-thrum, thrum-thrum, thrum-thrum."

He let it seep into his brain and radiate through his nerve endings.

Picking a flat spot on the wall, he began to tap out a counter rhythm, talking back to the mountain.

"Thrum-thrum, tickuh-tum. Thrum-thrum, tickuh-tum."

When the beat shifted, he did too.

"Thrum-thrum, tickey, tickey, tum thrumthrum."

He heard rock groan and grate and then Abby's jubilant cry.

"Noah. The ocean."

The rock slid back, revealing a ledge above the Pacific. The moon, a shade less than full in a clear sky, shone on the water. To the north, the lights of Port Anvil twinkled in the distance. The beach he and Abby had walked stretched far below them. Noah saw the glow of a campfire and flashed back to his encounter with Old Hannah (or Eve, or Melanie or the hermit, depending on the day), the dance, and the vision.

They stepped onto the ledge. The rock slid shut behind them.

"Home, Noah. We're almost home."

"Yeah, home," was all he could think to say, and a wave of anxious gloom crashed over him as they picked their way down a narrow trail that angled toward the landward side of the mountain and the road.

Glancing up at the distant stars, Noah asked Abby the question that had been on his mind since they returned from The Skin. "How did you know? How did you know how to break down the word from the Spiddle game to make the phrase that would persuade the Zezzue to catch me?"

"Well, I didn't *know*. Not exactly," Abby said defensively. "I, uh, made a logical assumption."

"You guessed?"

"It was a little more than a guess, big brother. Here's the way I figured it. As crazy and out of whack as everything was in there, it all made its own kind of sense. You just had to figure out the rules. It was just like any math or science problem. I knew it had been several words in an ancient language, so I took the letters and divided them up the same way I did the scrunched up sign over the door of The Last Place You Look. Three letters, then four, then five. Then three and then four again. The same pattern as your beats on the high drum. It had to be right. Just had to."

"And it was," he said quietly. "It was exactly right."

"But more important, I had to *believe* it was right. And *you* had to believe in *me*."

Noah nodded, thinking again how enormous his leap of faith had been. They didn't talk for a while after that. When the trail widened and then emptied into a grassy meadow near the bottom of the mountain, Noah knelt and ran his fingers through the grass. Not moss. Real grass.

Beyond the meadow, the trail wound through a stand of trees and then up a bank toward a small park beside the road. As they climbed the bank, Abby grabbed his hand. "Listen."

The voices of a man and a woman drifted on the night. Noah didn't recognize the woman's voice. But he knew the man's. Dad.

"We could try the west trail again." Dad's voice.

"Whatever you think, Sean. But you're exhausted."

"But they've got to be out here somewhere. They've got to be. I feel it. Stronger than I felt it before."

"That's Jennifer talking to him," Abby breathed.

Mrs. Ramsden. Out here with Dad, searching for him and Abby.

"Let's go."

He tugged free of Abby's grip, leaped up the bank, and strode through a patch of moonlight toward the couple sitting across from each other at a wooden picnic table. Abby followed at his heels.

As they drew near, Mrs. Ramsden looked up. Her eyes widened, sparkling in the dim light. Her mouth opened, but no sound came out.

"I'll never forgive myself for this, Jen," Sean Keene told her. "Noah was trying to talk to me for the longest time and I just didn't listen. I couldn't hear, I..."

Jennifer Ramsden gulped air and pointed across his shoulder. "Sean. Look. It's them."

"Wha...Noah? Abby?" He turned, legs tangling in the bench.

Noah saw tears flowing down his cheeks. "Dad," he heard himself say. "We're back."

Sean Keene raced toward them, arms open. "Noah. Abby. I...I'm so...Oh, you're safe. You're safe."

Noah felt himself encompassed by his father's right arm as Abby was enfolded in the left. He returned the hug, and felt tears rolling from his eyes. Over his father's shoulder he saw Mrs. Ramsden blotting at her face with a tissue. He smiled at her. It felt good. It felt right. Now for the next step. He took a deep breath. "Dad."

The word came out with a crack in the middle. Noah cleared his throat and tried again. "Dad, there's something I need to tell you."

His father didn't release the hug. "Noah, you don't have to—"

"Yes, Dad, I do."

Sean Keene released Noah and stepped back a couple of feet, his face tight. Noah saw Abby's brow furrow, her bottom lip curling into a pout. *She thinks I'm going to blow it. Well, I guess she needs one more lesson in trust.* He took the verbal leap. "Dad, I want to apologize to you. I was so hung up on trying to have my say that I didn't realize I wasn't listening to you, either. You were right about not giving me more responsibility. I hadn't earned it. And running away was a horrible, inconsiderate thing to do."

His father's face didn't change. Noah pulled in a breath. "Please don't get mad at Abby. She came along to keep me out of trouble. And..." He and Abby exchanged glances. "And she did. Mostly. But it was my fault, not hers. I'm so sorry for all the pain I caused you. I'll accept any punishment you come up with."

Mrs. Ramsden sniffed and blotted her face again.

Sean Keene's face didn't change.

Abby looked up at her father, then shrugged off his arm and took Noah's hand. "If you punish Noah," she insisted, "you'll have to punish me, too. I was the brains of the operation. So there."

Sean Keene threw back his head and roared with laughter. "Oh, Abby. Noah. What a pair you are. What a pair."

He rubbed tears away with his shirtsleeve. "I think we've all been punished enough since your mother died. I didn't... I didn't realize how selfish I was, how wrapped up in my own sorrow. I forgot I still had a family and a lot to be thankful for. I need to start showing that." He held out his hand to Noah. "And I need to listen better, too."

Noah raised his hand and grasped his father's. Abby wrapped her arms around both of them and squeezed. In a moment, Noah felt other arms, and realized Mrs. Ramsden, no, he'd call her Jennifer, had joined the embrace. If she made Dad happy, that was what counted.

"So, um, where were you guys?"

The question from his father carried no hint of accusation. It was almost matter-of-fact. But Noah felt his body stiffen. "We were lost, Dad. Really lost,"

Abby kicked Noah in the ankle. "But we found our way. We found our way home."

Sean Keene stepped back and studied them for a moment. Jennifer Ramsden laid a hand on his shoulder and he shrugged. "You're safe. That's all I really care about."

"Are you hungry?" Jennifer asked.

"We could eat," Noah and Abby answered together. "A lot," Noah added.

"We'll stop for something at the all-night diner," Sean Keene said with a laugh. "How about a clam basket?"

"Yum." Abby darted ahead to the truck, Noah in pursuit.

It was a tight fit, but, with Jennifer sitting in the middle and Abby perched on Noah's lap, they managed to wedge themselves into the cab.

Half a mile from the diner, the headlights illuminated a figure walking toward them on the shoulder of the road. As they came closer, Noah saw it was an old woman pushing a shopping cart filled with boxes and plastic bags.

"Old Hannah," Sean Keene said. "Wonder where she's going in the middle of the night."

Abby nudged Noah and giggled softly.

Hannah paused, one hand on the metal cart handle, the other around a thick wooden stick. Her fingers were long and delicate, not gnarled with age. Noah wondered why he hadn't noticed that at the campfire. He assumed it was because he simply hadn't opened his eyes and looked.

As they rolled past, Hannah smiled. Eve's smile. Melanie's smile. She raised the stick in a salute and winked.

EPILOGUE

The inky blackness of the Realm of Exponential Darkness hugged Spid like a skin-tight, sensory-deprivation suit. His only tactile sensation was a feeling of clamminess on his skin. When he lifted his hand, he couldn't tell if he was touching his own face, or Yurk's, or even if he'd lifted his hand at all. From the second the Zezzue dropped him into the penetrating blackness, he hadn't been able to touch, see, hear, taste, or smell anything.

But considering Yurk was dropped in alongside him, he could count the smell part of the equation as a blessing. The troll fought an unfamiliar emotion—fear. Unless he found a way out, he would die here. And why? Because of a bratty, precocious girl.

Anger, escalating into rage, smothered his dread. "She cheated."

He thought he felt his lips move, but he heard nothing. He tried again. "She cheated."

His words rang inside his head, but no sound reached his ears. The utter darkness sopped up the words like a sponge.

How could she do this to him? Especially after he offered to spare her life?

And how could he, Spid, the Grand Exalted Garboon, the towering intellect of The Age of Trolls in the land of Beneath, a ruler so wise, so benevolent, so...so...inarguably right, be so misunderstood? After all, he'd only wanted the best. He'd only wanted to illuminate and enlighten the misguided souls of the world with his ultra-omnipotence.

He felt a prickle in his mind, a sort of psychic vibration inside his skull. "Yurk?"

The sound of his voice was instantly extinguished, unheard. But the thought must have made contact. He felt the psychic prickle again. It grew stronger, buzzing and tickling. Then it formed into a voice, a tiny and hollow voice, deep inside his ears. "Dittoes, Boss. Dittos to the forty-ninth power."

"Yurk!" Spid probed the darkness with his brain wave.

"Here, Boss," the ogre thought back.

"Ah." Spid imagined a smile. Or perhaps he actually did smile. Things would be fine. After all, he had Yurk. The ogre was practically family. No, more loyal than family. More caring.

Of course, Spid admitted, it was easy to be more caring than a gammit mother who refused to look at him and a troll father who chained him to a rock for a hundred years just for using his battle hatchet without permission.

He tamped those memories down. This was no time to get into all that. No, he needed to think only positive thoughts. He had to remain in perfect command of his mind. His mind was the most powerful weapon ever devised. He would escape and he would triumph. The world would recoil in fear from the terrible revenge of Spid the Devious.

Filling his lungs with dense air, he opened his mouth and roared "I'm the king of the world!"

The sound was so loud it actually penetrated the darkness, but so much of it was absorbed he heard only "foof."

But Yurk must have sensed it. Spid felt the psychic prickle again, and the ogre's voice filled his brain. "You duh troll, Boss. You duh troll."

Also by Carolyn J. Rose and Mike Nettleton

The Big Grabowski

Sometimes a Great Commotion

By Mike Nettleton

Shotgun Start

By Carolyn J. Rose

A Place of Forgetting

An Uncertain Refuge

Hemlock Lake

Through a Yellow Wood

No Substitute for Murder

Mike Nettleton grew up in Bandon and Grants Pass, Oregon. A stint at a college station in Ashland led to a multi-state radio odyssey with on-air gigs in Oregon, California, and New Mexico under the air name Mike Phillips. In 1989 he returned to the Northwest and in 1994 joined KEX Radio in Portland. Recently retired, his hobbies are golf, pool, Texas hold-em poker, and book collecting.

Carolyn J. Rose grew up in New York's Catskill Mountains, graduated from the University of Arizona, logged two years in Arkansas with Volunteers in Service to America, and spent 25 years as a television news researcher, writer, producer, and assignment editor in Arkansas, New Mexico, Oregon, and Washington. She founded the Vancouver Writers' Mixers and is an active supporter of her local bookstore, Cover to Cover. Her interests are reading, gardening, and not cooking.

Surf to www.deadlyduomysteries.com for more information.

And stop by their blog:
http://deadlyduoduhblog.blogspot.com/

www.ingramcontent.com/pod-product-compliance
Lightning Source LLC
Chambersburg PA
CBHW062013170626
46813CB00001B/148